MICHAEL ALBRIGHT

IT BEGINS

PART II

LitPrime Solutions
21250 Hawthorne Blvd
Suite 500, Torrance, CA 90503
www.litprime.com
Phone: 1-800-981-9893

Published by LitPrime Solutions   10/27/2022

ISBN: 979-8-88703-076-0(sc)
ISBN: 979-8-88703-077-7(hc)
ISBN: 979-8-88703-078-4(e)

To the center of my universe,
my family, and to all those
who run toward danger rather
then away from danger.

CONTENTS

PREFACE

O N A BRIGHT SUNNY DAY, a Transvaal passenger aircraft was on the last of several trips across Zambia. The flight was largely uneventful when suddenly a pure white light appeared in front of the aircraft and moved to swallow it up. In mere seconds, the aircraft and its crew and passengers were surrounded by the light. Abruptly, the aircraft rose vertically into the sky. An intensive land and air search of Zambia and the surrounding countries was in vain. The aircraft and all of the people simply disappeared.

Meanwhile on the other side of the world, in Brazil, a country well-known for UFO sightings, a Brazilian passenger aircraft disappeared into the heavens. This time, however, the bodies of the missing were returned. Neatly arranged, the bodies were placed in multiple rows. When discovered, the horror became evident. All of the internal organs had been removed. A young girl was left alive to give statement of the horrific acts of desecration.

In response to the alien threat over the years, a top secret organization known as Space Command was established within the United States Navy. During the preceding years, Space Command armed itself with advanced weaponry and was staffed with the best of the best. It's new commander, Rear Admiral Michael "Scotty" Scott, had experience with the alien threat and was committed as were the men and women of Space Command to beat the threat back and defeat the aliens no matter the cost. No stone would be left unturned in their determination.

Due to recent events, when two Space Command flights were intercepted by UFOs, Admiral Scott became convinced that their secured communications were not that secure. He knew that somehow the aliens had a spy in Space Command. To combat this threat beyond doing a complete security check of the personnel, he enlisted the help of an old friend, Jonesy, who is a master computer hacker.

OKAY, SO SEND ME TO THE PRINCIPAL'S OFFICE

Throwing all caution to the wind, Scotty disobeyed his own orders and did not take a meandering route back to Colorado. Instead, he and Doreen left their security detail behind and went to Newark Liberty Airport and took a direct flight to Denver.

Once they arrived in Denver and entered the terminal, Scotty and Doreen were warmly greeted by two Marines dressed in civilian clothes. They did a good job of pretending to be friends of the traveling duo. As they began walking through the terminal, two other Marines fell in behind them, and another pair walked in front of them. Scotty couldn't understand what the fuss was all about and asked the Marine next to him, "How did you know that we were on that flight?"

"Sir, when Major Whitney found out that you left New York without your escort, he went nuts. He had Jonesy hack all of the transportation systems leading back here. When he found out that you were on the plane, he dispatched us here. But he thought that your reservations might have been a blind, so we have security teams covering the bus and rail terminals as well," the Marine replied.

"I'm sorry for all the trouble," Scotty offered.

"No trouble, sir. I'm just glad that we found you safe." The Marine hesitated and then added as an afterthought, "I'd hate to be your security escort in New York. The major is going to kill them when they come back."

"Don't worry about them. The fault is all mine. I'll straighten it with JW," Scotty offered, feeling guilty that he and Doreen left the security team behind.

Once outside of the terminal building, Doreen and Scotty were ushered into another one of JW's special vehicles. This one was an old battered four-wheel drive Suburban that looked like it was about to fall apart from rust. Once inside, though, each person sat in a racing-type bucket seat with a five-point seat belt restraint. When the driver started the engine and pulled out into traffic, one could immediately tell that it was built like a tank and as fast as a race car.

"One of the major's special cars?" Scotty asked.

"Yes, sir. The camo job on the outside makes it look like junk, but the entire vehicle is armor plated, the windows are bulletproof, and even if the tires are shot out, we can run on the rims at sixty miles per hour. Oh, yeah! We also have a satellite linkup for communications and tracking," the driver offered.

"Impressive!" Scotty answered, knowing that JW didn't miss one little detail in the design of this vehicle.

For the next hour, Scotty and Doreen sat back and enjoyed the ride as the beautiful scenery passed by. Once they arrived back at the base, Scotty glanced over at Doreen and wished that they were back in New York City. But in a strange sort of way, he was a little elated that they were now making progress. Scotty reached out and squeezed Doreen's hand and smiled. Doreen smiled back with a warm, sweet smile and blew him a kiss, just as JW opened her door.

"Welcome back, sirs!" JW called out as Scotty and Doreen exited the vehicle. Not one to let an opportunity slip by, JW spoke up, "Sir, I hesitate to remind the admiral, but how can I protect you if..." but Scotty cut him off.

"I know, JW. I should be keel hauled for disobeying my own orders.

It was not the security team's fault in New York. Right now, I want to see you, Jonesy, Captain Clark, and Beverly in my office. Kindly get them together in fifteen minutes," Scotty ordered as he and Doreen hurried to the elevator.

"Yes, sir!" JW hollered out as Scotty and Doreen quickly walked away. In frustration but thankfulness that they were all right, JW put his hands on his hips, lowered his head slightly, and shook his head from side to side. Recovering quickly, JW went to notify every one of the meeting.

When Scotty and Doreen were alone in the elevator, they didn't speak but rather, they embraced in a passionate kiss and held onto each other tightly, not wanting to let go of the moment or last night. When they reached their floor, Scotty broke their embrace and pushed the button that holds the door open. Scotty reached down and grabbed his overnight bag as Doreen took her bag and left the elevator. Together, they hurried to their individual quarters for a quick shower before the meeting.

Scotty entered his quarters and immediately went into the bedroom. As he crossed the room in a hurry to get to the bathroom, he tossed his overnight bag onto the bed a little too strongly. The bag tumbled across the bed and onto the floor. At first, Scotty was going to walk over and pick it up, but since he was in a hurry, he left it where it was and went into the bathroom. Quickly, Scotty undressed and entered his shower. Bending over slightly, Scotty turned the water on, a little cooler than normal. As the invigorating water sprayed over him, Scotty reached for the soap when he suddenly remembered the last time he took a shower. Scotty felt alone, very, very alone.

YOU'RE KIDDING! THAT'S HOW THEY DID IT

R UNNING THE LAST FIFTY YARDS to his office, in a failed attempt to be on time, Scotty burst through the outer door, gave his secretary a big hello, and entered his office.

"Attention on deck!" JW shouted out as everyone left his or her seats, stood erect, and saluted.

Scotty stopped dead in his tracks, returned the salute, and answered, "At ease!"

Everyone approached Scotty and welcomed him back as Doreen stood off to the side, wishing that she was somewhere else. After returning the greetings, Scotty directed everyone back to their seats. He walked around to the other side of the table and sat down next to Doreen. Finding himself across from Jonesy, Scotty had trouble seeing him since there were file folder after file folder stacked in front of his friend's face.

"Well, Jonesy, you did a hell of a job. Now, can you please tell us what you found out?" Scotty directed.

A little nervous, Jonesy cleared his throat, removed a folder from the top of the stack, opened it up in front of him as he pushed the others aside, and began, "As all of you know, Admiral Scott suspects that there is a spy or spies operating inside of the base. This suspicion is based on two separate instances. The first one being the incident involving Admiral Braddock and the second one involving Admiral Scott on his return from Brazil. If you were to treat each incident separately, then, yes, maybe both cases could be attributed to chance encounter. However, if you take them together, then the conclusion is obvious. These encounters were deliberate.

"The question, therefore, became how did the aliens know our every move and precisely where the two aircraft were when the intercepts took place. It's true that they could have been monitoring the aircraft's movement and radio transmissions, but that would leave an awful lot to chance. The movements of both aircraft were monitored, of course, by the civilian air traffic control system as well as our military system. Additionally, this complex as well as the Washington, DC, office was also monitoring the progress of both flights in a real-time sequence. The flight plans of both aircraft were also known in advance by both offices. Therefore, there was adequate time to transmit that data to whomever. The sixty-four-thousand-dollar question then is how could this be done in facilities, that for all intent and purposes, the most electronically secure areas in the world. There is not a fax line, office intercom, computer, telephone line, or radio transmission that is not checked and rechecked constantly.

"On the day of Admiral Braddock's incident, the Washington facility was controlling five of the satellites while this facility was in control of the rest. On the day of Admiral Scott's encounter, this facility was controlling all of the satellites. Admiral Scott felt that the satellite net was being used by the aliens as a means to transmit their intelligence. All things considered, it was the only possible way to get intelligence out.

"Scotty...err...I mean Admiral Scott instructed me to examine the computer record of the satellite transmissions to see if there was a carrier signal attached to a transmission." Jonesy looked around the table and saw a puzzled look on Beverly's face. Deciding to rephrase his point, Jonesy asked, "In other words, was it possible that there was a transmission hidden within a transmission to a satellite?

"In order to examine this possibility, I had to first write a complex computer program. I couldn't run it through the central computer for fear that a spy might realize what I was doing. I also couldn't utilize one of the supercomputers in our laboratory for the same reason. What I needed was a stand-alone unit with plenty of processing power. I didn't want to order one because that would mean that I would have had to tell procurement why I needed such a computer. So, instead, I went shopping," Jonesy looked at Scotty, winked, and then turned back toward the group and continued as Scotty closed his eyes, afraid of what was coming, "by hacking into the government supply net. I found just what I needed. A quad processor computer with loads of memory. The computer was destined for the Army War College to run combat simulations. However, I was able, shall we say, divert the shipment to someone who needed it more. Me! You have to see this thing. It has…" Jonesy was interrupted by Scotty.

"Jonesy!" Scotty cried out and ordered, "Could you please just get to the point? You're going to give us all heart attacks."

"Oh…yeah. But can I keep it?" Jonesy asked.

"Yes, Lieutenant. You can keep it as long as no one knows where it is." Scotty gave in.

"No worry there, sir. As far as the Army knows, the CIA grabbed it and has it locked away in Langley," Jonesy proudly answered.

"That's good, Lieutenant. Now get to the point!" Scotty ordered.

"Yes, sir. As I was saying, once I received my new computer," Jonesy began then looked at Scotty with a big smile on his face, looked back at the group, and continued, "I was able to run the program much faster and away from prying eyes. First, I examined the transmissions for the two days of the intercepts. I found nothing unusual there. To be on the safe side, I then began checking backward, but again, nothing. I thought perhaps the admiral was looking in the wrong place, but then, by accident, I found out about the atomic time clock transmissions. As you may know, the atomic time clock is broadcast from Canada on a constant basis. This base picks up that transmission, boosts the signal, and constantly feeds it to the central processing unit on each satellite. Piggybacked onto that transmission, I found what we were looking for. In the case of Admiral Braddock, a transmission left the base attached to the atomic time clock broadcast, precisely six minutes before the intercept." Jonesy turned toward Scotty and added, "In your case, Admiral, the hidden transmission went out nine minutes before the intercept. You were right, Admiral. There is a spy operating on the base, and indeed there might be more than one."

Anxiously, Scotty asked, "Any idea who he or she is?"

"I'm afraid not. I know that the transmission was sent from our main control room, but, and this is the really brilliant part, the spy made it appear as if the piggybacked transmission was sent from every computer terminal in the room. I'm in the process of working on a computer program to filter out the dead ends and locate the exact terminal," Jonesy answered with a slight tone of disappointment and then added, "On the bright side, once I get the new program written, we should almost instantly determine when a hidden transmission is sent out and the computer terminal it originated from."

"Is there any chance that you will have the program done before the conference?" Scotty asked, with a hint of hope in his voice.

"I doubt it, sir. But I will try like hell. Sir…" Jonesy paused, looked down at the table, and then back up at Scotty and added, "Admiral, there is one other thing."

"Yes, Lieutenant." Scotty anxiously replied.

"Scotty…I mean Admiral, when I found the transmissions, I took the liberty of going back and running the program on all of the copies of the atomic time clock transmissions." Jonesy paused and then added, "Sir, since the base became operational, there has been a total of two hundred and thirty-one other hidden transmissions."

That revelation left everyone in shock. After what seemed like five minutes, but was actually only seconds, Scotty spoke up, "Jonesy, is there a pattern to the transmissions?"

Jonesy took a moment to gather his thoughts and then answered, "No, there is no discernable pattern, either by date or time. It appears to be random. I don't know the full history of the base, so I can't tell if the transmissions are tied to some kind of event the base was involved in. My gut feeling is that the transmissions are probably just regular intelligence reports."

"Jonesy, I know that right now we are shooting in the dark. We have no idea about their language, other than the symbols that are in the saucers that we have, but do you think that we might be able to read their transmissions?" Doreen asked.

Jonesy sat back in his chair for a moment, pondered the question, and then answered, "I have been hoping for the same thing. Let me explain the approach that I am using with that part of the investigation. When I wrote the program to find the piggybacked transmissions, I did so with a couple of assumptions. First, if I were sending the transmissions, I would want them to be very short and woven within the regular data stream to the satellites. Therefore, it follows that such a message would have to be compressed and sent out in bursts. Secondly, any message sent out would have to be hidden within another transmission and not sent out over dead air. I've separated out the transmissions that I have found so far and filtered them through a decompression program. And guess what? It worked. So in the future, we will be able to detect a transmission when it happens. But there is more.

"I know that the two transmissions relative to the intercept of the flights were formatted on one of our computers. In other words, the transmission itself was first typed into a computer here and then sent through an encoding program. Once that was done, the message was further compressed into a burst transmission format and downloaded to a disk. The spy, at his leisure, would then simply insert the disk into one of our computers and execute the program into the time data stream to the satellites."

"Fucking great!" JW exclaimed and then added as he looked around the group, "I'm sorry. I guess that I was thinking out loud. Sorry to interrupt."

"That's okay, JW. I think you expressed what we are all thinking," Scotty answered and then turned to Jonesy. "Any good news in all of this?"

"Not all that much, but I am making progress. There is something else which may give us a starting point. Since the basic format of transmissions were based on our computers, I was able to reduce them to binary code. You know the ones and zeros that each computer keystroke represents. I feel that now we may have a starting point to eventually being able to read their transmissions." Jonesy concluded.

"Any comments?" Scotty asked the group.

"Sir, we can't let what we just heard out of this room. Otherwise, if the spy finds out what we know, he will go deeper and become impossible to find," Beverly contributed.

"I agree. The only people that we can trust right now are the ones in this room. So we are all going to have to work a little harder now," Scotty commented and then looked at Jonesy and added, "Jonesy, you did one hell of a job. It may have just saved our collective butts one day."

Everyone in the room expressed their agreement, much to the embarrassment of Jonesy. To escape the awkward moment, he asked, "So you're not mad about the computer?"

Scotty laughed and ordered, "No. If you can, try and get a few more. You're going to need them. If you can't acquire them, let's do it honestly and order them."

"I'm sure that I will be able to find a few. It's a big world out there!" Jonesy quickly replied, with a devilish grin on his face.

Scotty laughed slightly again and commented to the group, "You are right, it is a big world out there. But from what we have learned in the short time that we have been here is that it is all that we have and the alien's want to take it away. We have to assume that the aliens know everything about this base, its capabilities, our defensive and offensive posture, our plans, and in short, everything that we know." Scotty then turned deadly serious and spoke, "Jonesy, we need that program as soon as possible. Yesterday would've been good, but just as soon as you can." Turning his attention back toward the group, he added, "Once the program is in place, Jonesy's workstation in Space Command will have to be manned twenty-four hours a day. Since we can't bring anyone else into this, we have to do the work. I know that it is asking a lot, given our current workload, but it's the only way to keep it a secret."

Turning toward JW and Beverly, Scotty directed, "JW, I want the base brought up to full-alert status. In the next few days, I want you to gradually filter in some additional security people into the main computer room. They can pretend to fix computers or, perhaps, do some custodial work. Whatever they do, I don't care. I want them there now and around the clock. You and Beverly work out the details and make it happen.

"Beverly, I want you to coordinate the overall combat readiness of the base. Get together with Captains Kendall and Bone and enhance our readiness. We are still in a defensive mode, but it may be time to prepare for an offensive posture." Turning his attention to Doreen, Scotty pleaded, "Doreen, we need more aircraft, pilots, and technicians, and we needed them yesterday. Light fires under the manufactures. If possible, double up on the training schedules and feeder programs so that we have enough pilots and technicians."

"Will do!" Doreen immediately replied, already thinking of how to complete her assignment.

Scotty then turned toward Linda Clark and ordered, "Captain Clark, I want you to coordinate all security matters outside of the base. That includes all teams we have operating on missions around the country and throughout the world. Also, all requests for leave are to be filtered through you. You have the complete right to deny any request based upon operational need or if the person requesting leave is a possible security risk. In essence, our safety is in your hands." Turning his attention back to everyone, Scotty added, "JW will continue to oversee the security for the conference and then concentrate on catching our spy or spies."

"Thank you, sir. I'll not let you down," Captain Clark replied, smiling to herself and proud of the fact that she was given such an important assignment. At last, Captain Clark felt that she would be contributing, rather than being an assistant to JW and a mother hen to the Marine contingent.

"Two more things," Scotty announced and turned toward Jonesy and ordered, "Jonesy, after you have the program up and running, I want you to work on cracking the alien language. Carolyn Gibbs would probably be a big help, so see her." Almost as an afterthought, Scotty added the news that would make Jonesy happy, "Oh, and, Jonesy, you have a blank check right now. So whatever you want, see Beverly and she will order it for you. Unless, of course, you want to go shopping on your own!"

Scotty saw the gleam in Jonesy's eyes and wondered what hell he had just unleashed on the world. But there was another item on his list he almost forgot about. Turning his attention to Beverly once again, Scotty directed, "Beverly, you once expressed reservations about Captain Kendall. If he throws roadblocks in your way or doesn't seem committed to the program, you have full authority to relive him and get someone you can work with. Understand?"

"Five by five, sir!" Beverly eagerly replied.

Scotty then looked around the room and announced, "Good luck, ladies and gentlemen. That will be all."

As everyone was leaving, Scotty asked Beverly as she walked by, "Beverly, is Admiral Morrison still on the base?"

"No, sir. He returned to Washington when he learned that you were on your way back," Beverly answered.

After everyone left, Scotty and Doreen sat there for a moment and just held hands in the quiet and emptiness of the room. Scotty was looking deeply into her eyes. After a minute, he spoke, "Doreen!" He wanted to express his feelings, but words seemed inadequate.

Doreen was likewise looking into Scotty's eyes and finished his thought, "I know. I wish that we were somewhere else too." Pausing for a few seconds, she regrettably added, "But we are not. It's time to get to work again."

Doreen stood up quickly, followed by Scotty. They just stood there for a moment gazing into each other's eyes. Slowly, they embraced, not caring that the door to the room was open. Scotty wanted to pick her up and carry her to his quarters, but that was not to be.

The electronic ring of the telephone on the conference table broke their embrace. Scotty didn't want to let go of Doreen, but the damn thing just kept ringing. Doreen told Scotty that he better answer it. Reluctantly, Scotty reached for the telephone as Doreen left to go and check on their little patient. But Doreen didn't escape before Scotty reached out and softly slapped her on the butt. Doreen turned around and smiled as she blew Scotty a kiss and then left.

Letting out a sigh, Scotty picked up the receiver. With regret in his voice, Scotty answered, "Yes." For the next thirty minutes, Scotty brought Morrison up to date on the latest developments. In the back of his mind, though, Scotty's thoughts were only of Doreen and their little escapade in New York City.

THE SHELL GAME

Vinson had returned to Space Command a full five days prior to the international conference on terrorism and, more importantly, the diversionary meeting on the alien problem. Based upon the communications traffic the base was monitoring, as well as receiving and answering, Scotty knew that Vinson had accomplished his mission. The members of the association were busy sending and receiving messages about a meeting, which would never take place.

What alien in the cosmos wouldn't want to eavesdrop on a meeting that discussed what the world's response would be to the alien invasion? Scotty thought to himself. But Scotty felt that something was wrong. Things were going too well. There simply wasn't time to go back and review everything to see if there was a flaw in the plan. Events were now taking on a life of their own, and things were moving too fast.

On the same day that Vinson had returned, JW began to move his security teams into the hotel and the immediate surrounding area of the meeting. Over the next few days, the security teams staying in the hotel performed a security sweep of the entire structure and declared it to be free of any electronic-listening devices. One security team, dressed as telephone workers, entered the hotel and began to "rewire the structure with optic cable to upgrade the system," a benefit the management welcomed and didn't question. While they made a great showing of bringing cable into the hotel and looking busy, they were actually sneaking in the inflatable manikins and electronic equipment that would allow an electronic blanket to be draped over the entire hotel. This blanket would detect any attempt of electronic eavesdropping and would be able to pinpoint the direction and location from where the electronic attack was coming from. With such capability in place, JW was sure that if the aliens tried to penetrate the meeting, and he was convinced that they would try, security forces could immediately be dispatched to catch the aliens.

JW was sure that he had all of the bases covered. He had security forces in the hotel, around the hotel, flying over the hotel, and hell, he even had people patrolling the ancient sewer system under the hotel. Right now, JW believed that the hotel was one of the safest places on earth right now. He had saturated the area around the hotel with his people and in the past few days had come to know more about the people in the neighborhood than they probably knew about themselves. But, like Scotty, JW also grew uncomfortable when everything seemed to be going so well.

The hours passed with agonizing slowness for Scotty as the day of the conference approached. Doreen recognized his tenseness and did what she could to lighten his mood. Together, they had stolen moments away from the reality of the base. They would meander through the atrium and cautiously held hands when they felt that no one was looking. Sometimes, they were even lucky enough to escape among the plants and shrubs and share a short but passionate kiss.

Other times, when people were around, they would settle for an occasional touch, or as they walked, their bodies would lightly brush up against each other.

Each night, Doreen would lie between her sheets thinking only of Scotty. For his part, Scotty would endlessly replay in his mind the night they shared in his home. For the first time in his life, Scotty was in love. Not a casual first-interest love but a deep love, in which he felt incomplete without Doreen. Both of them wished that they were back in New York City, but that was a memory now to be cherished by each of them and something to look forward to.

JUST ONCE AROUND THE PARK, GEORGE

WITH JUST ONE DAY TO go before the start of the conference, Scotty was ready to explode. He knew that he was driving everyone crazy, constantly asking for updates on the conference and the diversionary meeting. Scotty just had to do something to relax. Since it was impossible for he and Doreen to escape the base, he did the next best thing. Scotty went flying. Today, Scotty would transition from flying the simulator to actually flying the X-aircraft.

Captain Kendall anxiously waited for Scotty on the hangar deck. While he waited, he checked and rechecked the aircraft Scotty would be flying. He didn't want anything to go wrong with the boss's first flight. Kendall was checking the aircraft for the fourth time when Scotty walked up beside him.

After saluting, Kendall immediately launched into a mini lecture on the flight systems of the aircraft and a detailed review of the safety features. Scotty stood there patiently and listened as best he could. When Kendall finished, Scotty put on his flight helmet, winked at Kendall, and climbed aboard the aircraft. After being helped into the seat, and strapped in, Scotty connected his oxygen and the communications line to his helmet. He then waited as an aircraft tug pulled him onto the elevator for the short ride to the surface.

Once Scotty was on the runway, he eagerly pushed the engine start button. Tension began to melt away as he felt the vibration of the powerful engines. While he waited for permission to take off, Scotty did a last-minute check of the instrumentation and the aircraft control surfaces. Satisfied that all was well, Scotty looked up at the sky and watched as soft, pale blue clouds drifted by.

"Tango 1, you are cleared for takeoff." Scotty heard in his headset. A smile crossed his face as Scotty edged the throttle forward and was airborne in a matter of seconds. He had requested a flight path out over the Gulf of Mexico at an altitude of sixty thousand feet and from there a jump into space and back down.

"Easy on the throttle, Tango 1," Kendall radioed.

"Relax, CAG," Scotty answered as he pushed the nose of the aircraft upward and dramatically increased his speed. Unable to control his excitement anymore, Scotty let out a scream of joy and radioed, "This is great!" Adding a little more speed, Scotty crossed the threshold into space and turned his engines off. He eased the aircraft over into a low orbit over Earth with the help of directional thrusters. Once that maneuver was completed, silence overcame him, for he learned the lesson of humility, as he gazed upon our fragile world. To some, such an experience would be religious, and perhaps that would come later, but to Scotty, it was wonderment and a reminder of man's place in the universe. He was roused from this dreamlike state when he received instructions to correct his flight attitude to maintain his orbit. Flight control asked if they could program his flight computers to fly the aircraft, but Scotty refused. He wanted the whole experience, and that included him manually flying the aircraft.

His attention was then drawn to the stars. From earth, they would never look the same again. Scotty felt that he could reach out and touch them, or at least be able to fly around them. The urge of adventure grew within him once he sighted the moon in the cold dark vastness of space. Thinking out loud, Scotty radioed, "I think that I will fly around the moon."

"Er…no can do, sir! There is not enough fuel or oxygen onboard. This was supposed to be a short hop, Admiral," Kendall replied.

"Sure know how to ruin a moment, CAG. After one trip around the block, I'm coming in," Scotty replied with disappointment in his voice. Settling back into flying the aircraft, Scotty watched as the continents and oceans of the world slipped by below him. As he approached the western coast of North America, Scotty began preparations to land.

Approaching the atmosphere of Earth, Scotty eased the nose of the aircraft upward at a thirty-degree angle. The heat of reentry was then dispersed over the outer shell of the aircraft and the protective composite material. Once in Earth's atmosphere, Scotty restarted the engines and increased his speed as he did a few barrel rolls in celebration of his flight and the exhilaration he was feeling.

Following the instructions of the flight controller, Scotty was on the ground in a few minutes and lowered down to the hangar deck.

Once the aircraft was parked, Scotty climbed down from the cockpit and was welcomed back by Doreen's open arms. They hugged and kissed, forgetting where they were. Surroundings didn't matter, they were together lost in another place at another time.

Kendall coughed loudly, reminding Scotty where he was. They broke their embrace but held onto each other. After discussing his flight with Kendall, Scotty and Doreen walked toward the elevator. As they walked, Scotty asked what would happen if a pilot were to become stranded in space. Doreen explained that the pilot would be able to fly the aircraft down as the orbit decayed, and, once in Earth's atmosphere, the aircraft would be able to glide to a safe landing.

Scotty could see that she was right, based upon what he just experienced, but he also wanted to know what would happen if a pilot was stranded in deep space. In such a situation, the pilot would not be able, absent an operating engine, to establish an orbit close enough to the earth.

To answer his question, Doreen first bit her lip and then replied,

"We have plans for a deep-space rescue aircraft. All of the designs are done and ready to go."

"Ready to go? You mean it's not built yet?" Scotty asked, afraid of the obvious answer.

Doreen looked down at her feet as they walked, then looked at Scotty and answered, "I argued with the admiral that the rescue aircraft should be built at the same time as the fighters. The plan calls for the construction of four rescue aircraft to be in operation once all of the fighters were deployed." Doreen hesitated and then continued, "Michael, the admiral, saw things differently. He ordered that all assets be committed to the fighters. The rescue aircraft would then come later." Doreen hesitated again and then concluded, "At the rate that deployment of the aircraft is going, we should be able to begin construction of the rescue aircraft within a few months."

Scotty stopped walking, looked at Doreen, and ordered, "Do me a favor. Start construction of the rescue aircraft immediately, and I mean right now!"

"I'll give the order immediately. But what about the admiral?" Doreen asked.

"Let me worry about him," Scotty quickly replied and then directed, "Now, let's get some lunch."

Doreen looked at Scotty as they waited for the elevator. She saw something new on his face. It was a new excitement. Doreen knew that there was a new maiden in their lives. It wasn't another woman although some pilots call them "she," but rather, it was an aircraft.

"What was it like up there? In space, I mean." Doreen jealously asked.

"It was knockdown great! Those astronauts sure have been keeping space travel a secret. I'd like to say that it is the best feeling in the world, but it sure wasn't. The best feeling is being with you," Scotty replied, winked at Doreen, and then lovingly slapped her on the rear just as the elevator door opened. Doreen, slightly flushed, wanted to hug Scotty, but there were people in the elevator.

Once they were in the elevator, Scotty asked, "Have you come up with a name for the aircraft yet?"

"Well, kind of. I was thinking about Pegasus," Doreen replied and then asked, "What do you think?"

"I like it. The winged horse. Sounds good," Scotty replied as the elevator stopped, and they began walking toward the mess hall.

As they approached the entrance to the mess hall, Doreen spoke up, "Oh, I asked JW and Jonesy to join us. I knew that you would bother them anyway, so I thought that they might as well eat with us."

"You're beginning to scare me. You know me too well!" Scotty replied with a laugh in his voice for which he received a loving elbow to his abdomen.

"There they are," Doreen declared, pointing to the two of them sitting at a table eating. She then directed and asked, "You go and sit down and I'll get our lunch. Hamburger, okay?"

"Sounds good. But…" Scotty began to answer but was interrupted by Doreen.

"I know, cooked very well done until it can be used as a hockey puck, coleslaw, and onion rings on the side and a Pepsi," Doreen replied as she turned away and headed for the mess line, shaking her head.

"You're really scaring me, woman!" Scotty called out after Doreen as he watched her walk away and felt desire in his heart. Recovering from his momentary daydream, Scotty walked over to JW and Jonesy, who were eagerly attacking some hot dogs and a very large platter of fries. Jonesy was the only person Scotty knew that ate coleslaw on his hot dogs rather than the usual toppings. Scotty always wanted to try Jonesy's concoction, but somehow never got around to it.

"You, guys, look like you are enjoying yourselves!" Scotty exclaimed as he reached the table and began to sit down.

JW looked up as he bit a large piece out of one of his hot dogs, dropped his lunch onto his plate, and stood up at attention. Jonesy managed to mumble something through a mouthful of food and also stood at attention.

Scotty was a bit embarrassed and ordered, "Guys, I told you that no one gets saluted in the mess hall. Now sit the hell down." Once they sat down, Scotty didn't waste a second and immediately asked JW for an update.

JW finished chewing his food and then answered, "Everything is on schedule, Admiral. So far, there is nothing unusual. All teams are in place and ready for anything."

"If the aliens are going to do something, then when do you think that they will act?" Scotty asked.

"If I were them, sir, I would be in the area now and would be getting ready to eavesdrop on the conference. But I wouldn't begin until about five minutes after the conference is set to begin," JW answered, with conviction in his voice.

"Will your security team be ready to act fast?" Scotty asked then realized that it is a stupid question to ask this man.

"Yes, Admiral. Besides the teams in the buildings around the hotel, I have three other teams, each consisting of six agents in full-body armor and armed to the teeth, secreted in vans around the area ready to move on a moment's notice," JW replied as he mentally reviewed his plan looking for a weakness.

"Good! Their orders are to try and capture the aliens unless they resist," Scotty prodded.

"That's correct. In fact, two men on each of the teams have special weapons for capturing people. One of the men has a foam gun that shoots hardening foam at a high velocity. It will encase an individual in less than two seconds and will prevent the person from moving. The other weapon is a net gun. This weapon shoots a weighted net around an individual, and again, the person cannot move. Either one is very effective. Also, each team member carries a Taser weapon that will shoot fourteen hundred volts of electricity through a person. It shouldn't kill an alien, but we don't know for sure," JW explained.

"I like it, but I want to be clear about something. If any of our agents are fired upon, their orders are to fire back and eliminate the threat with extreme prejudice. Is that clear?" Scotty ordered, more concerned about his men than the damn aliens.

"Crystal clear, sir," JW replied, proud to be working for this man.

"Good. Ah…here's lunch," Scotty replied as Doreen placed a food tray in front of him. Scotty picked up his hamburger, took a bite, and then asked, "Jonesy, any progress yet?"

"Not yet, Admiral. Nothing has gone up the data stream to the satellites. I now have every computer that is used to communicate with the satellites running through an electronic filter or trap, if you will. It will instantly detect any carrier signal and pinpoint the computer that sent the signal," Jonesy replied, confident that his computer program will work.

"That's great!" Scotty answered and then asked, "Any luck with a translation yet?"

"Not really," Jonesy replied in a low tone and then explained, "Since we broke the transmissions down into binary language, I am trying, with the help of the two code breakers JW sent me, to reformulate their language from the function identification labels in the saucers. Luckily, they suffer from the same phobia as our military. Every little switch and lever are labeled. From there, we can move onto the computers in the saucers although we have to figure out how they work first. Overall, though, we are making progress as slow as it is."

"If you are able, one day, to read their language, will we be able to speak it?" Doreen asked.

Jonesy thought for a moment and then answered, "Hopefully, yes. But there is another wrinkle. Their language may be tonal. By that, I mean it may be similar to Chinese. For example, in Chinese, depending on the tone of a spoken word, you could call a person a pig, but apply a different tone and you have another whole different word. What we need is an alien to teach us or a set of their first-grade language books."

Scotty picked up on the dilemma and added, "I can't promise that we can get the books, but I sure as hell will get you some linguists. Who knows, maybe after tomorrow we will have some alien prisoners." Turning his attention back toward JW, Scotty continued, "JW, I'm afraid that I am going to thin your ranks again. I want to send Vinson to Hawaii right after the conference is over tomorrow. His orders are to meet Captain Montgomery and the USS *Salisbury* at Pearl Harbor Naval Base. He will be our eyes and ears on the scene. Make arrangements for him to get to Hawaii aboard a commercial airliner. Have some agents escort him to the airport and meet him in Hawaii. Their job is to get him to the *Salisbury* ASAP."

"Will do, Admiral!" JW exclaimed, paused, and then asked, "Sir, if I may, Vinson looks like he hasn't recovered from his last trip. Do you think that it is a good idea to send him?"

"Originally, I wanted to send you, but I can't spare you right now. We do need someone on the scene, and that is Vinson. He can rest up when it's over. Get him there in one piece, JW, and make sure he meets the *Salisbury* before she sails," Scotty directed. Looking at everyone, Scotty ordered, "Okay, now I want you all in bed asleep by dinnertime. Report to Space Command by two hundred hours (2:00 am). We will monitor the conference first and see what shakes out. Then we will see what interest our diversion attracts. I'll be in my office the rest of the afternoon meeting with my exec, and I'll give Vinson the news. So if that's it, I'll see you all later." Scotty and Doreen then stood up together and walked out of the mess hall.

As they approached the elevator, Doreen told Scotty that she was going to check on their visitor and spend some time with her. Scotty knew that Doreen was spending as much time as she could with the girl and was comfortable in the knowledge that if the girl was to fully recover, it would be due, in a large part, to Doreen. Kindness and compassion are what the girl needed most, and Doreen supplied that in abundance.

Once the elevator doors closed, Scotty and Doreen found themselves alone. Passionately, they locked in an embrace for the few seconds it took the elevator to reach the medical level. As the doors opened, Doreen broke their embrace and whispered something, which Scotty couldn't hear. Doreen left the elevator but not before Scotty lightly slapped her on the rump. Once in the hallway, Doreen turned around and faced Scotty. She blew him a kiss and in a teasing tone of voice said, "Why, Admiral, I didn't know you cared." As an added tease, Doreen lifted her skirt up more than a few inches and coyly smiled at Scotty. He felt himself get aroused, but the elevator doors closed on his desire.

I ALWAYS WANTED TO HAVE A TWIN

As time ticked by, Dustin grew a little anxious. When it was only six days to the passage of DG122, Dustin stopped going home. He would either sleep at his desk or on the couch in Victoria's office. Dustin still had a burning desire to go to Japan to observe the asteroid, but something didn't seem right. While he didn't tell anyone about his feeling, at this point, that's all it was. Dustin felt that he had to somehow broach the subject with Victoria. Deep down, he knew that this feeling of his was an interruption, no, it was a blockade, to his plans of going to Japan and on vacation with Victoria. If they could only go on a vacation, Dustin vowed, he would finally make a positive move to win the heart of his affections.

Dustin was sitting at his desk reviewing radio telemetry when Victoria walked up behind him and put her hands on his shoulders. Gently, Victoria began to massage his stiff, tired muscles. Dustin closed his eyes and momentarily imagined himself and Victoria lying next to each other on a beach somewhere in a paradise not yet imagined.

After a few moments, Victoria stopped her spontaneous massage and leaned over Dustin's shoulder, pretending to look at his computer monitor. Actually, she just wanted to be a little closer to the center of her affections. Dustin still had his eyes closed as he breathed in the sweet, alluring smell of her perfume. He wanted to turn toward Victoria, put his arms around her, and kiss her. But that was his dream world and not reality.

"Do I have a surprise for you!" Victoria declared.

Opening his eyes and looking into her eyes, Dustin replied, "We are going to a beach?" Dustin immediately realized that he had spoken his innermost thoughts and was a little embarrassed.

"What?" Victoria asked, not believing what she thought she heard.

"Er…we're going somewhere? Er…I mean…what? I mean what?" Dustin struggled.

"How did you know?" Victoria asked as she reached into the pocket of her miniskirt and withdrew some papers. She then announced, "What I have here is two first-class tickets to Japan. Just you, me and our friend, DG122."

"That's great, Vick," Dustin replied in a somber tone.

Victoria was a bit thrown off by Dustin's reply and asked, "What's the matter, Dustin?" After pausing for a few seconds, she added, "As an added bonus, I booked us a mini vacation in Hawaii!"

"That's great, Vick. There is nothing in the world I would like better than to go on vacation with you." Dustin surprised himself with his candor. He saw a slight smile on Victoria's face, but he again recovered quickly. "It's the radio data. Something is wrong. I'm getting most of the data that I expected, but some of the readings on the back curvature of the asteroid are…well…not what one would expect."

"What do you mean, Dustin?" Victoria asked in a deadly serious tone.

"I don't know. You see, as the asteroid gets closer, the radio data becomes stronger. But as we adopted the signal to wrap around the back of the asteroid, the data should fall off. But just the opposite is happening," Dustin replied, trying to think through the problem.

"I understand what you mean. But wouldn't that indicate…"

Victoria stopped in midsentence and stared at Dustin who was staring back at her.

Suddenly, at the same moment, they reached the same conclusion. "Oh my god!" Dustin spoke up in an excited voice.

"DG122 has a hitchhiker!" Victoria declared.

With feelings of dread and horror, Dustin immediately began checking over his data. Victoria suggested that they take all of the material into her office where they could have some relative quiet. Victoria turned around and walked through the somewhat sterile environment of the computer room. Some of the other astronomers watched the gently sway of her hips as she walked away. Other astronomers saw the look of dread on Dustin's face as he gathered up stack after stack of papers.

Dustin lifted the reams of paper, which reached from his waist to his chin, with both arms. As Dustin walked to Victoria's office, he often had to peer over the stack of paper or shift the load to see where he was going. The last thing he wanted to do was trip over a desk chair or something, which would launch his precious papers all over the floor.

When Dustin reached Victoria's office, he gently placed his papers on the conference table. Standing up straight, Dustin looked around and saw Victoria standing in front of her office window, staring at the assemblage of news trucks in the parking lot. Slowly, Dustin walked over to Victoria's side and peered out the window.

Victoria saw his reflection in the window glass, turned toward Dustin, and asked, "What are we going to tell them?"

Dustin knew the only possible answer. "The truth!"

"But, Dustin, they will make us look like fools. Now all of a sudden, there are two asteroids. You don't think that the sudden knowledge of the second asteroid will make them wonder if the basis of your findings is flawed to begin with?" Victoria asked.

Dustin turned and faced Victoria as he answered, "Look it. We tell the truth and explain how we found out about it. Let them draw their own conclusions. The important thing is that we do tell them. My only problem is that I have no idea what the effect of the meteor shower will be on the hitchhiker."

"How's that?" Victoria asked as she stared in Dustin's eyes.

Turning back around to look at the media trucks in the parking lot, Dustin wished he was somewhere else as he answered, "If it wasn't for the meteor shower that the asteroids have to pass through, I would be confident that the hitchhiker would continue on its present path. It would just remain where it was, being pulled along by the gravitational pull of DG122. The problem is that we have no idea of the relative mass of the hitchhiker. Without that little fact, it's anybody's guess what will happen. But there may be a hint in the data. So why don't we sit down and review all of the material knowing that there is a hitchhiker there."

"You're right. I'll order up some coffee," Victoria replied with a hopeful tone in her voice.

"And some chocolate chips." Dustin pleaded with a smile on his face, which seemed to break the tension.

Laughing slightly, Victoria answered "And some chocolate chips!" as she walked over to her telephone and placed the order.

For the next four hours, Victoria and Dustin reviewed the research material again and again. Each time, they reached the same conclusion, DG122 had a hitchhiker. The main problem they were confronted with was the fact that they were dealing with an unknown quantity. From the data available to them, it was impossible to determine the mass of the new asteroid. This was further complicated by the impossibility of being able to determine what influence the meteor shower would have on the smaller asteroid.

After considering all the known facts, they decided to run computer simulations to see what would happen when the new asteroid, now designated as DG122A, came in contact with the meteor shower. Since they did not know the mass of the asteroid, they decided to run three simulations. In the first simulation, they would assign the mass of DG122A as one eighth the mass of DG122. The other two simulations would then be run at one quarter the mass of DG122 and finally at one half of its mass.

While Dustin returned to his computer to begin working on the simulations, Victoria sat at her desk. She turned her chair around and stared out of her office window. Unconsciously, she began drumming the fingers of her right hand against the armrest of her desk chair. Victoria became totally lost in her thoughts, wondering what in God's name she was going to tell Washington and the reporters gathered below in the parking lot. As she pondered her dilemma, only one thought came to mind, *Dustin was right, just tell the truth as it happened. No one could have guessed that the asteroid had a hitchhiker.*

THE LIGHT…HEY, IT'S NOT THE PARTY LIGHT

NESTLED AMONG THE GREEN HILLS and valleys of northern Alabama rests a small town, not unlike countless others across the country but yet unique unto itself. In the eyes of the world, it is not important, but to those who live there, it is very important in their minds and in their hearts. Immigrant farmers, mostly from the high hills of Bavaria, settled Heyitvill in the 1800s. They came to America seeking not only their fortunes, though very few found one, but a new way of life based upon the concept of freedom and the excitement and challenge of a new beginning. What those intrepid early settlers found was a hard land where winters were short and the hot, oppressive heat of the summers lingered well into later fall. But fields had to be cleared of timber, plowed, seeded, and time would hold the key of their failure or success. Fortunately for them, nature was kind, and, as the sands of time passed, a community grew rooted in agriculture but strong and wise enough to embrace industrialization.

The social, economic, and political ills of the past century were a dark page in the history of the country as a whole. But Heyitvill emerged into the new age, mindful of the word toleration, but went better and embraced inclusion as their watchword. Today, it is still a place where people can walk the streets and sidewalks of the community without fear, where neighbors mostly care for each other, and where the want of one person may frequently becomes the want of all. It is truly a place lost in time and bypassed by the interstate.

Arty chose this location for the first meeting between himself and Commander Cunningham with great care. They could have met in a big city or a resort town, but it was always better to keep a low profile. In fact, the location Arty chose was about as low profile as you could get as long as your cover story was plausible should any of the locals bother to inquire. And inquire they would in a town where everyone is either related somehow to just about everybody or where the community is so tight-knit that strangers do not pass unnoticed. As a cover story, Arty decided to portray his little group as members of the "Scientific Advancement for Farming Foundation" charged with the goal of establishing hydroponic farms throughout the United States. True, Arty, didn't know anything at all about the practice, other than what he was able to gleam from the internet, but he wouldn't have to since nobody else really did either in a farming community rooted in traditional methods. Most importantly, the cover story would allow him and his team access to the farms throughout the community as they ostensibly searched for locations to start their "farms based on advanced scientific methods."

What attracted Arty to this area was not the location itself although it was easy to get to since it was close to Huntsville along Interstate 65. But rather, it was because two of the people he had to investigate were from Heyitvill. The first was a Mrs. Martha Nesmith, who had her implant removed a little over a year ago by her local doctor.

Mrs. Nesmith had reluctantly gone to Dr. Sabine complaining of a constant pain in her wrist. Thinking that she would receive a prescription for arthritis, Mrs. Nesmith became alarmed when the doctor first x-rayed her hand and told her that there was something in her wrist causing the discomfort. Being positive that she had never broken her wrist, hand, or for that matter her arm, Mrs. Nesmith became even more alarmed when the doctor told her that it should be surgically removed. After a lot of coaching and pleading on the good doctor's part, Mrs. Nesmith agreed to the surgery.

On the appointed day, Mr. And Mrs. Nesmith arrived at the hospital early and patiently waited for their turn. Mrs. Nesmith was laying on a gurney while her husband of fifty-one years sat patiently alongside, tenderly holding her hand. When the nurse interrupted their repose and told them that they were next, Mr. Ed Nesmith slowly stood up, bent over his wife, and kissed her. He stood by while she was wheeled away and watched as his wife disappeared behind a pair of swinging hospital doors. Ed declined the kind offer of coffee from the nurse and didn't want to wait in the assigned area for surgical patients. Instead, Ed meandered down the hallway and went outside. Slowly and with purpose, he put on his well-worn straw hat fashioned somewhat similar to a cowboy hat and shuffled over to a park bench located not fifty feet from the hospital entrance.

Once he sat down, Ed looked around and took in his surroundings. People were rushing here and there. A few pregnant women were walking together and entered the hospital. *Probably for childbirth classes*, he thought. But it was the sight of a mother struggling with her twins that caused him to smile. One of the twins was screaming that he left his toy in the car and wanted to go back for it, but the mother would not hear of it and pulled her young charges along. When they passed, Ed tipped his hat and said good morning to the mother and offered to the upset child "Son, now you listen to your mother and try and help her" in a soft, whisper-like voice. The young child stopped crying and momentarily stared at the old man in front of him grinning ear to ear, but the wails of childhood began again once they were past.

Ed sat back and crossed his legs and still smiled to himself. He could never understand why people always turn around in a restaurant, or any public place for that matter, and glance disapprovingly first at a child who is crying or fussing and then at the embarrassed parent. You see, to Ed, the wails of children were the sounds of life, and if they want to cry in a restaurant, well who on God's good earth could blame them?

Still smiling, Ed reached into the top-center pocket of his bib overalls and withdrew a pouch of tobacco and his homemade corncob pipe. After tamping the tobacco down in the bowl of the pipe, Ed reached into the same pocket and withdrew a box of wooden matches. After removing one match, Ed put the box on top of the tobacco pouch and put them back in his pocket. After putting his pipe between his lips, Ed bent over and struck the match against the concrete. Bringing the lit match up to his pipe, Ed sucked vigorously until he was satisfied that the tobacco was lit. He shook the match out and flicked it away with his fingers. Ed then sat back, and as he puffed, he thought about his wife, and he silently prayed to his God for her life.

Dr. Sabine began the operation routinely enough, but once he exposed the offending material in Mrs. Nesmith wrist, he knew that the removal of the item was probably beyond his ability. Somehow, the object was connected to her nerve endings. Instead of closing the surgical cut up and try another day, Dr. Sabine called for a doctor skilled in microsurgery and a specialist in the nervous system. After a brief consultation among the three doctors, the decision was made to proceed. After seven hours of delicate work, the operation was completed to the satisfaction of the three physicians, and Mrs. Nesmith was wheeled into the recovery room.

Dr. Sabine found Mr. Nesmith outside still sitting on the bench quietly holding his pipe between his lips, staring straight ahead. Sitting down next to him, Dr. Sabine explained that his wife had come through the surgery in excellent condition and was recovering nicely. Mr. Nesmith inquired about the object, but to his disappointment, Dr. Sabine could not offer any explanation what the object was and how it could have gotten there. As they were talking, Dr. Sabine's alphanumeric beeper came to life. Unclipping it from the pocket of his white smock, Dr. Sabine became alarmed when he read the message: Rec Code Red (recovery patient in distress). Dr. Sabine, trying to remain calm, excused himself and told Mr. Nesmith that he would be able to see his wife shortly, but as a precaution, he wanted to keep her overnight. Mr. Nesmith simply replied that he also thought that wise given his wife's age and all.

When Dr. Sabine entered the recovery room, he couldn't believe his eyes. Mrs. Nesmith had somehow pulled out her saline drip and the wire leads attached to her body to monitor respiration, blood pressure, and her heart. She was wildly flailing about in the bed. Four nurses were trying to hold her down but were losing the battle. Dr. Sabine quickly ordered a sedative even though she was still feeling the effects of the anesthesia administered during her operation. After the sedative was administered, her muscles relaxed, and Mrs. Nesmith laid still and began mumbling. Dr. Sabine bent down over her and could hear the words: "White light. See it. It's coming. The light…the light."

Dr. Sabine didn't know what to think. As a precaution, he ordered Mrs. Nesmith to be put in restrains to prevent a reoccurrence. Three hours later, Mrs. Nesmith awoke, the restraints were removed, and she was taken to her room. Old Ed shuffled into his wife's room, walked over to the bed, and slowly bent over and gently kissed his wife on her forehead. He then pushed one of those uncomfortable visitor's chairs over to the side of his wife's bed and sat down. Ed reached out for his wife's hand and tenderly grasped it in the palm of his hand. Throughout the night, Ed remained in this position watching his wife's chest rise and fall under the thin white blanket with each precious breath. The night passed quickly for Ed as he was lost in thought; thoughts of their life on the farm together. The good times and the bad times didn't matter as long as they were together.

As the stillness of the night transformed into the activity of the day, preparations were made for Mrs. Nesmith to be discharged. Dr. Sabine came in to examine his patient and satisfied that all was okay. He signed the discharge papers. A volunteer wheeled Mrs. Nesmith down to the front entrance of the hospital while Ed went to get the old station wagon.

As Ed parked his old car in front of the hospital entrance, his wife emerged in her wheelchair. Once Ed was out of the car, he took over from the volunteer and helped his wife up, and while holding her arm, he slowly walked her to the passenger side. Once his wife was safe in the car, Ed thanked the volunteer and then sat back down behind the wheel of the car. Slowly, after putting the car in gear, Ed pulled away from the hospital for what he hoped would be the last time. You see,

Ed and his type of person don't trust doctors. They have no reason not to trust them, but they know that they do.

The second case that drew Arty to this town was the case of Simon Payne. Simon's case was similar to Mrs. Nesmith but was different in one regard. True, they had both claimed to see a light come out of the darkness, and they both had objects removed from their wrists, but Simon seemed to remember. Just what he remembered he wasn't so sure of. It was more like frozen images in his memory rather than a sequence of events, and it was impossible for him to adequately connect those images. Simon wasn't shy about these images; in fact, he would tell everyone he could about them, but he seldom found a sympatric ear. Some people would at least pretend to listen, and when he was finished, they would immediately make up an excuse to leave his company while others would do their best to avoid any contact with Simon.

Most people regarded Simon as a bit eccentric, and by most standards, he was. Simon was not a rich man, and you couldn't really call him poor, but rather, he walked the thin line between survival and poverty. Simon's only source of income was his military pension and that was a pittance, considering a lifetime of dedicated service to a country that in a larger sense didn't even know his name. But the small amount of money he received allowed him to exist on his own, and Simon was grateful for that.

Simon lived alone on a small hill a few hundred feet from a road that anyone hardly traveled on a regular basis save the ever-faithful mailman, but even he avoided contact with Simon. His house was a simple one. It was, more or less, a platform elevated off the ground on rocks so that snakes and other varmint could not easily enter the home. The house was made out of scrap lumber that others cast off and was probably salvaged from the local landfill. But Simon was proud, and the one room home he constructed served his needs. One day, he hoped to have electricity, but the local power company wanted too much money to run the power lines to his house. Simon also wanted to have a heating system one day, and running water would be nice, but that cost money, and there was far too little of that to waste on such comforts. He also had thought about getting a telephone, but then he realized that he really had no one to call. His family was dead and his friends, well Simon really had no one he could truly call a friend. In reality, a town that prided itself on friendliness failed him. Simon was a person that mostly everyone hurried by, and no one ever lent a hand or extended a smile to this gentle creature.

When Arty and his escort first arrived in Heyitvill, they settled into the local motel and immediately began looking for Simon. The only paper trail of Simon they had to go on was the medical file, which detailed the removal of the object from his wrist and his pension and military service records from the government. After a few hours spent on the military net, they were able to pinpoint Simon's home and obtained a high-resolution satellite image of his house, which showed in great detail the property and the surrounding area. Arty couldn't believe the contrast between Simon's home and those of his neighbors on either side. Simon's home appeared to be, what could best be described as, a poor man's shack. On each side of Simon's home, about three hundred feet away, were sprawling ranch homes with the required pools in the backyards. Immediately, Arty felt sorry for Simon and wondered what went wrong. How could a highly decorated veteran of Vietnam and the Gulf War come to live out his days like this? Sure, Arty had to interview this man, but he was determined to help Simon in some way. Just how he would help him, Arty didn't know, but help him he would.

When Arty and his team arrived at Simon's home, Arty thought it best if he went in alone and instructed his team to remain in the vehicle and park at the end of the driveway. As Arty walked up the washed-out trail leading up to the house, he looked around and observed that the grounds were immaculate in appearance with all bushes trimmed and flowers planted and attended to along the walkway. Upon reaching the house, the first thing that caught his eye was a large American flag hanging on the wall next to the front door. *A proud man*, Arty thought to himself. Arty continued on and ascended the few steps up to the home. As he walked, a sick feeling was forming in the pit of his stomach. His brain, at first, didn't register the smell, but the memory of the smell crept into the present. It was a smell Arty was familiar with and would never forget. It was the smell of death.

As Arty walked to the front door, he reached in his back pocket and withdrew some tissues. He held them over his nose and mouth with one hand while he opened the unlocked door with his other. The smell overcame him, and Arty felt like running out the door as the bile rose within his stomach, but instead, he pressed on keeping down the urge to vomit. Quickly scanning the room, Arty saw Simon lying on his bed in a corner of the room. Arty slowly walked over to his side and stared down at the man he did not know but had come to respect. *What brought this man to this?* Arty wondered. Slowly, Arty reached down with his free hand and pulled a sheet over Simon's face and silently said a prayer for the soul of this gentle creature.

Arty then turned around and began to walk outside when his attention was drawn to a picture hanging on the wall. He then noticed a piece of wood next to the picture upon which was mounted a Silver Star medal. From the government service records, Arty knew the story well. The closing days of Vietnam found Simon and his squadron of Recon Marines doing sweeps of the countryside just outside of Da Nang…

On one such mission, Simon's squadron was patrolling alongside a road sweeping the area in anticipation of a friendly truck convoy coming down the road in the next few hours. Their main concern was the jungle that was approximately one hundred and fifty feet from the road and the waist-high grass along the road, which they were walking through. Their mission was to make sure that the area was clear of any unfriendliness. His squadron proceeded cautiously in a single file with at least twenty feet between each man. According to the action report, the squadron came under fire as they were proceeding around a bend in the road. The point man (the man leading the squadron and who was approximately one hundred feet ahead of the main body of the column) had already turned the bend in the road and the rest of the squadron had just reached the bend when all hell broke loose. Simon, who was the last man in the column, heard the first shots fired and looked up the column. He watched in almost slow motion as two of his friends and fellow Marines were gunned down. Everyone who was left alive fell to the ground and started laying return fire in the direction of the jungle where the shots apparently came from. Mortar shells began to fall around them, and it would only be a matter of time until the enemy gunners found the range and zeroed in on the Marines.

Lifting his head up cautiously, Simon took in the situation and realized that the enemy had not yet discovered his position. The middle of the column was taking the brunt of the attack. Looking toward the jungle, Simon was able to locate the flashes of the enemies' rifles as they fired, and instinctively, experience and the years of training overcame him.

Slowly and with as much stealth as possible, Simon crawled on his stomach toward the jungle. As he crawled, Simon was careful to part the tall grass as he proceeded so that the grass would bounce back to its original position once he passed. This way, he would not leave a depression in the grass that an enemy soldier could observe and immediately know Simon's position. After what seemed like an eternity, but in fact it was less than two minutes that had passed, Simon reached the edge of the jungle growth and began edging his way toward the enemy firing position.

After a couple of minutes, Simon could see two mortar teams and beyond them approximately fifteen North Vietnamese regulars. Simon took a second to check his weapons, an AK-47 he had taken from an enemy soldier, a .357 magnum pistol, and a few grenades. Simon checked to see that the magazine in the AK-47 was full and his spare clips were within easy reach. He then checked that the pistol was fully loaded and placed it back in his chest holster, being careful to make sure that the snap closure was open. Reaching up to the left side of his shoulder harness, Simon also opened the snap closure to his combat knife. Lastly, Simon reached up to the right side of his shoulder harness and withdrew two grenades. Looking at the grenades, Simon hoped that he guessed right when he shorted the fuses down to about four seconds. (It was a somewhat common practice among soldiers in Vietnam to remove the fuse from grenades, which was set at ten seconds, and shorten the fuse down to around four to five seconds or to whatever time delay the individual preferred.)

Purposely, Simon edged closer, crawling on his stomach, until he was approximately twenty feet from the first mortar team. Slowly, trying not to make any noise and remain unseen, Simon stood up and then crouched down. Carefully, he laid the AK-47 on the ground in front of him within easy reach. After taking a deep breath, Simon pulled the pin on the first grenade and tossed it toward the mortar team. He then pulled the pin on the second grenade and tossed it with more strength so it would carry further. Simon put his head down as he counted. One, one thousand, two one thousand, three one thousand …the jungle reverberated with the sound of an explosion. As Simon reached for his AK-47, the second grenade exploded. Looking where he threw the grenades, Simon quickly took in the scene. Both mortar teams lay dead, strewn in all sorts of odd shapes. Looking beyond them, Simon could see the other North Vietnamese were momentarily stunned by his attack, and he knew that he had to strike now. Simon rushed the line of men, firing his machine gun as he ran toward them. In his initial burst of fire, Simon killed six more of the enemy. It took the enemy that long to realize what was happening, and the remaining North Vietnamese turned their fire toward the wild man running through the jungle toward them. Simon pressed on toward the enemy firing his weapon. He could now hear the somewhat familiar sound of bullets whizzing past him, but yet he continued onward. In seconds, he had killed five more of the enemy before his Ak-47 ran out of ammunition.

Throwing the AK-47 to the ground, Simon withdrew his pistol and fired the first shot wildly, but his second and third shot slammed into the chest of one of the enemies. Simon then leveled his pistol at another soldier and fired again, striking him in the forehead. Running toward the last two remaining North Vietnamese, Simon fired his weapon, but the shots missed their marks. He fired again, but the hammer of the pistol struck a spent cartridge, and Simon instantly knew that he was out of ammo. While still running toward the enemy, Simon threw the pistol aside, withdrew his knife, outstretched his arms, let out a hellish scream, which startled the two North Vietnamese. He crashed into the one closest to him, and as they fell to the ground, they together somehow managed to knock the other North Vietnamese also to the ground.

Simon found himself on top of the North Vietnamese he crashed into. For one brief second, both of these men stared at each other, each knowing that if they weren't enemies and they had met each other on the street, they might have been friends.

Reacting first, Simon in one quick motion shoved his left elbow into the throat of the enemy and with his right hand thrust his knife into the man's chest, where he hoped his heart was. Drawing upon all his strength, Simon then twisted the knife in a clockwise motion and felt his enemy's body go limp.

The last remaining North Vietnamese soldier was on his stomach, clawing with his hands at the floor of the jungle, trying desperately to get away from this madman who had seemingly appeared out of thin air and killed all of his fellow soldiers. Simon immediately jumped on this man and thrust his knife between his shoulder blades.

Knowing that he had not delivered a death blow, Simon reached for the man's face with his left hand and pulled his head upward. With his right hand, Simon already had removed the knife from the man's back and then drew the knife across the man's throat and felt life leave the last of his enemy.

Completely exhausted, Simon fell over on his left side and rolled over onto his back. Staring up at the sky, Simon breathed hard, quick, deep breaths, trying to relieve the pounding in his chest as he felt that his heart was about to burst.

The members of Simon's squad had stopped their firing when he had begun his attack and inched their way cautiously forward. When the firing had stopped, they came quickly and stood in amazement around Simon as they realized just what he had done. No one spoke for a few moments as they each knew that Simon had saved all of their lives. One soldier broke the silence when he said with a smile on his face "Fucking A, Simon. Fucking A" and then walked away to examine the carnage.

Arty let out a sigh as he recalled that Simon did not take the offer from his superior officer in Vietnam to safely sit out the remainder of his tour. Simon, true to himself, preferred to stay with his squadron and for the next three months placed himself in harm's way. When his tour in Vietnam was over, he returned to a country that somehow preferred not to recognize or thank him for his and his fellow soldiers' and sailors' sacrifice.

With compassion, Arty reached up and removed the Silver Star from the piece of wood. He held it preciously in the palm of his hand staring at it, and then he glanced over at the photograph and whispered, "Thank you." Arty thrust the medal into his shirt pocket, vowing to bury it on top of Simon's grave in Arlington National Cemetery. He then turned around toward Simon's body, saluted, and walked out of the cabin. Once on the porch, he removed the American flag, determined that it would one day fly in a place of honor. Where that was to be, Arty didn't know, but he tenderly folded it, kissed it, and placed it in the large pocket of his safari jacket.

Arty walked back to his vehicle and ordered one of his security forces to notify the local sheriff of Simon's death. While the call to the sheriff was being made, Arty placed a call to a longtime friend of his in the Veterans Administration. Arty informed his friend of Simon's death and his background. After a few minutes of conversation, he secured a promise from his friend that Simon would be buried in the hollowed ground of Arlington. After both calls were completed, Arty felt like going back to the motel and resting, but instead, he decided to visit the Nesmith farm.

The sun was just beginning to set when Arty and his team arrived at the farm. Turning into the long driveway, it would be a full minute and a half before they reached the house. As they approached the house, Arty tried to ready himself for the forthcoming interview; however, he kept wondering about Simon and what kind of a person he must have been like. Nearing the house, Arty looked out the windshield and noticed Mr. Nesmith walking across the wraparound porch of the old two-story farmhouse. Arty shifted his weight in the seat and thought to himself, *Oh well, it's showtime.* Once their vehicle came to a halt, Arty instructed the members of his team that they could get out of the car but had to remain near it while he went to talk to the Nesmiths.

As Arty walked up to the house and started up the front steps to the porch, he called out, "Good evening, Mr. Nesmith. I'm Arthur Giovine, but please call me Arty, everyone does." Arty reached the top step and walked a few feet across the porch and reached out and shook Mr. Nesmith's hand.

"Glad to meet you, Arty," Old Ed shot back and added, "Do your friends want to come up and sit down?"

"No, they're fine where they are," Arty answered back and then looked around and saw Mrs. Nesmith sitting in an old cane rocker, quietly rocking back and forth. Walking over to her, Arty introduced himself and studied her. She replied in kind, and it was then Arty saw a rather blank look in her eyes. Old Ed then directed Arty to sit in one of the porch chairs and offered him a glass of mint iced tea, which he gladly accepted. Sipping slowly, Arty wondered just how to begin.

Putting his glass down slowly, Arty began as he raised himself upright in the chair, "Mr. Nesmith, I represent the association for the Scientific Advancement for Farming Foundation. Our goal is the establishment of hydroponic farming in the southeast United States. We will accomplish this with generous grants to farmers to establish the methodology in the area and hopefully build upon those initial efforts. In this way, we feel that the average acre yield will increase at least by 100 percent and higher relative to the land used. Your farm has been identified as one such possible area for our program. Therefore, I would like to discuss with you your possible inclusion in our program."

Old Ed cleared his throat and for the next twenty minutes went on to lecture Arty about hydroponic farming, its successes, and its failures. Arty sat there and listened, at first amazed by what he was hearing; however, this quickly changed to boredom. When Ed finished talking, he asked Arty what tier or vertical stacking factor the foundation was recommending. Arty tried to sound impressive in his answer, but the look on his face and the pauses between parts of his answer gave the act away.

Old Ed was not one to be patient with others who try to deceive him. Slowly, he rose from his chair asking Arty if he could refresh his iced tea. Arty accepted Ed's offer eagerly and rose to hand him the glass. Ed took the glass and entered the house. A few seconds later, Ed emerged onto the porch without Arty's iced tea but rather, he was carrying a shotgun, which he quickly raised and aimed at Arty.

"Mind telling me just who in the hell you are because you sure in hell ain't no farmer much less one who believes in hydroponics." Old Ed declared as he pulled the firing hammer to the shotgun back and put his right index finger on the trigger.

"Hold on a second!" Arty shouted out and continued, "You're right, I'm not a farmer, and if the truth be known, I don't know squat about hydroponics. Hell, I'm lucky I can remember the word much less be able to talk about it." Arty saw a faint trace of a smile in the comer of Ed's mouth and relaxed a bit. "My name is Arthur Giovine, that much is true. My associates and I are members of the National Security Agency." Arty then glanced behind him and saw his security team with their guns drawn and pointed at Ed. Giving a hand motion to lower their weapons, Arty turned back around and continued, "Mr. Nesmith, we know about the object which was removed from your wife's hand. Your doctor had forwarded it to a research lab for examination and who in turn sent it to our agency for examination. We also know that during your wife's recovery from the operation, she mentioned something about a white light. I was sent here by the government to find out anything you may know about the object and the white light your wife saw."

For the first time, Mrs. Nesmith spoke up, "I have seen the white light at night in the woods over yonder."

"You don't have to speak to these men!" Ed quickly stated.

"But I want to. If the government sent them all the way down here to talk to me, then I'm going to talk to them. And put down that gun, you old fool! I swear he takes that damn thing out every time strangers come a visitin'. It's getting so no one comes to see us anymore. And bring this man his iced tea!" Mrs. Nesmith shot back, and when she finished, a warm smile crossed her face as she looked at Arty and then added, "Now what would you like to know?"

Arty watched Ed out of the comer of his eye as he slowly took his finger off the trigger and eased the hammer into the safe position and placed the gun standing up against the house as he muttered something.

"Excuse me, Mr. Nesmith, I didn't hear what you said," Arty spoke up.

"Never mind him," Mrs. Nesmith shot back.

Arty turned back toward Mrs. Nesmith and asked, "About the light, when was the first time you saw it and how often do you see it? Also, what happens when you do see it?"

Mrs. Nesmith sat upright in her chair and folded her hands in her lap, and with an edginess to her voice, answered, "I first saw…let me back up and start from the beginning."

"Take your time," Arty offered.

Mrs. Nesmith took a long sip of iced tea, cleared her throat, and began, "You see, Mr. Giovine, I was born in this house. My daddy built this house with his brothers, and I have lived here all my life. When Ed and I were married, we moved in with my parents, and when they both passed away, we decided to live here until we die. I love this house and all of the joyful memories it has. I watched as my children were born here and grew up here. Look around, have you ever seen a more beautiful place?"

"No, I can't say that I have," Arty answered, trying to get Mrs. Nesmith to relax.

"I know. This is a special place," Mrs. Nesmith replied and began to look around as if for the first time and then turned her attention back to Arty. "But that's not why you are here. You want to know about the light, and so you shall." Mrs. Nesmith shifted her weight in the chair and seemed to relax.

After taking another sip of iced tea, she continued, "As a child in grammar school, I, of course, used to hear the stories older children would tell us younger kids of a light that would appear in the woods, and as the story went, if you saw the light, you would die. I remember never wanting to go outside at nighttime, and every night, I would have the window shades pulled down tight. I thought that if I couldn't see the light because the shades were down, I wouldn't die. As I grew older, of course, the stories had no meaning, and it was forgotten about.

"When I was twenty-one, what I thought was a childhood fantasy became a reality. I was sitting right here on this porch when late one night I saw a ball of white light in the woods right over there." Mrs. Nesmith turned herself half around in the chair and pointed to the stand of trees about two hundred feet from where she was sitting.

"That was a long time ago," she added in a soft voice, lowered her head, and stared at her folded hands on her lap.

"Did anything happen when you saw the light?" Arty asked, trying to get her back on track.

Mrs. Nesmith looked at Arty and continued somewhat nervously, "The night that I first saw the light…well…the light moved toward me. I wanted to run, but for some strange reason, I just stood there. It is a beautiful light, but that's not why I didn't run. I…I…felt as if the light was talking to me and telling me to relax and not to be afraid. Each and every time, it's the same thing. The only thing I remember is seeing the light. I…"

"What? How many times has this happened?" Arty excitedly cut in.

"Oh, I used to see the light about once a month, no, it was more like once every three weeks," Mrs. Nesmith replied.

"Mrs. Nesmith, you used the word *used*. Does that mean that you don't see the light anymore?" Arty asked.

"Funny you should ask. Now that you mention it, I haven't seen the light ever since Dr. Sabine removed that thing from my hand," Mrs. Nesmith answered with a questionable look on her face as if she just heard something she didn't understand for the first time and asked, "What was that thing in my hand?"

"We have no idea. Our best scientists have examined it, and all of the results are inconclusive. Some think that you at some time, when you were a young girl, had nerve damage, and your doctor implanted it as a means of tying the nerves in your hand together. Others believe that it is an old surgical pin that was used to splint a shattered bone together. Do you remember having an operation on your arm, or do you remember breaking your wrist or arm when you were young?" Arty hated lying to Mrs. Nesmith, but it was better if she thought that the implant was related to some surgery when she was a young girl.

One thing was the truth though, Arty had no idea just what the implant was, but an educated guess was that it was some sort of monitoring and tracking device. This would mean that Mrs. Nesmith had something the aliens wanted. From the medical records, Arty knew exactly what it was.

"That's just it, I have absolutely no memory of ever breaking a bone, and I surely don't remember any kind of nerve damage. I'm quite sure my parents would have told me about it when I was old enough to understand if anything like that ever happened," Mrs. Nesmith confidently replied.

Arty had gotten the information he was after and was anxious to leave, but one other area had to be covered. "Mrs. Nesmith, when you have seen the light, was your husband ever with you?" he asked.

"Oh my, yes. I remember him being with me a lot when I saw the light, but he has no memory of it," she declared.

Arty turned toward Ed and asked, "Is that right? You don't ever remember seeing the light?"

"That's right. There were times we were sitting here on the porch, and Martha would stand up. She would look toward the woods and say that the light was coming. When I would say that I didn't see it, Martha would point to the woods, and I would look to where she was pointing, but I never saw it. At first, I thought that she had a problem with her eyes. After lot of trips to the eye doctor, we realized that it had to be something else. I knew she wasn't crazy or anything like that, so I just figured that it's easier to let her have her fantasy and let life go on, but then I later realized that something was going on," Ed replied in a soft, almost forgiving voice that portrayed his love of his wife.

"What do you mean?" Arty quickly asked.

Looking first at Martha, who returned his glance with a smile, and then back at Arty, Ed continued, "Well…err…I hope you don't think that I am crazy or anything, but weird things happened every time Martha said that she saw the light."

Arty's interest was piqued now, and he became impatient as he interrupted Ed again and asked, "What kind of weird things are you talking about?"

"Well, sir, every time Martha would say that she saw the light, I would get a tingly feeling through my body, and then both of us would wake up hours later sitting here on the porch. It was almost as if we both went into comas for hours at a time. For example, Martha would see the light at around 9:00 pm, I knew the time because I began looking at my watch when she said she saw the light, and we would wake up around three o'clock in the morning. We both assumed that we fell asleep, but I just knew that something had happened, but I never had a clue just what it was. Sometimes, we would be lying in bed asleep, and Martha would get out of bed, go over to the window, and just stand there looking out at the woods, and the same time lapse would happen.

"This may also sound a little crazy, but sometimes, when Martha saw the light, I would have a vague memory, kind of like a dream, of small creatures accompanied by a man come onto the porch or in our bedroom. They would surround Martha in a yellow light and sort of carry her away. I would try and fight them, but it was as if I was paralyzed or something. The whole thing was like a bad childhood dream of monsters that kept coming back."

Arty quickly interrupted by asking, "Could you describe the creatures and the man figure?"

"All right, but remember that I am not nuts! The man figure is similar to you and me, but he seems to have trouble breathing, in that he takes very deep quick breaths. His eyes, however, set him apart from you and me. They are noticeably larger than ours but look the same. What I mean is if you were to see him on the street, you would stop and take notice of his eyes. They are just large. The small creatures were no taller than four feet and seemed to take orders from the man. I would have to say that they resembled the aliens you see in science fiction films but different. Their eyes were not as large as the ones in the movies. They didn't seem to have any hair on their heads, and they only had four fingers. Oh, and they were all thin. There wasn't a fat one among them. Other than that, I can't remember anything else about them. Okay, so tell me I'm crazy," Ed replied in a voice that echoed confidence in his recollections.

"I don't think you're crazy, Mr. Nesmith, and I think that there may be others who may tell the same story. I just have to find them," Arty replied, feeling a kinship with this kind old couple.

"So you are looking for other people who may have had the same experience as us or have you already found them?" Ed asked.

"My agency sends me out to investigate all sorts of things, but I have never come across an incident like this one. But who knows what I will come across," Arty answered and drank the rest of his iced tea and then concluded the conversation and thanked Mr. and Mrs. Nesmith for their time.

As Arty was about to enter his vehicle, Ed called out with a chuckle in his voice, "Hey, if you ever want to get into that hydroponic business, give me a call first. I might save you from making some expensive mistakes."

Arty paused for a moment, smiled, and answered: "Good night, sir." And then he entered the vehicle. As they drove away, Arty felt sorry for what the Nesmiths went through due to the aliens. But he concluded that as long as there were people like that around, the aliens would never win.

Arty and his team then went to the local truck stop for dinner where the eating was always good, cheap, and plentiful. It seemed that everyone made an effort to be in good humor during dinner, which helped ease the tension for the moment. A laugh is truly the best medicine, especially when it is shared.

After dinner, the group returned to the motel for a quiet night's sleep and wait for the arrival of Richard Cunningham and his group tomorrow.

SO WHEN DOES THE SHOW BEGIN?

SCOTTY FOLLOWED HIS OWN ORDERS and retired to the comfort of his bed around dinnertime. After an hour of tossing and turning while replaying in his mind over and over again how he thought the events of tomorrow would play out, Scotty gave up and reluctantly left the comfort of his bed. He went into the bathroom and took a sleeping pill. Scotty knew that the next day would be a pressure cooker, and he simply needed his sleep. Returning to bed, Scotty rechecked his alarm clock for the fifth time and made sure that it was set for midnight. Lying on his side, Scotty adjusted his pillow and fell into the endless void of deep sleep.

A few minutes before midnight, Scotty awoke and stared at the alarm clock, counting down the minutes. When the alarm went off, Scotty sprung from bed, turned the alarm off, shaved, and took a shower. He shifted his weight under the pulsating stream of hot water in an effort to relieve the tension in his shoulders. For a moment, Scotty considered bringing a chair into the shower to sit under the water, like he used to do after a long flight. But time was short, and the aliens surely wouldn't wait. Regrettably, Scotty left the shower, donned a fresh flight suit, and walked to Space Command. He pushed all thoughts of the aliens aside for the moment as he daydreamed about Doreen.

Arriving a full hour before he told everyone else to report, Scotty thought that he would have some time to relax and read the morning intelligence reports as he savored some hot chocolate. When Scotty entered Space Command, he was surprised to find everyone at their posts. As he gazed across the room, Scotty saw Jonesy at his station in a fresh uniform, a rarity for him. JW was sitting in front of his computer station busily talking on the telephone. Vinson was also sitting in front of a monitor, which would later show a view of the hotel from a satellite. There was also a telephone in front of Vinson that was a direct line to the front desk of the hotel. The telephone was an added precaution Scotty had insisted on as well as an interpreter should the clerk of the hotel not speak English.

Scotty was happy to see his executive officer, Beverly Hocker, manning a computer station with Captain Bone. They were constantly monitoring the defensive posture of the base. Next to them, Captain Kendall was manning a computer as well. He had taken the precaution of having four F-18 fighter jets as well as four of the X-aircraft, armed to the teeth and ready for takeoff on a moment's notice. As an added precaution, CAG had also readied two Blackhawk helicopters and two Cobra gunships, also ready for immediate flight. JW contributed three squads of his Marines ready to man the Blackhawk helicopters and respond to whatever might happen. Finally, Scotty spotted Doreen, who was sitting behind the command desk coordinating all of the activity.

Scotty felt a little guilty about first walking over to the most important area in the vast room, the snack table. Trying to imagine how much coffee would be consumed that day, Scotty chuckled to himself and found the hot chocolate container. After pouring himself a large cup, Scotty picked up a cinnamon bun and walked over to Doreen.

Before he reached her, however, someone shouted out, "Admiral on deck!" Everyone that was not presently engaged in an activity stood up and saluted. Scotty carefully placed his cup on the floor and his cinnamon bun on top of the cup. He then stood up, returned the salute, and greeted everyone.

"Good morning. I know that today is going to be a difficult one for all of us. But I direct you to look around for a moment. What you will see is the very best this country has to offer in each of you. I fully realize the sacrifice that each of you is making for your country, and I thank you for it. We must stay sharp and at the top of our game this day and every day. I know that you are capable of it, and I know that you will each give your best. I thank you for it, and I salute you." After bending down and retrieving his hot chocolate and cinnamon bun, Scotty added, "By the way, there is a whole table of goodies up here, and there will be all day. So when you need it, don't be shy. Come on up."

The room erupted in applause and light laughter for a minute, but most importantly, the tension eased a bit in the room. Everyone then quieted down as Scotty proceeded to his command desk.

Doreen watched with admiration as Scotty made his little speech. When Scotty sat down next to her, Doreen greeted him with slight coyness in her voice, "Why, good morning, Admiral."

"Good morning, Captain," Scotty replied, drew himself near to Doreen, and whispered in her ear, "All that I really want to do is undress you slowly as we fall into bed and engage in some serious probing of the current situation." Scotty then sat up straight, took a sip of his hot chocolate, and noticed that Doreen had turned a pale shade of red. He watched her as Doreen nervously adjusted her thin uniform blouse in an attempt to cover up her now hardened nipples, which were clearly visible through her blouse.

Doreen could only respond in a high-pitched voice, "Me too!"

Scotty longed for what he had just said but instead settled for his hot chocolate and cinnamon bun. After a few seconds, Scotty asked Doreen if the news media was going to cover the conference on terrorism.

Doreen explained that the only American television station covering the conference was CNN. They were due to stay on the air from the opening ceremonies through the closing of the conference. The event was also going to be covered by the BBC and a French network. Then

Doreen explained, in great detail, the preparations the staff has done to cover every possible contingency.

Scotty listened with admiration for his crew. Every one of them had shown initiative and dedication. Scotty hadn't thought to bring the base up to full-alert status, but CAG, Beverly, and Bone had. JW seemed to be a human dynamo covering almost everything else. Jonesy was alert as ever, probably praying that the spy would use the satellite net so that he could pounce on him. Even Vinson had gotten into the act with enthusiasm, wanting to do much more than handle the telephone to the hotel. He was bothering everyone by asking constantly if he could help them.

During the morning hours of the conference, the wee hours of the morning in Colorado, a little boredom set in among the crew. Everything was going along as if it was just another boring day in corporate America. But this was not corporate America, and every day was unique with its own set of problems and challenges in the base.

As the day wore on, however, Scotty noticed a heightened sense of tension as the hours counted down toward the secret meeting. Scotty himself became more anxious and constantly asked JW for updates. He was surprised with himself as Scotty felt a sense of relief when the conference ended. *It won't be long now*, he thought to himself.

For some reason, Scotty started thinking about his grandfather. Most of the memories were pleasant enough, but Scotty centered in on the way his grandfather ate roast beef sandwiches. He would first butter two slices of bread, then add three, never more than three, slices of fresh cooked roast beef and some lettuce. He would then top off the sandwich by adding potato chips. He would then squish the sandwich together, breaking the potato chips. His grandfather would then eat hardy, really enjoying his food. Not being able to stand it any longer, Scotty rose from his chair determined to make one of his grandfather's sandwiches. As he began to walk to the snack table, his attention was drawn to a monitor that had been blacked out all day.

A satellite came alive, broadcasting a live picture of the hotel where the secret meeting was to take place. Scotty sat back down and watched as Doreen zoomed in a picture that showed the roof of the hotel in one quadrant of the monitor. In the other three quadrants of the monitor, Doreen somehow manipulated the satellite to show views of street in front of the hotel and the immediate surrounding area.

Scotty could plainly see people walking on the street, cars passing by, and deliverymen making deliveries. It was at this moment that Scotty thought of the people in the hotel and how he may have placed their lives in danger by scheduling the secret meeting there. He thought of two words in the English language that he hates. Taken apart, they are just two plain words, but put together, they mean unspeakable horror. Scotty struggled not to think of the words, but his mind formed them, collateral damage. The weight and implication of those two words hit him like a ton of bricks. All thoughts of his grandfather's sandwich disappeared from his mind. Scotty then donned his headset once again. The headset allowed him to hear all the orders being given to the security teams in and around the hotel as well as what was going on in Space Command.

Approximately thirty minutes prior to the start of the secret meeting, the human decoys began to arrive at the hotel. Scotty tried to imagine what was happening as he watched the satellite feed. The decoys would enter the hotel through the front door, go up to the first floor, down a hallway, then down another staircase, and exit through a side door, which JW's security men had secured. The agents upstairs in the conference room would be setting up the manikins and getting ready to run the audiotape. Once everything was ready, the agents would depart the hotel once the audiotape began. For a little added precaution, JW had one team of agents remain in the lobby of the hotel once the other agents departed.

BUT THIS ISN'T WHAT THE TRAVEL BROCHURE SAID

Admiral Morrison had been secreted away from the conference right before the closing ceremonies. He was taken to a waiting limo and directed to sit in the back seat by an unnerving character that looked more like he belonged in a motorcycle gang than the driver of a luxury limousine. Morrison was just getting comfortable when the car's tires screeched as the driver sped away from the conference. Swearing that the driver was a frustrated grand-prix-want-to-be, he held onto the passenger-assist handle for dear life as the car rocked back and forth, weaving through traffic. Once they emerged onto the highway outside of Paris, Morrison let go of the handle and settled back in his seat. He would have liked to have seen the countryside; however, the placid scenery was going by in a blur as the car rocketed down the highway.

After thirty minutes passed, Morrison was abruptly thrown from his seat onto the floor as the driver from hell made a sharp right-hand tum. Unable to contain himself any longer, Morrison let out a string of curse words regarding the driving skill of the devil in the front seat. As soon as Morrison repositioned himself in the seat, he noticed that they were entering a French air base. The driver did not slow down as he approached the gated entrance to the base, but rather, they were waved through. Two minutes later, after another series of high-speed turns, the car came to a screeching halt in front of the Air Operations Building.

Morrison opened the door of the car and for an instant thought about getting down on his hands and knees to kiss the pavement. Instead, he got out of the car, gently closed the door, walked up to the driver, who was still sitting behind the wheel, and politely thanked him for a most interesting ride. As he walked to the entrance of the building, Morrison said a silent prayer to his God, thanking him for his safe arrival.

Once inside flight operations, Morrison walked up to the operations desk and announced himself to the waiting clerk. He was asked to wait a minute as his pilot was summoned. Morrison looked around the lobby of the building and took notice of the drab military colors that seem present in countless military buildings throughout the world. There were also the required pictures of military aircraft adorning the walls, which seemed to blend in well with the clean Spartan presence of military business. When he heard someone walking down the hall, Morrison turned around and did not like what he saw.

The admiral had expected to see his pilot dressed in uniform who would then escort him to a waiting executive business jet for a casual and comfortable flight back to the United States. *Surely, after the car ride from hell, I deserve that,* Morrison thought to himself.

Instead, he was looking at a Naval aviator walking toward him, dressed in a flight suit with the accompanying G-force add-ons. The admiral's mouth was slightly agape as Captain Marcy Graham walked up to him, placed a small gym bag on the floor, and outstretched her hand as she introduced herself to him. The clincher was when she told him that she was his pilot for the trip home.

Morrison shook her hand and almost pleaded, "Pleasure to meet you, Captain. But why are you dressed that way. Do you mean that you are flying escort?"

Marcy momentarily studied the admiral and wondered what in the hell he was talking about. She then replied, "Admiral, what I am wearing is a standard issue combat flight suit. I pilot an F-14, and this evening, you are my passenger. You will be sitting in the rear seat, and for our safety, don't touch anything."

"Captain, there has been a terrible mistake. I am due to return on an executive jet," Morrison quickly replied, knowing that he was losing the argument.

"Sir, I have direct orders from Scotty…err…Admiral Scott. They state that you are to fly in my fighter. No disrespect intended, sir, but, come hell or high water, you will return with me."

Morrison slightly lost his temper and answered in a sharp voice, "I outrank Admiral Scott, Captain. What I say goes around here! Now get me an executive jet just as fast as you can! And that's an order, Captain!"

Marcy was surprised by his outburst but knew what she had to do. Looking Morrison squarely in the eye, she chose her words carefully and spoke in a soft voice but with a firmness the like of which Morrison had never heard before, "I have orders directly from Admiral Scott, who I know to be an admiral in the United States Navy. I don't know you, and I don't give a hoot in hell who you are. But Admiral Scott thinks enough of you to order me and my squadron here to carry you home." Marcy paused, reached for the gym bag, and threw it at the admiral as she continued, "In there is a flight and G-suit. I would suggest that you get dressed immediately. Otherwise, I'll have some very nasty people strip off your clothes and stuff you in the flight suit. Do I make myself clear?"

Morrison was equally surprised by her outburst. He also knew from her misstatement that she was a friend of Scotty's. Knowing that fact, Morrison was only too keenly aware that he would have to do as he was told. *Friends of Scotty seem to be so damn headstrong and are the best at what they do*, Morrison thought to himself and decided to try a new approach with "Ole Iron Pants" as he had silently nicknamed her. Taking a deep breath, Morrison spoke in a soft pleading tone of voice, "Now, Captain, take a long hard look at this well-nourished portly temple of fine food. Do you honestly think that I could fit into one of those flight suits, much less the cockpit of a fighter?"

"The flight suit will fit you. As for fitting in the cockpit, you'll fit fine. It will be a tight fit, but no worry there. We brought along a giant shoe horn to help get you seated," Marcy replied, trying to inject humor into a somewhat tense situation.

Morrison accepted his fate and entered a small bathroom off to the side and changed into his flight suit. While the admiral was changing, Marcy walked over to the window and looked outside. As if on cue, a Humvee pulled up in front of the building. Her attention was then drawn across the parking lot toward a few military police jeeps with their blue lights flashing. The Air Police were standing around a long black limousine with confused looks on their faces.

Marcy was interrupted when an officer walked up to her and introduced himself as Major Stills. He apologized for having neglected her but explained that he had been attending to the refueling of her fighter squadron. Morrison then came out of the bathroom and joined them. After introductions were made and pleasantries were exchanged, Marcy excused herself and the admiral. Together, they walked outside to the waiting Humvee.

Morrison stopped short and exclaimed, "Oh no. Not you again!" The limo driver from hell was holding the door of the Humvee open for the admiral.

"Why, hello, Admiral. Nice to see you again," the limo driver replied.

As Morrison entered the vehicle, he asked, "I suppose that you are a friend of Scotty's as well?"

"If you mean Captain Aldridge, yes. It's my pleasure to work for him," the driver replied as he raced around to the other side and sat behind the steering wheel. After Marcy sat in the back, the Humvee took off at a high rate of speed.

Morrison, once again, found himself holding on for dear life and asked, "Why was the Air Police around the limo that we came in?"

"It seems that some dastardly individual decided to take the Ambassador to Great Britain's car for a joyride. How it wound up on the base, I couldn't guess," came a quick reply.

"Are you in the Navy, son?" Morrison asked, afraid of the answer.

"Oh yes, sir," came a reply from a smiling face.

"Ours?" Morrison dared to ask.

"Of course, the best drunn outfit in the world," the driver replied.

"What exactly do you do for the Navy?" Morrison continued to probe.

"I'm in procurement, sir," he replied.

"What exactly does that mean. Wait! Don't answer that," Morrison stated while thinking to himself that he is really going to have a long talk with Scotty about the company he keeps.

Suddenly, the Humvee came to a screeching halt, throwing the admiral forward in his seat. Morrison quickly reached out with his hands and braced them against the dashboard, stopping his forward motion. Looking out of the window, Morrison saw that they were parked next to an F-14.

Turning toward the driver, Morrison offered, "Thanks for the experience. Just tell me that you didn't steal this vehicle as well."

"I prefer to think of it as borrowing, sir," he replied with a wide grin on his face.

"That figures," Morrison answered as he left the Humvee.

"Say hello to Scotty for me!" Morrison heard as he closed the door and walked alongside of Marcy toward the aircraft. He didn't know what to expect next but dreamed of the torture he would inflict on Scotty for the mess he found himself in.

Marcy directed the admiral over to the ladder leading up to the rear seat of the fighter. Carefully, Morrison climbed the thin ladder and gently placed his body into the seat. An aircraft technician quickly explained the function of the gauges in front of him while another technician adjusted the seat restrains. Morrison next received instruction regarding the ejection system, but he didn't listen. He was too busy praying. After his helmet was connected to the intercom and oxygen systems, he was again told not to touch anything.

When the technicians were finished, Marcy quickly settled into the cockpit and began her preflight safety check. Once satisfied that all was well, she lowered and locked the glass canopy. Morrison listened as she then radioed the tower for permission to take off. Praying that the plane would never leave the ground, Morrison's heart sank when Marcy received permission to taxi.

Marcy pushed the throttle gently forward and taxied her aircraft onto the runway. She was then instructed to hold at the end of the runway for final clearance for takeoff. While she waited, Marcy welcomed the admiral aboard and instructed him to remain calm, sit back, and enjoy the ride. Morrison, in the meantime, was looking wildly around the cockpit, trying to remember what the technician had told him about the gauges. His attention was then drawn to another F-14 as it pulled up alongside his aircraft and stopped. He then heard Marcy radio the control tower, and, as if by instinct, Morrison put his Nomex-gloved hands on his legs and dug his fingers into his flight suit.

"Sierra, Charlie 1-2, you are cleared…" Morrison heard over the intercom as Marcy pushed the throttle to the maximum. He felt his body being pushed into the back of his seat as the aircraft thundered down the runway. In less than a minute, they were airborne and climbed to thirty thousand feet. When Marcy leveled the aircraft, Morrison relaxed a bit as he looked out and saw three other F-14s flying alongside them. He felt the tension leave him as he gazed at the whisper-soft clouds above him. Looking forward, the admiral took in a beautiful sight few people ever see. He was flying at over five hundred miles per hour, streaking toward the United States, chasing an elusive vibrant sunset.

Major Stills watched from outside of the operations building as the flight of F-14s rocketed into the sky. He thought of Marcy and felt a pang of sorrow for her as he anticipated that the admiral would complain all the way home. Stills then laughed to himself as he visualized a mental image of the admiral in his flight suit. The admiral, he realized, was the classic definition of two pounds of bologna in a one-pound sack.

Major Stills then reentered the operations building and returned to his office. He sat down behind his desk, took a key from his pocket, and inserted it into the locked top drawer of his desk. Once the drawer was unlocked, he withdrew a four-inch square of orange plastic.

Holding it in his hands, Major Stills snapped the plastic square open along the scored line on its surface. He cast the two pieces aside as he withdrew a piece of paper from inside the square.

Major Stills unfolded the paper and placed it in the center of his desk blotter. He then picked up the receiver of his telephone and carefully dialed the number on the paper. Once a nameless and faceless person answered the telephone, Major Stills spoke one line, "The package is in transit."

After placing the receiver back on the cradle of the telephone, Major Stills sat back in his chair. He looked at the piece of paper and then reached for it. He stared at it for a moment as he held it in his hand. In one quick motion, Major Stills wadded the paper into a small ball and threw it in the air. He watched as the paper rose in the air. In an instant, the paper erupted in a flash of fire, and it was gone, without leaving the slightest residue. Major Stills shrugged and wondered what all the secrecy was about before he left his office for the day.

DON'T THESE GUYS EVER GIVE UP?

As time wore on, Scotty became edgier. He thought that the aliens would have shown their hand by now. According to JW, the audiotape that was playing in the fake meeting had only an hour more to run. So far, there was no indication that the aliens had made any attempt to electronically eavesdrop on the secret meeting. Inwardly, Scotty began to think that he had missed the obvious, but what that was, he couldn't imagine. His thoughts then turned toward the incident in Brazil. He remembered just how vicious the aliens could be. Then it came to him. In a flash, Scotty realized his mistake. The aliens weren't interested in listening in on the conference at all. The prize was way too big for that. Scotty put himself in their shoes and knew what they would do.

Quickly, Scotty rose out of his chair and was walking over to JW when his attention was drawn to the wall of monitors. A radar image of the upper atmosphere of earth appeared on three of the monitors. At the same moment, a radar operator announced over the intercom that six Z-1s were streaking toward earth. Based on their trajectory, the operator added that they would enter earth's atmosphere somewhere over Mexico.

Scotty didn't wait for events to unfold. He knew what was coming and had precious little time to react. Scotty donned his headset and spoke into the microphone, "Confirm upon execution! CAG, launch the 18s, weapons hot, repeat weapons hot. Orders to engage. Vector flight on your call. Mission to protect the base. Bring the X-aircraft on the deck (surface) and launch at your discretion, same mission. Launch two squadrons of X-aircraft and vector them to France. Mission to engage and destroy any alien craft." Looking over at CAG, Scotty was glad to see him busy talking on the radio and at the same time typing on his computer issuing the necessary orders.

As Scotty remained focused on the monitors, he continued, "Bone, bring the plasma cannons online…order to engage at one hundred out (one hundred miles away). Vinson, call your contact in the French Air Force. Advise him to expect an attack by Z-1 craft. Recommend engagement. Beverly, sound battle stations and seal up this base. Confirm that backup generators are brought online. Doreen, contact medical and make sure they are ready. JW, give your teams in France the evacuation order."

Scotty remained standing, watching the monitors and listening carefully as each of his orders were confirmed. Praying that he was wrong, but inwardly knowing that he was not, Scotty called out Vinson's name. He stopped from finishing his sentence when the radar operator announced that the saucers were dispersing over Mexico and heading toward the United States at seven hundred miles per hour at an altitude of sixty thousand feet. One second later, the same radar operator announced that another Z-1 was coming in over the Atlantic Ocean three hundred and fifty miles off the coast of Portugal. Its estimated speed was eight hundred miles per hour and accelerating. Instantly, another set of monitors showed the image of Europe with the location of the Z-1 displayed in real time. French fighter aircraft then appeared on the screen as they raced toward the coast to meet the threat.

For a few brief seconds, Scotty's attention remained on the monitors as he watched the French fighters close the gap to the alien craft. Turning toward Vinson, Scotty told him to contact the hotel and issue a bomb threat. Vinson hesitated and looked at Scotty. He saw Vinson staring at him with a look of puzzlement on his face. In a voice loud enough to wake the dead, Scotty shouted, "Now, Commander!" Vinson turned around, picked up the receiver to the telephone that was a direct line to the hotel, and nervously waited as the telephone in the hotel began to ring.

Hotel Intercontinental

If you knew Henri Gespard, you would know that working at a hotel was a bit out of character for him. His friends often thought of him as being more comfortable in the dust and thoughts of antiquity. But Henri was also one of those individuals that had a natural gift for languages. He seemed able, often to the frustration of the rest of us who labor over language tapes trying desperately to learn even the basics, to listen once to a language and instantly become familiar with it as he was with his native French. Over the years, he was able to become fluent in English, German, Spanish, and Italian.

Henri knew that he could have a better job as a translator for some corporate giant, but that was not Henri. He loves classic literature and, at present, was attending university to obtain his master's degree and probably later his doctorate in what else, classic literature. Henri took the job at the hotel for two main reasons. First, it did provide him with a source of income, and that, combined with student loans, scholarships, and whatever money his parents could afford, Henri managed to squeak by. He was making his educational dream a reality.

Secondly, because of his talent for languages, Henri was assigned to the front desk. The advantage working there was that the evenings were mostly his own. Often, he would sit behind the elegant marble reception desk with a book open. He would then become lost in the words of the ancient literary masters. His only interruption was occasionally answering a guest's question or returning guests their room key upon their return to the hotel for the night.

Today, Henri had come into work earlier than usual in order to help the day clerk check in over one hundred visiting foreign tourists who would arrive late in the day. Beyond the large influx of tourists, the only other activity in the hotel was a business meeting that was scheduled to take place at 6:00 pm. Henri knew the meeting would be no problem as long as the room was stocked with an ample supply of food and drink.

At 4:00 pm, the tourist buses arrived. Henri and the day clerk, Paul, worked furiously, checking the guests in. After an hour and a half, the last guest was in their room, and the hotel settled down into its ordinary routine. Henri checked the ledger to see what the meeting required in way of refreshments. He was surprised to learn that nothing had been ordered. Assuming that it was an oversight, Henri called the kitchen and ordered up a few trays of cheese, cold meats, crackers, and fruit to be placed in the room. He then called the bar and had them bring up a selection of dessert wines and a small dry bar.

When the food steward came to the hotel desk and told Henri that the person who came to the door of the conference room refused the food, he shrugged and directed the steward to place the food in the hotel's small bar. When the wine steward came and told the same story, Henri thanked him for his trouble and directed him to return the drinks to the bar. Henri wondered to himself who these rather odd people were. They apparently don't drink or eat, so Henri concluded that they were either monks or members of some weird diet club. In any case, the attendees were due to arrive soon. Concluding that the meeting would not require any of his attention, Henri thought about going home and then returning at his normal starting time at 9:00 pm. Instead, Henri told Paul to leave early and enjoy his evening.

Approximately thirty minutes later, some people began to arrive at the hotel. Instead of checking in at the front desk, the people just went upstairs. Henri thought them rude that they didn't even acknowledge his presence, but, in his own way, he dismissed them as one would a pesky fly. To his benefit, their lack of manners allowed Henri some time to himself. He bent down under the receptionist desk and withdrew his favorite book, *The Iliad*. With tender care, Henri opened the book to the place he left off and began reading. A smile crept across his face as Henri became lost in another time and in another place.

Henri looked up from his book when a guest left his room key on the desk and walked out of the hotel. It was then when Henri noticed two roguish-looking characters sitting in wing chairs opposite each other by the front entrance. He watched the men, with a keen interest, as they sat there pretending to read newspapers. But when someone would enter or leave the hotel, the two men would look the person over from head to toe and then communicate with each other in some sort of hand language, which they only understood. When Henri noticed, what appeared to be, a hearing aid in one of the men's ears, he concluded that they were policemen. His suspicion was confirmed when he saw the same man with the hearing aid talking into the cuff of his shirt. At that, Henri laughed to himself and wondered what was going on. His concentration was interrupted when the desk telephone rang.

Henri glanced at the ringing telephone and then back toward the policemen. He was disappointed when he saw the two policemen stand up and walk toward the front door of the hotel. As Henri watched them leave, he wondered what kind of a case they were on. He became excited, for a moment, as he thought of himself as a detective chasing a desperate criminal through the streets and back alleys of Paris, but that damn telephone kept ringing.

Henri abandoned his daydream and reached for the telephone. He let out a breath of frustration as he began his greeting in letter-perfect French followed by the same greeting in English, "Good evening. Hotel Intercontinental. How may I be of service?"

Space Command

Inwardly, Scotty knew that the saucers over the United States were a diversion, so he paid full attention to the monitors, which showed the Z-1 now crossing into France. He watched with anticipation as the four French fighters flew an intercept course toward the intruder. When the fighters were twenty miles from their target, each aircraft launched two missiles toward the saucer. The Z-1 managed to simultaneously explode all the missiles before they reached the saucer. The Z-1 then emitted a heat trail directed at the two lead fighters. Once the beam reached them, they disappeared into fiery balls of flame. The other two fighters broke off their attack and flew in opposite directions away from the Z-1.

Scotty called out to CAG and asked him the estimated time of arrival of the X-aircraft over France. He was disheartened to learn that the X-aircraft wouldn't be within striking distance of the Z-1 for another six minutes. Reluctantly, Scotty ordered CAG to recall all aircraft as he knew that the whole thing would be over within a minute or two. As if receiving confirmation of his decision, Scotty listened as the radar operator announced that the saucers over the United States were heading back out into space.

Hotel Intercontinental

Henri was surprised when he heard a madman on the telephone shouting in English that there was a bomb in the hotel set to go off in three minutes. Not believing what he heard, Henri inquired, "Sir, are you sure that you have the right number? This is the Hotel Intercontinental."

He was rewarded for his polite inquiry when the same voice shouted back, "Listen, you idiot! The bomb is going to go off in two minutes. Evacuate the hotel. Now!" The line then went dead.

Taking the telephone receiver away from his ear, Henri stared at it for a moment and then quickly returned it to its cradle. He then reached down and pressed a button under the desk to summon the police. Turning around, Henri then pulled the fire alarm. Instantly, automated bells started sounding in the hallways of the hotel but not in the bar and restaurant area. Seconds passed like hours as Henri waited for guests to come rushing down the stairs. But only a few heeded the alarm. Henri patiently instructed these guests to leave the hotel and stand across the street. When no one else came down the stairs, Henri wanted to go running through the hallways and knock on everyone's door. But he knew that there was not time for that, if the man who called was right. He listened for a moment for the reassuring sounds of police and fire units blaring their sirens as they headed for the hotel. But he didn't hear them. When no one else seemed to be paying attention to the ringing alarm, Henri ran into the entrance way of the small bar and restaurant area. At the top of his lungs, Henri shouted, "Get out! There's a bomb! Get out!"

All conversation in the bar and restaurant ended when Henri started shouting. No one moved. Henri then repeated himself but in a much lower tone of voice. Henri stared back at the people staring at himself and once again, in a normal tone of voice added, "You have to leave. There is a bomb in the hotel. Please leave immediately!"

After a few seconds, one of the patrons laughed and directed, "Turn off that damn ringing sound."

Everyone then turned back around and continued their conversations as they finished their meals and drinks. In utter frustration, Henri couldn't understand their reaction, but in reality, he didn't believe that there was a bomb either. He left the diners to their fate and raced back to the desk. Henri decided that he would call each guest room individually and issue a warning.

Nervously, Henri picked up the receiver and placed it to his ear. His other hand began to tremble as he dialed the first number. As he dialed, his other hand lost its grip on the receiver and dropped it onto the floor. As Henri bent down to pick up the receiver, he felt a vibration through his shoes and heard a low rumbling sound.

Space Command

Scotty stood in muted silence watching the drama unfold in front of him. He, as well as everyone else in Space Command, was transfixed as they watched the live satellite feed. The two remaining French fighters had managed to turn around, fly alongside of each other, and were now chasing the saucer. Scotty knew that their pursuit would end in failure. There simply wasn't enough time for the fighters to come within firing range of the saucer. In fact, there was nothing that could be done. Everyone was now an observer incapable of positive action.

As the saucer neared the hotel, it began slowing down until it came to a rest over the hotel. It seemed to hover there for a moment. Scotty held his breath as he knew what was going to happen next but prayed that it wouldn't. The saucer then emitted a concentrated beam of light onto the roof of the hotel. Two seconds later, the beam of light stopped, and the saucer speed off toward the west and out of view of the satellite. Scotty then heard a dejected voice over his intercom, announcing that the saucer was reentering space, away from earth.

Hotel Intercontinental

Henri stood up with the telephone receiver in his hand. Slowly, he replaced it back onto the telephone as he raised his head and stared at the ceiling above him. It was as if he was willing himself to see through the floors above, to find out what that the source of the now crashing sound was. Somewhere, in the recesses of his mind, a voice was shouting, "Run! Get out! Get away!" But Henri couldn't move. He stood there as the noise became louder and louder. After a few seconds, Henri realized what the noise was. Each floor of the hotel was collapsing onto the floor below it.

Henri looked down at the reception desk and picked up an errant pen and returned it to its holder. He wadded up a scrap of paper and threw it in the wastebasket. Seeing that the desk blotter was a little crooked, Henri adjusted it so that it was squared in relation to the surface of the desk. His last physical act was to adjust his tie and the hotel jacket he wore.

Henri smiled as he thought of his parents and then formed a mental image of his girlfriend, Marie, as tons and tons of concrete, steel, and wood came crashing down upon him. Henri's hopes and dreams of a future he would never know ended in an instant of pain.

Space Command

"JW!" Scotty called out.

"Checking, Admiral," JW replied.

Everyone in Space Command sat in silence and watched as a dust cloud formed around the remains of the hotel and then dispersed in the evening breeze. What was left for all to see was a pile of rubble on a street in France. There was nothing there that could even resemble what was once a proud hotel. Toward the back of the carnage, a gas pipe somehow stood alone above the debris spewing forth an eruptive flame.

The sight of the flame reminded Vinson of the eternal flame on the grave site of President Kennedy. He thought it would be fitting if such a memorial were to be erected in the spot where the hotel once stood. But he realized that it would not be so for economics always wins out. The property was just too valuable for it to be used as a memorial.

"Admiral," JW called out.

"Talk to me, JW," Scotty acknowledged him.

"All of the teams are accounted for, alive and well," JW replied with a smile on his face.

"Good!" Scotty replied and then turned his attention toward Doreen and Beverly. He ordered his two executive officers, "Secure the operation, release the satellite, and resume normal operations." Scotty didn't wait for his orders to be confirmed. Instead, he left Space Command and proceeded to the hangar deck. Once there, Scotty jumped into a Humvee and drove up the winding ramp to the surface.

Scotty waited for a fighter jet to land and then drove across the runway to a small knoll. After parking the vehicle, Scotty walked up to the crest of the knoll. He glanced over at the snowcapped mountains and wondered what it is all about. "Why do the innocent have to die?" he questioned. After a few minutes, Scotty raised his eyes to the heavens, extended his arms upward, and cried out, "Why?"

Later that night, an international news channel carried a thirty-second news story about a natural gas explosion that leveled a hotel in France. The newscaster then put a smile on her face and read a story about a herd of wild horses being saved from starvation in the American West.

For Henri's mother, her nine months of pain, joy, anticipation, and her dreams for his future ended as a passing footnote in life, brought to an end by a force known only to a few and understood by no one.

I WOULDN'T DO THAT

R ESTING UNEASILY IN HIS MOTEL room, Arty found himself pacing back and forth. Television didn't help much. Periodically, he would sit at the foot of one of the double beds in the room and scan the channels on the cable TV. Months ago, he would have found whatever the History Channel happened to be broadcasting of immense interest, but not today. Richard Cunningham and his security team should have checked in over two hours ago. The meeting had been set for late dinnertime, and now the light of day was disappearing fast. As the minutes passed into hours, Arty became worried. He had watched the news to see if there had been an airplane crash or perhaps if Cunningham was traveling by train maybe a train derailed somewhere, but nothing. Arty was frustrated by the fact that if they were traveling by car and had an accident, there was no way for him to find out. It was unlike Cunningham to be late for anything. *The man gave a new definition to the phrase "straitlaced,"* Arty thought to himself. He was painfully aware that they were both under strict orders not to communicate either between themselves or the base, but in conditions like the one he found himself, *Rules should be bent*, Arty concluded.

To help make the time pass, Arty once again took out his laptop computer and reviewed the cases he and his team had investigated.

On the surface, all the victims appeared to be normal average human beings making their way through life. They all worked hard for a living, they had the normal hopes and dreams shared by everyone, and they reveled in the joy and pleasure of their children. One among them, though, was quite a bit luckier than the rest. Twenty-seven-year-old Jessie Johnson was a lottery winner, and not an ordinary lottery winner. He had won a lottery worth one hundred and eighty million dollars. Of course, the taxman cometh and the tax man taketh, and in Jessie's case, he took seventy million of his winnings. But Jessie was still rich by any definition. He didn't squander his winnings but rather invested wisely and helped out his parents, siblings, and his friends. Arty thought about the interview he conducted with Jessie.

Under the pretext about writing an article about lottery winners, Arty interviewed him about his life. Jessie, when asked if he had any plans to settle down, replied that he probably wouldn't because how would he ever know if a woman loved him for himself and not because of the money. Arty pondered Jessie for a moment and then closed his file, thinking that Jessie may be the poorest man he had ever met.

As Arty pulled up the next file, there was a knock at the door. Arty crossed over to the door and looked out the peephole and saw one of his security team. Opening the door, he was greeted by Staff Sergeant Philip Stafford, a proud Marine, a veteran of Vietnam, the walk in the desert of Kuwait, the caves and mountains of Afghanistan, and the sands of Iraq.

"Dinnertime, boss," Philip called out as he entered the room and walked over to the small circular table and chairs and placed two brown bags down. As he began emptying the bags, he continued, "I got you favorite, outside cut barbecue, onion rings, American fries, and a Pepsi. Oh yea," he reached into the second bag and teasingly held up a large brownie wrapped in plastic wrap, "a brownie to die for."

"You didn't have to do that," Arty replied as he walked over to the table after closing and double locked the door.

"Well, if you would rather not..." Philip began to reply but was interrupted by Arty.

"Sit down, Marine, and eat. That's an order!" Arty cut in and then sat down, unwrapped the sandwich, and took his first bite. With a moan of appreciation in his throat, a smile crossed Arty's face as he reveled in the taste and then reached for his soda.

Taking a sip, he put the cup down, looked at the burly Marine across from him, and said, "Thanks, Phil. I needed this. I've been sitting here for hours now wondering where the hell Commander Cunningham and his crew are."

"I'm sure that they were held up for a reason, sir. They should be here any minute," Philip replied, trying to set Arty at ease.

"I hope so. But if they don't show by midnight, I want to head back to the base. We can't take any chances," Arty replied.

"I thought we were going to stay out for three months, sir," Philip stated but was really asking a question at this sudden revelation.

"It's time to head back. I found what we were looking for, and it's too damn important to waste more time. I wanted to see if Commander Cunningham found the same thing, but I'm beginning to wonder what happened to him," Arty replied in a dejected voice.

"I'll make the arrangements, sir," Philip replied and then tried to lighten the mood a bit, "What do you think about those Yankees? Looks like another World Series."

Arty laughed at the sudden change in conversation and then eagerly, as he ate, talked sports for the next half hour. As he talked and argued batting averages, box scores, and which players should and shouldn't be traded, Arty found himself feeling better and for a precious few moment forgot about the mission and what he had found.

This lighthearted banter was interrupted when Philip's radio crackled to life.

Philip and Arty held their breath when the voice on the radio announced, "Our late guest has arrived."

With that, Arty quickly gathered up the remains of their dinner and placed them in the garbage as he sucked the last drops of his Pepsi from the cup and then likewise tossed it into the wastebasket. As Arty crossed the room to the door, he instructed Philip to order a pot of coffee and some food, a turkey club sandwich would do nicely, for the long-lost commander. Philip stood up, grabbed his walkie-talkie, replied in the positive, and left the room as Arty held the door open. Arty walked outside and stood by the threshold of the door, first looking left and then right, searching for Richard.

A few seconds later, Richard walked around the comer of the building, and upon seeing Arty waiting, a broad smile crossed his face. "Arty!" Richard cried out as he closed the gap between them. Richard took his notebook computer out of his right hand, placed it in his left, and extended his right hand to shake Arty's hand.

"Richard, how the hell are you? God! It's good to see you. I was beginning to think that something happened," Arty replied as he shook hands and then motioned Richard into the room.

Richard crossed the room and stood at the table and chairs. Gently, he placed his computer on the table and then took off his light jacket and sat down. Once seated, Richard let out a big sigh and said, "Sorry we are late, Arty. We picked up a tail late this afternoon, or at least we thought so. We doubled back the way we had come and then headed east for a while. We finally lost them at a rest stop on the highway. Well, we didn't really loose them. One of the guys shot three of their tires out, and we took off like a bat out of hell. We didn't detect any other tails."

"Do you think it was the aliens?" Arty asked as he picked up his laptop computer and walked over to the table.

"I don't know. We got a pretty good look at them at the rest stop. All of us at once walked toward the bathroom and then turned around and walked back toward the cars. Both of them had also left their cars and followed. When we turned around, we walked right by them. One of them had sunglasses on, but the other didn't, and his eyes really didn't appear to be large or anything. Just in case, I wanted their automobile disabled," Richard replied.

Sitting down at the table, Arty replied, "For the sake of argument, let's just assume they were aliens. That means that they are onto us. It's time to pull the plug and head back. Besides, I think I found what we are looking for."

Richard perked up with that comment, opened up his laptop, and turned it on. "Me too. Every person we investigated was different in a lot of respects, but one thing was common in all of them." Once his computer was up and running, Richard made a few keystrokes and then turned it toward Arty and said, "Here, take a look at this chart. Is this what you found?"

Arty carefully looked at the screen and digested the data. Each column of the chart was mostly dissimilar for each individual in a respective category, but in one category, each individual was the same. Without looking up, Arty spoke what he was thinking, "My god! It's the same thing I found."

Richard sat there staring at Arty absolutely stunned. He suspected that Arty would have found the same result, but up to this moment, he hadn't realized or rather had refused to think of the consequences of what they had uncovered.

Carefully, Arty turned the computer off and folded the screen down until he heard the click that the screen was in the closed position. He, too, was momentarily stunned as the gravity of the situation sunk in.

"What do you think?" Richard hesitantly asked.

Looking down at the table, Arty replied, "I think we are in deep shit." Arty cleared his throat and then looked at Richard and continued, "Based upon what we found, it means that the aliens have been here for quite some time operating at will, at least up till now. But more than that, they are obviously looking to settle here permanently, and some of them probably already have. A little corrective surgery here and there and voila, what do you have? An alien that looks like a native earthling. Why else would they be trying to adapt to Earth? Scotty was right about the organ harvesting, but that now seems to be a sideline of convenience. Christ, Richard, this is scary stuff, and right now, only you and I are the only ones who know what the aliens need from us so that they can adapt to Earth's atmosphere. We have to get this information back and quick."

"I know." Richard rose from his chair and asked, "How far is Huntsville from here?"

"It's about fifty miles north of here. Why?" Arty asked.

"NASA has a base there. I'm guessing they have some private jets there for the big wigs. I'm gonna—" Richard replied but was cut off.

"Oh no, you're not. Scotty will eat you alive if you fly back," Arty pleaded.

"Look it, Arty, Scotty needs this information and damn quickly. Hell, I can commandeer an airplane and be back at the base in a few hours. It will take us two to three days to get back by car. And what about that tail I picked up today. We might not even get back," Richard likewise pleaded.

"You said it yourself. You are not sure that they were in fact aliens. It's best to follow orders," Arty retorted.

"Since when do you follow orders?" Richard shot back as he readied himself to leave.

"That's my point. Look it, Richard, what you want to do is something I would pull. But even I recognize that flying back is a bad move, especially when we are not even expected. And if I recognize it as being the wrong thing to do, then it must really be the wrong thing to do no matter what. Just follow orders, Richard," Arty pleaded.

"No, I'm going back right now, and... What the fuck was that?" Richard was stopped midsentence by what sounded like a gunshot.

Arty didn't wait for Richard to finish talking. Instead, he ran to the bed, withdrew a 9mm automatic handgun from under the pillow, and ran over to the door. Crouching down behind the door, Arty skillfully pulled back a corner of the curtain masking the picture windows of the room. What he saw he didn't like. One man was sprawled across the engine cover of a car and another was lying in the space between two cars. Both men appeared to be dead, and blood was everywhere. A few of his Marine escorts were standing over the bodies with their weapons drawn. Arty stood up and opened the door.

Philip immediately shouted at him, "Sir, stay inside!"

Not being one to listen to anyone, Arty walked outside followed by Richard. "What happened?" Arty asked of Philip.

"We saw these two men arrive at the motel. They first went to the office and then drove around here and parked. They stayed in their car for a few moments, then left their vehicle, and started walking toward your room. All of a sudden, they each took out a Mack-10 machine gun from under their sport coats. It was then I ordered them shot," Philip replied as two of his men searched the bodies.

Arty edged closer followed by Richard. Arty peered closely at the men and immediately noticed that the blood oozing from their wounds was frothy and looked pink. "Goddamn! What the hell is this?" Arty cried.

Philip then looked closer, looked over at Arty, and shrugged his shoulders.

Richard in the meantime bent down over the man, looked at his face, and said, "Oh shit!"

"What do you mean oh shit?" Arty excitedly asked.

"It's the guy from the rest area," Richard quickly answered.

The ever cool under pressure Sergeant Philip Stafford began issuing orders. Two of his men would stay behind to deal with the locals and declare it an NSA affair. They would demand that the incident really never happened. He then ordered Arty to get ready to leave within two minutes and likewise ordered Richard's escort to leave right away.

Arty and Richard looked at each other, and Arty again pleaded with him not to fly back, but he knew from the expression on Richard's face that his pleas were useless. Wishing each other luck and shaking hands, they went their separate ways.

When Arty reemerged from his room, less than a minute later, Philip was already waiting for him. Arty quickly asked if either of the dead men had anything in their pockets. Philip replied, "Absolutely nothing but this vial of pills." He handed it to Arty. Arty quickly looked at them and noted their orange color then put them in his pocket and entered his vehicle. Arty then waited for Richard's group to leave.

Richard's group quickly left the parking lot of the motel followed closely by Arty and his escort, now short of two men. Both groups entered onto Interstate Route 65 and headed north at a high rate of speed. Forty minutes later, Arty watched with resignation as Richard's group took the exit for Huntsville and headed toward the NASA facility. Arty turned his head forward when he could no longer see Richard's vehicle, reached up to the overhead center counsel. and pushed the rocker switch for the map light. He then reached down and withdrew a map of the central United States, unfolded it, and began to devise a twisted path back to the Colorado facility.

NASA Space Center, Huntsville

Richard and his crew followed the road signs for the Space Center which would direct the casual tourist to the visitor's center. Once there, a visitor could spend the entire day amid static displays of spacecraft that had actually flown in the cool chill and wonder of outer space. There were also interactive displays of space hardware. A venturesome tourist could even try his luck on some of the same equipment the astronauts train on, or one could immerse himself in the mock-ups of space vehicles like the space shuttle or the space station. Also, one cannot pass up the IMAX Theater, which offered exciting stomach-turning films on travel in space and its relative challenges. The Space Center in Huntsville is also the home of Space Camp where children and adults alike can experience firsthand what it is like to live and train as an astronaut. But it is also much, much more than a tourist attraction. Serious work and research were conducted here, which in no small way had contributed to the American space program.

Silently, Richard admired the hope, innocence, and spirit, which this facility offered to its visitors, and wished that this was truly a time of innocence. But this simply was not the case for Richard and the others in Space Command who could no longer view space solely as a challenge, but rather, they must recognize the deadly threat that was present in its vastness. The daydreams of childhood that carry forward into adulthood were now in the back of their minds as they faced an enemy that is their reality.

As they neared the facility, Richard directed Sergeant Hodges, the head of his security escort, to try and find the main gate. After a short while of driving around the Space Center, Sergeant Hodges located the main gate and pulled up to the guard shack and stopped the vehicle just short of the barrier blocking the road as he rolled down the window.

Three security personnel, dressed in black jumpsuits devoid of insignia or rank, exited the security checkpoint and approached Richard's vehicle. One of the men approached Sergeant Hodges while his two companions took up position about ten feet from the front fender, one on each side, of their vehicle. Richard watched as the individual on his side of the vehicle slowly and nonchalantly took his M-16 from his shoulder and held his weapon pointed toward the ground but definitely in the direction of the vehicle with one finger resting against the trigger. When Richard looked toward the officer approaching Sergeant Hodges, he noted that the other officer was holding his weapon in a like manner, but the barrel was a little higher and was definitely pointed at the vehicle.

"What is your business here?" the security officer demanded once he reached the driver's side window. He then began to shine a powerful flashlight into the faces of the four occupants and around the inside of the vehicle.

Sergeant Hodges very slowly raised his left arm and unfolded his NSA identification and handed it to the security guard and replied in a calm voice. "We need to speak with the senior official on duty right now. This is a matter of national security, and time is of the essence."

The security officer, to say the least, was dismayed. First, he had never seen NSA identification before beyond having seen a picture of one during his initial training, but there was an identification manual in the guard shack, which contained pictures and identifying features of all sorts of government IDs. Secondly, he wondered just why in the hell these people choose his gate and not the one a little bit further down the road.

"I'll need to see all of your IDs please," the security officer replied and then collected the identifications, examining each one to ensure the ID photographs matched the faces of the individuals. He then went into the guard shack and checked the IDs against the tests of authenticity in the identification manual. After approximately fifteen minutes, he was satisfied that the identifications were authentic. Just to make sure, he decided to double-check the identifications on the National Security Net—a small, often unheard of, office of the Defense Department which maintains a computer base of all government issued identifications along with photographs and physical descriptive data of the individuals issued such identifications. After another ten minutes of checking the identifications against the computer records, the security officer was satisfied that the people were who they said they were. He then looked at the daily duty roster and determined that Mr. James Schaffer, a middle manager who was unlucky enough due to his ranking to be assigned the night shift, was the senior official on duty.

Mr. Schaffer was idly sitting at his desk in his small office on the second floor of the administration building prepared to handle any problem that arose. In his case, those problems usually centered around a shortage of cleaning staff on any given night or such earth-shattering inquiries as to why the staff cafeteria was never open at night and making sure the candy and soda vending machines were well stocked. But Mr. Schaffer was content in his job and didn't lust after advancement or responsibility. He just wanted to exist.

On this night, Mr. Schaffer was busying himself with planning a fishing vacation to the Florida Keys. His desk was cluttered with brochures promising the fishing experience and catch of a lifetime. The odd thing was that Mr. Schaffer had never been fishing in his life. When the telephone on his desk rang, Mr. Schaffer glanced over at it with a frown on his face and with great reluctance picked it up.

"Hello," Mr. Schaffer meekly spoke into the telephone.

"Sir, this is security gate three. There are four agents from the National Security Agency here demanding to see you."

"Oh! Can't they come back tomorrow morning?" Mr. Schaffer replied, fearing that if they couldn't come back, he would have to make a decision.

"Sir, they are quite insistent…" the security guard lowered his voice to almost a whisper and continued, "and believe me, they don't look like the type of people you want to piss off."

James Schaffer hesitated, thought for a minute, and then in a frustrated voice replied, "Oh, very well, send them to the building, and I'll meet them in the lobby." Throwing the fishing brochure aside, the reluctant administrator stood up behind his desk, straightened his tie, put on his sport coat, and slowly walked out of his office toward the elevator.

As Mr. Schaffer exited the elevator, he was surprised to see three burly men accompanied by a thinner man waiting by the front door. As he slowly walked toward the door, James Schaffer wondered just what the hell they could possibly want at this time of the night. Upon reaching the door, James Schaffer smiled an uneasy smile as he reached for the swipe card suspended from his neck by an official NASA lanyard. As he swiped the electronic lock to open the door, Richard Cunningham pushed the door open, and all four men entered the lobby.

"Good evening, gentlemen. My name is…" Schaffer began to say but was interrupted by Cunningham when he shouted, "I don't give a hoot in hell what your name is. We are from the National Security Agency, and this is a matter of life and death. My life and your death. We need an airplane and pilots now! A business jet if you have one."

"Wait a minute. I can't do that. I'm in charge of candy and soda around here. I'm the guy that makes sure the place gets cleaned. I don't know anything about any airplanes!" Schaffer answered as he took two steps backward.

Cunningham reached out and ripped the plastic pouch attached to the lanyard from around Mr. Schaffer's neck. In the pouch behind the swipe card was Schaffer's official NASA identification card. After reading the identification card, Cunningham continued in a low voice that rose to the point of hollering, "Now look, Mr. Schaffer. We are agents in the NSA, and we need a plane now. If we don't get one, a lot of innocent people are going to die. Now get us a fucking plane!"

Schaffer saw the determination in Cunningham's eyes and walked over to the reception desk closely followed by his visitors. Nervously, he fumbled through the directory next to the telephone and found the extension for the aviation department. With a shaking, nervous hand, Schaffer dialed the four-digit extension number while mumbling to himself, "I ain't ever gonna get to take that fishing trip!"

Schaffer was surprised when someone actually picked up the telephone. "Hi, this is Mr. Schaffer over in administration."

"Yes, Mr. Schaffer, I know who you are. What can I do for you this evening?" the voice answered.

"I don't suppose that you would have a jet and a couple of pilots hanging around, would you?" Schaffer asked, sure that the man on the other end would say no.

"Why, yes, sir. There are four pilots on standby status, and all of our business jets are fueled and ready," the voice replied.

"You do? I mean…I need a jet right away for four NSA agents," Schaffer proudly demanded.

"Yes, sir. What is the destination?" the voice asked.

Schaffer turned around quickly, looked at Cunningham, and asked, "Where are you going?"

"That's classified. Just tell him 2,000 miles, and the pilot will receive the destination once we are airborne," Cunningham shot back.

Schaffer repeated Cunningham's reply into the phone and was told to send the agents right over. After hanging up the telephone, Schaffer turned toward Cunningham and stated, "Okay, the plane is waiting for you. If you exit the road you drove up to this building on and go left, you will come to a T. At the T, make a right and continue on for about fifty yards and then make a left…"

Once again, NSA Agent Cunningham interrupted Mr. Middle Manager Schaffer. Cunningham reached out and grabbed Schaffer on the right side of his sport coat and began pulling him toward the front door as he shouted, "You're coming with us, Schaffer!"

As they approached the entrance door, Cunningham tossed one of the Marines', Schaffer's identity card and door pass. The Marine quickly swiped the card and opened the door just in time for Cunningham to drag the unwitting Schaffer through the door and over to their vehicle. Cunningham opened the front passenger door and roughly pushed Schaffer into the seat and ordered, "Now just tell the driver where to go and no bullshit, just directions!"

Once everyone was in the sport utility truck, Schaffer humbly gave directions and held onto his seat for dear life as the vehicle sped off and almost flipped over as it negotiated high-speed turns. After a few minutes, Schaffer was thrown forward as they came to a screeching halt on the tarmac of the airport next to a small business jet that had its engines running.

Cunningham exited the vehicle and ordered Marine Sergeant Joseph

Stone to accompany him. As Cunningham withdrew his computer case from the vehicle, he paused, withdrew a disk from the accessory pocket, and put it in a zippered pocket of his light jacket. After closing the case, he ordered the driver and the other Marines to drive Mr. Schaffer back to his office. They were then to return as quickly as possible back to the base but to be on a constant lookout for someone following them. After saying goodbye and wishing everyone good luck, Cunningham and Stone climbed aboard the jet and took off.

Schaffer was relieved as he watched the jet take off and his escorts begin to drive back to the administrative building. To break the silence in the vehicle, Schaffer offered, "Boy, your boss sure is a hot head. Is he always that excitable?"

"Yea, he sure is a tiger that one. But you sure are a lucky man, Mr. Schaffer," the driver replied as he pulled into the circular drive of the administration building.

"How's that?" Mr. Schaffer politely inquired.

"Our boss has a funny habit we've been trying to break him of," the driver answered with a coy grin on his face.

"You mean because he hollers so much?" Schaffer hesitantly asked.

"Well, yea, he does that. But what I'm talking about is when he gets finished with someone, he usually shoots him in the head or orders us to do it. He didn't even mention it tonight," the driver answered, doing his best not to laugh.

"Think we ought to do it anyway? That way the boss keeps a perfect record," A voice from the rear of the vehicle offered.

"Nah! He told us to take Mr. Schaffer back to his office, and since we are here, we'll just let him go," the driver played along as he stopped in front of the administration building.

As soon as the vehicle came to a stop, Schaffer pulled the door handle open and jumped out, stumbling slightly, fought to regain his footing, and then ran up the few steps to the front entrance. Once at the front door, he began to feel around in his pockets for his entry card and then realized that one of the NSA agents still had it. In frustration, as if he could will the doors open, Schaffer pulled at the handles of the two glass doors to no avail. Turning around, he watched as the sport utility vehicle sped away. In total helplessness, Mr. Schaffer "Just Want to Exist" sat down with his legs crossed, leaned his back against the entry doors, withdrew a cigarette, lit it and took a deep drag as he thought to himself, *My god! I gave away a jet and two pilots, and I have no idea who I gave them to.* Shaking his head back and forth, Mr. Schaffer concluded, *Man, I am so fucked!*

Space Command

It had been a long hard day for Scotty. One of the longest and most pressure-filled he could remember since he began this job. He could not seem to shake the image, forever etched in his mind, of the hotel in Paris as it collapsed. But operations, that demanded attention, were continuing. The only thing that members of Space Command could do was to continue taking steps forward. There was no time to lick their wounds. Progress had to be made if they were to be successful and in the end victorious.

Vinson had left Space Command right after the incident in France was over and was on his way to Hawaii to meet the *Salisbury* before she sailed. All preparations were completed for the operation in the Pacific to begin. All the ships were in place, and now the really hard work was shortly set to begin. For a moment, Scotty thought of Vinson and the task that lay before him and the crews of the ships. True, the object on the floor of the ocean was the main objective of the project, but the sideline issue of possible alien response to the presence of the ships worried Scotty. He knew that the time for a fight with the aliens was still in the future, but if the aliens chose to attack the little flotilla, well Scotty was prepared to fight.

The highlight of Scotty's day was to be a quiet, relaxing dinner with Doreen in her quarters. This was later to be followed by a staff meeting. Scotty had fallen deeply in love with Doreen, and she with him. It was as if they were teenagers again and fell in love for the first time. For them, it was a return to the age of innocence. They both hated the time they spent apart from each other, and when they were together, well, it was time spent in a bubble. When together, they were both oblivious to the happenings around them, and nothing else mattered. The talk around the base of their affair quickly disappeared as most wished their admiral and his lady well.

Scotty walked to Doreen's quarters with a slight smile on his face in anticipation of some private time spent with his love. Doreen always tried to do something special for Scotty at times like this. Of course, she always tried to prepare a special meal for him, but to Doreen, it didn't matter if they ate hot dogs while sitting on the floor of the hangar deck. Sometimes, she would steal some flowers for the table from the atrium, or she would wear a special dress she knew Scotty liked (the white linen one), and on other occasions, she would take out a bottle of wine that she had smuggled onto the base, but she would only allow him a half a glass. To Doreen, the most important thing was the time they spent together, and if she could do something to make it more enjoyable, so much the better.

Scotty and Doreen spent the next few hours together having an enjoyable dinner and talking the time away, not about business but about each other and their childhood memories. No subject was too small to explore to the finest detail, but most importantly, they communicated and understood each other. But something special also was happening; they were growing much closer together.

After, what seemed like a moment in time to Scotty, he looked at the clock on the wall and realized that almost three hours had passed. Quickly, they cleared the table and packed the dirty dishes into the dishwasher. Before Scotty opened the door to Doreen's quarters, they embraced in a long passionate kiss that turned their attention, even more so, toward their personal desires. But duty is duty, and they both proceeded to Scotty's office for the briefing.

Arriving late for the meeting, Scotty strode in with an air of authority befitting an admiral while Doreen took her place at the conference table with the same air of authority but was a little flushed in the face. Scotty quickly called the meeting to order and asked each member to present an update of his or her individual areas of responsibility.

Following the protocol of rank and seniority, each member presented a summary of any progress or problems in their individual areas. Executive Officer Beverly Hocker presented an overview of the base and confidently expressed that they were ready for anything. Doreen was next and discussed the current status of the X-aircraft. Scotty interrupted her and asked, for the benefit of those present, if the space rescue vehicle was ready yet. Doreen informed the group that the aircraft were now in the initial stages of manufacture. Scotty visibly frowned as he was still upset that Morrison had delayed their construction.

Captain Kendall, the CAG officer, informed the group that all base aircraft were operational and commented that the two ready aircraft (fighter aircraft which are ready to take off on a moment's notice) should be increased to four aircraft. Scotty immediately agreed with that suggestion and gave the necessary orders. He was quite gratified that CAG had become much more serious in the past months and come to the realization, after the incident in France, that these aliens play for keeps and the threat was a very real one.

Next, Captain Bone, the weapons officer, gave a short briefing regarding the weapons stock presently on hand and the future projections. He also briefly talked about the disbursement missiles to the small fleet in the Pacific trying to recover the object on the ocean floor. Major Whitney then followed him. JW detailed the efforts his Marines were doing to try and ferret out the spy or spies who may or may not be present on the base and a basic review of ongoing security concerns. Lastly, JW detailed the combat readiness of the base and his Marines.

Scotty spoke very briefly about Commanders Giovine and Cunningham. Everyone expressed some concern for their safety but were relieved that they were following protocol and had not contacted the base.

The last subject on the agenda was the operation in the Pacific. Scotty started off by presenting a general overview of the operation supplemented by maps and a 3D graphical presentation showing the dispersed ships and a portrayal of the ocean floor where the object was located. Scotty then placed a video call to Admiral Laffey aboard her flagship, the USS *Abraham Lincoln*. Since she was able to see all of the people seated around the conference table, she greeted each one individually. After being prompted by Scotty, Admiral Laffey gave a briefing relative to the fleet and the degree of combat readiness. She finished her remarks by stating her belief that their mission would be successful, and if trouble came, she would not hesitate to deal with the problem when it arose. After answering a few general questions from the group, Scotty thanked her and wished her success before concluding the call.

Over coffee and some light refreshments, the group continued their discussions in a more relaxed mood. Each member also used this opportunity to catch up on each other's lives and how they were coping with living underground. When the meeting finally broke up, Scotty decided to go and check on Jonesy and see how he was doing.

Scotty knew right where he would be, in the main communication room of Space Command working on his beloved computers surrounded by empty wrappers from his new favorite snack food, chocolate cupcakes with the cream filling in the center.

As Scotty was leaving his outer office with the others following him, Marcy, who held her hand over the receiver of the telephone and had a very concerned look on her face, stopped him. Scotty looked toward Marcy and asked what was wrong. In a low monotone voice, she answered, "Admiral, there has been an open broadcast communication from Commander Cunningham. It seems he is on his way back to the base aboard a private jet. Lieutenant Jones is requesting your presence immediately in Space Command."

For a few brief seconds, Scotty stood still staring at Marcy, not believing what he had heard. The others in the group also had stopped in their tracks and had a stunned look on their faces. Scotty recovered quickly and started issuing orders. "CAG, launch the ready craft and prep another squadron. Bone, ready all defensive measures. JW, seal this place up tighter than hell. Doreen, alert medical and get a full staff on the ready." Before Scotty had finished issuing the orders, JW had already sounded the Klaxon alarm, which was sounding throughout the base, informing everyone that the base was on a full-alert status.

Scotty walked out into the hallway, and immediately, two armed Marines started following him. Before he took ten steps, Scotty turned around and hollered "JW, turn that damn alarm off" and then began running toward Space Command with his security escort in tow. Once there, Scotty pushed through the doors, disregarding the security checkpoint just in time to hear Jonesy shout out, "Shit!"

Before Scotty reached Jonesy, he hollered out, "Jonesy, talk to me!"

Jonesy turned around with a look on his face that made Marcy's expression seem like a smile. As Scotty approached him, Jonesy began talking, "A signal just went up the time telemetry to the satellites. I'm trying to pinpoint the sender." Jonesy was typing fast on his keyboard, executing the tracking program he had just finished a day ago. "It looks like…it's coming… Come on, baby, give it to me…it's…it's…station 32." Jonesy stood up and pointed to his right and two rows in front of him. Scotty and the Marines looked to where Jonesy was pointing and were surprised to see an individual standing in front of station 32 facing them. The individual raised his arm and pointed something at Scotty.

When the Marines saw this, they, at the same time, raised their automatic M-16s and fired. Their aim was perfect, and the individual collapsed dead as his body was repeatedly struck by bullet after bullet, almost cutting him in half.

Other people in Space Command looked on in horror as the scene unfolded in front of them, and a few screamed. Scotty turned toward them and shouted, "People, get back to work. I need you now more than ever. This is a war!"

Mostly, everyone returned to their work, and those who didn't were helped back to their work by the others. Scotty turned his attention back to Jonesy who was just staring straight ahead. "Jonesy!" Scotty shouted.

Jonesy turned back toward his friend and snapped out of it. "Scotty, you won't believe what happened," Jonesy stated.

"Jonesy, just tell me," Scotty pleaded.

"Cunningham is aboard a jet he conned NASA out of and is heading for the base. He's currently about two hundred and fifty miles out and is requesting landing instructions. His damn jet is broadcasting its flight code. Let me pull it up on the screen," Jonesy replied, and his computer instantly showed an infrared satellite image of a small jet as it flew over the ground. The image was also put onto one of the large wall screens on the far wall.

"Shit!" came a scream from someone in the room immediately followed by "Z-1's coming in. Two of them. Looks like they're headed for the aircraft. Images coming up now."

All attention turned toward the large screen as the saucers fell in behind the small jet. Immediately, a heat signature was detected going from one saucer to the aircraft. The aircraft didn't explode as one might have suspected, but instead, a broadcast from the aircraft was heard, "We are hit! Both engines out. We are going in. Broadcasting coordinates."

All eyes watched as the aircraft glided to earth and landed in what looked like a cornfield. The two saucers at first circled the aircraft from above and then landed within a few hundred feet of the stricken craft.

Scotty reacted quickly and contacted CAG, who had been monitoring the situation with JW. "CAG, get our aircraft over those saucers. I don't want them to lift off. Get me a helicopter strike force ready to go. I'll be right there. Tell JW I need his best right away. And launch that second flight and prep a third." Scotty didn't wait for confirmation of the orders. He bolted out of the room with his security force in tow and proceeded to the flight deck.

I FORGOT MY PLANE TICKET

When the elevator doors opened on the flight deck, Scotty paused momentarily and watched as organized chaos reigned supreme. People were running everywhere but somehow in an organized fashion. Two attack helicopters were being towed onto the massive elevator that would carry them to the surface. Two Blackhawk helicopters were likewise being towed to the same elevator. Squadrons of Marines dressed in full combat gear were walking alongside the Blackhawks, ready to board them when they stopped moving. Four of the X-aircraft were in the final stages of flight preparation. Two women medics ran toward the Marines and joined them. In the middle of all this, JW, dressed out in combat gear, was standing amid the chaos, chomping on a big cigar, hollering orders and giving prodding where necessary. Scotty noted that JW seemed to have a crooked smile on his face as if he was enjoying the action around him.

When Scotty stepped off the elevator and walked toward the helicopters, he was immediately approached by Carolyn Gibbs. Carolyn didn't say hello or good luck but instead walked along side of Scotty and began talking, actually pleading with him and at the same time giving him an order, "Admiral, I want you to put this on. It's something I have been experimenting with."

"What the hell is it?" Scotty shot back as he picked up the pace and looked at the strange piece of clothing, which resembled a vest.

"It's kind of a bullet proof vest that will absorb and reflect a shot from a laser. I tried it out, and all of the tests are positive," Carolyn stated with conviction.

"It looks like it's made out of glass. How is that going to stop a laser?" Scotty asked as Doreen approached.

"It is made out of small prisms ground to very specific angles that allow the laser to be reflected away from you. Look it, Admiral, it works. Trust me. Just put the thing on!" Carolyn shot back.

"If Carolyn says it works, then it works. Put it on. Please, Michael!" Doreen chimed in.

A smile crossed Scotty's face when he looked at Doreen and then returned his attention back to the vest. "What if they are shooting bullets? Do I ask the aliens to wait while I change into a regular vest?"

"I used Kevlar as a base material in the fabric which the small prisms are attached to. It will stop a regular NATO round. Just put it on!" Carolyn shot back.

"Michael, put the vest on, please," Doreen pleaded.

Scotty stopped walking and reluctantly put the glass vest on and zippered it all the way up to his neck. He then held out his arms shoulder high to his sides and spun around for the benefit of Doreen and Carolyn and asked, "It feels really light. Well, how do I look?"

"Like the man I love who is concerned for our future," Doreen stated, condemning Scotty to wear the vest.

"You look great. The aliens will want to know who makes your clothes," Carolyn answered.

Scotty looked at Doreen and announced, "Well, it's time to go. Wish us luck."

Doreen took a few steps closer and gave Scotty a short passionate kiss on the lips and whispered, "Good luck. Come back safe, my love."

Scotty turned to leave, but Carolyn grabbed his arm and turned him around toward her and said, "Admiral!"

Looking at the expression on her face and the sadness in her eyes, Scotty knew immediately what she wanted to ask. In order to give her some comfort, Scotty replied, "Carolyn, as far as we know, Arty was not aboard the aircraft. He may do some crazy things, but I am sure he would at least follow my orders this time."

Carolyn then stood on her toes and gave Scotty a kiss on the cheek under the ever watchful eye of Doreen and whispered "Thank you!" as tears appeared in the comers of her eyes.

Scotty looked once more at Doreen and kissed her lightly on her forehead and then turned around and ran toward the helicopters. As he passed JW, Scotty called out, "What are you dressed up for?"

"Where you go, I go!" JW replied as he also started moving toward the choppers.

Scotty didn't reply but merely smiled to himself and boarded the first helicopter and positioned himself in the doorway. He looked at Doreen again and saw her waving and as her lips moved and formed the words "I love you." Scotty winked with a broad smile on his face as the elevator started lifting the helicopters up toward the surface.

JW walked by the second helicopter as they ascended and shouted out, "Give them hell, Marines!"

An eager chorus of "Huh ra" met his cheer! JW smiled to himself and seated himself next to Scotty on the first helicopter. Scotty looked at JW, who had the cigar firmly locked between his teeth, and smiled as JW smiled back at him and gave him the thumbs-up signal.

God, he is really enjoying this, Scotty thought to himself.

In a few minutes, they were airborne and heading toward the crash site. Scotty put his headphones on and immediately asked how long before they reached the scene.

The pilot answered that they would be there in just a few minutes. Not satisfied, Scotty, instructed the pilot to give it all he's got. "Aye, aye, sir," came a quick response from the pilot even though he was flying at maximum speed.

Scotty then checked in with central communications to determine the status of the fighter aircraft. CAG informed him that the fighters were flying a circular pattern over the saucers. Scotty gave the direct order to destroy the saucers immediately. JW tapped Scotty on the shoulder and pointed off in the distance. Scotty looked to where JW pointed and watched as two of the X-aircraft swooped down and each fired one of the hypersonic missiles toward the ground. It was easy to see the fiery trails of the missiles as they raced toward their targets and impacted on the saucers. Anyone watching the encounter must have wondered at the sight of two large fireballs rising approximately three hundred feet into the air and then disappearing within a few seconds.

Moments later, Scotty was contacted by Space Command and informed that two more Z-1s were on the way. Immediately, Scotty gave the order to engage the saucers and destroy them. No one on the helicopters saw the engagement as it took place about two hundred miles away at the point the intruders entered the atmosphere. Four of the Xaircrafts were vectored to the expected point of entry of the saucers. When the saucers entered the atmosphere, they separated, and two of the X-aircraft followed each one. The pilots of the X-aircraft coordinated their attack, and on a given signal, all four planes each fired a missile. The speed of the missiles gave them the penetration power necessary to tear through the skin of the saucers and microseconds later explode. Both of the saucers exploded into fiery balls of flame as they tore apart in mid-flight. Most importantly, the pilots of the X-aircraft realized that the saucers apparently could not detect their missiles when shot from behind relative to their forward direction.

Scotty received word of the destruction of the two additional saucers and directed that a "well done" be passed onto the pilots. Then Scotty ordered that an additional four aircraft be launched to provide additional air cover by flying a circular protective ring at least one hundred miles from the crash site. The other aircraft on the scene would continue to provide an air cap (air protection) over the crash site.

As Scotty was finishing issuing orders to Space Command, JW tapped him on the shoulder again and pointed off to the right. Scotty again looked in the direction JW pointed, but this time, the sight was not one of victory but rather it sickened him. At first, his attention was drawn to a few small fires burning in what appeared to be a cornfield.

Once Scotty's eyes became adjusted to the light of the fires, as the helicopter he was riding in moved closer and closer, the shape of an airplane emerged. The fuselage was laying on its belly right side up with what looked like a blast hole in its side. It was as if someone blew open a hole to remove something. The starboard wing had separated from the fuselage and lay about fifty feet away, burning. The tail of the aircraft had broken off and was approximately one hundred feet from the main body. Scotty's heart sickened when he saw two motionless bodies lying on the ground by the hole in the fuselage.

Scotty held on tightly to the assist handle, built into the doorway, as the helicopter banked to the left and lost altitude as it prepared to land. When the helicopter was about three feet from the ground, and about one hundred and fifty feet from the crash site, Scotty leapt out of the doorway. After landing hard on the ground and momentarily losing his footing, he began running toward the downed aircraft. When Scotty was about thirty feet away, he stopped and froze in his tracks. He simply could not believe what his eyes were seeing. Silhouetted by the burning fires, two aliens had emerged from the large hole in the side of the aircraft. He knew instantly that they were the classic "grays" that countless people have reported seeing for decades. Their bodies were short and thin. They had large heads with slightly slanted eyes that made them appear almost comical. If he had to guess, Scotty would say that they were dressed in some kind of gray, almost silver, body suit.

One of the "grays" was carrying, what looked like, a laptop computer case. The other one had something in his hand that looked like a weapon of some sort. For the briefest of seconds, Scotty wanted to call out to try and make friendly contact with these aliens. But he quickly realized that these were the bastards that shot down Cunningham's aircraft.

Quickly, Scotty reached for his handgun, but it was too late. One of the "grays" saw him at the same instant, but the alien didn't hesitate and wonder if it should make contact with the earth man. Before Scotty could draw his weapon, the alien raised his arm shoulder high and aimed his weapon at Scotty. In less than a microsecond, a blue light emerged from the weapon and hit Scotty dead center in the chest.

Scotty felt the pressure of the hit as if a sledgehammer, a really heavy sledgehammer, crashed into his chest. Immediately, he was knocked off his feet and thrown backward about ten feet. When he came crashing down onto the ground, he was stunned. Scotty struggled to get up but couldn't.

A corpsman and two Marines ran over to him and unzipped the vest. The corpsman checked Scotty's chest but could not find a wound or a burn mark from the laser shot. Scotty could only shout "Son of a bitch!" in frustration.

With those words, the corpsman knew that Scotty was okay and helped him to his feet. As he was getting up, Scotty reminded himself to thank Carolyn Gibbs for inventing the damn thing. Her wonder vest actually worked.

In the meantime, JW and two other Marines who were running behind Scotty saw him hit by the laser. JW drew his handgun, and the two Marines leveled their weapons at the aliens. In an instant, the aliens, along with Commander Cunningham's laptop computer, were pulverized in a hail of automatic weapons fire.

Once on his feet, Scotty looked around the area and noted that the Marines had established a security perimeter around the stricken aircraft. Looking toward the aircraft, Scotty saw JW emerge from the large hole in the fuselage, with a look of disgust on his face. But Scotty, for the moment, was more preoccupied with someone who was lying wounded on the ground while a corpsman knelt over him giving him aid. Scotty decided to let JW handle the details for now and made his way over to the wounded person.

Amid the blood oozing out of the individual's chest, mouth, and forehead, Scotty recognized the person immediately. It was Commander Cunningham.

Scotty knelt down next to him across from the corpsman. Putting a hand on the commander's shoulder, Scotty tried to comfort him and offered, "You'll be fine, Commander. You have the best corpsman in the service helping you. Why in no time at all you will be chasing all of the girls around again."

Commander Cunningham, upon hearing Scotty's voice, turned his head slightly and looked at Scotty. As blood trickled out of his mouth and down his cheek, Cunningham struggled to talk, "Admiral…the blood…it's the," he struggled even harder, "B-L-O-O-D."

"Don't worry, son. The corpsman is stopping the bleeding. You are almost all fixed up," Scotty answered and then raised his head to look at the corpsman.

The corpsman looked at Scotty and slowly shook her head back and forth to indicate that the commander was not going to make it. Fighting back the emotion of wanting to cry, Scotty strengthened himself, looked back down at the commander, and in another attempt to comfort him, said, "You will be fine, son."

Commander Cunningham, with all of his strength, lifted his head up and struggled to say, "Ad…miral, no. The bl…ood, it's the blood." His strength gave out, and his head fell back down. Drawing upon whatever strength that was left in his body, the commander reached up, grabbed Scotty by the vest, and pulled him closer. He did his best to talk as the blood continued to trickle out of his mouth, "Admiral, Lev…iticus, 1714…1714…it's the bl…" Commander Cunningham stopped talking, and his grip on Scotty melted away.

Scotty looked at Commander Cunningham and watched as the commander's last breath formed a bubble of blood on his lips. The corpsman immediately tried to resuscitate the commander, but his wounds were great and the effort was futile. As the corpsman began to pack up her instruments, Scotty asked, "Did he say Leviticus 1714?"

"Yes, Admiral," the corpsman answered as she finished packing and stood up. Almost in passing, she added, "Funny thing. A man bleeds to death, and he quotes a verse of the Bible about blood."

"The Bible? What do you mean?" Scotty anxiously asked.

"Leviticus is a book in the Bible. Chapter seventeen verse fourteen is a passage about blood. It says something like, 'As for the life of all flesh…the blood of it represents the life of it.' Or something close to that, Admiral," the corpsman replied as she turned to walk away but then turned back around and said, "I'm sorry, Admiral. His wounds were fatal. There was nothing anyone could have done."

"I know. You made a great effort," Scotty replied and watched as she hurried away to see if there was anyone else who needed attention. Scotty looked at the commander and pondered the man's last words. *If blood represents the life of it, or to put it more simply, blood represents life, then I was wrong. What the aliens are after is our blood, and the organ harvesting is an added bonus for them.* His concentration was broken when Marines came over and placed Commander Cunningham into a body bag and carried him to a waiting helicopter.

Scotty stood there for a moment and looked around. Two more helicopters of Marines had landed, and they were on their way to secure the site of the destroyed Z-1 craft. Other Marines and corpsmen were searching the area for any more possible survivors. In the midst of all the activity, JW stood alone, still chewing on his cigar, directing the operation. Scotty walked over to him and simply ordered, "Report!"

JW turned toward Scotty and replied in a low monotone voice, "Admiral, both pilots are dead. One looks like he was killed on impact. The other pilot made it out of the aircraft and joined the commander and the sergeant in resisting the aliens. All three of them put up a valiant defense." JW paused and then added, "I'm sorry about the commander, Admiral. He was a good officer."

"Thank you, JW. I'm sorry about your loss as well. I didn't know your sergeant, but if he served under you, I'm quite sure that he was one hell of a Marine," Scotty replied in a somber tone.

"That he was," JW replied and then added, "Admiral, I want you out of here. The most important thing right now is that you are safe back at the base. I have a helicopter standing by for you. Don't worry about this mess. I'll have it cleaned up by morning."

"Thanks, JW, but I'll ride back with the bodies of the men that died here. It's the least that I can do," Scotty countered and then after a moment added, "Tonight, we fought back and won. But tomorrow… well, I just feel that we may need a bit more time to prepare before we can take the fight to the aliens. It seems though, the way things are moving, that we will be forced to make a stand soon." Scotty seemed to be in a reflective mood for a moment but then perked up and ordered, "JW, whatever you need, just ask. Also, I'll send out an additional one hundred men to help with the cleanup. If you need anything else, just call."

"Will do, sir," JW replied as he watched Scotty turn around and begin walking slowly toward the waiting helicopters.

As Scotty walked, he thought about Commander Cunningham. Given similar circumstances, Scotty knew that he would have done exactly what the commander did. At the same time, Scotty was grateful that Arty had not done anything foolish. He wondered where Arty and his team were though and wished that they would return shortly.

When Scotty reached the helicopters, he walked over to the one in which the bodies of the men were placed in. A crew member reminded him that there was another helicopter waiting for him. Scotty, more out of compassion than duty, replied, "No! It is my honor to ride with these men." He then climbed aboard and sat down. As the helicopter lifted off, Scotty took one last look at the crash site and wondered where and when it was all going to end.

When Scotty's helicopter touched down at the base, it was immediately ferried down to the hangar deck via the aircraft elevator. Scotty was glad to see that Beverly had ordered an honor guard for their fallen brothers-in-arms. Three Naval and three Marine honor guards in full dress uniforms approached the helicopter in a precision slow march. Together, they lifted each body bag out of the helicopter and placed them on separate gurneys. Each gurney was then pushed across the hangar deck by three other Marine and Naval honor guards toward the elevator for their final visit to sick bay. While this somber procession took place, a Marine bugler played taps, which hauntingly echoed against the concrete and steel walls of the hangar deck. The base personnel, who were off duty, had assembled in their dress uniforms and stood at rigid attention as the procession passed.

Once the procession was over, Doreen ran up to Scotty and threw her arms around his neck. She firmly kissed him on the cheek and whispered in his ear, "Oh, Michael, I love you!"

Scotty was more than equally excited to see her and warmly hugged Doreen as he, too, kissed her and whispered, "I love you, Doreen." They both had forgotten for the moment where they were until Scotty heard CAG softly clear his throat. Reluctantly, Scotty broke their embrace and turned toward CAG.

With a wide grin on his face, CAG exclaimed, "I sure am glad that you are okay, sir."

Scotty thanked him, and CAG immediately brought him up-to-date on the current situation and the disposition of the aircraft. Playing it safe, Scotty ordered that a squadron of the X-aircraft remain on patrol as well as a squadron of F-18s. All other aircraft were to be recalled immediately and readied for future flight. CAG suggested that an additional squadron of the X-aircraft standby to be launched if the aliens should return. Scotty, of course, agreed and issued the necessary order. As they continued talking, Scotty saw Carolyn slowly approaching them. Scotty excused himself and walked toward her.

When they were about ten feet apart, Scotty loudly proclaimed, "This is the genius that I owe my life to!"

"Thank you, Sir. But…but…I…" Carolyn tried to form her question as her eyes welled up with tears.

In a low compassionate voice, Scotty offered, "Carolyn, Arty was not among the casualties. I have no idea where he is right now, but I'm sure that he is safe."

Carolyn began to giggle slightly as she wiped away some tears of joy from her eyes and answered, "Thank you, sir. You're right, I'm sure that he is safe." Carolyn then turned away and continued to cry the cry that only happiness can bring.

"Carolyn!" Scotty cried out.

Turning around while still wiping her tears away, she softly answered, "Yes, sir."

"Carolyn, I really want to thank you for the vest. I would probably be dead right now if it wasn't for your invention," Scotty replied, hesitated, and then continued, "I can't thank you enough, Carolyn, you really saved my life!"

"And I want to thank you too, Carolyn," Doreen added as she joined Scotty by his side and put her arm around his waist.

"Oh, Admiral, I forgot. I would like to take the vest back so I can study the effect of the laser blast. Perhaps, I can lessen the force of the blast. I heard that the blast knocked you off of your feet. Was it a direct hit, sir, or a glancing blow?" Carolyn asked.

"It was a direct hit, and, yeah, the force of the hit knocked me back about ten feet onto the ground," Scotty answered as Carolyn began unzipping the vest to help him get it off.

Once Scotty was out of the vest, Carolyn began walking away. Scotty called out, "Thanks again, Carolyn." Raising one hand into the air and waving behind her, Carolyn was too busy to reply as she was already examining the vest.

Scotty looked toward Doreen with a smile on his face. He reached over and gave her a tender kiss on her cheek. Doreen smiled back and expressed her love for Scotty and her happiness that he was safe.

It would have been easy for them to spend a little time together, but Scotty knew what he had to do. He asked Doreen to call a meeting in his office with CAG, Beverly, Captain Clark, and herself. Doreen asked if it wouldn't be better to have the meeting in the morning, which would give everyone a chance to calm down after the day's events. Scotty felt that under normal circumstances that would be the right thing to do, but not now. He directed Doreen to have the staff assembled in one hour, which would give him time to shower and change his clothes. As he was walking away, Scotty turned around and asked her to find out where Vinson was at this moment.

After showering and leaving his quarters, Scotty raced to the mess hall and waited as a cook prepared a pepper-and-egg sandwich for him. Wolfing it down as he walked to his office, Scotty thought of the poor souls in Zambia and Brazil, the innocent people in the hotel in Paris, and now this tragedy. Scotty knew that he owed all of the victims something, but he hesitated to call it revenge. *But that is what it is, revenge in its purist form*, Scotty thought. But he was quick to separate the notion of revenge from logical action. If a person lets revenge guide his actions, then mistakes and tragedy will surely follow. *No*, he resolved, *revenge would be had, but it would wait until logic dictated the time and the place on his terms.*

Arriving at his office, Scotty stood in the reception area for a minute. He withdrew a tissue from one of the pockets in his flight suit and dabbed the comers of his mouth to wipe away any remnants of his snack. Once satisfied that all was well, he opened the door to his office and walked in. He greeted each person individually and then took his usual seat.

Before beginning the meeting, Scotty thanked Beverly for her foresight in arranging the honor guard for their fallen heroes. Scotty then directed that the men were to lie in state on the hangar deck for a day with full military honors. Then later a service would be conducted in order to bring closure for the crew.

Lastly, Scotty directed Beverly to prepare a cover story, such as a training flight mishap to explain away the crash and loss of life.

Scotty then turned his attention toward Doreen. He wanted to know the flight status of the X-aircraft that had flown over the crash site. What he really wanted to know was the mechanical status of the aircraft after they had flown. Doreen realized what Scotty was after and answered as best she could. She explained that for every hour of flight, the X-aircraft requires at least three hours of maintenance. Scotty let out a whistle of surprise at this revelation, but Doreen quickly cut off any follow-up question. She explained that the maintenance schedule is to ensure optimal pilot safety. Most of the down time was spent double-checking the flight, weapon, and computer systems. In reality, only one hour was spent doing mechanical checks and preventive maintenance. Scotty was surprised that so much time was spent maintaining the aircraft but realized its importance.

Turning toward CAG, Scotty declared, "CAG, it was a good operation. The pilots and the crews are to be commended. Their performance was exemplary. The training schedule has produced the results we wanted. Keep up the good work."

CAG smiled slightly and thanked Scotty for the praise heaped upon him, but he knew that Scotty was a hard task master. Many, many hours of training were called for if the air wing was to maintain their edge.

Scotty then asked Captain Clark for an update on the cleanup of the crash site. She informed the group that the site would be fully cleaned up, including the UFO debris, by morning.

Anxious to move on and hopefully get some sleep after this long day, Scotty switched gears again and asked about Vinson. Doreen told him that Vinson should be landing in Hawaii within a few hours. He would then be taken to the USS *Salisbury* by a security detail that JW had arranged. The *Salisbury* would then sail and join the small flotilla already assembled over the unknown object on the ocean floor. Not wanting to leave out any detail, Doreen added that the *Salisbury* would sail at full speed and join the rest of the group by late tomorrow.

Scotty cut Doreen off and asked, "That's great, but when will they start operations?"

Without skipping a beat, Doreen quickly answered, "Tomorrow night!"

"Okay, let's move on. Doreen, can we activate the video link with Admiral Laffey?" Scotty asked, sounding like a man in a hurry.

"Of course," Doreen answered as she rose from her chair and walked to the bank of monitors on the far wall of Scotty's office.

After pushing some numbers on a keypad, the video monitors showed a picture of the bridge of the USS *Lincoln*. Sitting in her command chair overlooking the flight deck, Scotty could see that she was, as usual, watching over every detail as aircraft were being launched for patrol duty. A seaman walked over to the admiral and apparently told her that the video link was on, then she immediately turned around, looked at her monitor, donned a pair of headphones, and spoke into the microphone, "Hello, Scotty. This is an unexpected pleasure. I was wondering when you were going to call."

Doreen bit her lower lip and wondered about Scotty's relationship to Admiral Laffey. He talked about her often, but Doreen had always thought that it was a professional relationship. Now, for some reason, Doreen thought that there might have been a prior love interest there, and she didn't like it. But her twinge of jealousy passed for the moment as Scotty began introducing everyone in the room to the admiral.

After the introductions were made, Admiral Laffey briefed the group concerning the status of the small combat fleet. Scotty interrupted her, as was becoming his habit tonight, and related the events of the hotel in Paris and the death of Commander Cunningham. As Scotty told her the story, it was easy to see from the expression on her face that her mind was already considering all the alternatives there would be with an alien presence in the area. Admiral Laffey told Scotty that she would increase the combat readiness of the fleet immediately and increase fighter aircraft patrols.

Scotty in a slow methodical way ordered her to fire at will if the aliens show up within the next twenty-four hours. After that, Admiral Laffey would have to evaluate her situation based upon the behavior of the aliens. Scotty added to his order that she should do whatever her gut tells her to. She knew what Scotty was saying, "Wax the bastards at the first opportunity."

For the next few minutes, they discussed what the USS *Salisbury* would do when she arrived. Both Scotty and Admiral Laffey hoped that the operation would be a quick one. Scotty wanted Vinson to quickly locate the object, determine what it was, and hopefully do a little exploration of the thing. He would like them to complete their work before the aliens found out that they were there. While Scotty wasn't sure what the object on the bottom of the ocean was, he inwardly knew that it was a space vehicle of some sort.

When the video link was terminated, Scotty looked around the table and could tell that Admiral Laffey had impressed them.

Beverly spoke up first, "She seems quite capable, Admiral."

"That and a lot more," Scotty quickly replied.

Doreen saw an opportunity and seized it. "I agree, Admiral Laffey seems quite capable. I'm sure that she has a lot of experience and her position speaks for itself, but I would like to know a bit more about her."

Scotty looked at Doreen and realized that she was fishing. Deciding to play along and heighten her senses, he began, "Admiral Laffey is a unique combination of talent, looks, and determination. No disrespect intended to anyone, but since it came up, to say the least, she is a very beautiful woman. But never let her outward beauty fool you. Underneath, she is a very smart, quick-thinking, analytical individual who is more than capable of accomplishing any task given to her." Scotty paused and took a sip of water, and Doreen seized another opening.

"Where does she come from? What's her background?" Doreen quickly asked.

Scotty inwardly smiled to himself and answered, "Well," Scotty paused for a second, wondering where to begin and then continued,

"Admiral Laffey is from Maine. She lived on a farm in a quiet corner of the state. For college, she attended a small midwestern university. At first, her grades weren't all that great due to an overindulgence of social activity, but through the years she matured. During her last two years of college, Maureen worked part time in the campus bookstore to offset her educational costs. Whatever money was left, she put into flying lessons. Upon graduation, Maureen entered the Navy and qualified for flight school. Once there, she excelled beyond expectation. Her natural-born talents of leadership and ability exposed themselves, and she finished first in her class.

"During her initial assignment aboard a carrier, Maureen was quickly recognized for what she is, a strong, decisive, more than a capable leader. In the years that followed, the old guard of the Navy couldn't help but recognize that she is just as capable, if not more so, than her male counterparts. There isn't an aviator who wouldn't want to fly with her. She has a reputation of always getting the job done. In both Afghanistan and later Iraq, Maureen was decorated for heroism way beyond the call of duty. Time after time, she risked her life for the sake of the guys on the ground. In the years that followed, Maureen's career took off like a rocket. Responsibility upon responsibility was heaped upon her, and always the results were the same, excellence. Finally, she was promoted to admiral and given command of the *Lincoln*." Scotty paused for a second and took another sip of water.

"How do the men that serve under her feel about having a woman for a boss?" Beverly asked.

Scotty smiled to himself and answered, "Every man and woman aboard the *Lincoln* know that if trouble comes their way, Maureen is the one to get them out of it. They recognize her as one tough individual who will stop at nothing to get the job done. The crew knows that Maureen has one standard, excellence, and they willingly give their best to her and to the *Lincoln*. But more importantly, her crew knows that their safety is always upmost on Maureen's mind. The Navy Department has file draws full of transfer requests to the *Lincoln*. Hell, a lot of people know that there is a long wait to transfer to the *Lincoln*, so what they will do is try and get aboard one of the ships in her fleet. I hope that answers your question," Scotty concluded.

"Yes, Admiral," Beverly replied and was about to say something else when Doreen asked, "What kind of effect does her service have on her family?"

With a straight face, Scotty replied offhandedly, "Oh, Admiral Laffey is not married." Looking around the room, but careful not to look at Doreen, Scotty concluded, "Okay, people, I need you sharp, so let's all get some sleep and pick it up later when the *Salisbury* reaches the object."

As everyone began to leave, Doreen lingered until she was alone with Scotty. They didn't speak but momentarily looked into each other's eyes. They then fell into each other's arms and kissed a long passionate kiss of desire and love. Doreen wanted him to come back to her quarters with her, but Scotty had to remain behind and finish his work.

As Doreen was leaving, she turned around and asked, "Michael, about Admiral Laffey—"

Scotty cut her off. "There never was and never will be anything between us. It's strictly a professional relationship!" Scotty declared.

Doreen raised her eyebrows and put a puzzled look on her face to confuse Scotty and said, "Oh, I was just going to suggest that we try and get her a few more missile cruisers for the fleet. But then I guess that you already thought of that." Doreen then added as she turned around and walked out. "Good night, my love."

Scotty stood there dumbfounded for a minute as he watched Doreen walk out of his office. The realization came to him that he had just been snookered. Scotty could only laugh and shake his head.

MID POINT OBSERVATORY, MINUS FIVE DAYS TO THE ASTEROID

Victoria found Dustin just where she knew he would be. He was at his computer station. His body was slouched over, leaning forward. Dustin's arms were crossed on the surface of the desk, and his head was resting on his forearm. He was fast asleep. Strewn around him, on the surface of the desk and on the floor, were hundreds of wads of crumpled up paper. Victoria took in the scene momentarily, walked over, and placed her hand gently on his shoulder. Her nose told her that Dustin really needed a shower while her eyes told her he needed a shave and a change of clothes. When Dustin moaned in response to her touch, he sat upright and struggled to utter. "Hi, Victoria."

Boy, he sure could use a breath mint, Victoria thought to herself as she took a step backward and asked, "How is it going?"

Dustin shook the cobwebs of sleep away and answered, "Terrific if you like bad news. But otherwise all screwed up as usual!"

"Okay, why don't you freshen up and come into my office so that we can talk," Victoria ordered more than requested. Without waiting for an answer, she turned around and headed back to her office.

"That's a good idea!" Dustin called out. Feeling as if a heard of elephants had run through his mouth, Dustin added, "Just give me ten minutes."

As Victoria walked away, Dustin stared at her retreating body for a moment, watching the gentle sway of her hips as she walked, no, glided across the room. Snapping himself back to reality, Dustin opened the bottom draw of his desk and withdrew what he refers to as his emergency kit. Rushing into the bathroom, he opened his toiletry bag and neatly arranged the contents on the sink. Arranged before him was shaving cream, a razor, underarm deodorant, toothpaste, a toothbrush, and most important of all, cologne.

Twenty minutes later, Dustin strode into Victoria's office feeling better about himself but dismal about the universe. Victoria was sitting at the conference table waiting for Dustin with a fresh pot of coffee and a selection of his junk food favorites. Before sitting down, Dustin poured himself a cup of steaming black coffee, gobbled down a chocolate cupcake, and tried to make small talk. He asked Victoria if she was okay as she seemed quieter than normal. Victoria replied that she was fine but seemed preoccupied. *Who wouldn't be?* Dustin thought to himself.

Once Dustin sat down amid his papers, Victoria didn't waste any time. "What have you found out?" she immediately asked.

Dustin was taken back a bit by her candor as she always likes to talk about other things before discussing business. But Dustin realized that she has to deal in the real world answering to bosses and, of course, budget constraints. Clearing his throat, Dustin recognized that the after taste of toothpaste and coffee really doesn't mix well.

"Well, there is some good news, but otherwise it is all bad," he began.

Before he could continue, Victoria cut him off in a curt manner and pleaded, "Please, Dustin. I need the facts and fast. I have to call Washington and then somehow we have to release the information."

Dustin readily perceived the tension in her face and more than recognized it in her voice. Leaning forward in his chair, he began, "I ran the computer simulations that we had agreed upon, and I have to tell you, it's not good. Although the one-eighth mass model is somewhat okay." Dustin paused momentarily as he saw the expression on Victoria's face grow even tenser.

He then decided to try a new approach, "Let me start over. When the asteroids encounter the meteor belts, it will not have any effect on DG122. However, DG122A will be affected. Its relative mass is its enemy. It simply is not big enough not to be affected by the meteor shower. With each model that I ran, DG122A will be thrown off course and escape the gravitational pull of DG122. The problem is trying to predict just where it will go. The one-eighth model shows that it will be thrown off into space with a probable elliptical trajectory that just may send it back to earth. While it is not a planet killer, it sure will change things around here. But that shouldn't happen for at least one hundred years, and by that time, mankind may be smart enough to realize the threat asteroids pose to the earth. At that point, they should be able to alter its course or simply blow it up. I think…"

"That's the good news?" Victoria interrupted.

"Well, kind of," Dustin declared and then continued, "If DG122A is one quarter or one half the mass of DG122, then we have a problem. DG122A will be a planet killer if it were to collide with the earth. But that is unlikely. From the data available, it would more than likely glance the moon. It won't destroy the moon entirely, but it will knock it off of its axis. The gravitational effect the moon has on the earth will also change. But just how much is anybody's guess. There simply is not enough data, at the present time, to make an accurate prediction. I know that this is not what you want to hear, but it is the best I can do right now. We should have more reliable data as the asteroids come closer. Then we might be able to get a handle on the situation."

Victoria sat there stunned, unable to move or talk. Dustin stared at her, appreciating what she now had to do, announce to the world that DG122A may collide with the earth or the moon. In either case, life would change. While Dustin saw the asteroid as a great danger, he did not want to be a doomsday alarmist. He emphasized to Victoria that there was also a possibility, however unlikely, that the asteroid might simply spin off on an endless track throughout the galaxy.

"Vicky!" Dustin spoke up but didn't receive an answer. Victoria was staring straight ahead, apparently lost in thought. "Hey, Victoria!" Dustin called out a little louder.

Victoria looked up, smiling slightly as she answered Dustin's plea, "I'm sorry, Dustin. I was just thinking. I know that it may sound selfish and all, but I'm worried about this facility. We do really important work here, and I'm afraid of any negative impact this new information may have on our work. You worked really hard, Dustin. Without you, this operation would have been closed down a while ago. But now, all of that good work could be destroyed by naysayers who don't know the first thing about astronomy. I'm just worried. That's all. I'm worried about the asteroid, but I'm more worried about what might happen to our project."

"Victoria, look, no one, but no one could have seen the second asteroid. It's there, and we have to deal with it. I only regret that we can't get a better feeling for it. There's no space shuttle up now that we could send over to the asteroid on a reconnaissance mission. Hell, there is not even a satellite available that we could send on a 'fly by' to capture some readings. So I guess the only thing to do is make your calls and see what happens," Dustin replied, trying to reassure Victoria.

"Dustin, are you absolutely sure about all of this?" Victoria asked, hoping for a negative answer.

"Yes," Dustin replied in a low voice and then added, "I am."

With equal resignation in her voice, Victoria directed, "Okay, I want you to sit here while I place the calls. That way, if someone has a question, you can answer it."

For the next hour and a half, Victoria and Dustin sat in muted shock as they answered question after question about DG122A for every official imaginable. When all was said and done, it was agreed that an announcement should be made as quickly as possible. The White House directed that the announcement would be made by an official spokesperson, who would arrive by private jet within a few hours. Victoria and Dustin were directed to stand behind the spokesperson when the announcement was made and look positive. Dustin would then be called upon to give a brief talk about DG122A and what it was expected to do.

Later that night, the impromptu news conference took place. Under the glare of video lights, the world learned of what DG122A might do once it crossed into the meteor belt. Dustin answered a few questions, being careful not to sound like an alarmist but rather a cool, levelheaded scientist. But the news media was after sensationalism, and Dustin knew that he provided more than enough of it. When the conference was over, the threesome reentered the observatory. Victoria retreated to her office, closely followed by the government's spokesman while Dustin shuffled back to his computer station.

SHARKS...THERE'S SHARKS IN THAT WATER

Vinson felt someone's hand on his shoulder gently shaking him awake. Reluctantly, he opened his eyes and looked around. When he looked up and to his left, Vinson swore to himself that he saw the face of an angel. Her hair was of crimson red, her face was soft but yet well-defined, her eyes were like deep pools of crystal blue water, and her smile, well to say she stopped men's hearts would be a vast understatement. This vision before him was beauty in its purest form, and yet Vinson could not move or speak. He sat there with his mouth open, but words would not come. This apparition shattered his dream when Vinson saw her lips form words and he heard, "Good morning, sir. Would you care for some breakfast?" His momentary fantasy was shattered into thousands of fragments as dreams and visions melted into reality.

Shifting his weight in the seat, Vinson could only reply with a very weak, "Yes." He reached out his arms and unlocked the tray stored in the back of the seat in front of him.

He then guided the tray down into the open position. As he was reaching to his right searching for the magic button, which would allow his seat to ascend to the upright position, his vision, dressed in an airline stewardess uniform, placed a food tray in front of him. After finding the button, Vinson pushed it and simultaneously shifted his weight off of the back of the chair. As if by some mysterious design, the seat back rose to the standard airline upright position. Vinson let go of the button once the seat back wouldn't go forward anymore and then rested his back against it. Instead of eating, what the airlines define as food, Vinson first glanced around the cabin at the other passengers and felt jealous that they were probably going to Hawaii to lie on the beach while he was here for God knows what. Reaching to his right, Vinson pushed up the plastic shade covering the window and was greeted with vibrant blues, reds, and violets, the colors of morning. He then glanced downward through the whisper of thin clouds and saw a placid ocean with just the barest hint of movement in the waves. As he continued to look downward, Vinson wondered what was ahead for him.

A UFO on the bottom of the ocean, who cares? he thought, but Vinson knew that it was fear clouding his thoughts. Scotty cared, and that was good enough. After all, they might find something to help defeat the aliens, Vinson concluded, shaking away the cobwebs of the unknown.

Turning back toward his breakfast, Vinson smiled at his epicurean delight and actually felt hungry. He hadn't felt like eating since the aliens did their deadly work, and there was the problem of his hesitation. Vinson never heard Scotty holler so loudly before. *If only I hadn't hesitated to carry out Scotty's order, a few more lives might have been saved,* he thought. That was something Vinson would forever carry around with him, but what hurt the most was the look on Scotty's face after he hollered. Vinson saw the look on his friend's face transform from concern to disappointment as Scotty stared at him. That one simple look hurt more than anything he had ever experienced.

Vinson shrugged and vowed to never again to hesitate. He thought of a poem that he had once heard but couldn't remember the whole thing. "For want of a nail the shoe was lost, for want of a shoe the horse was lost, for want of the horse the rider was lost…" Vinson silently recited and swore to himself that he will never be the missing nail. Again, looking down at his breakfast, Vinson grabbed the sealed plastic bag containing the silverware, opened the package, placed the spoon and knife down on the tray, and with his fork scooped up a small helping of powered eggs. For the next ten minutes, Vinson tried to enjoy his meal, but his mind was elsewhere, lost to the mystery before him.

An hour later, his airplane descended down through the thin cloud cover and emerged into the warm sunshine of Hawaii. Vinson stared out of the window as the islands continued to grow in size as his plane drew ever closer. In a few short minutes, the aircraft touched down very softly. *Must be an Embry Riddle graduate!* Vinson concluded, referring to the private aviation university in Florida and Arizona that prides itself on training what they rightfully refer to as the best pilots and aviation technicians in the world.

As the aircraft taxied to the terminal, Vinson disregarded the flight attendants' instructions and unbuckled his seat belt. Reaching down to the floor under the seat in front of him, Vinson grasped his soft-sided briefcase and placed it on his lap, nervously tapping his fingers on the top of the case. When the aircraft stopped at the terminal, Vinson immediately stood up, excused himself as he stepped over the legs of his seatmate, took his duffel bag from the overhead compartment, and quickly strode to the exit being the first in line to leave.

The flight attendant politely smiled at Vinson as she opened the doorway of the airplane and stepped aside as the obviously nervous man in front of her anxiously left the aircraft and almost ran up the passageway to the terminal building. Once Vinson emerged into the terminal building, he was immediately approached by two beautiful women, dressed in somewhat modern but traditional Hawaiian costume. As the women were about to greet him, two rough-looking men dressed in T-shirts and dungarees stepped in front of the girls and each one grabbed Vinson by an arm and led him away.

"Wait a minute, who are you, guys?" Vinson pleaded.

"We're the greeting party, Commander. You have a ship that's waiting for you," one of the men replied.

"Don't I get flowers around my neck? Hell, I'm supposed to look like a tourist. Don't you, guys, know anything about this undercover work?" Vinson tried to reason with his apparent escort.

"Where you're going, you don't need flowers. Now be a good commander and follow us," the other man replied, and simultaneously, both men let go of Vinson's arms.

Vinson did his best to walk alongside his escorts, but it was more like walking a foot race. Once outside, another man opened the back door of a black Chevrolet Suburban with darkened glass. Once they were all inside the vehicle, Vinson started to buckle the seat belt but was hampered from doing so as the suburban quickly sped away from the airport.

Ten minutes later, Vinson was still trying to connect the seat belt, but the vehicle continuously rocked back and forth as the driver navigated the traffic lanes on the highway. The driver was passing other drivers first on the left and then on the right, followed by the same thing over and over again. Finally, Vinson snapped the seat belt closed and looked out as the scenery sped by. The silence in the vehicle was broken when one of the men announced that they were at "Pearl." Vinson was a little surprised when they sped through the gate of the Naval Base and continued to race toward their destination. After a few minutes, the driver brought the car to a screeching halt beside a ship. The man who was sitting in the front passenger seat got out and opened the door for Vinson. As Vinson emerged, the man asked, "Enjoy the tour, tourist?"

Before Vinson could turn around and reply, the man had reentered the vehicle, and with the back tires screeching, leaving a trace of rubber on the cement, the Chevy Suburban turned around and sped off.

"You fucking maniacs!" Vinson shouted to the retreating vehicle. Vinson then looked up at the sun, squinted from the bright light, and turned around to face the ship.

A man dressed in a captain's uniform was coming down the gangplank waving to him. As the man approached, he called out, "Commander, hello, I'm Captain Montgomery. Welcome to Hawaii!"

Both men stood on the dock, shook hands, and exchanged polite pleasantries. Captain Montgomery then invited him aboard, and Vinson followed the good captain up the gangplank and to his assigned quarters.

Vinson was surprised by the roomy accommodations and the presence of a single bed. Walking over to the bed, Vinson placed his briefcase and duffel bag down on the mattress and turned to listen to the captain. Captain Montgomery explained that shipboard clothes were in the comer locker for Vinson's use. When asked if he would like some time to settle in, Vinson jumped at the chance and stated that he would like to relax for a while if that was okay. The captain agreed and invited Vinson to dinner in his cabin at nineteen hundred to which Vinson immediately agreed. He then did the mental calculations and realized that dinnertime, to nonmilitary types, was at 7:00 pm.

Once the captain left, Vinson looked around the room, opened the locker, and examined its contents. Inside were dungarees, sneakers, and shirts that were all his size along with a baseball cap embroidered with the name of the ship. Vinson smiled to himself, closed the locker door, and walked back to the bed. Reaching down, he pushed aside his briefcase and laid down. Staring up at the white-painted cold steel ceiling, Vinson quickly fell asleep.

A few minutes before six, Vinson woke up from a deep sleep having been startled awake by the rocking motion of the ship. When he first sat up in bed, he momentarily was disoriented and forgot just where he was. Quickly, he got out of bed and ran over to the porthole. His fear was confirmed when he saw movement of the ship's silhouette in the fading sunlight against the waves. Resigned to his fate, Vinson undressed, put on the white terry cloth bathrobe, which had been laying across the chair by the small desk in the far comer of the room or more properly the compartment as it is called on a ship, donned a pair of shower shoes, grabbed a towel, left his room, and headed for the shower room he had seen earlier when he first came aboard.

After showering, Vinson dressed in a pair of light blue dungarees and a soft-blue-colored cotton short-sleeve shirt and a pair of sneakers. Sitting on the corner of the bed, Vinson pondered just what the hell he was doing here. He knew the mission was important, but somehow, Vinson felt out of place. The men and women of this ship were professionals who knew their job. Ever since Scotty had first called him and invited him to go to Africa, Vinson had been winging it. Somehow, he had survived Zambia, the horrible mess in South America, the trip to see the inner members of the association, and lastly, the attack by the saucer in France. Vinson knew what was wrong. He was used to living in a black-and-white world where truth was truth and not in a world where everything was colored gray and was unknown. Now here he was again on another mission heading out into the unknown, unsure of what they would find and ignorant of danger.

Vinson felt alone. Scotty thought him capable, otherwise he would have been sent packing after his hesitation about the telephone call, Vinson convinced himself. He knew that he was Scotty's eyes and ears, but more than that, Scotty also demanded results. As he sat there and thought, Vinson, for the second time today, made a decision about himself. He knew that he had to reach down within himself and find what Scotty saw in him; he would not be the missing nail. *If these aliens were to be defeated, then by God, he would do his part and pity the man that stood in the way of his duty*, Vinson concluded, slapping his hands on his knees and stood up ready for dinner and Captain Montgomery.

Before leaving his compartment, Vinson, for reassurance, walked once again to the porthole and then knocked on the steel hull to test its thickness and reassure himself that it was sturdy enough to keep sharks and those giant squid, the documentary and science fiction shows keep portraying, out. Confident of the sturdiness of the ship, Vinson crossed to the doorway, ready to take on whatever may lay ahead and whatever the damn aliens had in store for him and his friends.

Vinson left his quarters and walked up one passageway and down another. He had come to the realization that naval architects were masters at creating a labyrinth. Pride kept him from asking for assistance from those he met in the passageways on his quest for the captain's quarters. After a half hour of meandering this way and that, up this ladder and down another, Vinson finally arrived at his destination.

Standing in front of the door, Vinson adjusted his clothing and wondered just how in the hell he was ever going to find his way back to his quarters. *If Scotty ever sends me aboard another ship, I'm either goanna bring a box of chalk to mark my way or a very big ball of string,*

Vinson thought to himself as he extended his arm and knocked twice on the captain's door.

"Enter!" Captain Montgomery called out.

Vinson turned the door handle, entered the room, and held the door open as a steward left the room. Quietly, Vinson closed the door behind the steward then faced Captain Montgomery and offered, "Good evening, Captain. Sorry that I am late. I'm afraid that I overslept a bit."

"Got lost, didn't yea?" Captain Montgomery asked as he withdrew his chair from the table, sat down, and motioned for Vinson to sit down.

"God, yes!" Vinson exclaimed as he crossed the room and sat opposite Captain Montgomery and looked down at the dinner before him. Once seated, Vinson looked up and continued, "I'm afraid my time in the Navy was not entirely spent aboard ships. I find it amazing that so much can be crammed in such small spaces on this ship, and just how in the hell do you find your way around?"

"Don't worry, Commander, it's the same for everyone when they first come aboard. In a few days, you will know every space onboard and where everything is," Captain Montgomery replied.

"I just thank God that this is not a carrier," Vinson replied, trying to inject humor into the conversation.

His attempt was successful as Captain Montgomery laughed slightly and replied, "The name is George. Welcome aboard," as he extended his hand over the table.

"My name is Vinson. It's my pleasure to be aboard," Vinson replied as he shook the outstretched hand and then picked up his knife and fork, ready to attack the steak before him.

As the two men enjoyed their dinner of rather large steaks, at least eighteen ounces each, mashed potatoes, baby peas, carrot salad, and biscuits, they swapped stories of their naval service. George told Vinson of his service aboard warships and how happy he was in his current assignment. Vinson didn't have a lot of sea stories to tell but held the captain spellbound with his exploits in the Naval Investigative Service and his civilian life as a polygrapher. *Funny*, Vinson thought, *I didn't think my life was so interesting. I always thought it was boring.*

Just as they were finishing dinner, the steward returned and cleared the dishes from the table and placed before each man a large helping of chocolate mousse ice cream drenched in an orange sauce. With equal vigor, Vinson attacked this delight and merely grunted in agreement to what George was saying as he enjoyed his dessert. Vinson, in an attempt to consume every last drop, swirled his spoon around the empty bowl and treasured this last tidbit of delight. Once finished, Vinson grabbed his napkin from his lap and carefully, with purpose, wiped his lips. Placing his napkin down, Vinson exclaimed, "Boy, that was good!"

"Would you like more?" George asked, disbelieving that Vinson could still be hungry.

"Oh. No. I'm stuffed…well maybe just a little," Vinson sheepishly replied.

George laughed and called the galley. A few minutes later, a portion equal to the one Vinson had just eaten, but with slightly more orange sauce, arrived and was placed down in front of him. With equal enthusiasm, Vinson picked up his spoon and ate with a smile on his face.

Once Vinson was finished and the table was cleared, George got right down to business. Getting up from the table, George crossed the room and picked up a chart from his desk and unrolled it on top of the table. To keep it from rolling up again on its own, George placed four circular weights in each one of the comers. Clearing his throat, George then poured two cups of coffee for them and gave one to Vinson who eagerly accepted the refreshment and gently placed it down on a clear section of the table. George, after placing his coffee down, remained standing, pointed to a place on the map, and told Vinson that this was the area that they would be searching. Vinson remained silent as George then sat down and took a sip of coffee. After placing the cup back on the saucer, George looked at Vinson and said, "Look it. I believe in talking direct. I find that good honest communication means good work. Can we level with each other and hold nothing back?"

Vinson studied the man for a minute and knew that George was correct. Braddock and Scotty obviously trusted this man. *Otherwise, he wouldn't be here,* Vinson concluded and spoke up, "Yes, Captain. As long as we both agree to hold nothing back as far as this mission goes. You must understand that I am not at liberty to discuss other matters."

George let out a big sigh, leaned forward, extended his arms on top of the table, folded his hands, and began, "I'll accept that, but if there is anything which could compromise the safety of this crew and my ship, I expect to told immediately."

"Fair enough, Captain. I'm probably the last person in the world that would want to see anything happen to this ship especially while I am aboard. But you have to understand one thing. From the very beginning, we have been shooting in the dark. There's no rule book on this matter. We learn and adapt as we go along. Some of the lessons have been hard, and along the way some lives have been lost, but we are learning." Vinson cleared his throat and decided that it was now time to set the rules.

Staring at George, Vinson spoke in an even flat tone of conviction, "Captain, your job is to get us to where we have to search. We are to then identify and learn as much as possible about what is lying on the bottom of the ocean. Is it dangerous work? You can bet your sweet ass it is. Do we risk being attacked? Yes. Can people get hurt? Hell yea. But get me there, and let's see what in the hell is down there."

George was taken back a bit by Vinson's declaration and knew that he was not one to be fooled with or taken lightly. Shifting his sitting position, George replied sheepishly, "Good. I can see that we will work well together."

At that, moment Vinson knew that the job would be done no matter what might happen. Inwardly, however, he hoped that the sharks would stay away. Vinson didn't know what to fear most, the thought of sharks in the water or the aliens. After taking a sip of coffee, without taking his eyes off of George, Vinson ordered, "George, please bring me up-to-date on the plan."

George felt the edge disappear and became a little more relaxed as he began, "Okay. As you know, Adm, Braddock came to see me in Puerto Rico and filled me in on what is going on. As I understand it, there is a rather large metal object lying right here." George pointed again to the suspect location on the chart. "In a little over four hundred and fifty feet of water. Once we locate the object, this ship will be anchored almost on top of it, and we can begin operations. First, we will employ side-scan radar to not only initially locate it but also to map its approximate size and shape. When we have that information, we will then launch an unmanned remote underwater vehicle equipped with a camera array to see what we have. If we are lucky—"

"Sorry to interrupt. But is it possible to try and grab a metal sample while the sub is down there?" Vinson asked.

"Yes, but it will have to be done on another dive. You see, the sub will be rigged with a total camera and light package for the first dive. We will have a total of eight cameras, three videos, and five still so we can get a precise idea of what's down there. On a second dive, we will take off a few of the cameras and attach a package, which contains a torch and two remote claws. We should be able to cut through the metal, and the claws will grab our sample."

"Sounds good. I just want to get a good clean sample before the salvage ships go to work. Sorry to interrupt. Please, continue," Vinson replied.

"No problem. Please, if you have a question just ask it, don't worry about interrupting. Where was I? Oh, yea. As I was saying, if we are lucky, there won't be too much growth on the object, and we will have a clear picture of what we are dealing with. If the object has been down there for a while, well that's a different story. In any case, let's see what develops. After what Admiral Braddock told me, I'm curious as hell to see what's there." George sat back, took another sip of his coffee, and then looked at Vinson for a reaction when he added, "I think your Admiral Scott must be expecting trouble or something."

"Why would you say that?" Vinson quickly asked with a deadpan expression on his face.

"Well, at o-three hundred, we will rendezvous with a Naval combat group already at the site. Some of these ships include two guided missile destroyers, the USS *Roosevelt* and the USS *Milius*, two guided missile cruisers, the USS *Lake Erie* and the USS *Port Royal*, one attack submarine, the USS *Tucson*, and lastly, the USS *Abraham Lincoln*, a carrier that will remain on station twenty-five miles away and provide air cover around the clock. There's enough fire power there in just the few ships I mentioned to take on the world," George replied, trying to make a point.

Again, with a straight face, Vinson replied, "Admiral Scott is a cautious man and is simply preparing for the unknown. Besides, you were worried about the safety of your ship. I would say that Scotty has more than provided for that. What about the deep-sea research submarine? You didn't mention her."

"Oh yea. The research submarine is aboard her tender, the SS *Carolyn Chouest*. There are also two salvage ships with her, the USS *Safeguard* and the USS *Salvor*. This is shaping up to be one hell of an operation," George replied, himself impressed at the assemblage of ships.

"There is one other thing you should be aware of. The British have quite generously loaned us the services of one of their carriers, the HMS *Illustrious*. She will be arriving shortly along with one more ship for good measure, the USS *Ruben James*, a guided missile frigate. And that should complete our little group unless, of course, Scotty can scrounge up some more help." Vinson added with a little smile from the comer of his mouth.

"Why the British? I thought that this was an American show," George asked.

"The *Illustrious* came to Admiral Scott's aid one time when he really needed it. He probably felt that they deserved to be in on the show, and they jumped at the chance," Vinson replied, not really knowing just why the British were here.

"Oh. Admiral Braddock told me about that incident. Err...say, Vinson, just how widespread is this problem, and do we have allies in this problem?" George asked, not really expecting an answer, and by the response, he was not disappointed.

"Sorry, George, but that is outside the boundary of this mission. I'm sure that you understand," Vinson replied with conviction and saw a flash of disappointment on George's face and then continued, "I'm sure that you and your crew were chosen for this mission based upon your ability and in the future will be an integral part of our mission."

George shifted his weight in the chair again and replied, "I thank you for that, and I assure you that there is not a better crew anywhere.

We will get the job done. If I could, let me explain the operation as I see it. If you disagree, just say so and I'll change it. I know that each captain has received their orders and that you have full authority to change those orders."

"Yes, of course. But you must understand that I have that authority in the event that we are out of contact with Admiral Scott or his executive officers, Doreen Stark or Beverly Hocker. As you know, we will be in constant contact with Admiral Scott, and he will receive encrypted video feed of the whole operation," Vinson answered, downplaying his role.

"Do you really think that all of these defensive measures are necessary?" George asked.

Vinson momentarily contemplated his response, hoping that the operation would be a walk in the park and then answered, "I sure hope the hell not. But if any saucers show up, I will be the first to thank God that Scotty sent these ships, and then I'll run like hell for cover."

George had to laugh at Vinson's response and hoped that he was kidding about running for cover. He then continued, "The last thing I want to explain is the ship disposition of our little flotilla."

Reaching behind himself, George picked up a transparent piece of plastic and overlaid it onto the chart on the table. Vinson examined the sheet and noticed ships drawn on the plastic in a somewhat circular pattern surrounding what appeared to be another ship.

He looked up when George began speaking again while pointing at the chart, "The *Salisbury* will be here once we locate the saucer, if it is a saucer." George held his finger on the ship in the center of the circle and then continued to point as he spoke of the other ships, "The salvage ships, the *Safeguard* and the *Salvor*, will join us in the inner circle as well as the *Chouest*. The *Salisbury* will be positioned over the target, and the other ships will anchor around us at a minimum distance of five hundred yards. Our guardians, the missile cruisers, will be our inner ring of protection approximately one mile from the center point. The *Lincoln* will sail around the inner ring at a distance of no more than twenty-five miles. I didn't know about the *Illustrious*. Where do you want her positioned?"

"Admiral Scott has already ordered her disposition plan, and she will serve as backup to the *Lincoln*. She will be sailing a course opposite of the *Lincoln* so that at any given time, both carriers will be no more than twenty-five miles away from our center point. Both carriers will supply air cover around the clock, and each will have eight fighter aircraft on alert status constantly. Admiral Scott has also arranged for their combat information centers to act as one with the *Lincoln* taking the lead. Oh, and the other ship, the missile frigate *Ruben James* will be coordinating with the *Lincoln*. Due to her speed, the *Rubin James* will be a roving support ship should one of our ships receive damage. One more thing, the attack sub, the *Tucson*, will act independently but will coordinate with the *Lincoln*," Vinson replied, liking the idea that he had something to contribute.

"Your Admiral Scott has thought of everything," George replied and then asked, "What if an airplane enters our area?"

"As you know, a radius of one hundred miles has been declared a kill area. If anything enters our airspace, it will be shot down or escorted away. But I don't think we will have that problem for two reasons. First, our airspace zone has been declared a no-fly zone for all commercial and private aircraft and will remain so for the next few days. And secondly, as an added precaution, tomorrow morning, it will be announced that NASA is desperately trying to stabilize the orbit of the Space Lab Aquarius. However, it will quickly become apparent that their efforts are in vain, and plans will be made to bring it down in a controlled reentry. Since the Aquarius is so large, parts of it will survive reentry and crash down in the South Pacific exactly where we will be. At the last minute, of course, the space lab will be saved. Warnings will again be issued late tomorrow for all surface ships to evacuate the area. As an added precaution, just in case the space lab cannot be saved, and for added realism, Admiral Scott has secured a few Coast Guard Cutters to patrol the outer zone and escort any shipping out of the danger zone. The Coast Guard activity will also be coordinated by the *Lincoln*," Vinson replied with conviction, thinking to himself that he was glad that he was not Scotty should something go wrong.

"Damn impressive!" George quickly exclaimed. Then while looking at Vinson, he asked, "The admiral on the *Lincoln* is new to the game. Do you think it wise to give all these responsibilities to the *Lincoln*?"

"I thought we had an agreement to talk directly to each other. What's your point, Captain?" Vinson tersely responded.

"Well, Admiral Laffey is somewhat new to her job," George replied, knowing that he should have never brought this up.

"You mean because the admiral is a woman?" Vinson asked as the muscles in his jaw tightened.

"Ah…yea, she is a woman, and I don't know if she has ever commanded such a task force before," George replied positive that he was going to regret his question.

Vinson tried to relax and dispel his anger as he sat back in his chair, folded his hands together, and touched his lips with his index fingers then withdrew his hands and stared at George as he replied, "If Admiral Scott were here, he would deck you and pick you up by your rear end and throw you overboard. And then he would do his best to attract some sharks. But thank heavens for your sake that I am not Admiral Scott." Vinson's jaw muscles began to tighten again as he continued, "Admiral Maureen Laffey is a graduate of the academy. Finished first in her class, I might add. She has flown F-18s in Afghanistan and Iraq. She has a much-deserved reputation of going below minimum altitude on her bombing runs to ensure that no friendlies were hit. When her flight career ended, she was assigned surface ships and excelled in not only ship handling but also in naval tactics. She has commanded the largest ships the Navy has to offer and was the captain of the *Kennedy* for two years. Hell, the officers under her swear that she chews nails rather than gum, but they all say the same thing about her. If there were a crisis, they would want her in charge. She is one tough cookie, cool as ice under pressure. Is she qualified? Hell, yes! Now, I don't expect that to ever be brought up again."

George swallowed hard and looked down as he replied, "It won't." George then looked up and said, "I was wrong."

"Good, now, when do we arrive on station?" Vinson asked, more relaxed now.

"Within six hours," George replied.

"Okay. Now, let's go over the plan again and see if we can find any shortcomings," Vinson ordered.

The two men remained at the table long into the night, constantly going over the plan and discussing what could possibly go wrong and the what ifs of an alien incursion.

ALIENS? WHAT THE HELL IS SHE TALKING ABOUT?

THE USS *SALISBURY* RENDEZVOUSED WITH the fleet almost precisely on time. The missile ships had already taken up their positions as directed by Admiral Laffey. The USS *Lincoln* began air operations as she settled into her routine of patrolling the outer protective ring. The *Illustrious* arrived on station a few hours late, having sailed through the backside of a nasty storm. But arriving safe and no worse for ware, the *Illustrious* fell into her assigned task and was ready to begin air operations. The salvage and research ships anchored close to the unknown object and prepared for their work.

As an added precaution, Admiral Laffey decided to hold a captain's meeting and discuss the disbursement of the small fleet and battle orders should an incident occur. Since she wanted to keep radio transmissions to the barest minimum, Admiral Laffey ordered all captains to the *Lincoln*. The ships, most of which carried their own helicopters, ferried their captains to the *Lincoln*. One by one, the captains of the remaining ships were picked up by a helicopter from the *Lincoln*. Some of the captains didn't like the idea of having to don a rescue sling and be hoisted into the helicopter, but orders were orders.

Once they were all assembled in the officer's dining room, Admiral Laffey arrived accompanied by her combat information officer, Commander Henderson. The room immediately quieted when one of the captains called them to attention. Admiral Laffey strode to the front of the room, returned their salute, and directed them to sit down. At first, she looked around the room, momentarily sizing up the assemblage before her. Satisfied that they all looked like men of conviction, she wondered though how they felt about taking orders from a woman. Some of these men were old time Navy, and quite frankly, Admiral Laffey was tired of having to prove herself to these naval dinosaurs.

As she stared at the men before her, Admiral Laffey began, "Gentlemen, I realize that this meeting is a bit unusual, but this is an unusual assignment. You have each received and read your orders. I know that in this time of relative peace in the world, they seem a bit unusual. That is why you are here this evening. Admiral Scott has directed me to share with you the prospect of what we will be facing. It will stretch your imagination. I ask you to accept what you may consider incredible, but I assure you that it is not." Admiral Laffey nodded to Commander Henderson, who took a disk out of his pocket and placed it into the DVD player on the television cart. She then glanced around the room and saw a puzzled look on everyone's faces.

Pausing for a few more seconds to heighten their curiosity, Admiral Laffey continued, "Gentlemen, what you are about to see is a shortened film version of the results of what an enemy, which we have scoffed at and dismissed as impossible for so many years, has wrought upon us. The film will show, in a satellite-tracking mode, what happened to a flight of Brazilian combat aircraft when they came in contact with this enemy. And then you will see, in full graphic detail, what happened when this enemy came in contact with innocent civilians. Commander, if you please."

Commander Henderson turned the television on and began the presentation. As the assemblage watched, no one spoke up, but Admiral Laffey heard murmurs. She didn't look at the film but instead studied each man's face. She saw looks of horror and disgust, but mostly, she saw determination. After the film had played for ten minutes, Admiral Laffey decided that enough was enough and directed Commander Henderson to stop the film. When he did so, Admiral Laffey looked back at the ship captain's and saw that a few of them obviously wanted to ask questions.

Rather than interrupting her flow, she continued, "Please, hold your questions until the end. Gentlemen, what you have just seen is real in all of its horror. We are faced with a new reality and a redefining of the word 'threat.' This new threat does not come from a foreign country, but rather, it comes from the outer reaches of the galaxy. It surely does not come in peace, but rather, it comes for us. It comes for our sisters and brothers, our mothers and fathers, our sons and daughters, and our neighbors. What you saw was the result of an airliner being snatched out of the sky, by this new enemy, and its passengers, for lack of a better description, dissected and most of their major organs removed. This new enemy, gentlemen, is of alien origin. I know it's incredible, but if it wasn't real, none of us would be here today."

Admiral Laffey paused and then went on to explain the history of what was known and suspected about alien incursion on earth. She supplemented her instructional talk with photographs and drawings of what suspected alien craft look like and the two types that they were likely to experience. Everyone accepted the concept of the Z-1 craft as they were what we have seen portrayed in science-fiction movies. The concept of the Z-2 craft, namely the long cigar-shaped craft, was a little harder for them to accept. The possibility of, for lack of a better description, a flying mother ship or airborne aircraft carrier stretched the imagination. Most of the captains realized that if they were to talk about the flying saucers to their subordinates, even though they were prohibited from doing so, there might be a mutiny aboard their ships due to their "psychological unstable condition." Therefore, they would keep the secret until it became an "operational necessity" for their subordinates to know.

After that tidbit of information was digested, Admiral Laffey told them of the real purpose of their visit to these waters. "Gentlemen, it is believed that a Z-2 aircraft crashed in these waters. It is this combat fleet's job to locate that craft, salvage it, and return it to port where it will be reverse engineered to find out its secrets. I know all of this sounds incredible, but it is our job. What we always thought of as fiction has suddenly become reality. I know each of you will perform your assignments to the highest possible standards. There is one among you who has had some experience with a flying saucer, and I would ask him to brief you about his encounter. Captain Montgomery!"

George stood up reluctantly, exactly unsure of what to say. Hell, he didn't even personally see the thing, but George was on the spot to say something. "Gentlemen, I am George Montgomery, the captain of the *Salisbury*. I can tell you that these things are for real." George stumbled for words and then recounted his ships encounter with the alien craft off the coast of Africa. What George emphasized was the shortness of the time interval between the *Salisbury* finding the object on the floor of the ocean and the appearance of the saucer. Most of those assembled squirmed in their seats at that news.

When directed by Admiral Laffey, George outlined for the group the work schedule as he saw it. "Since the object has been located, the *Salisbury* is presently being anchored over it. Side-scan radar will then map it dimensions and give us a somewhat 3D perspective of the outside of the craft. Once that is completed, we will descend upon the object to photograph it and hopefully give us some data as to its exact size. We will then look for an entry point into the object. If we should find a way in, we will then explore the object as much as possible before the salvage crews go to work. Hopefully, gentlemen, we can complete the work in a few days," George concluded, knowing that they would be there for a lot more than a few days.

Lastly, Admiral Laffey covered the possibility of combat with the aliens. Since they would obviously be subject to attack from the air, the plan was to first engage the aliens with fighter aircraft. Should the aliens penetrate the combat aircraft umbrella, the surface ships would then engage the aliens. The combat plan called for the commitment of four defensive missiles for each target, launched from different ships at the same time. In that way, each saucer would be attacked from multiple angles at the same instant. Commander Henderson, the admiral pointed out, would oversee the technical details and coordination. All of the combat ships would receive live intelligence data directly from Space Command, and they were expected to feed such data into their combat computers. Admiral Laffey reminded the captains that they were not free to independently commit their ships to combat and that all orders to engage the aliens would come from her. The only exception to this order was the possibility that the *Lincoln* was attacked and rendered incapable of action. In that case, command of the battle group would go to the senior-most captain and so on.

Once the presentation part was over, Admiral Laffey opened the discussion up for questions. Most of the inquiries centered on the aliens and what their combat capabilities were. Unfortunately, other than the Brazilian incident with the combat aircraft, little was known. The admiral thought that the questions were more than worthy of discussion. It was plain to see that each of the captains recognized the seriousness of the situation until one captain spoke up, "Is it necessary to remain on constant combat alert, or can we do it in shifts? Say the *Port Royal* remain at alert for four hours and they stand down and then the *Roosevelt* go on alert?"

Admiral Laffey hesitated for a moment, trying to control her anger and then with tight lips answered, "Captain, you have read your orders, haven't you?"

"Yes, Admiral," came a weak reply.

"Good. Then you know that they call for combat readiness and alert status around the clock. Perhaps, you have been asleep for the past hour and haven't heard a thing we have been saying or the discussion we have had. For your benefit alone, Captain, you are to be at alert status around the clock!" Maureen replied while staring directly at the offender and then added, "Captain, if you or anyone does not follow the orders and endangers the life of one crewman, rest assured that I will personally keel haul you and then cut your sorry ass up for shark bait! Is that clear, Captain?"

"Crystal clear, Admiral!" came a hasty reply.

"Good, then, gentlemen, if there are no further comments or

suggestions, this meeting is concluded. Good hunting, and may God be with us!" Admiral Laffey concluded.

Captain Montgomery and Vinson remained in their seats as the others left the room. When almost everyone was gone, George and Vinson approached Admiral Laffey, but she was too quick for them. Admiral Laffey walked up to them and held out her hand and said as she shook hands, "Ah, gentlemen, you two are the reason why we are all here. I hope what you heard will put your mind at ease and know that every precaution is being taken to ensure you and your crews' safety. But I must say this whole situation requires one to think in the abstract and anticipate what an unseen enemy, which up until a few days ago was pure science fiction to me, will do."

Vinson was taken back by her blunt and honest comments but recovered nicely, "You're absolutely right, Admiral. It's important to keep in mind what they are capable of. I was in Brazil with Admiral Scott, and I saw the results of their handiwork. You cannot assume anything with these creatures."

"I know, Commander. Scotty told me all about you and the great help you have given him. I guess that's why he trusts your judgment so much. And you, Captain, you also come highly recommended. I just ask you this, gentlemen, how long do you really think the recovery of the craft will take?"

All eyes turned to George as he glanced down at the deck and then back at the admiral and replied, "I really have absolutely no idea. I know I said a few days, but I think that it will take a while longer. We should be able to lift the entire craft off of the ocean floor in one piece and transport it back, but it's a monumental undertaking. I would guess that the operation will hinge on the weather forecast, which calls for clear skies and calm seas, and how long our cover story will hold. Do you have any concerns, Admiral, about the timetable?"

"My only concern is for the safety of the fleet. If the aliens attack us, I am quite sure that we will be able to successfully defend ourselves, but if they should attack in mass over a sustained period of time, well, that's a different story," Admiral Laffey replied and was interrupted by Vinson before she could continue.

"Excuse me, Admiral. But what exactly do you mean by a different story?" Vinson excitedly interrupted.

"Should the aliens attack in small waves, we can handle such an attack. If they launch a mass attack, even though this fleet has enough power to destroy the earth three times over, we could only sustain such an attack for approximately thirty minutes at the maximum. After that, we are simply out of ordinance except for our nuclear capability, and that is an option I would rather not use," Maureen replied, tongue in cheek, and added, "But I am sure, gentlemen, that will not be the case."

"Let's hope the hell not!" George thought out loud.

For a few seconds, the threesome stood in silence, each to their own thoughts about such a confrontation, and then Maureen continued, "The only captain that was not at our meeting was the commander of the *Tucson*. He and his submarine are at this moment patrolling around the inner circle of defense and at any given time will be no more than ten miles from your ship. Scotty thought that it was a good idea to have him handle any underwater attack by a saucer should that occur." Maureen hesitated, half not believing what she was saying, and then made her plea, not out of fear but out of concern for the men and women under her command, "Gentlemen, I'm not asking you to rush, but, please, let's do our work as quickly as possible. Let's grab that damn thing and get the hell out of here as quickly as we can."

"Believe me, Admiral. I'm the last one on earth to want to hang around here," Vinson offered.

"That goes for me too, Admiral," George added.

"Good, gentlemen. That being said, let's get on with it. I bid you good night and wish you the best of luck," Maureen concluded as she shook each of their hands and ordered her executive officer to show them to their waiting helicopter for the ride back to the *Salisbury*.

Once their helicopter lifted off and turned toward the *Salisbury*, Vinson looked out the window at the moonlit sky and the assembled naval ships below him. He wondered what would really happen if the aliens found out that they were there. Somehow, Vinson felt that the aliens would probably do nothing, but there was always the unknown, and it was the unknown that always causes the most problems.

CAN WE GO HOME NOW? I REALLY DON'T WANT TO BE HERE!

THE SHIPS GATHERED AROUND THE search and recovery site lay still in the water. An unusual calmness had overcome the seas surrounding the fleet. The water was more like a still lake than a moving ocean. One could only hear the gentle lapping of the water against the hull of the ship as it passed by on its never-ending journey into the night.

As Vinson walked on the deck of the *Salisbury* toward the research compartment, he took notice of the calmness of the ocean. In the back of his mind, he wondered if the still seas were better conditions for a shark attack. With that thought in his mind, Vinson edged away from the guardrail and walked as close as he could to the center of the ship. When he was almost at the bow of the *Salisbury*, Vinson found what he was looking for and entered the compartment.

Once inside, Vinson stood still for a moment and took in the hectic scene in front of him. He was in a room no larger than fifteen by twenty feet. It was crammed full of rack after rack of electronic equipment, computers, a large bank of monitors, and, what looked like, a very large plotting printer, the kind that can interpret raw computer data and print out a visual representation of that data. Technicians seemed to be everywhere working at their computers and talking to each other in some techy language. Vinson didn't understand this language, but everyone else did.

Captain Montgomery saw Vinson by the hatchway and motioned him over to a chair next to himself. From here, Vinson had a good view of almost every monitor in the room and the people operating the equipment. George explained to Vinson that they were about to launch the side-scan radar package, which would determine the size and shape of the object that they were anchored over. Then, pointing to the plotting printer, George explained that as the data was received from the radar, the computers would interpret the data and print a, somewhat, threedimensional picture of what the radar discovered.

Vinson was impressed with what he saw and heard. The realization of just what their mission was began to weigh down on him. Scotty had placed a lot of responsibility on his shoulders, and Vinson swore that he would not let him down. His thoughts and worries were interrupted when he heard George speak over the ship-to-ship radio, "Admiral, request permission to begin operations."

A few seconds later, Admiral Laffey answered, "Permission granted. Let's make it a quick operation. The hairs on the back of my neck tell me trouble is on the way if we linger to long."

Uncharacteristically, Admiral Laffey paused for a second and then added, "Commander James, just give the word when your assignment is completed, and we can then depart the area almost immediately."

George then handed the microphone over to Vinson. After taking the microphone from George, Vinson held it close to his lips, but he also paused for a second. He hated to think that the fleet was depending on his every move. *I just want to go home and forget about this alien crap*, Vinson thought to himself and then answered the admiral, "Will do, Admiral." Vinson then turned toward George and nodded.

"Launch the sled!" George bellowed, his voice bouncing off the steel walls of the small compartment.

Once a technician issued the command to begin the search, other technicians on the aft deck of the *Salisbury* began the delicate operation of moving the underwater equipment sled into the water.

Slowly, the sled was hoisted from its cradle and moved out over the water. With great precision, the sled was then lowered into the ocean. The operator didn't release the sled until she was satisfied that the umbilical, which provides power and two-way computer communication between the ship and the sled, as well as a live video link to the remote cameras, which would be placed on the sled for its second dive, was operating properly. Once satisfied that all was well, the sled was released to begin its descent toward the object.

Twenty minutes later, the sled drifted down to approximately fifty feet above the floor of the ocean under the watchful eye of its operator. At this depth, the operator engaged the electric thrusters on the sled, turned on the radar, and guided it in a search pattern across the floor of the ocean. In less than a minute, the sled found its prey.

All eyes watched the monitor as the operator guided the sled to one end of the object to begin the mapping process. No one in the compartment spoke a word. In fact, it was so quiet that Vinson wondered if anyone was breathing. At a dead-slow speed, the sled began its journey down the object. Immediately, the compartment became alive. Every technician in the compartment eagerly attacked their work. Some were bent over computer screens while others collected data from the sled. Everyone seemed to be in shock. No one could believe what they were seeing, but then, there it was.

Vinson's attention was drawn toward the plotting printer once the pen began moving. As the pen moved across the paper, a drawing of the object began to emerge. After a few minutes, one could easily see that the object was oval-shaped and had crashed into the ocean floor at almost a twenty-degree angle. As the object grew in length, Vinson just had to ask, "Captain, what would you estimate the size of this thing to be?"

George, who was likewise intrigued by the picture that was emerging, studied it for a moment and then answered as he scratched his head, "Beats the ever-living hell out of me!"

Turning around toward the back of the compartment, he called out, "Hey, Sandra. Could you please come over here a minute?" Turning back toward Vinson, George added in a low voice, "Sandra knows her shit. She will be able to tell us in a minute."

Sandra Billings, the recognized expert on the plot printer and its interpretation, looked up from her computer screen, which portrayed a computer model of what the plot printer was printing. Looking at George with a slight frown on her face and a hint of annoyance in her voice, Sandra answered, "Be right there, Captain."

Sandra was, to say the least, very surprised at what she saw. In her few but very busy years aboard research vessels, she had performed hundreds of side-scan radar searches. But she had never remotely seen anything like what she was now looking at. Reluctantly, Sandra pushed her chair back and stood up. She smiled slightly as she approached George and Vinson. Inwardly though, she wondered what these two idiots, standing by her equipment, could possibly want.

Once she reached the plot printer, Sandra clasped her hands behind her back and with a forced smile on her face asked, "Yes, Captain. What can I do for you?"

"Sandra, Mr. James here is interested in knowing what the size of the object is? Also, would you have any idea what it is?" George asked with a slight air of authority in his voice.

Sandra looked at Vinson and in a somewhat agitated voice replied, "Well, sir, my job aboard this ship is to see that the radar performs normally and accurately. From the data gathered, I am able to determine the measurements of the object and in most cases just what the object is." Her voice then changed at this point into an inquisitive tone as she continued, "So far, the object is more than five hundred feet in length, and we have not yet reached its end. As you can see from the picture, the object is basically an elongated oval-shaped structure with a relative height just less than one hundred and fifty feet." Sandra then paused and added, "As to what it could be, I have no idea. I have never seen anything quite like this before," Sandra concluded and then turned her attention toward George and asked, "Captain, if that would be all, I would like to return to my work."

"Of course, Sandra. Thank you," George answered, dismissing her.

Why don't those idiots take a long walk off a short pier and let me do my work? Sandra asked herself as she went back to her computer.

Vinson stood there transfixed as he watched the object continue to grow in size. His mind was full of questions: If Scotty was right, and this was a mother ship, then how many Z-1 craft was it capable of carrying? Where in the hell did this thing come from, and how did it get here? Most importantly, how many aliens did it hold and where were they? His last question to himself was the most disturbing of all: What the hell do I do now?

George saw that Vinson was in a contemplative mood and asked him if everything was okay. Vinson looked back at George and wanted to tell him the whole story but realized that he couldn't, at least not just yet. Instead, Vinson began to talk about the size of the object. After a few minutes of this idle banter, Vinson asked George to have the technicians prepare to change the underwater sled over to cameras as soon as the side-scan radar was recovered. George tried to talk Vinson out of such immediate action since it is standard procedure to fully analyze all of the data from the radar first. But Vinson would not hear of it and ordered the preparations to be done. Reluctantly, George gave the necessary orders, but he couldn't understand why Vinson was in such a hurry. Vinson, however, was convinced that their work must be completed quickly and the fleet dispersed before the aliens knew that they were there.

Three hours later, the side-scan radar reached the end of the object. As the equipment was being recovered and the changeover to cameras completed, the final data was fed into Sandra's computer. With an air of haste and intense pressure around her, Sandra worked feverishly to finalize the dimensions of the object. When she was finished, Sandra stared at her computer screen, unable to believe what she was seeing. After a few moments, Sandra regained her composure and pushed herself away from her desk. She then stood up and walked over to the plot printer and watched in awe as the object continued to grow in size. Looking up, she called out for Vinson and George to join her.

When George and Vinson stood alongside of her, they looked down as the pen continued to race across the paper. It was easy for them to understand the look of shock on Sandra's face. The object, as best they could tell, had doubled in size from the last time they looked at the drawing.

Vinson looked at Sandra and spoke first, "Don't tell me that this thing is now twice as big."

In a muted monotone voice, Sandra answered, "It's slightly larger than that."

"How big, Sandra?" George quickly asked.

Sandra looked at both George and Vinson and answered, "I make it out to be one thousand sixty feet long!" Sandra then paused for a second and, while looking first at the surprised looks on George and Vinson's faces and then back at the drawing, continued, "As we discussed, the object is resting at a twenty-degree angle into the seabed. Slightly over two hundred feet of the object is buried in the ocean floor. Gentlemen, it seems that your object didn't sink like a boat but rather fell out of the sky and crashed into the ocean."

Vinson and George could only look at each other with confused looks on their faces. But each of them knew that this was no longer a walk in the park and things have suddenly become deadly serious.

THOSE ARE NOT FIRECRACKERS IN THE SKY

"**Y**OU BETTER CALL, SCOTTY!" EDENAUSEGBOYE demanded more than suggested.

Auskile knew that his wife was right, but he didn't like the edge of fear he detected in her voice. He loved his wife and family more than his life and would do anything to protect them, but for the first time in his life, he felt a bit powerless. How can he possibly protect them from a force that comes quietly in the night and does who knows what? Since Scotty told him about the aliens, life as Auskile knew it was never the same. Suddenly, there was a force acting not only against his love ones, and his country, but against the world as a whole. Auskile had done what Scotty suggested, but still he knew it was not enough. And now the lights in the sky seem to be everywhere.

For the past few weeks, the lights have appeared usually in the wee hours of the morning.

Air Force jets were dispatched to investigate, and the result was always the same. The lights would move off at breakneck speed and disappear. But it wasn't only Zambia that was bothered. From the intelligence reports, Auskile knew that many other countries in Africa were experiencing the same thing. The official explanation across Africa was "unique atmospheric conditions." But Auskile knew differently.

"You're right. I'll call Scotty and tell him what has been going on," Auskile offered.

"You better tell him about the jets too." Edenausegboye directed.

"Jets? What jets?" Auskile asked, wondering how his wife knew about the fighter jets chasing the UFOs.

"The jets you sent to chase away the UFOs!" Edenausegboye replied, with a firmness in her voice still tainted by a degree of fear.

"Oh, and how is it that you know national secrets?" Auskile asked, trying to take the edge off the conversation.

With coyness in her eyes and an ever-so-slight grin on her face, Edenausegboye answered, "You talk in your sleep."

Auskile knew that he had been had. There was no way out, but he didn't mind. Trying to lighten the moment, Auskile inquired, "How is it that you never listen to me when I am awake, but the minute I say something in my sleep, you are all over me?"

With now laughter in her voice, Edenausegboye replied, "Now you know the secret of a successful marriage." Her laughter died away as she added, "You really should have told me. We're partners, and anything that may affect our family, we should talk about."

Auskile was lost. He didn't know what to say, so he spoke from his heart, "I didn't want to worry you. You and the children are the most important thing in my life. I would never allow anything to harm you or the children. I'm sorry, Edenausegboye." Auskile looked downward and then back at his wife with a hopeless look on his face.

With compassion and love in her heart and admiration for her husband, Edenausegboye added, "I know Auskile. Let's call Scotty." Edenausegboye sat down in a soft leather chair across from her husband and added, "I'm going to sit right here and make sure you tell him everything. Scotty will know what to do."

With laughter in his voice, trying to again lighten the moment, Auskile asked, "Can't I have any privacy around here?"

With conviction in her voice mixed with a slight laugh, Edenausegboye replied, "You can have all the privacy you want at your office, but not in this house! Now, let's call Scotty."

THICK CHOCOLATE CAKE TOPPED WITH FUDGE— IT WORKS FOR ME!

I N A WAY THAT WOULD resemble a sacred ceremony, Scotty poured himself a glass of thick creamy chocolate milk. With the utmost care, he placed it on the kitchen table next to his "energy snack," two very rich chocolate brownies. After putting the container of milk back in the refrigerator, Scotty sat down in front of his treat. But there was one little detail missing. He reached over and retrieved a napkin. After placing it down on the table, on his left side, Scotty was ready. Gone from his mind were thoughts of aliens and, for the briefest of seconds, dreams of Doreen.

Carefully, he picked up one of the brownies with his left hand and lifted it toward his mouth. Salivating in anticipation, Scotty opened his mouth, moved the first of his brownies closer, and was about to take a bite when the telephone, mounted on his kitchen wall, rang.

Scotty closed his mouth and looked at the telephone with contempt. Looking back at his brownie and then back at the telephone, Scotty knew what he had to do. Slowly placing the brownie back on the plate, he reached for the source of his disdain. "Yes!" Scotty greeted the caller with a tinge of anger in his voice.

"Admiral, I have a call for you from the president of Zambia. The line is secure, sir. Ah…Admiral…I have no idea how he managed to call our central number."

"Don't worry about it, Sailor. Just put the call through," Scotty ordered as the frown from his face faded and was replaced with a smile. After hearing a click on the line, Scotty spoke up, "Mr. President, you don't know how good it is to hear from you. It has been too long since we talked."

"Yes, my friend, it has. But, Scotty, quit calling me Mr. President. You know my name," Auskile ordered.

Scotty knew from the tremor in his friend's voice that this was not a casual call. *Something has happened*, Scotty thought to himself. Disregarding culture, Scotty decided to get right to the point rather than spend a few minutes asking about his friend's family. "Auskile, I can tell that this is not a social call, so why don't you just tell me what is wrong. I assume that it has to do with our visitors."

There was a long pause, and Scotty could hear his friend taking short breaths. Finally, Auskile let out a sigh and began, "You're right, Scotty. It has to do with our uninvited guests…" For the next ten minutes, Auskile told Scotty about the lights that would appear in the night sky.

When fighter jets were directed toward the lights, the lights would move off at a high rate of speed and disappear. He went on to detail that it wasn't only Zambia that was experiencing the night visitors, but his Air Force was picking up reports all over Africa about lights in the sky. With a bit of hesitation, he detailed for Scotty mysterious radar blips that would suddenly appear during the day, and when fighters were sent to the area, their combat radars confirmed the blips, but the pilots couldn't see anything even though their instruments told them differently.

Scotty told Auskile about his experience over the Gulf of Mexico and how the UFOs were able to be invisible in daylight as long as they remained level in flight. Not wanting to scare his friend, Scotty told him that the UFOs were probably just testing the air defenses of the countries in Africa. This seemed to reassure Auskile, but like Scotty, he also knew his friend.

"There is more, isn't there, my friend?" Auskile probed.

This time, it was Scotty who hesitated. "Yes…a…lot more." Scotty detailed for Auskile what he saw in Brazil and the attack on Commander Cunningham's aircraft. When Scotty was finished, there was not a sound on the other end of the telephone. Auskile was lost in thought, and Scotty let him think.

After a little more than a minute, Auskile cleared his throat and in a nervous tone asked, "Do you think that they are preparing to invade and kill us all?"

Scotty wanted to answer his friend directly and say yes, but he chose instead to reassure Auskile that for now, the aliens were doing what they have always done, watch and observe for the most part.

"What about Brazil?" Auskile almost shouted.

"Like I said before, I think that Brazil was a warning not to meddle in their affairs. They showed us what they are capable of, but remember we showed them what we are capable of when we attacked and destroyed the craft that shot down Commander Cunningham's aircraft. So I think that we are kind of in a stalemate right now. I don't think that either side wants to take any offensive action." Scotty didn't believe what he just said, and for right now, a somewhat little lie was not a bad thing.

Auskile didn't feel reassured; he surely didn't feel safe, but rather, he felt afraid. But his friend told him that things should be all right for the present. "What can I do to prepare?" Auskile asked.

"Just do what we talked about. Keep your Air Force on top of its game. Train them and train them again. The same thing with the army. Prepare them. Always be prepared," Scotty answered, not knowing what else to say and then added, "I will keep you informed of every new development and you do likewise. In that way, we will both be prepared."

"Okay, my friend. I will…" Auskile was interrupted by Edenausegboye. "Scotty, Edenausegboye want to say hello."

"Hello, Scotty. We sure do miss you. When are you coming back?" Edenausegboye quickly asked.

"I miss you and your family very much. I hope all is well. I'll be back as soon as I can," Scotty answered and left an opening when he paused for a second.

"Everyone is well. So how is Doreen? Tell me, when shall we prepare for the wedding?" Edenausegboye left nothing out.

Scotty nervously laughed for a second and then replied, "Doreen is fine. In fact, she is just great. And, no, it's a bit early to start planning a wedding."

"Oh well. Don't let this one slip through your fingers!" Edenausegboye ordered.

"I won't," Scotty answered and then paused again. This time, Edenausegboye didn't make use of the opportunity. He then continued, "Edenausegboye, Auskile needs your help. I'm afraid that I have placed a great burden on him, and he will need your strong guidance. Keep your family well and safe."

"I will, my friend. Let me go now. We will call again real soon. You be safe also." To lighten the moment, Edenausegboye added, "And for the sake of God, ask that lovely girl to marry you. You two belong together!"

Scotty laughed and answered the challenge, "I will." He stood there and stared at the receiver in his hand after Edenausegboye hung up. Scotty wanted to protect his friends, but he realized that there was nothing he could do other than what he has already done, tell them the basic truth.

After hanging up the telephone, Scotty looked down at his brownies, which a few minutes ago were the center of his universe. However, he wasn't hungry anymore. Instead, he wrapped them in a paper towel and decided to go to his office early before the others would arrive. Taking his treasure with him, Scotty opened the front door to his quarters. He was greeted by a saluting Marine Security Guard.

Scotty returned his salute and offered, "Sergeant, I asked you not to salute me every time I leave my quarters!"

The Marine didn't answer, and Scotty knew that he would never win the argument. As he walked down the hallway toward his office, Scotty turned around and walked back to the Marine. He didn't return his salute this time but instead placed his brownies in the Marines hand and said, "Here, have a couple of brownies. They might take your mind off saluting for a while." Turning back around and walking toward his office, Scotty heard the Marine call out, "Thank you, Admiral." Scotty kept walking and mumbled to himself, "Yeah, yeah, at least somebody will enjoy them."

SAY CHEESE

A S THE PHOTOGRAPHIC SLED BEGAN its journey down through the depths of the ocean, the research compartment was a beehive of activity. The technicians attended to their individual duties while at the same time everyone was talking to each other about what they might find. Some swore that they would find an old giant pipe or tunnel section that somehow was forgotten in the pages of time. Others thought that perhaps it was some weird kind of experimental ship the Navy lost track of. While this banter was going on, George explained to Vinson that they would be able to determine how long the object had been on the bottom of the ocean by the amount of marine growth on the "doohickey." Suddenly, everyone stopped talking when one of the technician's announced that the sled was close to the object and the underwater lights could be turned on.

Vinson sat erect in his chair and stared at the monitors. George looked at Vinson and smiled. He then stood up, clasped his hands behind his back, turned around and faced the monitors, and bellowed, "Power up the sled, and let's see why we are here!" Smiling to himself, trying to hold back laughter, Vinson thought that George more than overplayed the moment and thought, *But what the hell, it's his ship.*

When the lights on the sled were turned on, everyone let out a collective sigh. Some were more vocal and spoke up "Holy Shit!" or "That's impossible!" One person almost hollered, "What the fuck!" Whatever the comments were, one thing was obvious, no one could believe what they were seeing. Displayed on everyone's monitor was a shiny silver elliptical-shaped object totally devoid of any marine growth. None of the technicians could detect any kind of rivets, which would hold the object together. In fact, the metal appeared to be seamless as if it was made out of one continuous metal sheet.

As the photographic sled made its way down the hull, one could see, what appeared to be, indentations that bent the metal inward as if it was hit by something. Further down along the hull was a large hole, approximately thirty feet across and at least fifty feet high. The metal on the edges of this hole was bent outward as if there had been a large explosion on the inside of the object.

Slowly, the sled continued on its journey down the hull, taking pictures every few seconds. When it reached the part where the object entered the seafloor, the sled operator directed it to the top of the object and down the other side. Nothing remarkable was found on the other side beyond similar indentations in the metal.

When the sled completed its photographic survey, Vinson directed George to obtain a sample of the metal from the blast hole. The operator moved the sled to the hole and chose a piece of metal bent almost to a ninety-degree angle to the outside of the object. When the sled was close enough, the operator extended a claw and grabbed onto the piece of metal. Once satisfied that he had captured the metal, the operator extended a small nozzle and placed it next to the piece of metal. He then executed a computer command, and a sharp pinpointed flame came out of the nozzle. But the torch had no effect.

Vinson asked George what was happening, but he was as puzzled as anyone. A discussion ensued among the technicians because this was new to them. Never has their cutting torch, which radiates a temperature of nearly seven thousand degrees, failed them. Vinson suggested a rather low-tech solution, namely rocking the piece of metal back and forth with the claw. This way, it might just break off. At first, the technicians scoffed at the idea as they sought out another high-tech solution. Finally, lacking anything better, they tried Vinson's idea.

At first, light thrust was applied to the sled and then the power was increased. Over the next twenty minutes, the metal became more pliable and finally gave way. Trapped in the claw of the sled was a piece of metal that had been on the floor of the ocean, for how long no one knew, or could even suggest where it came from.

"Recover the sled!" George shouted out.

"Belay that order!" Vinson shouted even louder and then added, "Bring the sled to the large opening in the hole of the object!"

George turned toward Vinson with an angry look on his face and said in a very quiet but strong voice, "Commander, we have to bring the sled up now. The memory banks in the digital cameras are full, and besides, a trip into the object should be done with the research submarine. You have to remember that the sled is tethered. If we send it into the object, we run the risk of cutting the cable and losing the sled."

Vinson answered George in an even firmer voice, "Captain, if you listened to what I said, I did not give an order to enter the object but rather maneuver the sled to the opening of the hole. I am well aware of the risk of losing the sled. Further, you forget that we have a live video feed, which we are recording. If need be, we can make stills from the tape." Vinson paused, waiting for it sink in and then ordered, "Now get the damn sled over to the opening!"

George turned back around and directed in a soft voice, "Proceed as the commander has directed."

Another technician slowly maneuvered the sled to the edge of the hole and held it steady against the current. She then glanced over at Vinson who met her look. He held up his thumb and forefinger close together to indicate a little and winked at her. The technician winked back with a slight smile on her face.

She then redirected both of the video cameras straight ahead. With the skill of a surgeon, the technician edged the sled forward into the hole, just over the threshold. She then redirected all the lights forward to peer deeper into the space beyond. All eyes in the room strained to try and make out what the shapes were looming in front of the sled.

When the technician reduced the zoom on the video cameras, everyone suddenly jumped back a bit as a great white shark charged at the sled. At the last second, the shark veered to the left while showing his razor-sharp teeth of death.

As the surprise of the moment wore off, everyone began concentrating on the cloudy shapes that were at the edge of the effective range of the lights. (At this depth, the lights were only effective for five or six feet.) Without urging from Vinson, the technician again inched the sled deeper into the void. As the sled moved forward, the shapes began to become clearer. After a few more seconds of moving the sled forward, the technician stopped the sled and cried out, "Shit! I don't believe this!"

The technician then moved the sled from side to side. Everyone knew immediately what they were looking at. Everywhere, right out of the sci-fi movies, were flying saucers. Not just one or two but a lot of them. Some were in pristine condition while others appeared to have suffered some sort of battle damage or were damaged as a result of the explosion that probably took place. The area that the saucers were in seemed to be large, very large.

Vinson wanted to send the sled even further into the cavernous space, but he knew that it would be foolish to do so. "Begin recovery of the sled. Make prints of the video, please," Vinson ordered and continued to watch as the sled backed up.

"Stop!" Vinson cried out, and immediately, the sled stopped.

Vinson thought he had seen something and wanted to make sure that it was not an illusion. Being a little nervous of what the result could be, Vinson directed, "If you could direct a light and a video camera to the left and stop if you see anything."

In a very slow, gradual movement, a video camera and a light turned in sync. In an instant, Vinson knew that he did not see an illusion. In front of him, displayed on the monitors, was some type of a control panel mounted on a bulkhead. But what made it remarkable was the fact that it was lit up.

George and Vinson both looked at each other with fear on their faces. Vinson spoke first, "I know. The damn thing still has power!" Vinson paused, looked at the monitor, then back at George again, and ordered, "Recover the sled, George, and give the order to prepare the research submarine for a dive. I want to get inside of that thing."

OH WHERE, OH WHERE HAS VINSON GONE?

SCOTTY THOUGHT THAT HE WOULD get to his office first and have some time to himself. He planned on checking in with Admiral Laffey and Vinson. Scotty was anxious to get this little excursion over with as soon as possible. In the back of his mind, he was not worried but was more than a little curious about all the asteroid talk. It seemed unclear what was going to happen. *Can only do one thing at a time*, Scotty thought to himself as he entered his outer office.

While saying hello to his secretary, Marcy, he could hear voices coming from his office. "They are all waiting, Admiral," Marcy offered and then added, "We are getting a tremendous amount of pictures of what Commander James found in the Pacific. Sir, it looks like he hit the jackpot. There are loads of Z-1 craft inside of that thing. It's all on your desk." Marcy paused and then almost in a hush asked, "Admiral are we going to be all right?"

Scotty felt like saying that he didn't know but instead put on a confident look, put his palms down on her desk, bent over, looked her in the eye, and said, "We are going to kick their butts back to where they came from!" Scotty then smiled and winked at Marcy.

"Go get them, Admiral!" Marcy exclaimed as Scotty walked into his office.

Scotty didn't waste time on pleasantries but instead went right to work. "I understand there are Z-1 aircraft in the object. Analysis?"

"You are right, Admiral! It looks like it is an airborne aircraft carrier," Beverly was quick to speak up. All the others quickly agreed as Scotty sat down and began reviewing the photographs.

After a few minutes of silence as Scotty absorbed what he saw, Bone spoke up, "Sir, we have a couple of the saucers here, but I was wondering if it would be possible to grab a few from the craft so that we can compare the technologies. Perhaps, the ones on the bottom of the ocean are a newer version or even an older model. But in any case, if we had one, it sure would be interesting to study and learn its secrets."

Scotty looked up and around the table. He saw Doreen smiling at him, and he really just wanted to walk away from all this with her and live their lives in peace. That dream lasted less than a second as he turned to Bone and answered, "That would be ideal, but for now, I think we should just recon the situation and get out of there and then go back later. This is a look-see situation to learn what we can quickly. We are in a shooting war now with the aliens, and our main focus should be on that for the immediate future."

"Yes, Admiral," Bone replied, a little dejected knowing that Scotty was right.

To break the obvious silence that followed, Scotty directed Doreen to establish a link with the *Salisbury*. Doreen walked over to the bank of monitors and established a link that allowed for instant communication between Space Command, Admiral Laffey, and the *Salisbury*. Scotty first checked in with Maureen and after a brief discussion of the combat readiness of the fleet turned his attention to the *Salisbury*.

Scotty was surprised to see Captain Montgomery on the video link. "George, how are you?" Scotty greeted him and without waiting for an answer ordered, "I was expecting to see Commander James. Could you send for him, please?"

George cleared his throat before answering somewhat nervously, "Admiral…sir…Commander James is not aboard the *Salisbury*. Er… Admiral, as you know, we located the object, and, boy, it sure is large. Excuse me, sir. In any case, there is a large, what appears to be, a blast hole in the side of the thing. We sent a remote camera just inside of the thing, and, well…you wouldn't believe it, sir. There appears to be a hangar deck in there. I mean it looked like a large area. Believe it or not, there were flying saucers in there and not just a few. But what really perked our interest was a control panel that was lit up. Sir, that would mean that the thing still has power."

Impatiently, Scotty cut George off and asked, "Yes, Captain. I am aware of that, but just where in the hell is Commander James?"

"Oh, yes. Sorry, sir. Commander James is aboard the *Carolyn Chouest* getting ready to go aboard a small research submarine that will fit through the hole of the thing, whatever it is," George quickly replied and then added, "Commander James wants to explore the interior of what he thinks is a flight hangar deck inside of the object. You know, sir, just like the hangar deck of an aircraft carrier."

"How soon before they are ready to launch the submersible?" Scotty asked, a little frustrated.

"They should be launching right about now," George answered and then added, trying to save the moment while wishing that he was somewhere else, "We will have a live audio and video feed to you momentarily."

"Good, Captain. We will await the feed. And, Captain, please standby," Scotty ordered.

"Will do, sir," came a quick but reluctant reply.

YOU SURE THAT THIS THING ISN'T MEANT FOR THE BATHTUB?

AFTER CLIMBING UP A TEN-FOOT ladder on the aft deck of the *Carolyn Chouest*, Vinson found himself standing on a narrow catwalk even with the entry hatch of the small submarine. Vinson examined the hatch and the thickness of the metal and pondered his predicament. On the one hand, he was anxious to get into the object and see what was there, but on the other hand, he really didn't want to get into the tiny submarine. A member of the crew was urging him to climb down the hatch, but Vinson had to ask a couple of questions first.

"Is this thing shark-proof? And what about a giant octopus?"

"Ah…don't worry about that, sir. If a shark comes by, we have anti-shark weapons mounted on the outside of the sub. And, hell, if a giant octopus grabs onto the submarine, why, we will shoot an electrical charge through the hull and take care of him. You know, just like they do in those science-fiction movies. Now, would you please get in, sir?" the crewman answered as he bit his lower lip to keep from laughing.

Vinson seemed to like his answer and climbed down into the submarine. Once inside, Vinson was directed to lie down, on his stomach, on a foam rubber pad next to the pilot, Captain Johnson. Vinson was given a quick briefing about all the levers and valves surrounding him and understood the underlying theme of the lecture: don't touch a thing. Propping himself up by the elbows and looking out of the front of the submarine, Vinson was amazed at the wide view he was afforded out of the bubble glass in the front of the submarine.

Wanting to make sure of a few things, Vinson fired away some questions, "Are the cameras and the live video feed ready to go? How long have you been doing this? Are the anti-shark weapons loaded? How long can we stay down? Do you think a shark could eat this thing?"

Captain Johnson was a little surprised by the sudden barrage of questions but put it all in perspective since this was Vinson's first ride in a miniature submarine. "Yes, all of the cameras are ready to go. We will turn the live video feed and the external lights on when we drift down close to the object and are ready for our approach. No, a shark can't eat the submarine. It's too large for his stomach. We have enough oxygen and enough power for approximately four hours, and I have been piloting this particular submarine for the past three years. And what shark weapons are you talking about?"

"You know, the anti-shark weapons mounted on the outside," Vinson shot back, wondering just how long the captain has really been piloting the submarine if he doesn't know about the shark weapons.

"Oh, those anti-shark weapons. Yes, Commander, they are loaded and ready to fire in case we should encounter one of those submarine-eating sharks," Captain Johnson replied and turned away so Vinson would not see the big grin on his face as he desperately held back his laughter. Once he composed himself, Captain Johnson ordered, "Now, Commander, just lie back and enjoy the ride. We are ready to launch."

Vinson watched with great interest as the submarine was hoisted off the deck of the ship and for a few brief moments was suspended in the air. The submarine was then swung out away from the ship and over the ocean. Slowly, the submarine was lowered until the ocean almost entirely engulfed it. As Vinson was gazing out of the bubble glass at the water and an errant fish that wandered by, he heard Captain Johnson's radio "Disconnect" and then turning toward Vinson, he continued, "Just enjoy the ride, Commander."

Once the tether to the ship was separated, the little submarine slipped below the waves and began its descent. Captain Johnson studied the radar blip of the object on his scope and gently manipulated the dive planes so that his vessel slowly closed on the target in a gentle, slight dive. When the submarine was a few hundred feet from the object, Captain Johnson started the electric motors, switched on the underwater lights, and activated the live-video camera. With a delicate touch on the controls, Captain Johnson guided his submarine toward the large hole in the side of the object.

As they closed to a distance of about three feet, he turned toward Vinson and asked, "Are you sure about this, Commander?"

"Dead sure, Captain! Now, let's go in real slow and look around," Vinson replied while staring out his bubble glass view.

Inch by agonizing inch, the submarine crept forward until they were through the hole and into the alien craft.

"Holy shit!" Captain Johnson cried out and added, "If I didn't see it, I wouldn't believe it. They are flying saucers. I can see why you were so anxious to get down here."

"That's right, Captain. Now, let's go look around," Vinson ordered, anxious to get this little adventure over with.

For the next hour and a half, they explored every inch of the cavernous, what could only be called, hangar deck. They rode over, under, and alongside of the parked flying saucers. Some of the saucers had their access hatches open, and some pretty weird-looking fish had set up housekeeping in the alien craft.

SOMEBODY PINCH ME!
THIS HAS TO BE A DREAM

S COTTY WAS STUNNED. HERE, RIGHT before his eyes, was the Golden Fleece. Row after row of Z-1 spacecraft were simply parked, waiting for someone to come and take them away. Allowing himself to dream a little, Scotty thought about the prospect that if these saucers were in relatively good condition, then just maybe the mother ship could be in the same condition. *A little tweaking and who knows? That would be some coup!* Scotty allowed himself to hope. In any case, Scotty felt vindicated. His earlier premise had been correct, the cigar-shaped craft were in fact a sort of flying aircraft carrier and who knows what else.

Bringing himself back to reality, Scotty realized that there were some central questions that the answers must be found too. Quickly, he went over them in his mind. Why was the spacecraft here? Why were most of the Z-1 craft in good and probably flyable condition? If most of the craft are in flyable condition, then why were they not launched to protect the mother ship if indeed the ship had been attacked? If the mother ship had been attacked, then who attacked it? If it had been attacked, then what kind of weapon was used against it?

Scotty pondered these questions while he continued to stare at the monitors. His concentration was broken when his eye noticed an image on the bulkhead behind one of the saucers. A few microseconds later, his brain registered what his eyes saw. Excitedly, Scotty called out "Vinson!" hoping that the audio feed would work.

After what seemed like an eternity to Scotty, but in reality was only a few seconds, Vinson replied, "Admiral, is that you?"

"Yes, Commander. It's Scotty," he answered.

"Scotty, you wouldn't believe what I am looking at. There's row after row of Z-1 spacecraft down here. Man, we could start our own alien air force with this stuff. I'm telling you, Admiral, you just have to see what's down here. It's like…" Vinson replied but was interrupted by Scotty.

"Commander, I can see it. We have a live video feed. We can see what you are seeing, and we have been listening to your conversation and comments," Scotty replied and was interrupted by Vinson when he exclaimed, "Wow! I didn't know that."

"Okay, Commander. Let's settle down and get back to work," Scotty ordered and then directed his attention to something else. "On the video monitor, I am looking at a saucer that you seem to be hovering in front of."

"That's right, Admiral. It's the one that has a small hole in it by the entryway," Vinson stated, asking confirmation of what Scotty was looking at.

"Yes, that's it. Now on the bulkhead directly behind the saucer, there seems to be a star map of some kind. I want you to move your submarine over to the bulkhead and let me see what is there," Scotty directed.

"I see it, Admiral," Vinson answered and then directed the captain to take it in really slow and gentle.

Vinson kept his eyes on the map as the submarine inched forward. After a few minutes, Vinson realized what Scotty had seen. Stretched out in front of him was indeed a map. Vinson scanned a small monitor as he manipulated the video camera across the map. Vinson shuddered when he saw what he was looking for. Frozen on the monitor screen was a map of Earth's galaxy.

Excitedly, Vinson called out, "Scotty!"

Scotty had been watching the monitor with undivided attention. When he saw Earth's galaxy, a rush of emotions overcame him. This confirmed that the aliens had been coming to Earth for a long time. *Why else would a star map of our galaxy become a mere decoration on an alien flight hangar? And what of the other galaxy maps? Were they also that well-known to these creatures?* These were question's Scotty ran over in his mind and shook him to the core. *These damn aliens had probably been killing different races for time immortal*, Scotty thought and pondered the situation. Hearing Vinson calling him, Scotty sat upright in his chair and acknowledged, "Yes, Commander."

"Admiral, these bastards have our galaxy all mapped out as well as other galaxies! Hell, there is no telling just how long these creeps have been raiding our world as well as others. What's interesting is that our Earth is colored red. On the other maps, there is also one or two planets also colored red. In one galaxy, there are five planets colored red. Just taking a guess, I would say that the color red would indicate their hunting grounds. Goddamn these bastards," Vinson answered with anger in his voice.

Scotty could also feel the anger rising within himself, but he had to refocus Vinson. In a firm and commanding voice, he directed Vinson to photograph each of the maps. Once satisfied that Vinson was doing as he directed, Scotty relaxed a bit but remained glued to the monitor. He couldn't believe what he was seeing. For the next hour, he watched as galaxy after galaxy crossed the screen. When Vinson was done, Scotty had counted nine hundred and sixty-three galaxies.

Satisfied that his job was completed, Vinson called Scotty, "All done, Admiral. Is there anything else?"

"No, Vinson. Go back to the ship. You, guys, did great!"

"Home, James," Vinson announced and then settled down to enjoy the ride back.

The captain of the submarine turned it around and slowly made his way toward the same large hole they had passed through. As they were about to leave the spacecraft, Vinson noticed the lighted control panel the remote sled had located. Wanting to make sure that he did a complete job, Vinson directed the captain over to the panel. He wanted to get some close-up pictures of the panel.

As the captain edged the submarine to within ten feet of the panel, Vinson directed him to move in a little closer. Vinson wanted to see if he could decipher the markings on the lighted panel and hopefully understand what they meant. When they were about two feet from the panel, Vinson directed the captain to stop and hold the submarine steady.

Vinson stared at the panel and tried to understand the symbols, but after a minute or two, he realized their meaning eluded him. He then began taking some close-up photographs of the panel. His concentration was broken when for the briefest of seconds, Vinson felt the back of the submarine rise ever so slightly. This sensation was then closely followed by a forward momentum.

Vinson turned his upper torso and looked toward the back of the submarine but didn't see anything wrong. His first thought was that they were being attacked by a shark. Before he could verbalize his thought, Vinson heard the captain utter, "Oh, shit!"

As Vinson turned back around to look forward, he asked, "Was that a not so bad 'Oh shit' or was it a really bad 'Oh, shit'?" As Vinson regained his view out of the bubble glass, he immediately braced himself and exclaimed, "Oh, shit. It's a really bad 'Oh, shit.'"

In the heartbeat of a second, the submarine collided with the panel.

"What happened?" Vinson cried out.

As the captain began backing away from the panel, he told a nervous Vinson, "A small pressure wave hit us and pushed us forward. No harm done though."

"Well, nothing seems to be leaking, so I guess that we are safe," Vinson added, unsure of just what to say and then asked, "Say, Captain. You don't think we did anything, do you? Like turn the thing on or something?"

"Nah. We just tapped the thing. Besides, this thing has been down here for who knows how long. It can't possibly be working. The lighted panel is just a fluke," the captain replied, trying to reassure Vinson and then added, "Just relax, Commander. We will be topside in a few minutes."

As the captain backed the small submarine away from the panel, two lights came on above the panel. "On second thought, we seemed to have turned on some lights," the captain offered as he turned the submarine around.

"Shit!" Vinson replied and added, "I guess we hit a light switch."

"Yeah, that's it. No harm in that," Captain Johnson answered as he began to guide his submarine out of the craft.

Together, the intrepid explorers left the spaceship and guided their submarine back to the *Carolyn Chouest*.

OKAY, SO I LIVE TO EAT

S COTTY SAT BACK FOR A moment and let out a big sigh. He was trying desperately to relax. All the pressure of the past few days seemed to be building within him. He knew of one way to relive all his pent-up energy, but that was something to be savored and not used as a relief valve. But the thought of he and Doreen alone, for even just an hour, just added to his dilemma. Beverly broke Scotty's train of thought when she asked if anyone wanted something to eat.

Thinking of food as a diversion, Scotty was the first to speak up and asked for a roast beef sandwich, on white bread with butter, and a large pot of coffee. As the others placed their orders, Scotty noticed that Doreen was looking at him with one of those disapproving stares. He answered her stare by adding a helping of onion rings to his order. Doreen ignored Scotty for a moment and ordered a grilled chicken salad and a cup of tea. She then glanced at Scotty and stuck her tongue out at him. Scotty returned her gesture, threw his head back, and with both hands ran his fingers through his hair.

While they were waiting for their food, Scotty pulled Doreen aside and discussed calling Admiral Morrison. Scotty had a slight sense of foreboding due to recent events, and given what Vinson found inside of the spaceship, well, something was bound to go wrong. Doreen felt the same way and felt that Morrison should be brought up to the present in case something really went wrong.

Together, they went into a small office next to Scotty's larger office and sat down around a small conference table. Doreen and Scotty stared at each other for a moment, lost to their own thoughts. Doreen then extended her arm and pushed the number three button on a hands-free conference telephone in the center of the table. Within seconds, Morrison's telephone began ringing.

The admiral answered on the fourth ring after he recognized the calling code on the caller ID, "Scotty! Things must be really bad if you have to call an old warhorse like me!"

"Hello to you too, Admiral," Scotty replied.

"Hello, Admiral," Doreen added.

"Ah! Commander Stark. It's always a pleasure to hear your voice. If you are both calling to check on my diet, don't worry. Let me assure you both that I am turning into a real veg head," Morrison joked and then asked, "Tell me, Commander, did that son of a sea dog ask you to marry him yet?"

Doreen became slightly flushed in the face and momentarily stared down at the table and then looked up with a grin on her face. While looking directly at Scotty, who was now squirming in his seat, replied, "No, Admiral. But he is working up to it."

Morrison laughed to himself while trying to picture, in his mind, what Scotty must look like at this second. Wanting to torture Scotty a little more, he answered, "Hell, son. You must be dumber than dirt!" Morrison followed his statement by more laughter and then suddenly turned serious, "Okay, Scotty. You didn't call to see how my diet is going. What's going on?"

For the next twenty minutes, Scotty brought the admiral up-to-date on recent events. The admiral listened intently and offered suggestions where he could, but he knew that Scotty had things well in hand. Scotty, however, also had another agenda. He felt that things were heading on a one-way street toward a major confrontation with the aliens. Scotty wanted to push the admiral into informing the president of the United States of the existence of the force.

The admiral had a different view. While he did agree that the president would one day have to know about the existence of Space Command, and its related interests, now was not the time. Morrison favored a gentler approach. In other words, the admiral would have to somehow get the president to order the establishment of a department or command to examine the UFO phenomenon. Only then could Space Command reveal its existence.

Scotty quickly pointed out that he doubted that this approach would work because what president, given politics, would suggest the establishment of such a department. This would first require a president to somewhat acknowledge the existence of aliens. Such acknowledgment would be political and social suicide. But Scotty knew that he was beat and that it would be the admiral's way or no way.

As the goodbyes were being exchanged, Beverly knocked on the door, and Scotty immediately called out, "Enter!"

Beverly placed Doreen's salad in front of her and handed Scotty a brown paper bag. Scotty thanked her just as Doreen was saying goodbye to the admiral. Looking first at Doreen's salad and then at the brown bag before him, Scotty put a big smile on his face. He then tore the brown bag open and spread it out to serve as a place mat. Picking up the sandwich, which was wrapped in wax paper, Scotty held it under his nose, breathed in, and loudly proclaimed, "Ah! Smells like roast beef with a light touch of butter."

Placing the sandwich gently down and unwrapping it, Scotty then opened a Styrofoam food container. He bent his head forward and again made a deep breathing sound and declared, "Ah! What have we here? Looks like deep-fried succulent onion rings."

As Scotty was going through his menu, Doreen bowed her head slightly so that she wouldn't have to look at him and began to quietly eat her salad. However, Scotty didn't let up. After he took the first bite of his sandwich, and began to chew it, he let out a small groan to accent his enjoyment of the food. When he finished his first bite, Scotty couldn't help himself and asked Doreen if she would like a bite.

In a voice as cold as an arctic wind, Doreen replied "No, thank you, dear" and continued to eat her salad.

Scotty then picked up an onion ring and, while dangling it in front of his mouth, asked, "Ah! The small pleasures of life are the important ones. Wouldn't you agree, my queen?" He then quickly gobbled down his treat.

Anger was rising in Doreen and in another very cold monotone voice replied, "I would say that is true in most cases. But then I am not as well-versed in small things as you are, my king!" Doreen then smiled slightly as she picked up a spoon and scooped up an artichoke heart from her salad.

Scotty's mouth was agape. Suddenly, the tables had turned. In a somber, hurt voice, Scotty asked, "Is that what you really think?"

With a big smile on her face now, Doreen looked at Scotty. She then raised the spoon and flung the artichoke heart at Scotty, striking him on the forehead as she answered, "No! You idiot!"

Beverly quickly opened the door to the small office just as Doreen let go of her food missile. She could only stand there in amazement. Beverly, for the moment, had forgotten why she entered the room.

Scotty, as the artichoke heart slid down his face, turned toward her and asked, "What's wrong?"

"Ah…Ah…Admiral, you better come in here quickly. It looks like four Z-1 craft are about to enter the atmosphere. Could be the Pacific, sir!" Beverly stuttered at first but then recovered quickly.

OKAY, SO YOU WANT TO FIGHT?

Scotty rose out of his chair, reached for a napkin, and wiped his face as he ran into his main office. For a moment, he stood in front of the monitors and studied the display as he watched the Z-1 aircraft slip into the atmosphere of Earth. Quickly, he contacted Admiral Laffey and confirmed that she was aware of the situation. The admiral replied that she had ordered full-alert status, with all weapon systems up and operating, and had launched ten more aircraft with additional fighters being readied on the flight deck for immediate launch. Satisfied that Admiral Laffey was indeed ready, Scotty issued an order to prep up the California group of X-aircraft for immediate launch. Should the aliens be interested in more than just looking, he wanted to be ready.

Scotty was then informed that the alien craft were indeed on a flight heading toward the battle group. Contacting Admiral Laffey again, Scotty, in a controlled voice, issued the order to fire only if the aliens either fired first or appeared to be a threat to the fleet. Knowing that part of the order was a bit ambiguous, Scotty added that whatever decision Admiral Laffey made on the scene, he would back her up.

Admiral Laffey acknowledged the order and asked herself, *My god, what does "appear to be a threat" mean?* She was the senior officer on the scene, and Admiral Laffey was used to command. She would exercise her best judgment. For Scotty's part, he was glad that Admiral Laffey was the officer in charge. He knew that she had a unique ability to quickly assess a situation and take the appropriate action.

THIS SURE ISN'T
A LOG CABIN

Admiral Laffey stood in the CDC (Combat Direction Center—a centralized location aboard naval vassals where all offensive and defensive actions are directed) scanning the different monitors and listening intently as various reports were coming in from the different ships and fighter aircraft. She was absorbing information so fast that to Admiral Laffey, it appeared as if everything around her was happening in slow motion. She was hearing reports as to the combat status of the other ships while she listened to the calm voices of the combat pilots. Knowing that her combat group was ready to handle any situation, well no one has really fully engaged the aliens before, Admiral Laffey remained cool as ice and issued last-minute orders in a calm businesslike manner.

Her attention was drawn to one radarscope by CAG (the Commander of the Air Group of the combat aircraft). CAG explained to her that the representation she was watching was the combat aircraft of the Interceptor Air Squadron 801 from the HMS *Illustrious* as they joined a squadron of F-18s from the USS *Abraham Lincoln*. Once the aircraft were flying together, they executed a sixty-degree turn as they climbed to an altitude of twenty-three thousand feet and closed on the approaching alien craft. Admiral Laffey knew that the next few seconds would determine the fate of her command as well as the fate of mankind in handling the alien problem. If the Z-1 aircraft were just coming for a look-see and turned away at the last second, then they would recognize their own vulnerability. But if the aliens engaged the combat group, then that would indicate their recklessness and inflated egos that they were superior. This was not just a test of will, but rather, it was a test of determination and survival.

ALL I REALLY WANT TO DO IS FLY

FEELING RESTLESS AND UNABLE TO do anything, Scotty was wishing that he was in the cockpit of one of the aircraft. One of the disadvantages of command is the frustration of being a witness to an event. Of course, the one in command directs the situation and issues the necessary orders, but you are not a participant and that in itself is like spending moments in a frozen hell.

Like Admiral Laffey, Scotty absorbed what was being said around him and watched the real-time radar displays on his monitors but events for him also passed slowly as if time itself had somehow slowed down. Without looking at Doreen, Scotty instructed her to contact Admiral Morrison and send a live feed to his office at home. Since Morrison wouldn't listen to his pleas, Scotty figured that he might as well see what they are up against.

Air Squadron 801

Squadron Leader Basil Thome radioed the flight leader of the American

F-18s and in the compressed language of naval aviators decided upon a battle plan. When the saucers appeared, the American group would break off to the right, descend, and arc around to the left and approach the saucers from below and attack. The British would make a head-on pass while the Americans were preparing for their attack and then break right to avoid being shot down by a stray missal from the F-18s.

Time also passed slowly for Basil Thome as he watched his radar and listened to reports from the combat information center. "One hundred miles and closing…eight zero and closing, straight intercept"—both the aircraft and the saucers were at the same altitude thundering toward each other—"six-zero…four-zero, five by five." (Both the aircraft and the saucers were closing on each other on a collision course. Note: the term five by five usually means that a pilot has positioned his aircraft down the center of an approach line for landing, but it can have many different meanings.)

When Basil heard the combat information center called "four-zero," he looked over to his right and returned the salute of the American flight commander seconds before his counterpart banked his aircraft to the right and descended as the other three planes in the American group followed their leader. Basil watched for a few seconds as the American planes grew smaller as they lost altitude. For the briefest of seconds Basil thought to himself *What a thing of beauty* and knew why he loved flying so much. But his attention was immediately refocused when he heard the combat information center called out "three zero."

"Weapons hot!" (All missiles to be armed!) Basil called out to his flight and knew that when the saucers were twenty-three miles away from him, which would be in a few seconds, the search radar on his aircraft would go for missile lock on the approaching saucers.

"Break! Break! Break!" came a frantic call from the combat information center aboard the USS *Abraham Lincoln*.

USS Abraham Lincoln

Admiral Laffey heard the same frantic call as Air Squadron 801. Turning her head to look at the operator who issued the call to break off the attack, Admiral Laffey appeared pensive. The operator felt her stare and looked up at her. He reported that the satellite feed detected on an infrared scan of the saucers, a heat surge building up in each one of the saucers, and felt that it was a sign that they were going to attack. Admiral Laffey simply nodded her head in recognition of the operator's assumption and turned back toward the main display. She stood frozen in a time warp as suddenly the four saucers became five. The fifth saucer, which had been flying almost touching another saucer, dove toward the sea.

"That new saucer, does it have a buildup of heat?" Admiral Laffey asked as she turned toward the operator again.

"No, Admiral!" the operator called out without looking up.

Admiral Laffey felt as the operator felt, the damn aliens were about to start a shooting war. *Damn them to hell! And if it's hell they want, then it's hell they'll get*, Maureen thought to herself. Reaching up to garb a microphone, Admiral Laffey put it close to her lips, pressed the talk button on the side, took a deep breath, and ordered her executive office to issue the order to all ships and aircraft to attack the alien craft. For mere seconds all naval ships readied their missile launchers to fire should the saucers fight their way through the fighter aircraft. The ten additional fighter aircraft the admiral had ordered launched earlier formed into two groups. One group flew toward the impending air battle while the other group remained around the fleet to provide a defensive screen.

Air Squadron 801

Basil and his pilots heard and understood the frantic call from the combat information center. Practiced procedure called for the two fighters on his left to bank their aircraft to the left while going into a gradual descent while Basil and his wingman were to bank to the right and gain altitude. But Basil knew that it was too late for mere seconds, the distance between his flight group and the aliens would close to nothing, and if all the aircraft stayed on their course, there would be one hell of an explosion as earthbound aircraft collided with intergalactic spacecraft.

There was, of course, another alternative. For the mere fraction of a second that fighter pilots have to make life-and-death decisions, Basil decided on the other alternative. He would attack. He knew that his decision would end not only his career but also put him in jail for the rest of his life. But simply put, there was no way in hell he would allow one of these saucers to attack his ship and his shipmates. As he instructed his pilots to engage the saucers, his career was saved when the battle order was received to engage the saucers.

Each pilot in Basil's group worked their attack computers, locked onto their targets, and received a confirming tone that their missiles would strike the targets, which they aimed at. In this case, the exercise was simple since the attack computer was capable of attacking twenty-three targets at once, but there were only four targets available. The fifth saucer was now out of range. At this point, Basil had no idea where it could possibly be and was not concerned about it. There was a powerful armada down there, and surely, they could take care of it.

Once Basil had a confirming tone on his targets, he gave the order to fire. All the aircraft launched their missiles. As the missiles left the aircraft, three of the pilots did what they were taught to do. When a missile is launched from an aircraft, the pilot has to compensate for the sudden loss of weight, in this case over a thousand pounds, if the aircraft was to maintain level flight. Basil was too busy watching the heads-up display (an electronic portrayal of the screen of the attack computer at eye level to the pilot so that he will not be distracted by having to look down at the computer and then back up) of his attack computer. At the exact same instant that the air-to-air missiles left the fighter aircraft, the saucers emitted a bluish light which reached across the sky and struck all four of the aircraft of Air Squadron 801.

Basil did not compensate for the loss of weight from his aircraft, and since his aircraft was now lighter, it rose slightly higher. This mistake gave Basil a chance at survival. When the blue light washed over his companions' aircraft, they and their aircraft were vaporized into an instantaneous cloud of dust. Since Basil had allowed his aircraft to rise, the blue light hit his aircraft in the rudder assembly and blew it away. His aircraft was then thrown into a downward spiral loop. Basil instantly heard alarms going off in his headset and was momentarily stunned.

Once he realized what had happened, Basil fought hard to reach the ejection handle. Slowly, he fought the effect of Gs on his body as he forced his hand downward toward the handle. Once he was able to grasp it, Basil pulled the handle with all his strength. In an instant, explosive bolts blew off his cockpit canopy, rockets then engaged under his seat, and he was ejected from the aircraft at over two hundred miles per hour.

Due to the sudden acceleration, Basil's mind didn't really register what was happening until the seat rockets burned themselves out. Basil was then separated from his seat, and his parachute opened. Slowly, he began his earthward journey. Once again, Basil disregarded his training and instead of working the parachute handles to control his direction and rate of descent, he looked around. He saw the flight of American fighters chasing the fifth saucer, but they lost the pursuit as the saucer entered the sea and was swallowed up by the ocean. Further to the west, Basil saw wreckage burning on top of the water. He incorrectly assumed that the wreckage was the remains of his squadron. What Basil didn't know was that their new hypersonic missiles had penetrated the saucers, and when the warhead exploded, the saucers were blown from the sky. Round one belonged to the humans, well sort of.

CAROLYN CHOUEST

T HE MINIATURE SUB SURFACED ALONGSIDE the *Carolyn Chouest*, and divers nervously jumped into to the water and attached lifting cables to submarine. Slowly, the submarine was hoisted aboard the ship. Vinson anxiously watched as the captain of the submersible opened the hatch and climbed out. When Vinson emerged from his confinement, he noticed that activity on deck was hurried as he watched the technicians rushing back and forth completing their assigned tasks. He was also curious that the deck was washed in very soft light as if the ship was trying to mask or hide its appearance. When the technicians completed their work, they all entered the interior of the ship, and the lights on rear deck were turned out. Vinson then glanced up the superstructure of the ship and for the first time noticed that the ship was dark except for the soft glow of red lights. He knew that red lighting was used on ships to protect the eyes of the sailors and maintain their night vision and that it also meant that the ship could be under some kind of combat alert. Fighter jets streaking over the ship and disappearing into the darkness of the night interrupted his observation of the ship. Trying to follow the flames of the fighter jets' engines, Vinson just stood there and wondered what was going on.

After a few minutes, the captain of the miniature submarine came up to Vinson, handed him a hot cup of coffee, and brought him up-to-date on what was happening.

"You don't think that we caused the aliens to come and attack us when we accidentally hit that control panel?" Vinson anxiously asked and then sipped his coffee.

"Nah, when we hit the panel, the lights came on, but who knows maybe it sent a signal of some type to the craft's main computer which in turn sent out a broadcast," came the answer Vinson really didn't want to hear.

"You really think so?" Vinson asked afraid of the answer.

"Who knows," came a very quick reply.

"Great!" Vinson muttered, and both men watched as another flight of fighter jets roared overhead. Taking another sip of his coffee, Vinson thought to himself, Shit, *Scotty is really goanna be pissed now.*

USS Tucson

Captain Jeffrey Bonner was a hunter. That is, he was a hunter of other submarines and ships which would do the United States wrong. His job, during war, was to seek out and destroy such transgressors. Today, he was protecting his country in a way that he was not familiar with. Up until his present assignment, he never gave aliens or their threat much thought. But if Admiral Scott said that aliens were for real, well then, they were for real. Captain Bonner positioned his submarine four hundred yards south of the object on the bottom of the ocean. He didn't know what the object was, but he didn't really believe that it was some sort of alien spacecraft. That is, until the events began to unfold on the surface. He watched his monitors with great interest and was aghast when the aircraft attacked the alien craft. When the fifth saucer broke off from the other four saucers, Jeffrey kind of knew that his boat was in for some action. For over two days, the *Tucson* rested on the bottom of the ocean, trying desperately not to make a sound. His orders called for independent judgment and action, when necessary, and now, he would have to exercise those directives.

Jeffrey Bonner was not a "ring knocker." He came up through the ranks the hard way. He attended a small midwestern college and joined the Navy ROTC Program. At first, he looked upon the Navy as a means toward an end. The income he received as a Navy ROTC cadet supplemented his tuition payments and as such was an integral part of his overall financial survivability in college. But as time and maturity progressed, Jeffrey Bonner became Navy, 100 percent Navy.

After graduation from college, Jeffrey, enthusiastically entered naval service. His first assignment was to the surface fleet. There he served as a junior officer aboard a missile cruiser. He found this assignment rewarding in itself, and he strove to do everything right, balanced with the usual mistakes a first-time officer makes. But his superiors saw something in him that set him apart from the rest. They saw a young man mature beyond his years and a natural leader. Jeffrey Bonner was a man who somehow managed to get along with everyone and led by example. The men respected him for who he was rather than what he was. At times, senior officers would even seek out his council. He was a young man who was right where he wanted to be and among people he wanted to be with.

The Navy then transgressed from being a job to joining a family. But that was not to say that he was soft on his men. Jeffrey Bonner quickly gained a reputation as one who ran a tight ship and who was fair in his dealings with the men. For that, his crew loved and respected him.

As the years passed by, Jeffrey saw his career, for surely his life in the Navy was now a career, grew in challenges. His superiors always gave him more than favorable fitness reports, which meant advancement in rank and responsibility. While he never really gave the submarine force much thought, his reputation had spread beyond the surface fleet. In the middle of a reassignment, Jeffrey had received orders to proceed to New London, Connecticut. No reason was given for the order, and while he tried his best to find out why, but couldn't, Jeffrey thought that there must be a mistake somewhere.

When Jeffrey arrived at the New London submarine base, he realized that he was in another world. It was the same Navy, but these sailors talked a different language and behaved differently. It was as if these men and women were members of a close-knit family rather than regular sailors. This intrigued Jeffrey, and he wanted to know more. His wonderment was satisfied when he was directed to Admiral Bruce Johnson's office.

For the next three days, Admiral Johnson gave Jeffrey an introduction into the submarine force. A man of Jeffrey's caliber was what the submarine fleet sought out and recruited. At the end of the three days, Jeffrey's head was spinning. He knew that submarines offered challenges that were not found anywhere else in this man's Navy. Knowing what he had to do, Jeffrey went to see Admiral Johnson and requested a transfer to the submarine force.

For the next six months, Jeffrey mastered a whole new world of skills and a new language, the language of a submariner. After completing the classroom training, Jeffrey experienced his first cruise, serving as third officer aboard a nuclear-powered attack submarine. Jeffrey enjoyed the thrill of the hunt as he cruised the Pacific Ocean in pursuit of Russian nuclear missile submarines and other targets of opportunity. Like all sailors, Jeffrey hoped and prayed that there would never be a need for his skills and his boat. For that would mean that the world was once again at war.

The years that followed passed quickly for Jeffrey. His skills grew, and his renown as a skilled tactician spread throughout the force. He rose in rank to executive officer and finally to the venerated rank of captain. Jeffrey felt that his life began when he took command of the *Tucson*. His superiors knew that his star would not rest there and fully expected him to rise to squadron commander and beyond.

Space Command

Scotty stood in the center of his office watching the monitors as events unfolded. When the fifth saucer broke off and headed for the surface, he knew that they were not looking this time but were here to extract a price for the human's boldness of searching their fallen spacecraft. But if they were so upset, it must be for a really good reason. That craft on the bottom of the ocean must contain something that they were afraid of should it fall into human hands. True, there would be a price to pay, but Scotty knew that it was already very expensive. Four naval aviators were killed in seconds, and that fifth saucer, where the hell was it?

Turning toward Doreen, Scotty gave the orders to launch the California group of X-aircraft or Pegasus, as Doreen liked to call them.

"How long until they are on station?" Scotty quickly asked.

"Twenty minutes, Admiral, on cruise speed with a hang time (the time the aircraft can stay airborne around the fleet) of thirty. If you prefer full throttle, five minutes to the fleet but a hang time of only nine minutes," Doreen quickly answered, smiling at the man she loved.

Scotty turned toward Doreen with a big smile on his face. Doreen, as usual, had managed to break the tension within himself with her usual efficiency and smile. "Twenty will be fine," Scotty answered and while still smiling turned his attention back to the monitors.

"Anything on the fifth saucer?" Scotty asked aloud.

"Sir, it entered the water six miles from the object," Beverly Hocker called out.

USS *Tucson*

Captain Bonner was on the bridge of his beloved command, listening to the reports and monitoring the activity. "Sir, the craft has entered the water. It is at a depth of four hundred feet and heading toward us at 263 degrees, now eight thousand yards out. Speed 20 knots," came a report from the sonar operator.

"Give me fifty feet up," Jeffrey called out and heard his orders repeated as it was executed immediately. "Ready all tubes," Jeffrey added. Turning toward his executive officer, Jeffrey instructed, "When the saucer is two thousand yards out, fire one and four, and three seconds later, fire two and three."

"At two thousand, fire one and four, wait three seconds and fire two and three," the executive officer repeated and by doing so confirmed the order.

Jeffrey stood ramrod straight, with his hands clasped behind him, on the bridge of the submarine. He was trying his best to maintain his composure and direct the attack in a calm and orderly fashion. The last thing the crew needed to see was their captain in an excited state. Like an immovable rock, Jeffrey remained glued to the deck and listened to the reports of the saucer closing on their location. Time also seemed to slow down for Jeffrey. The trap he designed was about to be sprung.

Slowly, it seemed, the sonar operator called out the distance, "Seven thousand yards, six and on intercept course, five out no course or speed change, four, three no change," and finally what Jeffrey was waiting for, "two straight and true."

Milliseconds later, the executive officer ordered the firing of the torpedoes, "Fire one and four!"

As the torpedoes were fired and their propulsion system engaged, the torpedoes began to unwind a fine wire no thicker than a human hair, which linked the torpedo to the ship's combat computer. Last-minute course adjustments were sent to the torpedoes along this wire, which allowed the torpedo to be guided to its target. Three seconds later, torpedoes two and three were launched and went racing toward the saucer.

Jeffrey remained in his position as the torpedoes raced away from his boat on their deadly mission. "All four running straight and true," came the announcement from the weapons technician who added, "Will arm at nine hundred yards. Seven seconds till contact."

Counting to himself, one, one thousand, two, one thousand, three one thousand, four one thousand, five one thousand…Jeffrey's counting was interrupted by the sonar operator who announced, "Target has changed course, turned left twenty degrees, same speed and depth!"

Within a second, Jeffrey did the mental calculations and figured that he still had a chance. He thought it odd that the saucer didn't fire something at the torpedoes, considering what they did to the fighter aircraft, but who could ignore a gift like this?

Torpedoes two and three changed their course to follow their target, but in the next instant, torpedo number one slammed into the saucer, penetrated its hull and exploded. Torpedoes two and three collided into the explosion and detonated. Torpedo four didn't have a target. The operator pushed the self-destruct button, and in an underwater flash, torpedo number four exploded.

Jeffrey allowed himself to show some emotion and cried out, "Yes!"

Looking around, he saw everyone staring at him. Regaining his composure, he turned toward his executive officer and commanded, "Put us back down on the bottom, gently if you please, remain at silent status, keep everyone alert, and give out a well done."

Remaining in his position, Jeffrey concluded that they were lucky this time. It was possible that the saucer simply didn't see them or didn't expect an underwater attack. He knew that the next time would be different.

Space Command

For a few precious seconds, Scotty stood alone staring at the monitors. He knew the commander of the *Tuscan* and silently congratulated him on his coolness under pressure. He could imagine the scene on the bridge as Jeffrey Bonner probably didn't even crack a smile at his ship's victory but rather stood there conducting business as usual in a calm cool voice. Scotty then thought of the aircraft that they had lost this night and of the aviators who wouldn't be returning to their ship. Silently, he said a prayer for their families and knew that their sacrifice would not be in vain. True, they had died defending their ship, but in a much larger sense, they had died so that the laughter, hope, and dreams of mankind would continue for yet another day.

When Scotty came out of his repose, he turned toward Doreen and smiled slightly, looked around the room, and walked the few steps to the conference table. While standing over the table, he placed his outstretched palms down onto the table. Bending over slightly, Scotty called out so the intercom connection would pick up his voice, "Maureen, well done. I need your assessment right now."

Admiral Laffey's mind was racing a mile a minute thinking through probable scenarios when she heard Scotty's transmission. She didn't need an instant to frame an answer and replied, "I know what I would do, Admiral, if there was something I wanted to protect."

"I was thinking the same thing. Are you ready?" Scotty asked, already knowing the answer.

"Yes, sir. We are at full-combat alert. All systems armed and ready. Total of sixty birds (combat aircraft) in the air. Another twenty are being launched to be held in reserve," Admiral Laffey replied, knowing that the next few minutes would be critical if they were to stand a chance. The reserve aircraft had to be launched and ready to attack in case the saucers started ripping through the fighter umbrella protecting the fleet.

Standing in the same position for a few minutes, Scotty stood up with a thoughtful look on his face and spoke out, "Maureen, I want to see something. I see by the ship disposition read out that the guided missile frigate, *Ruben James* is on the outer defensive circle. I want the *Ruben James* to set sail for Pearl at half speed. Also run an air cap over them but not in too close. I want to see if the aliens will attack the ship or let it go because it is leaving. Also give orders for the salvage ships to make all preparations to get under way."

Admiral Maureen Laffey executed Scotty's orders and then used the intercom to contact him. "The *Ruben James* is proceeding to Pearl at half speed, and all salvage ships are making preparations to get underway." Maureen paused for a few seconds and then continued, "Admiral, what are you thinking?"

Bluntly, Scotty replied, "Maureen, I think that we are in deep shit! Whatever is down there is valuable to them, and they are not going to let us walk in and take it. We know that the vessel is, for lack of a better description, a flying aircraft carrier. That's no big deal, but there is something more sinister on board that thing that they do not want us to have. I think that they are going to come back in force and keep coming until they see us moving away and abandoning the salvage operation. The aliens are going to come back and keep coming back until we leave. We know that we can take out their saucers and protect the site, but in a dragged-out battle, we are limited by our weapons at hand, and they know that. The ninety-million-dollar question is what the hell is in that spaceship and what are they afraid of. It's just too damn early to get into a prolonged shooting match with these bastards. Our survival right now is dependent upon hit-and-run tactics in a defensive mode. So stay alert and let's see if the bastards come back, and I think they will."

As Scotty was talking, Maureen was continually scanning the status boards to make sure that her combat fleet was up and ready. When Scotty finished, she replied, "Admiral, your reasoning is solid as ever. We are ready for whatever comes our way."

"Good luck, Maureen, and please don't forget to duck," Scotty added, knowing that Admiral Laffey would forget to duck because to her, the most important thing in the world was lives of the men and women under her command, but even with that, she would never waver in pressing an attack. She was old-time Navy embracing the modern world.

Scotty walked over to the phone bank and picked up the telephone receiver, which would put him in instant contact with Morrison. "Admiral, what's your assessment?" Scotty asked, knowing that the cunning ole war dog had been monitoring everything.

"Your reasoning sounds solid as ever, but I hope you're wrong and they don't come back," Morrison answered, feeling a bit out of step with the whole situation. The events of the night so far were becoming too much. First, the attack on the aircraft and now the attack on the fleet. This wasn't the way things were supposed to be happening. But one thing was crystal clear, the teacher had now become a full-time student. Scotty was able to go from one situation to another very quickly and remain cool and in command. Truly, Scotty was the right man for the job.

"Admiral, I think that the aliens are after something in that object on the bottom of the sea. I noticed that when the mini submarine was on its way out, it struck a panel or something that lit up the area, but it must have triggered something else, which resulted in the saucers turning up. I—" Scotty was interrupted while he was talking to Admiral Morrison.

"Admiral, they are coming back!" Beverly Hocker called out.

Scotty, while holding the telephone in his hand, turned around, looked at Beverly, and then his eyes looked up and scanned the monitor showing a bunch of orderly blips moving across it. "Report!" Scotty demanded.

"We count two five (25) alien craft entering the atmosphere with a projected flight path toward the fleet."

Without taking his eyes from the monitors, Scotty called out, "Maureen, do you copy?"

"Got them, Admiral. We're ready!" Admiral Laffey replied and immediately began issuing orders to fend off the attack.

"Doreen!" Scotty next called out without looking at her.

"Ten out, Admiral. Just issued orders for them to go to full speed. ETA two minutes," Doreen replied.

Scotty slumped his shoulders slightly, bent his head down and around, looked at Doreen with a trace of laughter, and thought to himself, *Goddamn, she's reading my mind again. She is one hell of a challenge.* Turning back around, Scotty placed the telephone receiver down on the conference table, folded his arms, and waited for the inevitable.

USS Abraham Lincoln

Admiral Laffey made last-minute preparations by placing her fighter aircraft in position and ordered a last-minute status check of her fleet.

"Admiral!" came a cry from a radar technician.

"Report!" Maureen demanded.

"Multiple targets at thirty-eight thousand feet coming right at us, ETA forty seconds," the radar technician replied.

Immediately, Maureen ordered her fighters to intercept the saucers at a distance of ten miles from the fleet. She stood transfixed and watched the monitor as the gap between the fighters and the saucers continued to close at an alarming rate. Her concentration was momentarily interrupted by a radio call.

"Admiral, this is Commander Stark from Space Command. We have a flight of four X-aircraft arriving your position in four zero seconds, call sign Tango X-ray."

"Commander, four more aircraft don't amount to much. This whole thing will be over in a few seconds. Now go away!" Maureen ordered.

"Excuse me, Admiral. But you don't know what these aircraft are capable of. Admiral Scott ordered their disposition," Doreen replied rather curtly.

Maureen was going to reply, but she was interrupted when the radar operator called out that five of the saucers had ascended to forty-one thousand feet and three more saucers had broken off and were heading for the *Ruben James*.

"Order the *Ruben James* to fire only if fired upon," Maureen ordered and silently said to herself, *I hope you're right, Scotty.*

Turning toward her executive officer, Maureen ordered him to send a signal to the *Tucson* to engage if threatened and then evade. She added that the *Tucson* was not to defend the object if the saucers entered the water.

As Maureen turned back toward the monitors, a radar operator announced that the engagement had begun. Maureen silently said a prayer as sixty F-18s ran headlong into seventeen alien spacecraft from God knows where.

In the blink of an eye, before the fighter aircraft had time to fire their weapons, the saucers attacked in unison, and twenty-one, the pride of Naval aviation, F-18s and their pilots vanished into oblivion as if they never existed. When the remaining F-18s fired, most of their missiles were intercepted by flashes of light from the saucers, but four of the invaders exploded in the air.

When the fighter aircraft and the saucers had flown by each other after the initial exchange of fire, the F-18s looped back around and perused the saucers as they raced toward the fleet. In a few seconds, the remaining F-18s were ordered to break away as the battle would now take place directly overhead of the fleet.

The group of five saucers that had gained altitude before the air-to-air exchange took place suddenly turned and headed toward the HMS *Illustrious*. In mere seconds, before the defensive air group could react, one of the saucers broke off and approached the proud British aircraft carried from the bow toward the stem. The defensive weapons of the *Illustrious* began to fire, but it was to no avail. Using lightning-fast speed, the saucer emitted, what looked like, a blue light onto the deck of the ship, and as it passed overhead, the light remained constant as it proceeded down the length of the deck.

Immediately, the landing deck exploded in fire as the thick steel deck plates were thrown into the air, and the area below the flight deck was exposed and destroyed. Men screamed in horror and pain as explosion after explosion ripped through the ship.

Exploding jet fuel and munitions added to the holocaust. In less than half a minute, a proud ship was transformed into a burning twisted hulk that began to slip beneath the waves.

USS Ruben James

Captain Brian Webb was in the waning days of his naval career. He had been passed over for promotion three times now and didn't want to face a fourth review, which usually meant retirement on the Navy's terms rather than his own. Wanting to remain in control, he was going to retire to the coast of Maine and live by his mistress, the ocean.

Lately, he had been reading books on lobster fishing and had decided that this endeavor was not for him. Oh, he would buy a boat to sail around in; however, it would be purely for pleasure and not for work.

He suddenly found himself and his ship involved in a shooting war against of all things, creatures from outer space. In reality, he thought that the young commanders he now served were probably insane and out of touch with reality. Now, his ship was alone heading toward Pearl Harbor, and he was ordered not to fire unless fired upon.

As he stood on the combat bridge of his ship and looked out at the sea before him, his radar operator radioed that three unknowns were approaching his ship at nine hundred feet at a speed of six hundred miles per hour, seventeen miles out. Brian Webb put a smirk on his face and wondered if the insanity was spreading and if he alone was an island of sanity in a world gone mad. But what the hell, orders are orders. Turning toward his executive officer, he ordered all weapons hot and continuous tracking of the unknowns.

Executive Officer Shelly Abrahms turned toward her captain, a man she had come to deeply respect and she suspected fall a little bit in love with, and said, "Captain, we were ordered not to fire unless fired upon."

"I know, Shelly. Let's just track them and get lock on them. If we can't fire, we can sure as hell scare them to death," Brian replied.

USS Abraham Lincoln

Admiral Laffey swallowed hard as she said another prayer and, in a strong authoritative voice, turned toward her executive officer and said, "Send this to all vessels, fire at will." Maureen then took five steps and stood while looking at the monitors, rigid, with her hands clasped behind her back as she watched the battle unfold.

This time, the aliens did not have the comfort of firing the first shot. Radar-guided guns aboard the naval vessels tracked and fired upon the saucers as they moved closer to the fleet. Barrage after barrage of missiles rose from the combat ships and began their deadly journey toward the intruders. The aliens were somewhat overcome by the deadly onslaught, which they ran into, and their return fire seemed erratic. Streaks of blue light crisscrossed the sky as desperation overcame a skilled well-coordinated attack.

Admiral Laffey watched in awe as those under her command performed their duty not well but beyond expectation. All the years of training and acquired skills were paying off. Like all good commanders, Maureen was thinking ahead. She knew that this attack was a follow-up to the initial probe by the aliens, but she knew that the defense her small fleet was putting up could not last. Sooner or later, the initial store of munitions and missiles would begin to wane. This was not yet a full-scale attack. With great reluctance, she picked up a red telephone handset and ordered the preparation of offensive air-to-air nuclear weapons.

Maureen knew the consequences of such action, but she thought of the security of the world and in a smaller sense her little fleet.

These aliens had to be stopped, and if it meant letting the nuclear genie out of the bottle, then she would. Mentally, she reviewed the manual in her mind, a low-grade offensive nuclear device fired in a missile from a fighter aircraft at a large group of hostile aircraft would explode in the immediate vicinity of the oncoming aircraft and wipe the skies clean of the invaders. At least that's what in theory was supposed to happen.

Maureen shuddered at the thought but knew what had to be done. Maureen then turned her attention back toward the attack. She asked for an update and was told that of the seventeen saucers that entered over the fleet, six were taken down immediately. The remaining eleven were flying over the fleet but were not engaging the warships as they seemed totally occupied in trying to shoot down the missiles coming at them.

"There go three more!" a technician cried out in the confines of the combat control room.

"Shit!" another voice called out. "Motherfucker! Those bastards!" the same voice cried out again.

"Two more are down!" another technician cried out, but Maureen turned her attention toward the panicked voice.

"What happened?" she demanded.

"Shit!" the technician again spoke out and didn't notice his admiral standing over him.

"Report!" Maureen demanded.

"One of the saucers hit the *Port Royal* in the forward missile bay. The bow is completely cut off from the ship and is sinking. The ship itself is still afloat but is also sinking. They need help, Admiral, and now."

Maureen padded the man on the shoulder and then turned toward her executive officer and was about to speak when the room erupted into a sea of sparks as some electronic equipment apparently overloaded as if an electrical surge went through some of the apparatus. The room then went dark as the lights and the remaining equipment turned off. Immediately, a few emergency lights came on, and in a few seconds, they also went out.

No one cried out as everyone was momentarily in shock. "Talk to me," Maureen demanded and looked around the room as a few lights came back on and then the attack computers and monitors came alive.

"Admiral, we were hit with an EMB (electromagnetic bomb which will cause total failure in all non-shielded electronic equipment) right over the fleet," her executive officer called out.

"What's our status?" Maureen demanded, knowing that her own ship should be okay since they had recently undergone an enhanced shielding retrofit as a precaution against such an event.

"All major systems online, Admiral. We're still in the fight. All ships recovering and defensive barrage going up again," came a quick reply.

"Order the *Roosevelt* to disengage and get to the *Illustrious* and begin rescue. Send the *Milius* over to the *Port Royal* and…" Maureen was interrupted by an excited voice.

"Fuck, here they come!"

"No commentary, just report if you please," Maureen coolly ordered.

"The five saucers that went high came down during the EMB blast. Three entered the water and the other two are on the deck (an expression which indicates that an object is just above the surface of the ocean) and making a run at us. I make it speed at 660 knots at eight thousand yards and closing on the port side," the voice replied in a much calmer tone.

Turning toward her combat control officer, Maureen asked in a dead-calm voice, "Are the Sea Whiz's up and running?"

"Yes, Admiral. They are tracking and should engage in two seconds or less."

Maureen and everyone in the Combat Control Center seemed to hold their breath in anticipation as the saucers raced toward the ship while they hoped and prayed that the Phalanx Sea Whiz system would provide their salvation.

USS Tucson

"Sir, three bogies just splashed down and are coming at us," a voice bent over a radar screen called out and then added, "Range five thousand yards and closing at thirty knots."

Captain Jeffrey Bonner checked the status board of his torpedo tubes and confirmed that all tubes were loaded and ready to engage. Turning toward the two men seated by the steering controls, Jeffrey ordered that the submarine rise off the bottom of the sea sixty feet and remain in silent running mode. He then called the engineering department and ordered them to bring the reactor up to full operating capacity and to be ready to cut in flank speed on demand.

Jeffrey walked the short distance to the radar operator, bent down, and glanced at the screen. Seeing the small blips heading toward the circle in the center of the screen, which represented his submarine, Jeffrey calmly ordered that all data be fed into the firing board and the computers onboard the torpedoes. Jeffrey listened closely as the firing solutions were worked out and relayed by word of mouth to him.

"Fire all forward tubes at two thousand yards in a wide spread at depths separated by three feet," Jeffrey ordered and then contacted engineering, "Talk to me. Are you ready?"

"Give me one more minute," a desperate voice answered.

"In one minute, we may all be dead. Get that power up quick!" Jeffrey demanded.

"Range three thousand, five by five!" a calm voice called out.

"Get ready!" Jeffrey ordered to no one in particular.

"Range two…" the same calm voice called out, but Jeffrey shouted out, "Fire!"

Immediately, all torpedoes in the forward tubes were fired, and upon reaching a distance from the ship of one hundred yards, they armed themselves. Data was being sent to the onboard computers of the torpedoes through the wire they were trailing behind, which was linked to the *Tucson*'s combat computer.

"Let's have that flank speed now and steer thirty degrees to port," Jeffrey called out.

"Flank speed, aye, thirty degrees to port, sir," came confirmation of Jeffrey's order.

To Jeffrey, it seemed like an eternity as he stood on the deck of his ship. When he felt the vibration of the increased speed under his feet and the turn to port, Jeffrey breathed a sigh of relief and was about to ask for a status report when he heard, "All fish running true to targets. Make it five seconds, four, three…"

All of a sudden, the entire submarine seemed to shake and vibrate. Anything loose went flying around the compartment as alarms began sounding and cold seawater entered the submarine in the bridge area. Jeffrey lost his footing and wound up flat on the deck with a couple of his fellow sailors.

Getting up quickly, Jeffrey called out, "Damage report! And turn off those damn alarms. Get a repair party up here!"

"Sir, we were hit in the sail. But otherwise, we're okay." A calm voice called out. (Note: The sail is the highest part of a submarine. It houses the antennas and periscopes. Mostly, it is commonly called the conning tower.)

"Two direct hits!" the combat officer called out.

"What's the track on the third?" Jeffrey quickly asked.

"He's not following. He's going toward the object," the radar operator quickly answered.

"Load all forward tubes. Do we have a firing solution on him?" Jeffrey ordered and inquired as his mind was operating at a million miles an hour.

"Yes, sir, tracking, and we do have a solution," a voice called out as others on the bridge looked at each other with a smirk on their faces knowing that their captain was not a man to screw around with. The smirks changed to smiles as Jeffrey ordered the submarine to come around at flank speed, increase their depth, and hug the bottom of the sea.

Jeffrey's plan was to come in low hugging the seafloor and pop up right before firing and hopefully surprise the aliens. It is a dangerous maneuver to skirt the bottom of the sea at flank speed, but Jeffrey knew the capability of his crew and believed in them. As the *Tucson* came around and raced toward the alien saucer, which now was stopped in the water close to the object, everyone's survival rested in Jeffrey's hands.

"Bring us up thirty feet," Jeffrey ordered when the *Tucson* was three thousand yards away from the saucer.

"Up thirty," a voice spoke out, confirming the order.

"Steady…steady," Jeffrey spoke out as the distance closed.

At fifteen hundred yards away from the saucer, Jeffrey spoke up a little louder, "Fire one through six."

Once Jeffrey felt the last torpedo leave the ship and confirmed that the torpedoes were on their way, he gave the order for a sharp turn to starboard and whispered, "Get us the hell out of here."

Once the turn to starboard was completed, Jeffrey felt the shock wave as it passed through the submarine from the exploding torpedoes.

"Direct hit on two of the torpedoes. Target destroyed. The other four impacted into the object. No secondary explosions," the weapons officer called out.

"Well done. Damage report?" Jeffery asked as his heartbeat returned to normal.

"All leaks have been repaired. The sail, as best we can tell, is filled with water and is slowing our speed by twenty percent," a member of the damage control party called out.

"Okay, let's keep her steady and stay around the fleet until we receive orders. Since we can't go topside and don't have a periscope anymore, we have to stay alert. Reduce speed to dead slow and give me a course toward the *Abraham Lincoln*," Jeffrey ordered and closed his eyes for a second, counting his blessings as he heard his order being confirmed.

SO WE ARE GOING TO FIGHT, ARE WE?

"GIVE ME A TRACK ON the unknowns!" Brian ordered as he picked up his coffee cup and took a sip of his magical elixir, which somehow calmed his nerves during times like this.

"Thirteen out altitude dropped to three hundred feet and on a gradual slope downward," The combat information technician called out a little nervously.

"Okay, son. Take a deep breath and keep the reports coming. Continue to track and confirm when you have lock on the target," Brian replied while trying to take the edge off the pressure-filled atmosphere on the bridge.

"Aye, sir. Nine out and holding at one five zero feet, direct intercept bow to stem," a now somewhat calmer voice replied.

"Sir, we have lock on all three objects!" came another report.

Brian remained standing on the bridge sipping his coffee and staring straight ahead, wondering just when he would be able to see these so-called flying saucers. Just to remind everyone, he stated in between the distance reports, "Okay, everyone, just be cool. Remember we are just tracking these objects. We will not fire. Repeat…do not fire!"

Shelly Abrahms looked over at Brian and saw that he was the picture of calmness and confidence and wondered how he did it. They were about to be, hopefully, not attacked but overflown by aliens from outer space. Here was Brian calmly drinking his coffee staring out of the window. It was then she realized that it was as she suspected; she was in love with him. Somehow, admiration and respect made the leap to love.

"Seven out, altitude holding at one five zero, straight track. Locked on targets," came a quick report.

In the time it took for the report, the saucers were two miles closer, and Brian saw a reflection of light in the distance. While still sipping his coffee, Brian left the bridge and walked out onto the adjacent wing bridge, a small area that is for the most part open to the air, and watched as the objects grew larger as they approached.

"I don't believe this!" Brian said to no one in particular.

In less than a minute, the saucers were overhead and flew over the ship. As they passed overhead, Brian turned around and threw his coffee cup at the saucers and hollered out, "You bastards!" Turning back around, Brian was confronted with Shelly Abrahms standing in the hatchway, which led back onto the bridge.

Shelly had a slight smile on her face as she said, "You missed."

Brian laughed a little and while still having the smile of laughter on his face, he winked at Shelly and replied, "Well, yea. Did you see how scared they were? That will teach them not to mess with the *Ruben James.*"

Once back on the bridge of his ship, Brian notified Admiral Laffey of his encounter with the aliens. Instead of continuing onto Pearl Harbor, as he was originally ordered, Brian received new instructions to reverse course and aid in the rescue effort of the *Illustrious.*

The following morning, as Brian entered the "crew's mess," as it was his habit to eat his meals with the enlisted ranks rather than in the officer's dining area, his attention was drawn to a plaque that had been hung on the bulkhead. Mounted on the plaque was a coffee mug inscribed with the ships crest, and below it was a brass engraving that read: In Commemoration of the Battle of the Cup and Saucers. Captain's Cup 3, Saucer's 0. Well Done, Captain.

When Brian finished reading, a broad smile with a slight laugh overcame him as he turned around only to find the sailors in the mess now standing and suddenly applauding him. Brian raised his arms to quiet the crowd and in a very loud voice said, "Thank you. Hey, we won!" The room then erupted in laughter as Brian walked to the breakfast line, picked up a tray, and stood in line. He was proud of his ship and the sailors that sailed her.

USS Abraham Lincoln

"Phalanx's locked on, Admiral," a hopeful voice called out.

Maureen turned around quickly and watched a monitor that showed, in a screen divided into four sections, the four Phalanx Sea Whiz weapons on the port side. It seemed like an eternity for Maureen as she waited for the weapons to engage. Maureen recalled the demonstration she had seen of the firing of a Sea Whiz weapon. A drone missile was launched at an aircraft carrier. When the missile was six thousand yards from its target, the Sea Whiz, which tracks a target independently, locked onto the drone and fired a short burst of tungsten penetrator rounds at the target. The missile blew up before it even had a chance to come close to the carrier. Maureen silently prayed that the demonstration she saw would happen in real life.

A blinking light in each quadrant of the video monitor indicated that the Sea Whiz's were tracking the saucers. In an instant, each weapon began firing. The aliens didn't have time to react as over forty thousand rounds per minute were fired from each of the Phalanx's. In seconds, the saucers were literally pulverized into slivers as if they were paper being fed into a crosscut shredder.

A cheer went up in the Combat Direction Center as the Phalanx's went silent and returned to their passive mode to await a new target. Maureen breathed in deeply and let her breath out slowly, trying to relax a bit amid an atmosphere of pure tension. But there was no rest for the weary. She went right back to directing the defense of her fleet. *How much longer could they keep up the fight?* she thought. Maureen listened intently as the fighter pilots talked among themselves as they attacked any saucers which strayed into the kill zone the fleet was establishing by their defensive fire. She was elated to hear that the aviators had shot down an additional three saucers without any losses to themselves.

"*Lincoln*, this is Tango X-Ray, do you copy?" a voice over the radio net called out.

Maureen turned around quickly toward the commander of the air group and directed him to answer the call. "Tango X-Ray, this is *Lincoln*, over," he answered.

"*Lincoln*, we are one hundred out, please advise where you want us," the flight leader called in.

"Tango X-Ray, who the hell are you?" the commander of the air group pleaded just before Maureen grabbed the microphone and spoke, "Tango X-Ray, who sent you and why are you so special?"

"That would be Admiral Scott, madame, and we can clear up your problem in a few seconds," the flight leader answered.

"So could Superman!" Maureen answered.

"Admiral, we need you to shut down your defensive fire now. We have acquired all targets and are ready to fire. We are closing fast on your position," their flight leader pleaded.

"Negative!" Maureen shot back.

"Admiral, it sure would be a lot easier if we had a clear sky to shoot in," the flight leader pleaded.

"Negative, Tango X-Ray. Repeat, negative. Do your best," Maureen now pleaded.

"Will do. Tango X-Ray out," came a voice of resignation.

"Admiral! I can't find Tango X-Ray on the scope. It's as if they don't exist. They must be stealth aircraft," a frustrated radar operator asked more than made a statement.

"They are some kind of new stealth aircraft I suppose," Maureen offhandedly remarked and went back to directing the battle.

A few seconds later, a now excited radar operator called out, "Holy shit! I have a multiple missile launch from the sky. I count fifteen missiles heading for the saucers. Shit, one of the missiles was just downed by friendly fire. Impact in four, now three seconds, in one. I'll be a son of a bitch. Admiral, all of the saucers were taken out."

"Are you absolutely sure?" Maureen hurriedly asked.

"All gone, Admiral. They all exploded due to missile impact. I have no idea where those missiles came from, but thank God they showed up," A much happier radar technician answered, followed by, "Man, I don't believe this. Who the hell are those guys?"

Maureen told her executive officer to order a cease-fire but to remain on full-combat alert status. What this meant for the sailors was that it was time to rearm their weapons systems and prepare for the next attack, which everyone felt sure would happen shortly. Grabbing the microphone, Maureen radioed the phantom aircraft, "Tango X-Ray, this is *Lincoln*. A big *well done*! Can I buy you a cup of coffee?"

"Negative, Admiral. We can sweep the area for only one more minute and then we have to return to base," the flight leader replied feeling a little bullish after the successful attack.

Maureen knew she couldn't ask but did so anyway, "Where is that so I can contact your boss and thank him?"

"That would be telling, Admiral. Tango X-Ray out," the flight leader replied and smiled to himself as he banked his aircraft to tum around and head back home. After all it, wasn't every day you could refuse to answer an admiral.

Maureen smiled a little smile and whispered to herself "Thank you, Scotty" and then turned her full attention back to the combat weary fleet.

OKAY, WHO LEFT THE LIGHTS ON?

OPENING HIS LEFT EYE, SCOTTY glanced at a gray wall of his quarters. His first thought was a question, *Who in the hell ever decided that everything in the Navy had to be painted gray?* For at least a minute, he pondered the question and then focused on the unbearable truth that he had to get up. But he concluded, *Oh, how comfortable this bed is.* As he lay on his stomach with the pillow scrunched up under his head on his right side, the mental battle of duty and the sheer joy of comfort and sleep raged on.

Scotty swore that he just laid down, but the clock told a different story. *And who turned the lights on?* A little over six hours had passed, but was it day or night? Pushing himself up with both of his arms, Scotty realized that he was still dressed in his flight suit. That would account for the lights still being on, and he remembered lying across the bed and then "voilà," he must have fallen asleep. Getting out of bed, Scotty bent over trying to find the AM or PM illuminated on his electronic alarm clock. Finding the PM indicator light lit, Scotty breathed a sigh of relief, knowing that he did not sleep through the meeting he had called. He even felt a little better when he realized that there was still a little over two hours yet to the meeting. His body told him to get back in bed, but it also told him that it was time to eat.

The clock told a different story. It told Scotty that it was almost time for dinner, but he wanted breakfast. Reaching for the telephone, he called the mess hall and asked for Chef Sal.

"Yes, Admiral," came a hurried breathless reply.

Man, this guy needs to exercise and eat a little less of his food, Scotty thought.

"Sal, I'm sorry to bother you. I know it's close to dinner time and all, but I just got up and I was wondering if I could get some breakfast?" Scotty asked.

"Let me guess, Admiral. You want four thick cut slices of French toast, stuffed with fresh mozzarella cheese, topped lightly with honey and crushed walnuts, and, of course, some bacon, cooked crispy. Is that about it?" Sal knew the answer since Scotty always called him first when he requested this dish.

"You got it. Oh! And two glasses of rich chocolate milk will do just fine. If it's not too much trouble," Scotty replied, chuckling to himself.

"No problem at all, sir. Just give me a half an hour," Sal replied with a smile on his face.

"Thank you, Sal. I'm going to shower and shave and then I'll come down," Scotty replied as he unzipped his flight suit.

"It's always a pleasure to see you eating with the crew, Admiral. Say, Admiral...err..." Sal began to stumble over his words.

"Yes, Sal. What is it?" Scotty asked, knowing that news of the two battles must have already spread throughout the base.

"Are we going to be okay, Admiral?" Sal asked nervously.

"Yea, Sal. We are going to be just fine. I promise you. Besides I would never let anything happen to this base. I like your French toast too much," Scotty replied, trying to cheer him up.

"Thank you, sir. See you shortly," Sal replied, laughing, grateful to have a man like Scotty as his commanding officer.

"See you then, Sal," Scotty answered as he slipped out of his flight suit.

After showering and shaving, Scotty put on a fresh flight suit and made sure that he looked neat and that everything was in its right place. He even checked his appearance in the mirror to make sure that his patches were perfectly squared up. He knew that as soon as he entered the mess hall, all eyes would be on him. People would look at him to see if there was any trace of worry or concern on his face. He had to appear to be a leader of determination and confidence. For him, that was easy. But yet Scotty worried that if he gave anything away that could create, in the least bit, a negative impression, morale throughout the base would sink immediately. Vowing to take the complete opposite approach, Scotty left his quarters.

As he approached the mess hall, Scotty began to encounter some members of the crew. Putting a big smile on his face as he returned their salutes, Scotty then followed that up with a big hello. He tried to tell himself not to oversell the cheerfulness, and so Scotty held it in check a bit. Once he entered the mess hall, he continued to greet all he saw, grabbed a tray, and stood in line. Sal, upon seeing Scotty in line, told him to come to the front of the line and he would get his French toast. Scotty, however preferred to stay in line and talk with the crew members that watched his every move. After Scotty picked up his meal and a very large cup of coffee, he looked around the mess hall for an empty table but then thought the better of it and walked over to a full table. He asked if those seated would like some company. Immediately, those around the table made room, and Scotty sat down and ate his French toast while everyone else ate steaks, hamburgers, and fries or some kind of chicken dish. In no time at all, everyone around the table was telling jokes and most importantly laughing. Scotty knew that he had pulled it off.

After forty-five minutes, Scotty excused himself and thanked those around the table for the pleasure of dining with them. Everyone replied that it was their pleasure and invited him back anytime. It wasn't every commander that preferred to eat with the enlisted ranks, a practice Scotty was having great success with among the other officers of the base.

As Scotty was leaving, he stopped by to see Sal, not only to thank him for the special meal, but also to order refreshments for the conference.

Scotty asked Sal to bring up to his office a few large urns of coffee, some bottled water, and a selection of soft drinks. In addition, Scotty requested some light snack foods including some doughnuts and pastries.

Sal knew what Scotty really wanted and asked, "What about some brownies?"

Scotty slapped his stomach with both of his hands, smiled, and replied, "The body says no, and the mind also says no, but the taste buds say yes. Some brownies would be great and err…some of those delicious chocolate chips would be really appreciated," Scotty answered instantly, feeling a little guilty over the snacks he was about to eat.

"Would you like some walnuts on those brownies, Admiral?" Sal asked, knowing the answer.

"That would be great!" Scotty immediately replied and then added, "Say, Sal, if Commander Stark should ask, I didn't order the brownies or the cookies. Okay?"

Sal chuckled and then said, "Of course, my wife is the same way. Don't eat this and don't eat that. Trouble is they just don't know what's good in life." Sal kept the smile on his face as Scotty thanked him and walked away. Sal felt good that everyone seems to have the same concerns and undergo the same arguments about what to eat and not to eat.

As Scotty almost disappeared, Sal called out, "I'll add some fresh fruit too." Scotty turned around and waved with a smile on his face and then turned back around and continued on his way. Sal, with the smile still on his face, then walked back into the kitchen and began to prepare the snacks.

Sick bay

Another normal day had come to an end. There were, as usual, too few aliments and too many doctors and nurses. Most of the medical staff assigned to the sick bay spent most of their day cleaning up the area when they were not reading medical journals or playing cards. Dr. Hewitt tried to break up the monotony with what he called "In Service Training." These were, at best, mini seminars mostly on trauma medicine. A lot of the staff found them to be a welcomed diversion; however, the instruction by Dr. Hewitt always seemed to be a half-hearted effort. Today had been one such day. Somehow, he had managed to turn a lecture on treating a heart attack victim into a boring, fall-asleep talk. It was almost as if Dr. Hewitt was reading from a script when he lectured.

When the day shift had left and the evening crew arrived, Dr. Hewitt retreated to his office and finished off his paperwork for the day. Reports had to be filled out and filed. But no one ever seemed to come and look at the endless reams of paper neatly typed and signed. *It must be for something,* he concluded and continued on with his work. As Dr. Hewitt crossed his Ts and dotted his Is, he wondered about the meeting that was taking place. Scuttlebutt around the base was that important decisions were being made about the alien attacks and how that would impact upon Space Command.

After completing his paperwork, Dr. Hewitt closed the file he was working on, reached up, turned his desk lamp off, and stood up. He put his hand in the pocket of his white smock and felt for the needle. Assuring himself that it was there, Dr. Hewitt walked out of his office and down the hallway toward the patient wards. He stopped in front of the door, which led to the little girl's room. Trying to gather his strength, Dr. Hewitt reminded himself that he had his orders, and to disregard them would be treason. Taking a deep breath, he pushed the door open and entered the room.

The little orphan heard Dr. Hewitt enter, lifted her head off the pillow, and looked at him. Her smile stopped the good doctor in his tracks. He was unable to move. Logic told him to follow his orders, but emotion told him something else. Dr. Hewitt smiled a simple smile in return and then hurried out of the room. *What does the life of a small innocent child matter in the grand scheme of things? Why was she left alive while all the others were killed?* Dr. Hewitt wondered as he hurried back to his office. No thoughts came to him as he sat in the darkened office. It was as if the emotion of the moment froze all logic.

DOREEN, COULD YOU PLEASE PASS THE BROWNIES?

ARRIVING AT HIS OFFICE a full hour before the meeting, Scotty was grateful that no one had arrived yet. He wanted some time to gather his thoughts. The past few days had been one for the record books, but it had accomplished something else that most people might have missed. For the first time in the unit's history, they had fought together as a unified force in a prolonged action with the aliens. All the independent parts and functions had come together as one, and as one, they had prevailed. Although Scotty deeply regretted the loss of life, from the death of the spy to Commander Cunningham having been killed, and the alien attack upon the fleet in the Pacific, something good happened. A new dedication, and the ideal of perseverance and eventual victory took hold in the hearts and minds of the service men and women of Space Command. The "raptors" had indeed lived up to their name.

While sitting at his desk, Scotty read the latest briefing report on the disposition of the fleet. It seemed that the entire fleet now was on their way back to Pearl. The search for possible survivors of the *Illustrious* had concluded and that made Scotty stop and think about the massive amount of life lost in a few seconds. The thought of so many men and women losing their life in an instant sent shivers up Scotty's spine. He swore to himself that never again would the aliens have the opportunity to kill so many people. *In fact, one life lost to them is too expensive*, Scotty thought. He knew that the tide of the battle had changed. He had resolved that no longer would the aliens have the freedom to roam the earth at will. At every twist and turn, they would aggressively confront the aliens until their threat was eliminated.

Before the meeting was to start, Scotty wanted to check with Maureen and see how things were going. When he contacted her, he was delighted to hear that the fleet was reformed and sailing toward Pearl together. Maureen expressed concerns about the seaworthiness of the *Port Royal* if they were to encounter heavy seas. Scotty agreed with her and issued an order for a floating dry dock to meet them. The *Port Royal* would be taken aboard the massive vessel and be ferried back to safety. Before they ended their conversation, Maureen told Scotty that Commander James had taken off from the *Lincoln* and would be arriving in Hawaii in less than one hour. Once in Hawaii, the commander will board an Air Force transport and should be back in Colorado eight hours later.

After talking with Admiral Laffey, Scotty put his feet up on his desk, leaned back in his chair, and put his hands behind his head. He then closed his eyes and for a brief moment let his mind drift. But thoughts of the current situation and the events of last night brought him quickly back to the present. Scotty wondered what was going to happen next but knew that whatever it was, well, they were prepared to handle it. When Scotty heard some noise in the outer office, he put his feet back down and stood up. As if on cue, all the meeting members arrive at once and quickly took their seats around the conference table. As Scotty was about to start, he heard a small commotion out in the hallway. Turning around toward the door, Scotty was greeted by a smiling Sal dressed in his chef apron and one of those tall white circular hats. Behind him were two of his cooks each pushing a cart loaded with food, urns of coffee, some chilled bottled water, and soda. Motioning for them to come in, Scotty announced to the group that perhaps they should get some coffee first and then begin.

Once the food was set up and Sal and his cooks had left, Scotty walked over to the food. Quickly, Doreen walked over to him and stood by his side. They looked into each other's eyes and smiled that knowing smile for the briefest of moments. Turning back around, Scotty hesitated at first and then reached for a bottle of water. Scotty felt Doreen looking at him as he reached for a paper plate and then quickly placed two fudge-coated brownies on the plate. As he turned back toward Doreen, Scotty felt the full pressure of her disapproving look and the expressive frown upon her face. Before Doreen had a chance to say anything, Scotty smiled, winked at her, and said "Brain food" and then quickly walked away and took his seat.

Waiting until everyone was seated around the table, Scotty began the meeting by giving a quick recap of the night's events and the current status of the fleet. Figuring that he might as well start at the beginning, Scotty turned the floor over to JW to bring the group up on the cleanup effort. JW was glad to report that the cleanup of the saucers was completed. All the pieces, at least he hoped so, have been recovered and are presently undergoing analysis by Carolyn Gibbs. Likewise, all the aircraft fragments have been cleaned up and transported to a storage facility within the base. Lastly, the area of the plane crash and where the saucers were blown up is being sanitized so that it will look like nothing ever happened.

When JW finished, Scotty turned his attention to Jonesy. What Scotty was interested in was the fallout from the spy that was killed in the communications room. Jonesy, the master of understatement, shrugged his shoulders and replied, "Everything's cool."

Scotty just looked at him and remembered when the both of them were in the Midwest and saw a tornado approaching. Instead of running for cover, the two of them remained in the open until the last possible minute before they were to become victims. Smiling slightly, Scotty recalled Jonesy's comment, "It's starting to get a little windy around here." Recovering from his remembrances, Scotty looked at him and asked, "Well, that's great, but have all the computers been checked? Are all the people back working? And has the place been cleaned up?"

Jonesy shifted his position in his chair and after careful consideration answered, "Yes, Admiral, the room has been fully cleaned, and all of our people are back to work. We had to replace some of the carpet though. A few of the computers also needed to be replaced, and the new ones are up and functioning. I ran a diagnostic on all of the programming, and each hard drive came up clean. As an added precaution, I checked our mainframe, and it also is clean. There are no hidden codes or any incursion into our system. The only anomaly I came up with was a hacker who tried to enter our system, but the automatic lockouts we installed blocked him."

"Hacker?" Scotty uttered.

"Yea, some kid in New Jersey, I think he was sixteen, tried to enter our system. He gained initial access from the Washington office. The system overrides went into operation immediately, and he was shut out and was probably pretty pissed off. Oh, excuse me, I meant angry. But he's cooling his heels now," Jonesy replied and was interrupted by Beverly Hocker.

"What do you mean pissed off and cooling his heels?" Beverly immediately inquired.

"Well, if someone hacks into our system, the program I wrote immediately detects it and upon detection downloads the hacker's computer and identifies his location. After that is done, which takes approximately from three to five seconds, the program sends an electronic bullet into the hacker's system. The bullet then overloads and short circuits his system while at the same time wipes his hard drive clean. Our wipe program puts on a five-layer tier of one and zeros. The hard drive could be reconstituted, but you need very sophisticated programming skills for that, and there are only a few people I know who are capable of performing such a thing.

"The kid was traced to a small town in western New Jersey along the Delaware River named Rosemont. Our agents raided the house under a federal warrant. The kid turned out to be eighteen, so we have him detained. We recovered his computer and a lot of computer manuals as well as very detailed notebooks he kept detailing his hacking escapades within the federal government and documents he viewed. A couple of computer technicians are going through the discs that were recovered to see if there is any sensitive material there. His parents are going a little crazy hiring attorneys and trying to get him released, but we moved him to a federal facility out of state. The federal attorney general responded to his parents and told them that under the National Secrets Act, their son can be held without arraignment for an indefinite period of time," Jonesy responded.

"Will the Attorney General's Office play along?" Scotty asked.

"They will up to a point. What they are interested in was how far he penetrated the federal computer system. From the review done so far, our little hacker has been pretty busy and has penetrated several systems pretty deeply. So his fate is almost sealed. He'll be in jail for a very long time," Jonesy answered.

"What do you think about him?" Scotty inquired.

"The kid is very impressive. I'd like to see if his talents would be an asset to our little operation. If he can hack a computer like I know he can, we sure could use him," Jonesy answered, hopeful that the kid could be saved.

Scotty thought for a moment and then looked at JW and then at Jonesy. "JW, have someone do a background check on this kid. Jonesy, I want this kid to stay in jail for at least six months to scare him a bit. After that, offer him, let's say, an alternative to a prolonged incarnation. If he is acceptable and you qualify him, offer him an enlistment in the Navy. But Jonesy let me caution you. He is not to become your playmate on the internet. In other words, don't steal the world." Scotty warned and then ordered, "Beverly, I want you to coordinate with the attorney general and see that the kid remains in jail."

Beverly nodded in compliance with Scotty's order, and Jonesy thanked Scotty.

"Oh, one more thing. What's this kids name?" Scotty asked as an afterthought.

"Brian Von Albrecht," Jonesy replied after looking at some papers.

"Okay. Give JW the particulars and let's see what we find out about him," Scotty ordered and then shifted his attention to the next item on his agenda. "Doreen, what is the status of our X-aircraft?"

Doreen was as usual right on top of things. "All aircraft are operational. The aircraft that took part in the battle have safely returned to base and are currently listed as operational. The additional aircraft you ordered to California have arrived and are also listed as operational. I would like to return those backup aircraft back to their bases as soon as possible. Just as a side note, I received a telex that fifteen more aircraft are now ready and will begin the flight certification process tomorrow."

"CAG, what about our status?" Scotty quickly asked.

Captain Kendall hesitated for a moment and then answered, "All of the X aircraft are operational as well as the 18s. Our combat helicopters are also combat ready, but two of our Blackhawks are down for servicing, which should be completed within twelve hours. It's due to the heavy use they received at the crash site. We do have five others that are flight ready though."

"Good work, CAG," Scotty replied and then turned his attention toward weapons officer, Captain Bone. "Bone, how is our inventory?"

Bone, who seemed to work miracles with the help of Jonesy in procuring all types of weapons both through regular channels and sometimes through some rather not so legal means, replied, "Weapons storage with the exception of the hypersonic missiles is at one hundred percent. Our missile supply is down four, but we have a shipment of fifteen new missiles coming in on the morning supply plane. The plasma cannons are operational and manned twenty-four seven. So we are in real good shape."

"That's great!" Scotty replied and pondered for a second. "I can't understand why they didn't coordinate an attack upon the base at the same time they took down Commander Cunningham's aircraft. Doesn't make any sense."

"Maybe, they just weren't ready yet," JW answered.

"I hope they are never ready," Scotty declared and moved on wanting to get through everything a little fast so that they could all hear from Arty. "Carolyn, I have to say again that you saved my life. When I took that laser shot, I thought for sure that I was dead. That vest you made saved my life. I can't thank you enough," Scotty declared and noticed that Arty was looking at her with a big wide grin on his face. "Is it possible to produce those vests for JW's men on a production level?" Scotty asked.

"Not yet on a mass production level. It's a little too early yet. I'm experimenting with a few different types of glass based upon what I've seen from the vest you were wearing when you were hit. I'm hoping to make them at least half or more than the weight of the prototype," Carolyn replied, a little embarrassed by Scotty's praise.

"Okay, whatever you need, just ask. I want to get them to the troops as soon as possible," Scotty emphasized and then asked Carolyn, "I know that I've come to look upon you and Doreen as our resident scientists, and indeed you both are more than qualified. I appreciate the excellent work you both have done. So that said, I have to ask you both, is there anything we should be made aware of regarding that asteroid, which is all over the news?"

Doreen and Carolyn looked at each other for a moment, and Carolyn nodded slightly to Doreen. Doreen spoke up, "Admiral, we have an astronomer that works in Carolyn's department who is up-to-date on the asteroids. Can we have her come up and give us the latest information?"

"Yes, but first I want Arty to brief us on what the results of the investigation revealed. Arty," Scotty ordered.

Arty looked first at Scotty and then at Carolyn, where his glance was met with a warm smile, and then around at the group, and began, "First, I would like to say how deeply sorry I am for the death of Commander Cunningham and the men who accompanied him. It must have been horrible for them. When I first came here, it was Commander Cunningham who, in no small part, showed or directed my way. When we were given our assignment, it was the commander who made me play by the rules. If he had left me to my own devices, it would have been me who is lying in state on the hangar deck. This man was a big influence on me, and I shall never forget him and his dedication to duty. He truly was a role model for the rest of us to follow. I shall miss him. That being said, I guess I better start from the beginning…" Arty commented but was interrupted by Scotty.

"Commander, that is indeed a legacy which Mr. Cunningham left behind and a dedication to duty which was outstanding. Commander Cunningham, with his last breath, told me that the secret to what the aliens want lies in human blood. We have not yet been able to reconstitute the hard drive of the computer. The disk that he gave me, as he was dying, was corrupted by a strong magnetic force, and the data is spotty at best. However, efforts are being exerted so we will be able to read the data on the disk. What we need from you is the conclusion you and Commander Cunningham reached when you met in Alabama. So if you will proceed with that in mind at the present time, we would be grateful. We will have time for a full debriefing later. Also, give your computer to Beverly, and she will see that your reports a re-downloaded, and you can write your final report later. Now, please proceed," Scotty pleaded.

Arty was taken back a little by Scotty's directness and reached into his pocket for the vial of pills that was taken from the dead aliens in the parking lot of the motel in Alabama. He started playing with the top of the vial by pushing up with his finger on the lid as he began to talk, "As you all know, we were assigned to do background checks on people who claimed to be abductees. We also were to examine the backgrounds of people who were known implant victims of the aliens. When Commander Cunningham and I were given the assignment, we decided to conduct an extensive examination of the backgrounds as quickly and expediently as possible. What we were looking for was some point of commonality among these people, which made them victims of the aliens. While we were given files that contained medical information, we decided to try and confirm that data as best we could.

"Initially, when we began the investigation, little discrepancies showed up. For example, a person's height was recorded incorrectly, a white female was recorder as being of Spanish descent, some dental records didn't quite match up, and in a lot of cases, the blood type was incorrect. At first, the discrepancies didn't draw our attention. Each file had something recorded incorrectly. After the first fifteen cases were completed, I knew something was drastically wrong. The blood types were always wrong. It was just too large of a coincidence for it to be a mistake. Someone was altering the records to hide the true blood types of the people. All the individuals I investigated were of the AB blood group. This blood group represents only 5 percent of the total population and by definition is a rare blood type.

"It was then that Commander Cunningham and I decided to meet and compare our findings. Sure enough, his findings were identical to mine. At that point, we decided that two things were happening. First, that there is a spy or spies in Space Command that have direct access to the records and, therefore, have the ability to alter the records. Secondly, that the real reason the aliens are here is to harvest a reliable blood supply.

"Out of curiosity, I contacted an old girlfriend…err friend," Arty stumbled over the word girlfriend as he looked at Carolyn and saw the disappointment on her face and then continued, "whose father is a general in the Air Force. I asked her to see if she could find out any information about the people on that plane the aliens attacked and subsequently harvested the organs and blood from the passengers and crew. What she found out scares the hell out of me.

"A computer analysis revealed that the people aboard that aircraft had two things in common. First, all the victims had an AB blood type. Secondly, they all had received a letter from a travel agency, which informed them that they had won a contest for a fully paid vacation package. The only thing they had to do was contact the travel agency, and their plane tickets were mailed to them. An investigation into the travel agency revealed that the agency was in business for a total of two weeks and then closed. The principles listed on the business license simply don't exist. Therefore, the conclusion must be reached that what we thought was a warning was indeed a warning but at the same time was a deliberate act performed in a cold and calculating manner.

"There is one other thing. When I realized the viciousness of these creatures with the Brazil incident, I wondered about the little girl down in sick bay. Today, I went down to see her, and with Doreen's help, we took a blood sample from her. Carolyn typed the blood for me, and her blood type is AB, just as her record shows. Why then did the aliens leave her? Benevolence? From what we know about them, they are vicious bastards incapable of compassion. No, they left her alive to send us a message. They are going to peruse their harvesting of blood and organs at their will, and the hell with us," Arty concluded.

"Wow!" Scotty declared and then continued, "Very good report, Arty. I agree with your conclusions, and at the same time, it worries me. As you know, we killed one alien that had penetrated Space Command and had sent the message revealing the location of Commander Cunningham's aircraft. But in a larger sense, it also makes one wonder why they reacted so fast and violently over the craft on the floor of the Pacific. Granted that they are two separate problems, but somehow, they must be related or linked in some way." Scotty was thinking out loud.

Turning toward JW, Scotty asked him what he thought. JW, much like Scotty, always thought that there probably were spies within the base. The question, though, for the moment was who had access to the records which were given to Arty and Commander Cunningham. JW knew that the list was probably going to be somewhat long. Scotty directed JW to turn the base upside down again if need be to find the spies. As an afterthought, he also directed that new blood tests be taken of all base personnel, but instead of typing the blood on base, JW was to have his second-in-command witness the drawing of the blood, secure the samples, and personally accompany the blood to an Army testing lab in Maryland. This process was to be followed until all the crew were tested. Scotty then asked for opinions about Arty's report.

Doreen was the first to speak up, "If they are interested in the blood, then why in God's name would they also take human organs? We saw the horror they wrought on those poor people in Brazil. Their actions were deliberate, and the organs were removed with precision. No, they must be after both."

"I agree with Doreen. The blood harvesting, I think, is secondary to the organs. The organs may allow them to adapt to the earth, especially the lungs, or simply our organs are adaptable to their bodies. If that is the case, then we may conclude that something is seriously wrong with their race, and our organs are used to replace dying parts of their bodies. It's really too horrible to think about. Our blood, however, from what we know, is different from their blood, so therefore, it must be used as some form of a substitute. Much like we break down blood into white and red blood cells and plasma, the aliens could be doing the same thing. They must need it to supplement their blood or to help them adapt to the transplanted organs," Carolyn added.

Scotty quickly commented, "That is my feeling exactly about the organs, and your conclusion makes a lot of sense about the blood."

"I'd like to just wipe these bastards out and be done with it," JW thought out loud.

"I agree with JW, but I think we have to be fully prepared. We have the firepower, we proved that, but the main question is, do we have enough, and what size force are we facing?" CAG volunteered.

"I agree with Admiral Scott. Let's fight them where we find them, but keep in mind that we must prepare for the day when we will fight a major battle with the aliens," Beverly commented.

Arty adjusted his sitting position and then spoke up while still playing with the vial of pills, "I know that we are talking in generalities and it's good to hear how you all feel. But what I want to point out is the human factor. I've met these people, and they are just like you and me. They are mothers, fathers, sons, and daughters. Somehow, we have to protect these people, but there is a however. If we defeat the aliens before we can fully understand the implants that some of these people have, what happens? What I'm saying is if the implants are somehow interwoven into the alien technology, if the tie between the aliens and the implant victims is cut, what happens?" Arty readjusted his position and continued, "What I am worried about is if the tie is broken, do the people die? I would like to eliminate the alien threat like all of you, but before we go to war with them, could we try and understand the implants a little better?"

Doreen looked at Scotty and then at Arty and replied, "Commander, we have studied the round implants placed in the sinus cavity and the nerve ending implants, and we determined that there is no threat to the people. Let me…" Doreen stopped talking and watched as the top flew off the vial Arty was playing with and the orange pills spilled across the conference table.

Arty quickly tried to gather up the pills with the aid of the others.

CAG picked up a few of the pills, looked at them, and handed them back to Arty and declared, "You must have a bad sinus condition. I guess you haven't gotten used to living underground yet."

Arty looked at CAG with a puzzled look on his face and replied, "No, I don't have a sinus problem, and living here doesn't really bother me. Why do you ask?"

"It's just that the night the admiral took over command of the base, I saw Dr. Hewitt taking the same pills. He told me they were for his sinuses because he was not use to living underground," CAG replied.

In a solemn even-toned voice, Arty, while first looking at CAG and then at Scotty, replied, "These pills were taken off of the body of an alien who tried to kill us in Alabama."

"Shit! JW!" Scotty declared as he rose from his chair.

"I'm on it, boss!" JW cried out as he rose from his chair and rushed over to the telephone. Quickly, JW issued orders for the arrest of Dr. Hewitt. Once the telephone was returned to its receiver, JW looked at Scotty who was checking to see if the sidearm he took from a cabinet was loaded and asked, "Are you ready?"

"Hell yea, let's go!" Scotty answered and as he ran from the room instructed the others to remain behind.

Mid Point Observatory

The floor of Dustin's small computer station was quickly becoming a sea of unknown depth of computer paper. Dustin had set his computer to automatically print each screen he viewed. He did this more for historical reasons than practicality. True, he would review and organize the printed pages, but in reality, his mind was now like a sponge absorbing each new fact and filing it away in a logical sequence. While he knew that the path of the asteroid would pass by the earth, Dustin did not like what he was learning about the hitchhiker.

Although he had settled upon three different scenarios for the effect the meteor shower would have on the hitchhiker, he now believed that anything was possible. No matter what he tried, Dustin could not get an accurate estimate of the mass of DG122A. The hitchhiker would not give up its secret easily. He still felt inwardly that the asteroid would spin off into space or at worst strike the moon. Recently, however, Dustin began to understand its true potential and worried that its orbit might become erratic. If that was to happen, then there was a distinct possibility, although remote, that it might collide with the earth. Not a hundred years from now, but rather, it might come back much, much earlier. Dustin now worried that should its path become erratic, it could strike the earth in less than a year.

As Dustin sat at his computer counsel, he became frustrated. Frustrated at the unknown. He was not used to unknown quantities. Dustin had always been able to find the elusive golden ring in a complex problem. But this time, the ring was out of reach.

Putting his elbows on the desk, Dustin lowered his head and rested it in the palms of his hands. Slowly, he massaged his temples, trying to push the tension away, which was giving rise to a head-pounding headache. Hearing the soft click of Victoria's shoes as she walked toward him, Dustin turned his head slightly and smiled as he called out, "Hi, Vicki." Turning back around, Dustin began massaging his temples again.

"Dustin, it's really late. Why don't you try and get some sleep? You can get back at it later after you relax," Victoria answered, stopped behind Dustin, and peered over his shoulder at the computer screen. After a few seconds, Victoria put her hands on Dustin's shoulders and began massaging them. A few seconds later, she added, "Dustin, your muscles are so tight. You really need to relax."

"Victoria, that feels so good. Is this one of your hidden talents?" Dustin declared and was so grateful for the massage.

"That plus a lot more!" Victoria softly replied in Dustin's right ear. She then kissed him tenderly on his head.

Dustin lifted his head up. His eyes were closed as he breathed in and treasured the smell of Victoria's delicate perfume. That combined with her gentle kiss was all he needed. Dustin was lost, logic was gone, and in a second, all the barriers between them melted away. Dustin moved his head to the left side, put his left hand behind her thin neck, and pulled her face toward him. In an instant, their emotions were lost in a kiss, and every instinct in their bodies awoke. As Dustin's tongue searched her mouth, he arose out of the chair, and they embraced. Victoria felt his excitement rise and press against her in the softest of spots. They pushed their bodies together, tenderly at first and then with an urgency of desire.

Breaking their kiss, Victoria whispered to Dustin to follow her. They walked in silence, hand in hand to her office. No one was there to notice their passage from being friends to lovers. Shutting and locking the door to her office, Victoria turned around to face Dustin. Dustin reached behind her and turned the light switch off. The soft reflective light of the parking lot outside softly lit the office.

Dustin stood there, ready to receive her with a smile on his face. He reached out for her and pulled her into him. Together, they inched their way toward the couch. Once there, Dustin lifted her cotton top over her head and flung it across the room. Victoria then began to unbutton his shirt and kissed his chest tenderly in a new area with the release of each button. Dustin reached for the closure of her bra. After a few awkward seconds, he found the catch, figured out how to release it, and freed her erect nipples from their captivity.

When Victoria undid the last button of his shirt, Dustin guided her upward, and she pushed the shirt off his shoulders and let it drift onto the floor. They hugged for a moment, each slightly embarrassed to say anything. Dustin bent downward and softly kissed her breasts. His mouth found her nipples, and he began to caress the left one with his tongue and then gently began to suck on her erect expression of desire. As Dustin turned his attention to her right breast, Victoria let out a soft deep moan and whispered, "Oh, Dustin."

As Dustin continued to gently suck on her breast. Victoria released his belt, undid his zipper, and as his pants fell to the floor, she reached for and then slowly stroked his expression of physical desire. Reaching down to Victoria's waist, Dustin unzipped her skirt and pushed it off her body. He then placed his hands on her waist and searched out her underwear. Grasping the lace of her thong, Dustin began to gently pull it downward over her thigh-high stockings. As Dustin removed her thong, he gently guided Victoria down to the awaiting couch. Victoria followed his guidance and laid down on the couch with her head on the armrest. Dustin knelt on the floor by her body and kissed her. He then guided his tongue toward her breasts and then downward. Victoria moaned and placed her hands on Dustin's back, gently rubbing him.

When Dustin reached her thighs, he gently pushed her legs apart and pulled her body toward him. Victoria placed her left leg over his shoulder as Dustin kissed her inner thighs as a tease of things to come. He then guided his searching tongue toward her prize of prizes. Slowly, his tongue massaged her lips. Victoria was no longer in control of her body. Desire overcame her, and she pushed her body closer and moaned a deep sigh of pleasure when Dustin's tongue entered her, slightly withdrew, and then reentered. Victoria pushed her pelvis slightly upward and down in response the pleasure she was experiencing. Her left arm reached out for Dustin's, and she guided his hand to her waiting breast. Desire and passion overcame her, and Victoria pulled him upward.

Their lips met once again in a long, searching kiss as their bodies pressed against each other. Her hunger grew deeper as she guided him to stand up. Victoria put her arms around his waist and sought out his erect passion. She sucked on its tip at first, and slowly, she took it all in as her tongue massaged downward. As her head went backward and forward slowly at first and then faster, Dustin was ready to explode, but he held it back; it just wasn't time yet. Dustin tenderly placed his hands upon her head and stroked her hair but knew that the ultimate pleasure was yet to come.

On a passionate high, Victoria laid back down on the couch and accepted Dustin. Wrapping her legs around his torso, she drew him in again and again until she was in another place, in another time.

Exhausted, the new lovers separated for a moment. Dustin laid down with his head on the opposite arm of the couch and breathed deeply. Victoria heard the breath of her lover, picked herself up, laid on top of Dustin and kissed him softly as their tongues danced their dance of desire and completeness.

Dustin whispered, "I love you," and Victoria replied, "I have always loved you."

Victoria slid down across Dustin a little, rested her head on his chest, and listened to his beating heart. Within a few moments, they were both fast asleep dreaming of each other.

Sick bay

Dr. Hewitt sat up in his desk chair and left his darkened office. He walked slowly, as if he was an old man, the distance of fifty feet from his office to the doors leading out into the main hallway. As he was about to go through the two stainless-steel doors that signified the entrance to sick bay, a Klaxon alarm went off. Dr. Hewitt stood motionless for a moment, wondering if the day he had always feared had come. When the Klaxon alarm went off after a few seconds, he relaxed. Pushing on one of the doors with his hand and taking a step forward, he froze in his tracks. The sound of the Klaxon alarm was suddenly replaced with the sound of booted feet running toward him. Peeking out into the hallway, he saw five armed Marines running toward sick bay. Stepping backward, Dr. Hewitt let the door go. Walking backward, he looked from side to side, trying desperately to find a hiding place. Quickly realizing that there was simply nowhere to hide, and in a state of panic, he reached into the pocket of his white lab coat.

Dr. Hewitt's hand closed around the needle that was intended for the little girl. Realizing that the sounds of the booted running feet were coming for him, Dr. Hewitt was overcome with the human trait of fear. Like a good soldier, he had followed his orders. For the past ten years, he had lived among the humans as one of them. He had taken care of them when they were sick and rejoiced with them when they became well. But he always kept his goal in perspective. After all, he was a spy sent to work his way into the most secret government installation in the world. Here he was to report on the progress of the humans as they learned how to fight the aliens. Report back he did, conduct minor sabotage, he did, sneak other spies into the base, he did, alter records to confuse the enemy, he did, learn their secrets, he did to a degree. Why then must he die? Dr. Hewitt tried to reason.

Dr. Hewitt had come, during his time among these creatures, to love and respect them. He admired their dedication, spirit, sense of duty to each other, and their world as a whole. Most of all, he enjoyed their laughter, something which was unknown in his society. He adopted this human trait and laughed at their confusion. On one hand, they pollute their planet while at the same time try to clean it up. No, Dr. Hewitt didn't want to die; he wanted to live among the humans. But how was that possible? He had his orders and a devotion to his own civilization.

Slowly, he backed up into sick bay as the sounds of the soldiers running became louder. Dr. Hewitt withdrew the needle from his pocket and held it up. With his other hand, he reached over and took off the protective blue cap on the needle. He stared at it for a moment and then in one swift motion stuck it in his neck. Quickly, he placed two of his fingers on the finger phalanges and with his thumb pushed in the plunger. In a couple of seconds, the deadly liquid was doing its job. As he felt the liquid spreading throughout his circulatory system, Dr. Hewitt stumbled and fell to the floor. He struggled to raise his torso and crawled along the floor until he reached the base of an examination table. Once there, he pulled himself up and rested his back against the base of the table.

Dr. Hewitt stared at the entrance to sick bay and waited for death to come, hopefully before his pursuers, but that was not to be. The Marines crashed through the doors, immediately surrounded him, and pointed their weapons at him. He was told to get up with his hands raised, but Dr. Hewitt laughed at first and then slightly coughed. Scotty arrived and ordered the Marines to move. Kneeling down next to Dr. Hewitt, Scotty noticed the needle sticking out of the good doctor's neck and knew that he was close to death.

Scotty bent over further, looked into his eyes, and asked, "Why?"

Dr. Hewitt struggled to lift his head and look at Scotty. He liked Admiral Scott and in his own way even admired him. He coughed slightly, and a pink frothy liquid began to come out of the left side of his mouth and flow down his jaw. Breathing deeply, which only increased the flow of liquid escaping, Dr. Hewitt tried to speak, "We… we…want…your planet. Our eco…sys…system…is …dying. Need…

yours…for the…the rest…of…our people." Dr. Hewitt eyes then closed, and his head slumped against his chest. He was dead.

Scotty stood up and, for a minute, stared down at this creature. JW noted that Scotty appeared a little ashen as if someone just scared the hell out of him. In reality, Scotty was scared. He guessed that the aliens wanted something and thought at worst that they wanted to populate the earth along with the humans. But now, for the first time, the true secret of Pandora's Box was revealed. The aliens were indeed trying to adapt to the earth, but humans were ultimately to be destroyed. This fight was for the survival of mankind.

The fear in Scotty would always be there, but he filed it away for the moment. It was good to fear because fear allowed you to accomplish the unobtainable. Turning toward JW, Scotty ordered him to have the area cleaned up and the body placed in the morgue. Once satisfied that the area was being sanitized, Scotty and JW left to return to the meeting after posting a guard in front of Dr. Hewitt's office.

Scotty's conference room

Scotty and JW returned to his office and found the others with pensive looks on their faces as they sat around the table nervously drinking coffee. Silence in the room prevailed as Scotty related what had happened. When he told them what the doctor had said, everyone looked at each other in silent recognition of the fact that they were in a virtual fight for the planet. No longer could there be isolated skirmishes. The aliens had to be stopped at all costs no matter what. Each encounter had to be fought as if it was a battle, and if a battle was to be fought, there was only one option—Win.

Through his finesse as a leader, Scotty unified the group and reminded them that there were still a few things they had to cover before they could adjourn to their own thoughts. Before he continued with the meeting, Scotty directed JW to have his second-in-command. Linda Clark work with Beverly and search the contents of the doctor's desk and his quarters. Turning toward Carolyn, Scotty directed her to lend whatever assistance she can to help them in the analysis of the doctor's belongings. Turning back to Beverly, Scotty directed her to appoint Flight Surgeon Shena Gordon in charge of the medical department. Lastly, he directed that JW coordinate with her the retesting of all base personnel to see if there are any more spies.

"I believe we left off with Arty concluding his remarks. Now, I would like to hear from the astronomer. Is she here?" Scotty asked while looking at Doreen.

"Yes, sir. Let me get her," Doreen replied as she rose from her chair and went into the outer office. Returning a few minutes later, Doreen introduced Mary Wesley to the group.

Mary went over to the wall and mounted a chart she had made to the fasteners available for such a presentation. Once satisfied that the chart was secured, she turned back around. Facing the group, Mary began to explain how the asteroid and its hitchhiker came to be discovered. She then explained the danger of the asteroid passing through the meteor shower and what might happen to the second asteroid.

Taking a deep breath, Mary announced that her findings differed with the conclusions of Mid Point Observatory in one respect. Mary prefaced her opinion by detailing how she and Doreen enlisted the help of Jonesy to hack into the data files of the observatory. Turning around to look at her chart, Mary pointed out the path of the asteroids and their intersection point with the meteor shower. Turning around again to face the group, Mary stood firm with her legs slightly apart in a position of authority and said, "When the hitchhiker, or DG122A if you please, comes into contact with the meteor shower, DG122A's orbit will most definitely be effected. While Mid Point Observatory believes that it will go off into space with a possibility of it striking the moon, it is my belief, based upon the data, that it will fragment, and some parts will definitely strike the moon somewhere on the dark side."

There was silence in the room for a brief second, and then Scotty spoke up, "Lieutenant Wesley, why are you sure that it will fragment, and if so, what will be the effects the impact has on the moon and its relation to the earth?"

Mary took a second to gather her thoughts and, then looking first at the group and then at Scotty, commented, "Admiral Scott, my analysis of the situation and the methodology I used to reach that conclusion differs from that of Mid Point in one main respect. Mid Point is an observatory, which for lack of a better word, observes. Their main focus is tracking the asteroids to determine their possible trajectory. I analyzed their data on the basis of their observations and agreed with their basic findings. But I focused in on the meteor belt that the asteroids will pass through at the point of intersection. Also, through the use of military satellites, I was able to get a fairly good idea on the mass of DG122A. I should point out that Mid Point does not have this data. That information, taken together with the mass and speed of the meteor belt, I was able to predict, with the aid of computer models, that DG122A will fragment. Some of those fragments will most definitely collide with the dark side of the moon. Other fragments will spin off into space while others will become part of the meteor belt or collide with DG122.

"What this will mean for the earth can only be a guess at this point. The moon will absorb the collision and may be slightly knocked off its axis by a one-percent shift. The gravitational pull between the moon and the earth will increase. Immediately, this will mean increased wave height and coastal flooding. Other than that, it's really too early to speculate on any other longtime effects." Mary paused for a second and then added, "There is, however, the very real possibility that some of the fragments will make their way to earth."

Scotty looked at Mary and for a moment wondered what else was going to happen. Wanting to lighten the mood in the room, Scotty asked, "Would you recommend buying beach-front property on the Pennsylvania side of the Delaware River?"

Mary and the others in the room laughed slightly. Her laughter left quickly as she replied, "That would seem to be a reasonable investment should the gravitational pull increase as a result of the impending collision. As you may know, New Jersey is predicted to disappear under the ocean in roughly a few million years. Taxis in New York City will become water taxis, much like in Venice. Around the East Coast, I might also suggest selling any property you may hold in an area near at or below sea level, like New Orleans. Parts of the East Coast might do well to study hydrology in Holland."

"Lieutenant, do you think that the aliens could use this event to mask or hide some sort of an attack?" Scotty asked, considering all possibilities.

Mary had considered this very question and had run a few computer scenarios two days ago and was prepared for this question. "The answer is both yes and no. Yes, it would be possible to try and sneak a force in behind or alongside of the asteroids, but that would be sheer insanity. The only reason I would say that such an action would be possible is because we will not have any satellites in the area of the passage of the asteroids. All satellites within or near the path of the asteroids are being redirected onto new flight paths which will take them out of harm's way."

"Jonesy, when will we lose satellite coverage?" Scotty asked as he turned toward his friend.

"In two days, we will lose all satellite coverage. However, we have hacked into NASA's two deep-space satellites and have redirected them toward earth. It will take NASA at least five days to figure out what is wrong. By that time, I will have released them and send them back into deep space. Of course, there will be absolutely no trace of my invasion," Jonesy replied with a grin on his face being the proud parent of a hack that no one will ever detect. With an even bigger grin, Jonesy continued, "You see, NASA takes forever to correct anything. Once they realize that they have a problem, all of a sudden, it's rule and diagnosis by committee, and that will take forever. Well, not forever, and they are very good at what they do, but I am better."

"Glad to see that modesty is one of your attributes," Scotty quipped back.

"Nah, I'm just real good!" Jonesy replied, not to be outdone.

"CAG!" Scotty called as he turned his attention toward the commander of the air group.

"Admiral, I'd like to go to full alert in two days and remain at that status for at least twenty-four hours past the event," CAG suggested.

Scotty was pleased with CAG's assessment and replied, "Make it so."

Being somewhat exhausted by the events over the past few days,

Scotty decided to end the meeting, but there was one other thing that was nagging at him. "There is one other thing I would like your ideas on. When we began the project in the Pacific Ocean, things went rather smoothly. Even the exploration of the object. Things went really bad when Vinson's mini submarine slammed into the panel and turned something on. It's their reaction that I find curious. I would think that due to the spies we had or may have on the base, they know of the technology that we have gleamed from them. Sure, we may have discovered the means for deeper-space flight and the ability to build a ship like the one on the floor of the ocean. But it would take us years to learn those lessons, adopt the technology, and actually build such spacecraft. No, I think there is some other secret down there that they want to protect. Otherwise, I don't think we would have fought the battle that we did. They bloodied us, and we in turn bloodied them. I'm interested to know if anyone has any ideas."

"Maybe, it has something to do with their weapons," Captain Bone offered.

"Yeah, but we showed them that we can shoot them down and overcome their weapon systems," Scotty answered and noticed that Doreen and Carolyn were exchanging knowing glances. "Do you two have something?" Scotty asked.

Carolyn nodded to Doreen who then faced Scotty and spoke up, "Well, maybe. One day, Carolyn and I were discussing the aliens as a whole and what they have been doing. We think that since the beginning of recorded history, and beyond that, one is able to readily ascertain that the aliens have been here, perhaps sporadically at first. In the twentieth century, their presence or visitations have increased rapidly over time. One might conclude that they have, in a sense, been cultivating their presence toward the day that they will take over our world. What we saw in Brazil was absolutely horrifying and showed us the level of their commitment. At that time, we thought, properly so, that organ transplantation was their only goal as they perused global domination. Now, thanks to Commander Cunningham and Arty, we know that they are truly after our blood to aid in their living on our planet. Human-organ harvesting is also being employed as an added avenue of adapting to Earth. From the death of Dr. Hewitt, if I may call him that, we learned that they have to come here in order to survive since their own planet is dying.

"The question, which begs to be asked, is the methodology in which they are perusing their ultimate goal. We often hear, what used to be in science fiction, the concept of terra forming or the process of constructing a planet's atmosphere so that a species can live on that planet. Why then aren't they reconstructing our atmosphere to adapt to themselves? The answer is that their science is flawed, or they were stopped from doing it. We can assume, from the blast holes in the ship on the floor of the ocean, that some force engaged in a battle with the aliens, which subsequently caused the ship to crash. Whatever race caused this to happen did so for a reason. Now, this is pure speculation on our part, but perhaps, this ship was engaged in terra forming our world, and our unknown benefactor may have simply shot it down as well as other alien craft. The alien craft on the bottom of the Pacific may contain such science. That is a prize they don't want us to have. But there is one more possibility that is far more likely.

"While Carolyn is far more qualified to talk about it than I am, let me just give you our basic idea. Our point is predicated on two main factors. That is the physiology of the aliens and how they manufacture their weapons, spaceships, and anything else they may need. First, let me discuss the physiology of the aliens we have encountered. As we discussed before, there seems to be an interdependence of the humanlike aliens and what we have come to call the grays. It appears that the grays are the worker force of the other aliens. Every time we have encountered the aliens, there seems to be one humanlike alien in charge over a group of grays. We can assume, for argument's sake, that this is due to a need. For example, the humanlike aliens may have been the ones who destroyed their planet. This is evident by the mere existence of Dr. Hewitt and the other alien. And what were Dr. Hewitt's last words, 'We need your planet for the rest of our people.' This would indicate that beyond his planet dying, his civilization is likewise dying out.

"But one other thing bothers me about his statement. He didn't say what their plans were for our planet. Do they want to settle here or rape our planet of its natural resources and move on? I know that I am getting off track, so let me refocus on the doctor's last statement. If we take his last statement and follow it to its logical conclusion, then we must assume that in all areas of his civilization, there are shortages. There would be people shortages in agriculture, military, civilian, and most importantly manufacturing. This then would explain the union or alliance with the grays. The grays fill in where the humanlike aliens are lacking adequate personnel. The problem though is the physiology of the grays as adapted to the manufacturing process. The grays are a small stature civilization with long, thin arms and short legs. Their bodies are disproportionate to any task they must complete. For example, how could such creatures construct such a ship as the one we were exploring on the bottom of the ocean? Yes, computer-driven manufacturing would account for the production of such vessels, but not for the construction technique employed."

Everyone around the table seemed to lean forward in their seats a little, paying full attention to Doreen as she continued, "Remember what was notated in the pictures we received of the outside of the craft? That the material, which the ship was made out of, appeared to be seamless. There were no indicators of the material being joined. Are we to assume that the ship was made out of one continuous roll, in a tubular fashion, of some sort of material? The construction and material production process to accomplish such a feat would have to be on a gigantic scale. No, the answer is the ship was constructed using nano-manufacturing techniques. That would account for the seamless material—"

Scotty had a somewhat confused look on his face as he interrupted Doreen, "Nano, what?"

Doreen looked at Scotty and then at the group and continued, "Nanomanufacturing techniques. In its simplest form, it is a process whereby an object is constructed one atom at a time. That would account for the seamless construction of the outer skin of the ship. Our science is in the infant stage of understanding and applying such techniques. But now I'm into an area that I am not qualified to talk about, so if Carolyn would please take over, I'd feel much better." Doreen yawned and looked at Carolyn.

Carolyn, in response to Doreen, also yawned and reached for her cold cup of coffee. Scotty looked around the table, saw that everyone looked pretty well-beat, and decided that right now, it would be better if they all were to get some rest. "I know that it is really late, and I think it might be better if we broke for the night. We can pick it up again in the morning when we are all fresh. I believe what Carolyn has to say is going to be really important, and I want us all wide awake for it. So let's meet back here at eleven hundred hours, and we will start with Carolyn."

Turning toward Mary, Scotty added, "Lieutenant, please have an update available for us on the asteroids at that time."

Mary nodded at Scotty in silent acknowledgment of his order.

Scotty then continued, "Also, let's think of any way we can possibly enhance our defensive position. Thank you all, and I'll see you in the morning."

As everyone filed out of his office, Doreen lingered. Scotty sat back in his chair, glanced up at the clock on the wall, and noted that it was almost 3:00 am. Speaking up, Scotty commented more than asked, "Just when I think it can't get any worse, it does." Pulling himself together, Scotty stood up, walked over to Doreen, and kissed her on the cheek and whispered, "I love you."

Doreen smiled at her lover and likewise expressed her love for him. Together, they left the empty conference room and walked toward their quarters.

As they walked, Scotty was deep in thought and asked, "This nano thing. Is it a really big problem?"

Doreen saw the worried look on his face, wanted to say no but knew better. "If the aliens are using nanotechnology, then Pandora's Box is opened. But right now, you need some sleep, so try and put it in the back of your mind. I'm sure that with people like Carolyn and Jonesy, we can overcome anything."

"How did you come up with this?" Scotty asked, half afraid of the answer.

"Carolyn and I went up to the hangar deck and closely examined the saucers up there, and you know what? Ninety percent of the outer skin is seamless. The only place where there is some kind of construction joint is where the entry hatch is. Other than that, it's one piece of material. We kicked the idea around and realized what they were doing," Doreen answered, reached up, and kissed Scotty on his cheek as they walked. She then reached out and took his hand in hers. Together, they walked hand in hand, not caring what others may think. Each moment was precious, and time was their only true enemy.

Mid Point Observatory

As the first warm red rays of the morning sun penetrated her office, Victoria awoke with a smile on her face. She pushed herself upward and kissed Dustin. Awaking, Dustin smiled and returned her affection with a tender kiss and softly spoke, "Good morning, my love."

Victoria smiled, slightly blushed, and echoed his words. Dustin put his arms around her naked body and hugged her for a few precious seconds, and then his mind returned to reality. "I guess we better get up and get ready. The day crew will be arriving shortly, and we should at least look presentable."

Victoria laughed but knew he was right. She stood up, grasped Dustin's hands, and helped him get up. Once standing, they embraced again, and walked into the private bathroom adjoining Victoria's office. Together, they showered, washing each other as an expression of affection but mostly exploration.

Once dressed, they decided to drive down to the nearest town, a short nine-mile drive, and have breakfast. But they didn't eat much. They mostly stared at each other and smiled. Dustin reached out, took her hand, and kissed the back of her palm. Victoria would smile that slightly embarrassed smile back and wish that they were away from this place and time.

Once breakfast was over, they drove back in silence, each lost to their own thoughts. Arriving at the observatory, their smiles turned to looks of disappointment as they reentered the real world of asteroids and all the related problems. Victoria returned to her office where she would sit in her desk chair, rest her head against the soft leather of the backrest, and dream of Dustin. Returning to his computer, Dustin dreamed of Victoria but was jolted back into the world of astrometry as he looked at the graph of the progress of the asteroids. *Three days to go and who knows, there may not even be a world*, Dustin thought and then allowed himself to momentarily dream of Victoria and the possibility of their life together.

NANO, NANO, WHO'S GOT A NANO?

ARRIVING A FULL HOUR BEFORE the scheduled meeting, Scotty was surprised to find Carolyn and Doreen already there. They had arrived early to set up a slide projector as a visual aid in trying to explain the evolution of nanotechnology. Scotty bid them good morning and retreated into his inner office. The first thing he did was review the morning briefing report and allowed himself to wonder why they use the word brief in the title. The damn thing was over thirty pages long and single-spaced at that. After twenty minutes of reading, Scotty put the papers down and relaxed a bit. A few minutes later, he called the communications room and requested a direct link to Admiral Laffey.

Once the radio link was established, Scotty was delighted to talk to his friend. Reassured that the remainder of the fleet would make Pearl a day before the passage of the asteroid, Scotty allowed himself a few minutes of general chitchat before breaking the link. Satisfied that all was well, he spent a few minutes preparing an outline of the speech he would give today in honor of Commander Cunningham, those who died with him, and the poor souls who died at sea. This was one part of command that Scotty disliked, no, hated. Realizing that words spoken from the heart and not from a prepared text were best and most true, Scotty wadded up the piece of paper and filed it in the circular file. Standing up, Scotty went into the conference room and was delighted to see that everyone had arrived a little early. After calling the meeting to order, Scotty along with everyone else took his seat at the conference table.

"I'd like to thank you all for coming early. As you know, this afternoon at thirteen hundred hours, we will have a ceremony for our fallen comrades," Scotty began and then continued, "Before we hear from Carolyn, I'd like to get an update from Lieutenant Wesley about the asteroids. Lieutenant?"

Mary remained seated and talked to the group, "I'm afraid that there is something new to report. I reviewed the most current data, checked it against my calculations, and the result is the same. It is still my belief that the asteroid DG122A will fragment due to the meteor belt. Some of the fragments will collide with the dark side of the moon. The other fragments will collide with DG122 while others will spin off into space." Mary took a deep breath before she added, "Some of the fragments will in fact collide with Earth."

"Are you sure about this?" Doreen quickly asked.

"Absolutely. The new data indicates that such an event is highly likely. I know that we are mainly dealing in unknowns, but Earth will take some hits," Mary replied, confident of her findings.

"Has Mid Point Observatory issued a warning relative to this new information?" Scotty asked.

"No, Admiral. As I said last night, we have access to information that they do not. I feel that we should somehow make sure that they are given our data so that they could make an announcement. You see, at present, the world knows of the asteroids, but they have been assured that they will safely bypass the earth. Sure, people realize that Earth will take some meteor hits, but a hit by part of an asteroid, no. So I would like permission to release our data," Mary pleaded.

"Request denied, Lieutenant," Scotty declared and then added "Give Jonesy a copy of your data on a floppy." Turning toward Jonesy,

Scotty continued, "Jonesy, what I want you to do is somehow make the lieutenant's data appear on the computers of Mid Point Observatory today."

"Will do, boss," Jonesy shot back and winked.

"Good," Scotty replied and turned back to Mary. "Lieutenant, do you have any idea where the asteroid could hit earth as well as any meteors?"

"With any degree of accuracy, no. The area of the earth that will be facing the asteroids when they pass through the meteor belt will be the Pacific Ocean basin. This includes all of the landmasses within or bordering the Pacific basin. The problem is when either a meteor or an asteroid fragment hits the outer atmosphere, it can skip or ride along the outer atmosphere and come down almost anywhere around the world," Mary answered and became frightened at the prospect of what she just said.

"It's now two days to the passage of the asteroids. Does anyone know what kind of preparations are underway?" Scotty asked.

"Yes, Admiral," Beverly Hocker spoke up, and after adjusting her sitting position to sit erect, she continued, "In the United States, all state and local governments as well as the federal government have declared the day that the asteroids pass by as an emergency. As such, all federal, state, and municipal employees have the day off. Private companies are starting to follow the governmental example. The thinking is that if the employees stay home, then the roads will be clear for emergency personnel should something happen. By doing this, there is also less chance of a catastrophe should a tall building get hit.

"In larger cities, such as New York, citizens will be urged to take refuge in the subway systems during the event. Otherwise, in rural America, people are being urged to stay in their homes. Further, all commercial airline traffic throughout the United States will be grounded on the basis of an emergency order. Private aircraft will also be grounded. The only aircraft that will be flying will be military flights, and it is doubtful that there will be a lot of that. Rail traffic, however, will be in service. Travel on the interstate highways will not be restricted. In each and every town across America, local governments are dusting off their emergency preparedness plans. Police, fire, and emergency units will be on alert with all their personnel on duty on the day of the event. Hospitals will likewise be fully staffed. All the telephone companies will also be ready with rapid response teams to fix, repair, or provide manual rerouting of their services.

"On the darker side, panic buying has started. Grocery store shelves are rapidly being emptied of staples, such as milk and bread. The large home hardware retailers are quickly running out of such things as batteries, flashlights, and for some reason, duct tape. Overall, the country seems pretty well-prepared. Other countries throughout the world seem to be likewise prepared. For once, the world seems to be of one mind, work together and survive the event," Beverly concluded.

"Thanks, Beverly. Are we also prepared?" Scotty asked.

"Yes, Admiral. Every effort is being made to preserve our assets, and hopefully, we will not take a hit," Beverly quickly replied.

"Thanks, Beverly. And I want to thank you for all of your efforts. I know that whenever you do anything, you always put your heart and soul behind it. Thank you." Scotty answered, knowing that no insignificant detail would ever escape her scrutiny. Turning toward Carolyn, Scotty asked, "Carolyn, would you please begin."

"Good morning, everyone," Carolyn began as she looked around the room and picked up the remote control to her computer, which would allow her to change the slides in the presentation she and Doreen had prepared. The notebook computer would send the picture to a plasma projector, which in turn would display the slide on the wall screen. "I hope all of you got a good night's sleep. Now, if I may, I would like to start at the basics of nanotechnology and give a brief outline of the science and where we are as compared to the aliens.

"Last night, Doreen touched on the idea of nano manufacturing. This is a relatively new area of science, which at present is in its infant stage. Like Doreen said, the concept applies to a manufacturing technique by which an object is constructed one atom at a time. The possibilities that such a process would open up are endless. But first, let me give you some background. In the 1990s, serious experimentation began on an age-old quest. We live in a world where miniaturization of any given object is desirous. Toward that goal, scientists first reduced the size of motors to the subminiature size." Carolyn pressed the button in her hand, and a picture appeared on the screen. "If you will look at the screen, you will see a motor. Now, it appears to be of a normal size, but as I bring up the next slide, you will see the same motor, but this time, its size is in perspective. The motor in the first slide is the same one you are looking at, but this time, it is resting on a dime. If you look closely, you will notice that it's about two-thirds the size of that dime." Pausing for a few seconds, Carolyn could see that she had everyone's attention. She then pushed a button on her remote and brought up the next slide.

"In this slide, you can see the next generation of these micro robot machines, which were one-eighth the size of the original. Once the devices were engineered, it was found that an electrical impulse could direct them to act in a certain way. Accordingly, they were constructed to accomplish a particular function. These are the devices which eventually became widely used in a variety of medical procedures. For example, people use to undergo open-heart bypass surgery. When these devices came into use, open-heart surgery became a thing of the past. Approximately, fifty of these devices are introduced into the blood system. They are then directed to the area where the arteries are clogged. Once in the proper location, these machines then go to work and remove the plaque. The devices also are used to target cancer cells, which they in a like manner destroy. Additionally, they are used in any area of delicate surgery, including brain surgery.

"The uses of these machines, beyond medical procedures, are almost endless. They are used to perform functions, which may be dangerous for a human to perform, such as inspection of an atomic power plant. They are currently used in manufacturing in areas of delicate construction and in fact are used in the manufacture of our own X-aircraft. Once these devices became commonplace, the thinking naturally turned toward subminiaturization. At first, efforts were made to reduce the size of the machines further, and in fact, there was some success in that direction. But then the idea took hold that the basic principles of engineering and manufacturing, as we know it, could be revolutionized."

Carolyn reached for a bottle of water and took a sip as she looked around the room to see if she was losing her audience. Satisfied that they were still paying attention, she continued, "It was a whole new way of thinking based upon solid scientific principles. The basic idea is a reversal in the way things are built. For example, if we were to build a computer, we would first manufacture a motherboard and then bring or add to that motherboard separate manufactured components until we had a working computer designed the way we wanted it. In nanotechnology, we would have another machine build the computer one atom at a time until the computer was finished. Basically, what we would be doing is taking the raw materials necessary to produce a computer and rearranging the raw materials one atom at a time with an exact precision that is not possible in today's world.

"We talked about the micro devices that perform medical procedures today. Well, if nanotechnology was to be applied to the medical field, it is theoretically possible that missing limbs could be replaced as well as a regeneration of nerve and muscular tissue. In effect, if a person loses a hand, let's say, another could be grown. Should a person become paralyzed and couldn't walk, nano-medical technology would be applied, and in no time, the person could walk or whatever. In other words—" Carolyn went on but was interrupted by Jonesy.

"Are you telling me that this nano stuff is the holy grail of medicine?"

"No, what I'm saying is that it is simply the application of a technology to aid in the regeneration of a human body. It is not applied to a total regeneration of a human body but is only applied to an affected area. For example, if a person's liver should start to go bad, it would be possible to repair that liver as long as the defect is discovered early," Carolyn answered.

"You gave the example of a computer before. The implants which we are finding in people, are they an example of nanotechnology?" JW asked.

"That's an excellent point. The implants, which were tied into the nerve endings of individuals and were extracted, could be a prime example of nanotechnology. Remember, when we cut the implants open, we found a silvery liquid material. This very well could be an example of building a computer one atom at a time. The resultant structure of the computer was liquid, encased in a housing and powered by the nerve endings of a human being. Such things are possible with the application of this science," Carolyn concluded and turned toward Captain Bone, the weapons officer, as she heard him speak up.

"What would the application of this nano stuff be in the weapons department, and am I out of a job?" Captain Bone asked with a slight grin on his face that was quickly replaced by an expression of concern.

"You wouldn't be out of a job as far as your ordering and inventorying weapons. But in the manufacture and design of weapons, the human being would be a nonentity. Let me explain. In order to apply this science, two things must first take place. Machines first have to be designed to produce nano-type products. Secondly, artificial intelligence then must be built into those machines and then into the process and end product. The result would be lighter and cheaper weapons produced rapidly. For example, if we were to take the basic combat rifle, the M-23 that weighs nine pounds, costs five thousand dollars, and takes three days to produce. Apply nano manufacturing, and the result would be a weapon that weighs in at just over four pounds at a cost of two hundred dollars and could be produced in sixty seconds. Apply that on a manufacturing scale, and thousands could be produced in a relatively short period of time. Nuclear-type weapons, equal in explosive power, could be created without the nuclear fallout.

"The application of artificial intelligence to the process would mean that weapons would be continuously more advanced as the machines learned. Now, this is the science-fiction stuff. The much-hyped smart bullet that could seek out an individual would become a reality in a very short period of time. It would be possible to create a virus-type weapon based upon a core of common DNA. Countries would be able to conquer countries with such a virus-type weapon, at very little expense, and never having fired a shot." Carolyn stopped and took another sip of water.

"You are right, this is science fiction, and quite frankly, it is scary. Can you tell me what the global ramifications are? But what I am really wondering is where could the end game be. If we grant or give artificial intelligence to such machines, where does it end?" Scotty asked.

"Those are questions that we can only speculate about. The scientific community has not addressed these concerns as the technology is only in the infant stages of development. However, the federal government has issued warnings about the technology disguised as position papers or studies, if you prefer. Let's first discuss the global ramifications. If the world adopts this technology, a world economy would become nonexistent. Any country would be able to produce its consumer needs nationally and much cheaper than it would cost to import them. No longer would there be international trade in goods. The science would be applied to food production, and trade in that sector would also end as aquaculture, and vertical-farming methods would be applied. All this, however, depends upon an adequate supply of natural resources, in which there might still be trade but on a very limited basis.

"Militarily, any third-world nation that applies this science, and has an adequate supply of natural resources, could become a superpower overnight. This would, of course, cause a shifting in the international power balance immediately. The weak would become strong and the strong may become the weak if they don't keep up or surpass the other countries. It's an arms race without precedence that will result in world chaos unless man matures above individual ideology and recognizes the purity of life and its natural pursuits." Carolyn concluded, a little depressed having voiced her thoughts out loud for the first time and then remembered that there was a second part to Scotty's question. "Excuse me, Admiral. What was the second part of your question?"

"I was wondering what happens when we give machines artificial intelligence. Is there something to fear? I know computer programs are a form of artificial intelligence, and some programs can actually learn. But where does it end?" Scotty asked.

Putting the cap back on her water bottle after taking another sip, Carolyn replied as she placed the water bottle back on the table, "The great danger in all of this is the giving of artificial intelligence to the machines that will construct the objects or machines made from the utilization of nanotechnology. For the sake of argument, let's assume we are using nanotechnology to purely construct a military defensive and an offensive system. You must keep in mind that we are using machines that have artificial intelligence. The machines we use to create our system must, as a matter of necessity, implant artificial intelligence into the weapon systems it creates and later builds. This is a result of the ability of the machine to learn and, in essence, think for itself. We then have an offensive weapons system capable of independent thought that will constantly evolve and improve on its own. Man will then become subservient and dependent upon the system for his own survival. If the system is self-evolving, what then would prevent the system from engaging in warfare if man should become the servant of the machine? If you—" Carolyn was going to continue but was interrupted by Captain Bone.

"That would never happen. Man would always be in control of the system," Captain Bone pointed out.

Carolyn considered his observation for a moment, wished that he were right, but disagreed. Looking at the group, she responded, "I would like to agree with you, but consider this. In a world where all countries are engaged in a military race to create a weapons system, which would guarantee their individual survival, speed becomes the key to that survival. As nations rush to create their offensive weapons, the temptation for the machines to be the guardians of survival becomes too great. On a similar course, when a nation builds an offensive system, it will also develop a defensive system. In this case, a machine created defensive system would also depend upon speed to react to an attack. I know you can point to the era of the 1980s and 1990s and the earlier period of the new century when man had to authorize and manually enable the launching of defensive missiles, but a very quiet revolution took place.

"In 2003, you may remember the war fought in Iraq. This points up the reality of the situation I am talking about. This was a war fought to overcome a despot who brutalized his people and threatened the world through his support of international terrorism. The bordering countries of Saudi Arabia and Kuwait were where the coalition of armies launched their attack. This then was a war fought over small distances. During this struggle, the United States deployed an antimissile, missile system, called the Patriot System. Due to the short distances involved, the Patriot System was set to full-automatic mode. This was done because there simply wasn't time for a human operator to track, analyze, and then react to the threat. By the time the human would react, the incoming threat would have delivered its deadly package. When the system was switched to operate on automatic, man then became the servant of the machine. His role was to provide for the maintenance of the system, rather than being the operator of the system. In a similar vein, it will become necessary for man to turn control of the defensive and offensive systems over to the machines."

"Carolyn, you have painted a rather dark picture of the future as it relates to this technology. Is there any plus side?" Scotty asked.

"Nanotechnology offers man almost an endless variety of advances. The secret to all of the possible advances is knowing at what point to turn the switch off or turn off the system. Each individual country would find it too tempting not to turn off the system as the longer the technology is allowed to expand, then that country gains an advantage over its neighbors. The temptation will become too great. Man will seek advantage over his neighbor and will be asleep the day the machines take over. Man will think himself in control, but as every day passes, he will become more and more the servant of the machine. Eventually, man himself will become unnecessary and extinct. On that day, the genie has escaped the bottle," Carolyn offered.

"Well, this just keeps getting better and better. Why are you convinced that the aliens have nanotechnology?" Scotty commented and hesitantly asked.

"I previously had analyzed a piece of the outer skin of one of the saucers we have on the hangar deck. While some of the materials in the metal are unknown to us, there were some materials common to our world. In particular, I found platinum, gold, chrome, and iron. What I found was that the molecular structure of the metals had been changed. This revelation puzzled me, and I spent endless hours trying to understand why. We have found a few of the metals on both Mars and the moon. The molecular structure of the off-world metals matched the molecular structure of the same metal found here on Earth. While I couldn't say for certain that the same would hold true throughout the universe or indeed other galaxies, I assumed, for the sake of argument, that it did hold true. What I was left with was an enigma.

"It wasn't until Doreen and I started talking about what the aliens were trying to hide when it hit me. The construction of the alien craft combined with the observation of what is on the ocean floor equaled the utilization of nanotechnology. The aliens must have some kind of manufacturing process aboard that vassal. It's the only thing that makes sense. If they are involved in deep-space exploration, they would have to carry with them some form of manufacturing to replace worn parts or to produce goods. Nanotechnology is the perfect solution to the problem. I checked with the leading expert in the United States, Regina Sawyer, on the capability of nanotechnology. Specifically, I inquired about the change in molecular structure of minerals. She confirmed that in the utilization of nano manufacturing, as far as her experiments have shown, would change the molecular structure of a mineral," Carolyn concluded, hoping everyone understood what she said.

"If nanotechnology has the capability to produce advanced weapon systems, then why are we able to defeat them?" Scotty asked.

"I can only speculate on that point. A nano-produced weapon system learns and then adapts to opposing weapons. It would then plan and build advanced systems to overcome the weapons the system it had just encountered. But here is the interesting part. I think the aliens realized the danger of a nano system and refused to surrender control of their weapons over to an impersonal system. That would account for the way we have seen them fight. Clearly, they are in control of their weapons. If they were using a system based on nanotechnology, we would have been beaten bad. This may be the way that they have kept the genie in the bottle. They probably just use nanotechnology to produce what they need. They may use it to produce weapons, but they maintain control over the weapon systems," Carolyn answered feeling that she was right.

"It seems to me that we are faced with a decision to make. On the one hand, we have an opportunity, provided that Doreen and Carolyn are correct, to leap ahead in technology. On the other hand, if we obtain this technology and utilize it, I'm afraid that it would cause a new industrial revolution, which might plunge the world into chaos. We do have a third option and that is to recover whatever we can and sit on the technology. I think that the best thing to do is to recover from the object the nanotechnology. We should also research whatever we find and tinker with it up to a point. Who knows it might prove useful. But we should heed the warnings that we have heard this morning. In the end, though, we should sit on the technology. I don't want this to be a purely command decision. There's way too much at stake. I want each of you to give your opinion," Scotty concluded.

For the next forty-five minutes, the dialogue went back and forth. Everyone agreed that another try should be made to recover any kind of new technology from the object on the bottom of the ocean. What they would do with it was a matter of contention. Some thought that if nanotechnology was obtained, then it should be exploited. Others thought as Scotty did, that the new technology should be examined then for the sake of humanity. It should be locked up in the darkest vault to protect humanity from the nightmare, which may lurk around the next corner. In the end, it was Doreen who put forth a compromise to end the impasse.

"Should we be successful in retrieving this technology, we should approach it not as a windfall nor as lucky happenstance. But rather, we should approach it with a caution as if we are the guardians of the future of mankind. Each thing we do in life has a ripple effect on those around us, and it spreads outward as if it was a wave crossing the vast expense of the ocean. Yes, we should try our best to recover this technology. Yes, we should examine it, step back, and evaluate its potential. If we find that we can control it, then we should use it. If we cannot contain it, then by God, we should then lock it away, lest man take the first step toward his own enslavement," Doreen spoke up and quieted the discussion in the room.

Noticing that everyone in the room seemed lost in their own thoughts after Doreen spoke, Scotty commented, "I take it then that everyone is in agreement. Recover the technology, examine it, evaluate it, and if it poses a threat, bury it." Looking around the room, no one spoke up, rather they just bowed their heads in agreement. "Okay, then that's it. At the first opportunity, we'll try again," Scotty concluded and then turned toward Carolyn and asked, "Carolyn, how do you read this Regina Sawyer? Do you think that we may possibly recruit her?"

Carolyn thought for a moment and then answered, "Regina Sawyer is the preverbal genius. Her résumé looks like a book. Having gone to all the right schools, combined with her talents and dedication, any corporation would be glad to have her on staff. Perhaps, her greatest strength is the fact that she thinks out of the box and in abstracts. While other people may be engaged in research and do things one at a time, she is always ahead of them. Coming from a family rich in service to the country, her father was a career Army officer, and her family has served in the military going back to the Civil War. I'm sure that she is dedicated to the country. As far as recruiting her, all we have to do is offer her a modern research lab with an unlimited budget, and yeah, she will work for us," Carolyn concluded and added one more thought, "Oh yes. One more thing. She is a very beautiful woman who will drive the men around here crazy."

Scotty laughed for a moment and noticed that Carolyn was looking at Arty with a look on her face as if she was saying "Don't even think about it, buster."

Smiling slightly, Scotty broke her concentration when he ordered, "Carolyn, start working on it. Give her whatever she wants."

"Yes, Admiral," Carolyn replied and then looked downward at her hands folded on the conference table.

"Good. Now, I think we ought to break. We have the ceremony for our departed friends in a half hour. What I want to do is start having these meeting every morning at the same time as long as we are not engaging the aliens. So I will see you all tomorrow morning," Scotty concluded and then ordered Mary to give him updates about the asteroids every six hours. After Mary acknowledged Scotty's order, he ended the meeting and directed everyone to return in the morning.

Mid Point Observatory

Dustin sat down at his desk and for a moment stared at his screen saver as pictures of motorcycles appeared and morphed into another picture of a motorcycle being ridden down a lonely, twisted road somewhere. He allowed himself the luxury of daydreaming about Victoria and he on such a road. They were on the identical motorcycles leaning into the turns and experiencing the thrill and exhilaration of the open road. Realizing that such dreams are in the future, Dustin sat up straight in his chair and pressed the *M* key on his keyboard. In less than a second, the picture of the motorcycle faded into blackness, and his computer came alive.

At first, Dustin's attention was drawn away from the computer as he straightened his desk out. After he neatly arranged his papers and threw out some unnecessary pages, Dustin turned his attention toward the computer screen. He began scanning the mathematical tables on the screen and wondered where the information came from. As he read and began to interpret the data, Dustin's heart began to race, and his blood pressure began to rise. At once, he realized that the situation had drastically changed, or had it. While he continued to read the data, it became obvious that the material did not come from the observatory, but rather, its origins were from several sources. The question soon became, was the material real or part of some weird sick joke? This material meant that asteroid DG122A was going to break apart and parts of it would likely fall to earth. Dustin knew that he had to make a decision fast. Gathering up a printed copy of the material, Dustin raced to Victoria's office.

After knocking a few times on her door, Dustin didn't wait for a welcoming "Come in." Turning the door handle, he simply walked in.

Victoria heard the light taps on her office door, but her full attention was occupied in reviewing some budget papers. After a few seconds, she looked toward her office door and was about to tell the person on the other side of the door to come in when Dustin barged through the door. Instead of being angry, Victoria's face lit up with a warm smile as she rose out of her chair and called out, "Hi, Darling!"

Victoria's greeting stopped Dustin in his tracks. Dustin smiled back and nervously replied, "Hi, Victoria." After taking a few steps forward, Dustin wanted to go over and kiss his love, but he was slightly irritated about something, and Victoria felt the slight tension.

"What's wrong, dear?" Victoria asked, somewhat puzzled by this new development.

"Victoria, please. This may seem rather stupid, but the waitress in the restaurant we eat in calls me dear, darling, or honey. It's just that it seems so impersonal and insincere. Some people like to be called those names, but I don't. I know that it is stupid, but people who don't know me seem to call me that, and I would just feel better if you would call me by my given name. I love the way you say it, and I know that you say it with such affection. I'm sorry, it's just a hang up with me." Dustin made his point.

"I'm sorry, Dustin. I only meant it in an affectionate way and not to hurt your feelings," Victoria replied, the affection evident in her voice.

"No, I'm sorry, Victoria. Just call me whatever you want," Dustin answered, sorry that he brought it up.

"Okay, dear!" Victoria replied, getting her point across with a slight smile on her face. Dustin looked at Victoria and could only laugh, not at his love but rather at himself.

Victoria knew that Dustin was hurt, and that was the last thing in the world she wanted to do. With an even bigger smile on her face, Victoria asked, "Dustin, my love, what's wrong?"

"I don't know where this came from, but somehow, this data was on my computer. It sure didn't come from here, and I didn't put it there," Dustin hastily replied.

Victoria couldn't imagine what he was talking about and tried to get him focused. "Dustin, please take a seat and explain to me what you are talking about. Would you like a cup of coffee or something?"

Dustin declined her offer of coffee but sat down in one of the office chairs. For the next twenty minutes, he explained his interpretation of the data, how the asteroid would shatter, and parts of it would more than likely strike Earth. Victoria followed his argument and agreed with his conclusion. But now what? Two days till the passage of the asteroid, and now they had to issue another press release saying that once again they had miscalculated.

Dustin remained in his chair as he watched and listened as Victoria placed call after call to the so-called big shots in Washington, DC. The impression Dustin gleamed from Victoria's words was that the people she was talking to were more concerned about their own reputations and lives than those of the citizens at large. All Victoria was concerned about was getting the warning out to the world, but it seemed to be an endless parade of red tape and stupid questions. After over an hour of endless dribble on the part of the people she called, Victoria finally reached the president's science advisor. At last, she thought an understanding ear. But his expressed concern was how the president was going to look in the eyes of the public by issuing another warning.

Dustin sat upright in his chair with a big smile on his face when Victoria, out of frustration, shouted, "Look it, you fucking idiot, who gives a shit how the president will look? So get that pea-sized brain of yours working, go in kiss your boss's ass or whatever it is you do, and issue the goddamn warning or I will." Victoria slammed the telephone down on the receiver and watched as the handset broke in two. She smiled slightly, looked up at Dustin, and in a stern voice with a hint of humor spoke, "Now, *honey*, what was it you were saying?"

Dustin smiled, laughed slightly, and answered, "Nothing, *dear*." Victoria also laughed as Dustin rose from his chair, walked behind her desk, bent down, whispered "I love you," and kissed her with a new passion.

Space Command

During the ceremony for the deceased warriors, Scotty spoke from the heart, just as he had planned. As he began speaking, Scotty realized that it was much more difficult than he had imagined. He knew what he wanted to say, and indeed the words came to him. But so did the emotion of the moment. At times, he hesitated to prevent himself from showing a physical emotion in the form of tears, but at times, his voice cracked as he talked. Scotty was afraid that his men might think him weak if he showed emotion, but just the opposite occurred.

The men and women of Scotty's command came to have a new respect for their admiral. They knew that he was a fierce fighter who simply doesn't back down, a leader who cares for his men, and a leader who is open to suggestion. But now, they saw their admiral as feeling the pain that they felt at the loss of their fellow servicemen. Each of them knew before that Scotty watched out for them, but this day, their admiration for him grew, and they felt a little closer to their admiral.

MOMMY, THAT MAN SAID THE SKY IS FALLING

People throughout the world come from different cultures, have different beliefs, dress differently, and talk differently in a multitude of languages. But in times of desperation, which threaten their natural survival, people are really the same. They have the same instinct to protect their children. They examine their faith and pray for divine intervention. They contact their loved ones and reaffirm their dedication and love for each other. As a last measure, they seek peace within themselves.

The day before the passage of the asteroids was like no other. People didn't bother to run to the grocery stores since they had already been cleaned out of everything. It seemed that everyone wanted to stockpile food as they prepared for what, they didn't know. Home stores had similarly experienced a shopping frenzy of building materials as people sought to fortify their homes. In reality, people didn't know what to do, so they did what people did best. They prepared for hard times, sought comfort in their families and in their religions.

Houses of worship were filled beyond capacity as people prayed for absolution and divine intervention. Religious leaders gave comfort where it was accepted but found themselves lacking. They simply could not overcome the undercurrent of fear. True to form, the doomsayers walked in front of places of worship carrying signs with messages of repent or predicting that the end was near. In some cases, people sought out religious belief for the first time in their adult life while others cast it aside and saw faith as a crutch of mankind.

That is not to say that everyone prepared the same way. The bottom feeders of society saw fear of the unknown as opportunity. Stores were looted, banks were robbed, and every sort of known criminal activity was engaged in as the police ran from emergency to emergency to stop the onslaught of the few. The weak were preyed upon as the strong fought off the assaults of these soulless devils.

HERE WE GO AGAIN

Victoria and Dustin stood by in muted silence as once again the representative of the federal government made an announcement. The news of DG122A splitting apart was received in an unenthusiastic manner. Not that the reporters weren't interested, but rather, they were in shock. There were follow-up questions, but it appeared that the inquiries were more of a formality then a real information seeking thought-provoking search for the truth. Their thoughts had turned inward.

When the announcement was made and the few questions which followed had been answered, Dustin remained behind and watched. He thought it interesting to see the reaction of the reporters and the television people. Expecting the media to remain behind and cover the story from the observatory, Dustin was surprised when they began to leave. But in truth, they were like anyone else. After their reports were filed, they simply went home to their families or their loved ones to await whatever would come.

With his hands in the pockets of his pants and his head hung low, Dustin shuffled back into the building. As he walked down the hallway to his work area, Dustin thought that he, too, would like to go home and be with his mom. Since his father passed away, his mother was alone. True, she lived in a retirement village and had a large circle of friends, but she really was alone. Her partner of forty-five years was gone, and a large void filled her life.

Dustin found himself at a crossroads. Yes, he wanted to run to his mother and comfort her fears, but then there was Victoria. Beautiful, enchanting Victoria. Dreams had suddenly turned into reality, and Dustin was happy. He deeply loved this woman, and he could not bear to leave her side. Trying to strike a balance, Dustin decided to call his mother and stay with Victoria. He knew that Victoria would remain at the observatory during the event, and that was okay with him. He would rather be here with her than anywhere on the planet without her. But he also recognized his responsibility to track the asteroids and somehow predict, if it should happen, where on earth errant rocks would fall, really, really big errant rocks.

Victoria also felt a deep sense of responsibility to her chosen career. She would remain at the observatory. Knowing that it would be almost impossible to predict with any degree of absolute certainty where a piece of the asteroid would land, Victoria knew that even if their predictions saved one life, then their efforts would not be in vain. And then there was Dustin. Victoria was in love. Not just a normal love but a deep, consuming love. She would remain at his side from now on. *Even if it meant riding motorcycles into the sunset, or was it the sunrise? Well, whatever as long as it included Dustin. What the hell,* she thought.

JUST ANOTHER DAY
IN PARADISE

WHILE THEIR PRIMARY THOUGHTS WERE of home and family, the members of Space Command were a dedicated lot. They recognized their duty and the importance of their work and commitment. Throughout the day, the women and men of Space Command performed their duties with a renewed sense of purpose. Each individual knew that the passage of the asteroids could be used as a cover for an attack by the aliens.

Scotty was seen all around the base. One minute he was in the communications area, and then he was seen in sick bay making sure that all was ready should the base be attacked. He even was seen examining the mess hall. The hangar deck was his last stop. Scotty wanted to make sure that all the aircraft were operational and that the aviators were well-rested. JW even came under the magnifying glass as Scotty double-checked the duty rosters and performed an equipment check. At the end of the day, Scotty was exhausted. As he stumbled into his office, Beverly entered, and Scotty immediately began questioning her as to the fitness and preparedness of the base. Somehow, she was able to cut through the anxiety her boss was feeling. Explaining that the finest collection of service men and women in the world were on the base and that each and every one of them knew their job seemed to calm Scotty as he sat down in his chair and let out a deep breath.

"You're right," Scotty replied and then added, "I've been acting like an idiot all day checking this and checking that. The people on this base are the absolute best that there are."

"Why don't you go and get some sleep, Admiral?" Beverly suggested.

"I will, but first, I want to check with CAG and Captain Bone," Scotty replied as he yawned.

"All aircraft are operational on all of the bases, and crews are standing by. All weapon systems are operational. Please, Admiral, get some sleep," Beverly suggested in a more authoritative voice.

Scotty looked up at Beverly and tried to smile, but a yawn smothered his effort. Getting up from his chair, he replied, "Good idea. Wake me if anything happens."

"Will do, sir," Beverly replied as she watched the man she had come to admire so much leave the office.

Scotty wanted to stop by Doreen's before he went to his quarters, but he decided that it was best to let her get the rest he knew she needed. Instead, Scotty headed for the mess hall. *Sometimes, you just have to have chocolate*, he told himself as his pace quickened in anticipation of a treat.

Grabbing a food tray off the stack, Scotty entered the food line and waited patiently as the line progressed toward the desert area. Chef Sal was inspecting the food line when he spotted Scotty. "Admiral!" Sal cried out and then added, "Is there something special you are looking for?"

Scotty smiled and then responded, "Just one of your world-famous brownies with the thick fudge topping and walnuts on the top. And a large glass of milk."

"You go sit down, Admiral. I'll bring one to you," Sal directed in a proud voice.

Scotty found an empty table toward the back of the mess hall and sat down. With his elbows resting on the table, Scotty put his hands on his forehead and gently massaged his temples, trying to rid himself of the tension he was feeling.

"Got a headache, Admiral?" Sal asked as he placed a tray on the table and sat down across from Scotty. "Mind if I join you?" Sal added as he took one plate containing two brownies and placed it in front of Scotty. He then took another plate off the tray with two more brownies and placed them in front of himself. He then placed a large glass of milk in front of himself and Scotty.

Scotty was about to answer Sal when Sal declared, "Little late in the day to be eating brownies."

"The brownies are for energy and the milk is to help me sleep," Scotty answered as Sal took a rather large bite of one brownie.

Sal moaned slightly in pleasure as he savored the taste of the brownie. After swallowing the tasty delight, Sal declared, "Man, these are damn good if I say so myself."

"The absolute best on the planet!" Scotty added and then ate.

For the next few minutes, the two men ate in silence and followed their feast with long sips of fresh cold milk. When he was finished, Sal wiped his mouth with a napkin, took hold of his now half-full glass of milk, and spoke up with a concerned look on his face, "Admiral, this asteroid business. They say now that the second one will probably break apart. I read this book once about asteroids, and it said that they explode just before impact with the earth. Well, sir, are we safe here?"

"Yeah, Sal. We're as safe as you can be. Don't forget were deep under the earth, and that offers us a lot of protection. Besides, the odds of a large chunk coming down here are pretty slim," Scotty replied, not fully convinced of what he just said.

"What's really gonna happen if a large piece of the asteroid actually hits somewhere?" Sal asked.

"I really have no idea, Sal. I would imagine, should a large piece fall, that there would be a lot of destruction. I just hope that the rest of the world is as well-prepared as we are. In any case, it will all be over in what?" Scotty hesitated as he looked at his watch and continued, "Twelve hours from now. By fifteen hundred hours (3:00 pm), the world will have witnessed an event that man, with all of his intelligence and capability, has absolutely no control over," Scotty concluded as he rose from the table, pushed his chair in, and added, "Good night, Sal. And thanks for the brownies."

"Good night, Admiral. I'll make up some more brownies and send them up to your office tomorrow," Sal called out as Scotty began walking away.

Scotty turned and told Sal "Thanks!" and then turned back around and walked toward his quarters.

WHO IS CHICKEN LITTLE, AND WHY DID HE SAY THAT?

T HE DAY BEGAN AS ALL days begin. The coldness and darkness of night faded into day as the warmth and light of the sun chased the shadow of night away. On parts of the earth that were to experience day, people ate breakfast while those where the twilight of night was coming sat down to eat supper. But this day, there was a change in the behavior of mankind. True, hunger and time dictated the need to eat, but meals were shared in anticipation of the unknown.

Throughout the world, a quiet hush overcame people everywhere. The rampant crime had suddenly stopped, churches that had been full a day ago were now mostly empty, streets were empty of cars, and in fact, it was as if people had simply disappeared. Most people decided to just to stay home and watch what they could of the event on television, and the television stations did not disappoint their viewers. Coverage was continuous, and somehow, the announcers never said the same thing twice. Stations continued to try and outdo their competition with dazzling graphics and a parade of experts who all said the same thing: "They had no idea what might happen."

IT'S NOT LIKE IT'S THE END OF THE WORLD OR ANYTHING

DUSTIN AND VICTORIA WERE SOMEWHAT excited about this day. It was Dustin who discovered the existence of DG 122 and later DG122A. But it was a hollow excitement. While he was a student, Dustin was alive with the prospect that when he left the theoretical world of education, he just knew that one day he would make a discovery and more importantly a contribution to the understanding of the universe. But who would have guessed that it would be a discovery that would hold the prospect of destroying the human race. *I guess that it is better than not knowing*, Dustin thought of his discovery.

As Dustin monitored the event that was about to unfold, Victoria walked up and stood behind him. Dustin smelled the sweet fragrance of her perfume, but his eyes remained riveted on the computer screen.

As she looked over his shoulder, Victoria slowly bent down and gently kissed Dustin on his head and asked, "How much longer?"

Dustin felt her kiss and wanted to stand up, take Victoria in his arms, and carry her off to some faraway place free of computers, responsibility, and other people. He fought hard to repress those thoughts and slowly answered, "In about an hour the asteroids should hit the meteor field." Pausing for a moment to gather his thoughts, Dustin added, "I know what the data says, but my god, I sure hope that rock doesn't fracture and split apart. I wish it would just keep tumbling into space and go away."

FIVE, FOUR, THREE, TWO, ONE, ZERO

SCOTTY KNEW THAT THE BASE was ready for the expected fall of the asteroids. Like countless millions of others, he hoped that pieces of the asteroid would not land here. But who knows, it could land anywhere. Doreen wasn't thinking about the asteroids. Instead, she was busy at her job overseeing the safety and disposition of the X-aircraft. But her thoughts were of Scotty and a life together yet unlived. CAG had done a good job of preparing the aircraft in case the aliens should try a sneak attack. Crews were on standby, ready to go at a moment's notice. JW had the base secured and, with the help of Bone, had the defensive plasma cannons warmed up and ready to go.

With less than an hour to go before the dreaded event, Scotty left his office and along with Beverly walked into the main communications room of Space Command. Together, they walked over to Jonesy and sat down a little behind him. Scotty glanced at all the monitors and realized that they were really powerless against the asteroid. All that anyone could do was standby and watch. Scotty wanted an enemy to fight, not some hunk of rock in space that was tumbling toward its own destiny.

For reassurance, Scotty asked Jonesy if the base was ready and if he could think of anything that might have been overlooked. Jonesy turned around, faced Scotty, and answered, "Hell, we're ready for anything." Jonesy hesitated and then added, "Hey, boss. I was just thinking. The whole world is watching this damn thing, which means the whole world is open. We could go on a thief's holiday and grab whatever we want. I'll bet that every computer system is wide open. All we have to do is knock at the door."

"What?" Scotty asked and continued, "I'm sorry, I wasn't really listening."

"I was just saying the whole world is watching this thing, and I bet we could get away—"

Scotty almost shouting interrupted Jonesy, "Damn! You're right."

Scotty looked at Jonesy with a look he knew well. It was the look a fighter pilot gets right before going into combat. The look of steel determination. "Get me CAG on the line right now!" Scotty ordered.

Jonesy quickly turned around, picked up the receiver, dialed in a few numbers, and handed the telephone receiver to Scotty. "CAG, here." Scotty heard.

"CAG! Activate the California group. I want four X-aircraft airborne now and headed out to the object in the Pacific. Those bastards are going to go after it," Scotty ordered and didn't wait for confirmation of his order but handed the receiver back to Jonesy. He then ordered Jonesy to bring up all the radar sweeps of the outer atmosphere. Within a few seconds, all the radar sweeps were on the monitors and were clean. The only thing remarkable was the tracking of the asteroids on a few of the monitors.

Beverly leaned over and asked Scotty why he thought the aliens would come now since it was just as dangerous for them to be flying as it was for their pilots. Scotty didn't have to think of answer. He immediately uttered, "Because that's what I would do. I'd wait for the last possible moment and go after what I wanted the most. They are not going to attack us now. That would be crazy, but they will go after that spaceship on the bottom of the ocean."

"God, I hope not," Beverly answered and then directed her remarks to Jonesy, "Jonesy, give the order that if any unknowns enter our atmosphere, plot their estimated time of arrival to the object."

"Yes, ma'am," Jonesy replied and issued the order. He then checked with CAG and learned that the X-aircraft were now fifteen minutes from the object. After informing Scotty and Beverly, Jonesy settled in and monitored the asteroids.

"How much time now?" Scotty asked.

Without turning around, Jonesy announced, "Nine minutes and forty-two seconds, Admiral."

Scotty sat back in his chair and waited. He wondered why the aliens were not yet here. It seemed to him that they would have acted by now. When the clock ticked down to three minutes, Scotty changed his mind and reasoned that it was now too dangerous for them to act. Getting up, Scotty wondered where Doreen was and was just about to ask Beverly where she was when a voice came over the loudspeaker in the room, "Z-1 coming. ETA to object one and a half minutes at current speed. Running track."

Quickly, Scotty looked up at the monitors and saw a display Jonesy had put up. Time to event: two minutes ten seconds. ETA of Z-1 to object: one and half minutes, fifty seconds. ETA of X-aircraft to object: Two minutes, forty-three seconds.

Scotty knew what the numbers meant. They would be too late to stop the Z-1.

Scotty bent over next to Jonesy and in a hushed but determined voice ordered, "Get CAG on the line and have him order our pilots back. There is no sense putting them in harm's way for nothing."

As Scotty stood up and turned around, Doreen walked into the room and over to him. She kissed him on his cheek, and he took her in his arms. They then sat down without speaking. While holdings hands, they watched the monitors to see what would happen next.

VICTORIA...VICTORIA... VICTORIA

USTIN COULDN'T TAKE IT ANYMORE. He stood up, put his arms around Victoria, and kissed her as their bodies almost melted into one. Dustin broke their kiss and, while his hands were around her waist and hers around his, spoke with determination and a hint of nervousness in his voice, "Victoria...I...I..."

Victoria interrupted him by saying, "The answer is yes, Dustin."

"You don't know what I am going to ask," Dustin spoke quickly.

"Oh, I think I do," Victoria coyly answered.

"Okay, then, will you marry me?" Dustin asked, with more determination in his voice.

"The answer is still yes, Dustin," Victoria excitedly answered.

A broad smile came over his face, and then Dustin pulled her close to him again.

As they kissed, Dustin reached behind himself and pushed the power button to his computer into the off position. They then walked arm in arm toward Victoria's office. They went to celebrate their engagement the only true way it could be celebrated. At that moment, their world was at peace.

CALLING ALL SPACE CADETS

WHEN WE FIND SOMETHING OR know something about an object or for that matter a person, man does first what he does best. He assigns it a name or perhaps a number or some type of designation. The asteroid, which was screaming through space, was not different. Nor was its hidden twin or the hitchhiker if you prefer. The asteroid was designated DG122, and the hitchhiker was designated DG122A. Some of the news media dubbed them Fat Man and the Little Boy. By doing this, they became familiar objects. But not familiar enough that man became comfortable with their presence. Man would look at them through a telescope but not be comforted. Some men would be intrigued but surely not comforted. And so this day, man would actually fear what he had designated or named. It was not for man to control. It was not for man to completely understand. It was not for man to look upon it as a friend. Nor was it for man to think of it as an omen. But it was for man to shy away from.

It is said by the sages of time that space is a cold dark place where man must tread lightly. There are no footprints in the sand to follow. There are no rules to follow except for one. If you disrespect it, space itself will remind you that man is a fragile creature that must walk lightly through the cosmos. This day, space would remind man just how truly fragile and vulnerable he is.

As DG122 pulled its hitchhiker along, it traveled on a pathway that was determined for millions of years ago. It had visited many worlds, some as cold as ice while others were as hot as the sun. And yet it prevailed. Luck was also on its side. Somehow, it had escaped the gravitational pull of each planet it passed. Some may call it karma or sheer luck, but its passage by Earth appeared as if it was meant to be.

Closer and closer the asteroids came. Their speed always remaining constant. When the two asteroids approached the beginning of the meteor belt, nothing really happened. Stray meteors slammed into DG122 without having any appreciable effect. Even DG122A proceeded on. The meteors would crash into the asteroids at incredible speeds. They would explode into hundreds of pieces on contact. Some of the pieces would then become part of the asteroids while many small fragments would career off into space. Some of these pieces would tumble and fall toward Earth only to be burned up when they entered the outer atmosphere.

As the asteroids traveled further, the intensity of the meteor belt increased. The number of meteors crashing into the asteroids went from few hundred a minute to thousands. When the asteroids were in the middle of the meteor belt, they were being pounded by millions of strikes per second. The meteors ranged in size from a particle as small as a grain of sand to pieces the size of a beach ball.

The effect on DG122 was minimal. Its mass was its savior. In fact, its weight increased as particles of the meteors became part of its mass. Its relative speed even slowed ever so slightly. But its path remained constant. Astronomers breathed a sigh of relief. The Fat Man would go away.

DG122A was a different story. The billions upon billions of particles striking it were doing their damage. It was as if a hot knife was cutting through butter. The tiny particles were cutting into the harden surface, and fractures or cracks were beginning to appear. The larger-sized meteors were acting as a hammer to further widen the cracks.

Slowly, the asteroid was beginning to come apart. If it could emerge from the meteor field, cracked but still together, there was hope. But time had simply run out.

At first, a small piece, the size of a large suitcase, broke off and tumbled toward Earth. Then another piece separated and went speeding off into space to eventually collide with some far-off planet in another galaxy. But then another piece broke off followed by even more pieces. In less than a minute, DG122A was no more. Instead, it became thousands of smaller asteroids. Some the size of a pebble, others the size of a tractor trailer truck. One piece was very large, experts would later say that it was over four hundred and sixty tons and as large as a small indoor shopping mall. This piece tumbled away following an erratic path toward Earth. The Little Boy had thrown his toys in the air.

OKAY...IT'S NOT TO THE SHORE, IT'S DOWN THE SHORE

J OSEPH FIELDS AWOKE EARLY THIS day, not with the feelings of the rest of the majority of the world. Instead of approaching the day with glumness and fear, Joseph saw this day as a once-in-a-lifetime opportunity. If the asteroid was to break apart, Joseph envisioned a spectacular light show across the sky. It was not an event to be missed and where else better to view it than the shore. He was interested in astronomy and was an amateur stargazer, but he didn't quite understand the difference between an asteroid and a meteor. To him, they were just tiny black rocks. After waking his family up, Joseph hounded them to dress quickly, gobble down their breakfast, and get into the family car. His destination was Seaside Heights. From Philadelphia, the trip would take roughly an hour and twenty minutes. Across the Ben Franklin Bridge, a boring trip down Routes Seventy and Thirty-Seven, cross the connector bridge between Toms River and Seaside, and presto, you are there.

Ann Fields felt just the opposite. For the past few days, the television carried nothing but stories on the possibility of the asteroids hitting the earth. Some television commentators said that pieces of an asteroid might fall to Earth while others promised that the asteroid would pass safely by. Ann just wanted to stay home with her two young daughters. They could watch what happened on the television. She didn't need to see it in person. Besides, the two-year-old wouldn't remember it anyway, and the four-year-old would rather play with her toys. But Joseph was insistent, so like a good wife, she dressed the children, packed some refreshments for her family, and off they went.

POP GOES THE WEASEL

W ITH RESIGNATION IN HIS VOICE, Jonesy called out the position of the Z-1 craft, "Alien over target, building up a large heat signature."

Scotty looked up at the monitor and knew what this meant. The Z-1 was about to destroy the spaceship on the floor of the ocean. The opportunity to reap the benefits of the derelict spacecraft was about to disappear.

Since the meeting about nanotechnology, Scotty had been pondering the problem over and over. He came to one basic conclusion. As he had previously thought, Scotty knew inwardly that they had to take advantage of the opportunity to acquire the technology. And the existence of the vessel on the bottom of the ocean would give them a large head start. But the technology scared him a little. In a way, he was almost grateful that the aliens had come to destroy the aircraft, but at the same time, it was an opportunity lost.

"The Z-1 is firing," Jonesy announced and, like all the other people in the communications room, watched as a large heat signature appeared on the deep-space radar. Looking down at his screen, Jonesy, in a monotone voice added, "Z-1 moving away. Heading back into space. Track should be clear of the meteor belt. Target was destroyed."

Scotty looked down at the floor in frustration and felt Doreen's hand as she tightened her grip on the palm of his hand. Looking up at her, Scotty smiled and knew what he had to do.

Standing up, Scotty bellowed out, "Okay, people. Let's get back to tracking the asteroids and any debris that may fall our way."

TABLE FOR TWO

ON THE BOULEVARD IN SEASIDE was a world-famous Irish Bar, O'Learys. It is well-known for serving great food at reasonable prices. On any given day, a line will form from outside of the building as hungry people wait their tum. Inside, there was a hubbub of activity as waiters and waitresses run back and forth trying to please the hungry patrons. Of course, one was able to wash down their dinner fare with a wide variety of beers and ales. But the Irish beers were the best treat of all.

Yesterday, O'Learys hung out a banner across the main entrance. The sign simply read "Asteroid Party." But the sign was very misleading. The owner of O'Learys knew that most people would stay at home the day the asteroids would pass. He wanted to give back to his patrons and offer them a place where they could be with other people and enjoy themselves. Today, O'Learys would treat their patrons. Families always ate here, and families came this day. There were no alcoholic drinks served this early. The only drinks were plenty of coffee and fruit juices. The people who came were treated to a breakfast fare unmatched anywhere. There were mounds and mounds of eggs cooked every way imaginable, what was now called French toast, and, of course, pancakes. Added to this were pile after pile of bacon and sausages. To entertain the children as they ate, there were clowns and magicians. The atmosphere was as it always is, friendly.

DON'T LOOK NOW

"S COTTY! WE HAVE A PROBLEM!" Jonesy called out.

Scotty let go of Doreen's hand, stood up, and went over to Jonesy's computer. "What's going on?" he asked, trying to remain calm for the benefit of those around him.

"We've got the preliminary track on the pieces of the smaller asteroid. Like predicted, some of the pieces will hit the moon but on the dark side. Other pieces are coming our way. And, Scotty, there are some very large pieces of rock," Jonesy replied.

"Okay, put up the track of Earth and the moon, and let's see what we have," Scotty ordered.

Jonesy went to work and quickly transferred the radar data into a computer and calculated the trajectory of the debris fields going toward Earth and the moon. Turning back around to Scotty, he translated the data into plain English. "Just like we thought. Earth and the moon will both take hits. But the moon will not be hit that hard. The debris heading toward the moon is somewhat small in size. The biggest ones are about two feet in diameter, but it will be hit by approximately four hundred pieces."

Jonesy seemed to lower his voice almost in reverence and continued, "Earth, however, is going to be a different story. We are going to take a lot of hits although most of them are small. However, there are a few pieces about forty feet long and massive in weight." Pausing for a moment, Jonesy swallowed hard and then added, "There is one more thing. I've checked it twice. There is one massive piece headed toward Earth. It's not a planet killer, but it sure as hell will wipe out a large area."

Scotty at first bowed his head downward and then looked over at Jonesy. Almost afraid of the answer, Scotty asked, "Do you have any idea where the debris will come down?" and then clarified his question, "Where will the big piece come down?"

"Mary is working on the problem now, but it doesn't look good. The problem is, as we discussed before, the debris will skip across our atmosphere and can fall anywhere. The good news in all of this is that a lot of the debris will burn up in the outer atmosphere. There is just going to be one hell of a light show. Each piece should have a long white trail behind it. The largest piece and the others that are about forty feet long will definitely get through," Jonesy answered.

"Okay, then. What you are telling me is that Earth is going to take some big hits, but we have absolutely no idea where," Scotty concluded.

"That's right," Jonesy replied.

"Are you tapped into NASA?" Doreen spoke up.

Jonesy turned toward Doreen and replied, "Yes, I hacked into their system, and we're getting a direct feed from their deep-space telescope in Hawaii. They show the same thing. They don't have any idea where the pieces will come down."

Scotty then ordered, "Send out what we know after Mary updates the data. Send it to every government in the world in plain language. Make it appear as if it came from some well-known institute."

"London Observatory, okay?" Jonesy asked.

Scotty chuckled and shot back, "Only the best!"

"Will do, Scotty," Jonesy replied and confirmed the order.

DID ANYBODY SEE BOX 14?

YEARS OF PLANNING AND DREAMING had finally come to an end. After what seemed like a lifetime of scrimping and saving, Thomas and Lydia Cathcart had purchased their first home. Their main concern was to move into a house before their first child was born. Lydia was four months pregnant, and part of their dream had been fulfilled. They both felt that when the house hears the first screams of a new life, it would truly become a home.

It wasn't one of those overly larger homes that were built to impress who knows who, but rather it was a modest cozy home where a family could be comfortable and happy. The home was located on a quaint little street where mature maple trees spread their branches above the sidewalks and street. It was as if the trees formed a protective canopy over the neighborhood. The trees helped block out the endless swishing noise from cars as they sped by on the New Jersey Garden State Parkway. This annoyance was a mere three blocks from the house. But when noise was constantly present, one tends not to hear it after a while.

Yesterday was moving day, and today, well today, was unpacking day. All throughout the house, boxes were piled everywhere. Nothing seemed to be in order except for the furniture, which the movers had arranged. Tom and Lydia went from box to box looking for different things. They were not, by nature, unorganized people. Before the move, they had packed and numbered each box. Tom would then enter the number of the box and list its contents in a notebook. As luck would have it, the notebook disappeared on the day of the move. So much for planning.

As they ran around the house, they, like others, had the television on. While they didn't pay much attention to it, Tom and Lydia listened to it as they moved from box to box. Lydia was impatient to set up the kitchen while Tom just wanted to find the box with his shoes in it.

HEADS UP

PLUNGING THROUGH SPACE, THE FIRST piece of large debris hit the outer atmosphere at a low angle. At first, it hit the upper atmosphere and skipped slightly and then reentered at a sharp-enough angle to begin its fiery descent. At the same time, millions of smaller pieces began their fiery death. On the dark side of the world, people stared in awe as millions of streaks of light crossed the sky. Their attention was drawn to one large stream of white light as a piece of debris that had begun its flight at over forty feet long was being burned down to twenty feet. When it reached the inner atmosphere, people stood still in fear as they followed the white contrail toward Earth.

In Northern Germany, people ran in all directions as they knew it was going to hit close by. But they were not quick enough. When this piece of the asteroid was two miles from the surface of Earth, in true asteroid fashion, it exploded. The energy released by the explosion was extremely intense and directed downward. When the energy from the explosion reached Earth, everything within a ten-mile radius was instantly vaporized. Homes at first leaned away from the blast and then exploded in intense heat and flames. The gasoline tanks of automobiles at first exploded and then what was left of the cars melted. Steel bridges melted from the heat where they once proudly stood. People and animals unlucky enough to be inside this circle of death were instantaneously incinerated. Everything was gone.

Beyond the ten-mile circle of death, fire spread quickly. Everything was on fire.

As the concussion of the blast spread outward, it wore the mask of destruction. Onward, it spread until time and distance became its enemy. When the force of the blast reached fifty-two miles away, the energy of death and annihilation had spent itself.

Help for the misfortunate was slow to come. Everyone outside the circle of death was in shock. Eventually, fire and rescue units reached the area and began their work. But it was as if their minds were numb. There was no central coordinated effort. No one in charge seemed capable of understanding the degree of destruction that had been wrought. Death and destruction had come for a visit.

WHAT AGAIN

L ETTING GO OF DOREEN'S HAND, Scotty stood up, wanting to do something. He felt helpless against the onslaught. But what could he do? "How bad is it?" Scotty asked in a monotone voice.

"Bad. Real bad," Jonesy replied without looking up.

Scotty turned to his weapons officer, Bone, who had just walked in. Excitedly, Scotty asked, "If one comes across our area, is there a chance that we could hit it with the plasma weapon?"

Hesitating for a moment to think, Bone then replied, "We can surely hit it. But, Admiral, I can't guarantee that we would destroy it. We might create a lot more rocks coming down. Smaller, yeah, but just as potentially deadly."

"What about using missiles?" Scotty followed up.

"Same problem, Admiral. We couldn't guarantee complete destruction," Bone shot back, thought for a moment, and then continued, "If we were to use nukes, and at least three for the smaller one and at least ten for the monster-size one, well that should do the job."

Scotty thought about what he said and instantly knew that any such plan was risky. But it was worth considering. His thoughts were interrupted when one of the technicians in the room announced over the loudspeaker, "Number two is coming down. Entering the atmosphere over the North Land Islands in eastern Russia…hitting the upper atmosphere…now over the New Siberian Islands…crossing into Alaska…over Tanana, Alaska…now in British Columbia…"

"Project its course…and give me the speed…how high?" Scotty cried out.

"Altitude eight five thousand and dropping fast. Speed, estimate at Mach 12 and slowing. Course on the wall!" Jonesy answered.

BY THE SEA, BY THE PEACEFUL SEA

J OSEPH AND ANN FIELDS PASSED by O'Learys while they were looking for a parking space close to the beach. Ann saw the sign declaring an "Asteroid Party" and suggested that they stop and give their daughters a break.

"It would be nice to relax and have something to eat, honey," Ann pleaded in a soft voice.

But Joseph just glanced over at his wife and with a frown dismissed her suggestion. A few minutes later, his persistence paid off, and Joseph found a parking place less than a block from the beach.

Once parked, Joseph again hurried his family along. Being careful to lock the car and put some money in the parking meter, Joseph picked up the picnic basket and blanket and ordered his family to follow. Ann let out a sigh of frustration, held her daughters' hands, and followed the love of her life, the reincarnated Napoleon, to the beach.

Crossing over the boardwalk and walking down the few steps to the beach, Joseph was amazed at the amount of people who were there. Some would say that the beach was actually crowded. Walking first to the left and then to the right, Joseph plodded on until he found a spot away from most of the people. Once the blanket was spread, Ann and the girls sat down followed by Joseph. The girls were more interested in playing in the sand than watching a light show. But Joseph explained to his captive audience that there was a good chance that they would see things streaking across the sky. Not being impressed with their father's talk, the girls giggled as they dug their hands and feet into the sand. And Ann, well, Ann just wanted to go home and relax.

NO! I DON'T KNOW WHERE THE HAMMER IS

"Tommy!" Lydia Cathcart called out and added, "Can you bring me the hammer?"

"Oh, boy," Tom whispered to himself, stood up, and kicked aside the twenty-third box he had opened, hoping to find his shoes. Walking into the kitchen, Tom saw his wife holding up, against the wall, an antique cookie mold. Tom walked up behind his wife, put his arms around her waist, and softly kissed her on the neck. Lydia blushed slightly, loved the attention, and turned around.

Tom let go of Lydia and stated, "I don't have the hammer."

"You did bring it, didn't you?" Lydia asked coyly.

Tom knew from the tone in her voice what would happen next. A hammer would have to appear as if by magic, or he would be going somewhere to buy one. Playing the game through, Tom replied, "Yes, of course. It's packed in one of the boxes somewhere."

"But I need it now," Lydia insisted.

"Can't we hang that thing later?" Tom pleaded.

"Well, yeah. But then it would be bad luck if it is not hung up right away," Lydia answered with humor in her voice.

Tom chuckled and replied with a smile on his face, "I guess that if it's bad luck, we better go get one."

"Okay!" Lydia quickly answered.

As Tom hugged his wife, he struck a deal, "There's a home store where Route Nine goes under the Parkway. We can go there. Also, there is a pizza place there so we can get something to eat."

"Like pizza with onions, sausage, extra cheese, and bacon?" Lydia asked as she leaned back and looked at her husband.

"It's a deal. Let's go!" Tom replied and grabbed his wallet off the kitchen counter.

JUST KEEP THE GOOD NEWS COMING

SCOTTY LOOKED UP AND SAW the course projection on the monitor wall. Concluding that number two was going to hit in the ocean somewhere, Scotty breathed a sigh of relief. But that was short-lived when he heard, "Number three coming in…it's the monster!"

"Where?" Scotty shouted but wasn't heard when another announcement rang out, "Number two passing over Indianapolis… now Knoxville…now over Charlestown …passing east of St. John's Island…now east of Natal…into the South Atlantic…falling fast!"

"The monster! Where is it?" Scotty cried out.

"Number three is entering the upper atmosphere over Manchuria… now passing over the northern island of Japan…" a nervous voice spoke up and added with some relief, "Now heading over the Pacific."

"What's the altitude?" Scotty demanded.

"Just under seventy-three thousand feet…slow descent!" the voice answered. "Number two is now southwest of Cape Town, South Africa. Coming down fast," a voice in the room called out.

Scotty looked up at the monitors, trying to keep track of both pieces. In this excited tense atmosphere, lesser men and women would have sat back by now and watched helplessly. But the members of Space Command remained at their computer stations collecting data.

"Admiral! We have impacts on the moon!" another voice called out.

Scotty looked down at Jonesy and instructed him to track the moon impacts and put the graphics up on the monitor.

"Number two is down to ten thousand feet, dropping fast!" an excited voice called out then added, "Atmospheric explosion at two thousand feet directly over Marion Island."

"Where the hell is Marion Island?" someone was heard to ask.

Someone else answered sharply, "In the Southern Indian Ocean. What did you do, fail geography?"

"The monster is approaching Eugene, Oregon. Altitude fifty-three thousand," Jonesy called out with resignation in his voice.

"Where is it going to come down?" Scotty asked.

Jonesy looked up at his friend and in a monotone voice answered, "Based upon the track, it is following and its loss of altitude somewhere east of the Mississippi."

Scotty just looked at him for a moment and then ordered, "Notify everyone we can. And get Carolyn and Mary up here. I want them to monitor the moon."

Jonesy turned back toward his computer and followed his orders. Scotty clasped his hands behind his back and watched the monitors and realized that the damn monster will probably pass just to the north of where they were.

OKAY, WHO TOOK IT?

T HE PEOPLE OF SPACE COMMAND and, indeed, the rest of the world would not learn the details of what had happened to Marion Island for days to come.

When the asteroid fell to two thousand feet, it exploded with devastating force directly over the highest point of the island, State President Peak. The focus of the explosion was so intense that the top layer of rock melted. Once the full effect of the explosion was felt, the mountain itself exploded. As the shock wave rippled through the land, the island began to crumble. It was as if the ancient volcano, which formed the island, had come back to life and exploded. Within seconds, the island disappeared from existence.

In nearby Prince Edward Island, the shock wave knocked over trees and crumbled buildings. But the island survived the first onslaught. A few minutes later, a tidal wave washed over the island, killing everything in its path. The tidal wave continued on its deadly course and killed millions of innocent people as its fury spread to land boarding the Pacific and Indian Oceans.

I'LL TAKE ONE OF THOSE— OH, AND ONE OF THOSE!

WHEN TOM AND LYDIA ARRIVED at the home store, they were surprised to find the parking lot at the strip mall almost deserted. Parking in the first space nearest the entrance, Tom wondered if in fact the store was open. But his apprehension quickly disappeared when they strolled through the front door. The store was strangely quiet and deserted. In fact, there was only one cashier working, and he was sitting on the checkout counter reading a magazine.

After picking out a hammer, no easy matter with Lydia asking a thousand and one questions because there was so many to choose from. The mother-to-be then announced that she wanted to look at some window curtains. Forty-five minutes and two full shopping carts later, their bargain hunting was finished for now. While they were checking out, Lydia kept a careful eye on the prices the computer was charging and the running total.

When the clerk finished tabulating the three hundred fifty-three dollars and nineteen cents bill, Lydia leaned over and whispered to Tom, "I guess we should have bought the cheaper hammer."

Tom chuckled a little and handed the clerk his credit card.

Once their purchases were loaded in the car, they drove the one hundred yards down to the pizza parlor. They were once again rewarded with a parking space right in front of the store. For the second time today, they were the only patrons. Choosing to sit in the last booth away from the front door and the counter, Tom and Lydia talked for a minute about the asteroids and hoped that they would harmlessly crash into the oceans of the world. Their talk was interrupted when the clerk called Tom up to the counter to pick up their slices of pizza. After paying the bill, Tom struggled while carrying their bounty back to the table. Once he was seated Tom picked up a knife and fork. Cutting a piece off of a pizza slice, Tom held it out to his wife. Lydia accepted the offer and smiled at Tom for his gentle attention.

OH WHERE, OH WHERE DID THE ASTEROID GO?

A S IF HE WAS NAILED to the floor, Scotty stood rigid with his hands clasped behind his back watching the monitors. "Any idea where it will come down?" Scotty asked.

Jonesy looked up at Scotty and answered, "No definite idea. It could be close to Philadelphia or somewhere in New Jersey."

"Did you get the warnings out?" Scotty asked softly.

"Everyone we could reach was warned, but I'm not sure anyone was listening what with the television stations speculating on everything from the asteroid debris missing the earth to worldwide devastation," Jonesy replied, resigned to the fact that it didn't matter one bit to anyone that they warned them.

"Is there anything on the hit in Germany in the news yet?" Scotty asked a little puzzled at Jonesy's answer.

"Nothing yet—" Jonesy was interrupted by the announcement, "Asteroid passing over South Dakota...coming up on Madison, Wisconsin...crossing Lake Erie...altitude five thousand gradual descent...speed Mach 2.5."

"Looks like a land hit, Scotty. We still can't predict where because it continues to make very small course changes. I guess it's because of the resistance it encounters as it moves through the air," Jonesy speculated.

"Our group in Willow Grove Naval Air in Pennsylvania, are they out?" Scotty asked, knowing they probably weren't.

"No, Scotty. There was no time," Doreen spoke up.

Scotty turned around, looked at Doreen, and smiled slightly, but his face told a different story. It was plain to see that Scotty was worried. Worried not only for those under his command but worried about what was going to happen when the monster did strike Earth.

COULD I HAVE A PHILLY CHEESESTEAK?

IT WAS NOT A NORMAL day in Philadelphia. The streets were mostly deserted. There was no one selling the famous Philadelphia pretzels in the street. No one was attending the Hot Rod show at the new Convention Center. The Gallery Downtown Shopping Mall was mostly deserted. In the restaurant district, waiters attended empty tables. For the first time in history, the Reading Terminal Market vendors outnumbered the customers. In a like manner, the animals in the great Philadelphia Zoo looked out of their enclosures and did not see any visitors. The bus and train stations fell silent. Penn's Landing was deserted. Independence National Historical Park was empty. There were no lines to see the Liberty Bell or Independence Hall. The ghosts of history were free to wander around the Betsy Ross House as it was devoid of visitors. No one was trying to throw pennies on the grave of Benjamin Franklin. The paintings in the art galleries and the exhibits in the many museums went unseen. Fairmont Park and the area of Boat House Row was deserted. Traffic signals changed and the Walk and Don't Walk signs lit up on cue, but no one was there to heed their warnings. The people in the City of Brotherly Love had simply disappeared.

By the time the monster reached the area of Philadelphia, its altitude had dropped to roughly twenty-five hundred feet. The altitude continued to erode; however, its speed had increased slightly. As it crossed the land, a sound wave was pushed out in front of it. People would later say that it sounded like a high-pitched whistle sound. When the piece of the asteroid passed overhead, there was a trailing concussion that would pick people up off their feet and cast them aside as one would a piece of paper. At the two-thousand-foot altitude, the concussion knocked down houses and other such weakly constructed commercial buildings as it passed by. Those buildings and houses which had natural or bottled gas as an energy source would inevitably explode and catch on fire. This swath of destruction was at least four miles wide and expanded as the monster came closer and closer to hitting the ground.

The asteroid entered Philadelphia from the west and seemed to follow Market Street as if it was a tourist looking for the historic area. As it passed above, what unfortunate people that were on the street were instantly killed either from the concussion or flying and falling debris. Buildings collapsed but not before their windows were sucked out by the onrush of air that raced to fill the void in the sky the asteroid had just occupied. As expected, fire was the next plague to be bestowed on the city as block after block ignited within seconds of the asteroid's passage.

When it flew over city hall, the statue of William Penn on top of the building was lifted from its pedestal and wound up in the shipyard a few miles away. The Philadelphia Convention Center crumbled as if it was made out of matches. The Gallery Shopping Mall was no more. The once proud stores of major retailers disappeared as if they were never there. The glass windows of the Constitution Center vanished, but the bastion of freedom, the Liberty Bell, remained in place, ringing on its own.

When the asteroid reached the Delaware River, the city was in ruins. As it crossed the river, the asteroid caused a thirty-five-foot wave up and down the Delaware. Penn's Landing was destroyed, and the USS *Olympia* was tossed about as if a child picked it up and threw it away. The nearby Benjamin Franklin Bridge felt the concussion and at first swayed toward the direction of the asteroid and then swung back and collapsed.

As the asteroid crossed into New Jersey, the wave hit the USS *New Jersey*, moored at the Camden Waterfront Park. The tough old lady rode out the wave and remained tied to the dock area. But the new baseball park, concert center, and state aquarium disappeared in the blink of an eye. Newly renovated luxury waterfront apartments crumbled along with the hopes and dreams of Camden's waterfront revival.

As the asteroid moved eastward, the towns of Cherry Hill, Haddonfield, Marlton, and Chairville were erased from the topography of New Jersey. When it crossed over the Brendan Byrne State Forest, the pine trees were lifted out of the loose sandy soil and became deadly missiles themselves as they were thrown about. Trees crashed into houses as far as ten miles away. In some cases, the occupants of those homes were crushed by the weight of the trees or by the collapse of their own homes.

By the time the monster reached the Garden State Parkway, its altitude had fallen to a few hundred feet. As it passed over the Parkway, speeding automobiles were picked up and tossed about. It was as if each car was picked up by its own personal tornado and thrown away at will. When it reached Route Thirty-Seven, the trail of death and destruction continued.

As the monster raced toward the shoreline, it swept through the heart of Toms River as if it was a broom sweeping away the past. Death, fire, and destruction were its calling cards left on each side of the highway. In an instant, the commercial district along this busy road was no more. Gone were the car dealerships, the hotels, the restaurants, the banks, and the hundreds of other commercial enterprises.

When the asteroid reached the end of Toms River, it crossed over Barnegat Bay and on into Seaside. As it crossed the bay, the twin bridges connecting Toms River and Seaside were no more. The concrete structures simply vanished as the concrete was pulverized into dust, and the steel melted by the force and heat of the concussion. When it crossed into Seaside, the asteroid was only seventy-five feet in the air traveling faster than a jet fighter.

PLOP

THE PEOPLE IN O'LEARYS BAR heard the passage of the asteroid. The building shook, and glasses neatly arranged on the counter and glass hangers fell from their perches. Televisions, arranged throughout the bar, broadcasting the latest news fell off the walls. Pictures came crashing down, and the glass windows were sucked out in an instant. But as the sound of the asteroid and its effects passed, the people started clapping because they knew that they had survived the worst of it. After all, most of the experts on the different television stations, which had been on, predicted a safe passage of the wayward rocks. The noise of their clapping, whistling, and hollering covered the sound of collapsing buildings as the effects of the asteroid were felt closer to the shore.

The people on the beach in Seaside heard the same noise as the people in Philadelphia had except it was approximately four or five times louder. As the whistling sound engulfed the beach, everyone stood up and faced the direction the sound was coming from. Most stood with their hands covering their ears as they watched an irregular-shaped rock, white hot in the front and trailing flames, came into sight. Mixed in with the noise of the asteroid was the terrible sound of homes near the beach collapsing.

As the asteroid came closer, Joseph Fields felt real fear for the first time in his life. Like any father, he knew that he had to protect his family, but at this moment, he felt powerless. The only thing he could do was force his wife and children to lay down in the sand. He laid down between his children and covered their heads with his arms. Ann Fields laid down next to one of the girls and placed an arm over her daughter and across her husband's back. Joseph managed to reach across and place his hand onto the back of his wife's head. Together, they lay there, trying to protect their family while awaiting their fate. Joseph struggled to look up and saw the asteroid fly less than one hundred feet above him. When the asteroid had passed, Joseph felt the concussion, which knocked those still standing down. He then felt a suction of air over his body. He struggled and fought successfully to protect his family from being lifted off the sand. All around him, people were flying through the air in all sorts of contorted positions, but somehow, Joseph managed to keep his family safe.

Joseph was about to move when all of a sudden debris that had once been houses started landing all over the beach. As he looked around Joseph saw a few cars come sailing through the air, crashing onto the beach, killing some of the people. Joseph knew that they had to get out of there and fast. When the debris stopped falling, he quickly gathered up his family, and they started running toward their car. Together, they crossed over where the boardwalk once was and began running down the street. Joseph held his children's hands as they ran. Ann ran behind her husband, holding onto the back of his pants by the belt.

SOMEONE PLEASE WAKE ME UP

Everyone in the vast room was silent. They knew that people were dying from something that was predetermined millions of years ago. Frustrating of all was the bare fact that there was nothing they could do. These were people who could fight an enemy against the worst of odds and win. But this, who knew how to fight this? Two planets collide before the dawn of man, and millions of years later, pieces of those planets come visiting.

Doreen had gotten out of her chair and stood next to Scotty. When she did, Scotty put his arm around her waist and drew her near. Without taking his eyes off the monitors, he bent down and kissed her on the head. Momentarily, he was lost in the fragrance of her perfume, but reality was in front of him. Doreen placed an arm around his waist, and together, in silence, they awaited the inevitable.

"It's going to land about a mile offshore. For some reason, this rock is not going to explode," Jonesy announced, almost choking on the words.

"How bad will it be?" Scotty asked.

"Real bad!" Jonesy relied with utter dread in his voice.

"Admiral, we're getting some really weird readings on the moon impacts," Mary spoke up, anxious to tell what she thought she knew.

Scotty turned toward her and shook his head in the negative and said, "Not now." Turning back around to the monitors he added, although he was speaking to no one in particular, "Christ, I learned how to surf there."

SURF'S UP

J OSEPH AND ANN DID NOT see the asteroid when it hit the ocean. The sound concussion from the collision sped across the water, up the beach, and into the streets, knocking the fleeing family down as they ran. Momentarily, they were stunned. The girls began crying, and Joseph saw fear in his wife's face. Joseph knelt down in the street facing the beach. As he helped his girls up, Joseph glanced up at the sky and in the distance saw what looked like a pale green wall of water. At first, he couldn't comprehend what water was doing in the sky, and *Why did it appear to be getting closer?* he wondered. It was as if a very large curtain was coming toward him.

As Joseph stared at the wall of water, the answer came to him, tidal surge. The sky was almost gone now, obliterated by the water. Joseph knew that there was no place to run. He knelt there in the street. Joseph faced the water and didn't want his daughters to see it. Taking his daughters into his arms and his wife kneeling behind the girls, Joseph and Ann hugged their family and each other. Joseph held on tight to his family, praying to his God as he awaited death.

As a three-hundred-plus-foot wall of water swept them up, Joseph thought of his family and then the odd beauty of the sea. It was the last thought of his life. The family would later become a statistic of the bean counters who keep such records.

The patrons at O'Learys heard a few new sounds. At first, they heard a crashing sound when the asteroid had hit the water. But soon, that sound washed over the building and was gone. They went back to eating and drinking, all agreeing how lucky they were. But a few seconds later, all went quiet in the bar as a new sound could be heard. A swishing noise was heard at first, followed by what sounded like a train engine barreling down the tracks, and finally, a crunching sound.

All eyes in the bar stared out of the spaces once occupied by windows toward the beach. Suddenly, those with an unobstructed clear view dropped their eating utensils or coffee mugs and ran out of the nearest doors. Others, in the back of the restaurant, quickly followed as building debris pushed forward by the towering wall of water came closer. Some ran up to the dining area on the second floor. It was too late. The wall of water demolished every building in its path. Automobiles and trucks were crushed and became part of the wall of debris. People were swept away in a heartbeat as the wave moved forward.

In less than a minute, Seaside was no more. The giant wave crossed the bay and continued inland. People in their homes had no warning of what was to come. Firemen and rescue workers were heading toward the devastation left by the passage of the asteroid on Route Thirty-Seven and the surroundings area. It seemed that fires were burning everywhere out of control. People were dying in collapsed buildings and crushed cars, but rescue would never come. The wave raced inland, destroying everything in its path. Block after city block was decimated. What had once been a thriving community was quickly becoming a wasteland of hope and dreams as the wave pushed on.

The only hope of salvation was distance. For every inch the wave moved forward over the land, its height diminished. By the time it had reached the downtown area of Toms River, the wave was slightly less than one hundred feet high. What saved the area from even more death and destruction was the Garden State Parkway. The Parkway in this area rises above the elevation of the city. When the wave hit the Parkway, its high earthen embankments broke the back of the wave. Billions and billions of gallons of water washed over the Parkway, but its power as a deadly destructive force was gone.

COULD I HAVE A GLASS OF WATER, PLEASE?

"You know, Tom, I shouldn't really be drinking soda. What with the baby on the way and all? I know it's not bad for you, but I would really rather just drink water," Lydia declared in between bites of her pizza.

Tom was distracted by a rumbling noise and had turned around to look outside just as millions of gallons of water suddenly appeared in front of the restaurant. Being quick-witted, even in a situation like this, Tom turned back around and said "You want water? You got water!" as he stood up and went to somehow help his wife.

Lydia's attention was then drawn to the noise and the sight of the water. "Shit! Tom, do something!" Lydia cried out as Tom reached her side and was pulling her out of the booth by her arms.

Suddenly, the water crashed through the glass doors and windows of the restaurant and cascaded in. Tom lifted Lydia out of her seat and pushed her on top of the table, face up in a prone position. Tom lifted himself on top of her. Lying of top of his wife and holding her down with his body weight, Tom tightly held onto the sides of the table. Not knowing what else to do and awaiting the momentary onrush of water, Tom kissed his wife.

Lydia shook her head to break the kiss and shouted, "Are you crazy or something? Not now, Tom!"

Tom looked down at Lydia with passion, love, understanding, and a thousand emotions yet unnamed in his heart and in his eyes. He then glanced toward the front of the building and noticed that the water appeared to have leveled off and was not rising. The water had risen just under the height of the table and stopped. After looking around and being reasonably sure that the water would not go higher, Tom pushed himself off the table and stood in water just over his kneecaps.

Tom reached over and pulled his wife up. Bending over slightly, Tom picked Lydia up in his arms and carried her out of the restaurant through the glassless doors. Lydia reached up and put her arm around his neck and held on tightly. Looking around, they saw that the parking lot was full of water. Automobiles that moments ago had been parked were pushed over to a comer of the lot in one mangled heap. Approximately two hundred yards away, there was a small hill in the parking lot where a drive-up bank was. Since the area around the bank was dry, Tom carried his precious bundle there as he pushed his way through the water.

For the first time in her life, Lydia didn't have anything to say. As they walked toward the dry speck of land, they just held each other. Their thoughts were unexpressed, but they felt each other's love. When they almost reached the hill, Lydia's silence had given way, "You just had to have pizza, didn't you? Next time, I pick the restaurant!"

Tom at first didn't hear her, but then the words processed through his shocked brain, and he softly answered, "Yeah, but it was good pizza. The floor show stunk, but the food was good."

Lydia giggled and then together they laughed. Within a few minutes, they reached the dry part of the parking lot. Tom put Lydia down, and together, they stood hand in hand as rescue vehicles began to arrive. The rest of the day, they never left each other's side, and they held onto each other. Each feared that if they let go of each other, one of them would disappear.

A FLOOD OF TEARS

"OH MY GOD!" JONESY EXCLAIMED to no one in particular.

"What's going on?" Scotty asked in a demanding voice.

"The New Jersey coast is gone!" Jonesy replied and then added, "News reports are starting to come in. I'm monitoring the news channels, and it looks real bad."

"Put the main television channels up on some of the monitors. Let's see what is going on," Scotty ordered as he tightened his grip slightly on Doreen.

"Death toll is expected to reach in the millions. There is no way to adequately describe the disaster that has struck the East Coast of the United States, especially New Jersey. The center of the tidal surge caused by the large piece of the asteroid that crashed one mile off of the coast struck Seaside, New Jersey, with nature's full fury. The tidal wave then spread death and destruction inland. As the wave spread across the east coast, the story is the same. Disaster…"

The story was the same on each of the news channels. It became apparent that almost the entire East Coast was affected. In Boston Harbor, the water rose an unprecedented twenty feet, causing minor flooding. While in New York City, the rivers rose almost fifty feet at one point, flooding lower Manhattan and the subway system. The city was at a virtual standstill. In New Jersey, the coastal area was flooded from Keyport down to Cape May. In Atlantic City, the tidal surge was over one hundred feet high. A few of the casinos collapsed while the others were helplessly flooded. In Cape May, the historic area was destroyed. Gone were the Victorian homes and a vibrant community. Similar reports echoed throughout the state: flood, death, and total destruction.

The outer banks of North Carolina were simply gone, washed out to sea. People would no longer be vacationing in Myrtle Beach; it didn't exist anymore. Charlestown was under water. Churches which stood the test of time failed miserably the challenge of the asteroid. Daytona Beach was underwater, but it would survive to host another Bike Week. In Key West, the ocean caused a ripple in the normal tides. The effect of the asteroid had played itself out the further south, and north one was from Seaside, New Jersey.

The room again went silent when news helicopters were over flying the New Jersey coast. It almost looked as if a drunken giant had walked up and down the coast, crushing everything in sight. There simply were no buildings left. Water seemed to be everywhere. Where there wasn't water, there was fire. And the fires were burning out of control. Rescue efforts were few at first and then became many as fire companies throughout the United States converged on the East Coast. But the task was too large, and the effort was in vain. Everywhere, there was death. In New Jersey, the National Guard and Army troops from Fort's Dix and Monmouth secured the areas affected and brought order and coordination to the effort. The governor of New Jersey declared a day of mourning as there was hardly anyone in the state who wasn't related to or knew someone who lived in the devastated areas. Flags were flown at half-mast, and it began to rain. Even the angels were crying.

KNOCK, KNOCK

Dustin and Victoria were laying on the couch in her office, each wrapped in the other's arms. They weren't speaking, but communication was not necessary. In a manner of speaking, they had just communicated more than words could express.

Victoria was the first to speak, "Dustin, how many children do you want to have?"

Dustin kissed her on her forehead and diplomatically replied, "As many as you want."

"I like a large family though," Victoria answered, testing the waters.

"I do as well," Dustin quickly added.

Victoria reached up and whispered in his ear, "Well, I guess we really have a lot of work to do. We better get started right away."

"I agree!" Dustin enthusiastically replied and kissed Victoria.

Suddenly, there was a knock on the office door. Victoria jumped up off the couch and reached for her bra and underwear. Realizing that there wasn't time to put them on, she threw them behind the couch and then pulled her dress on over her head. Dustin scrambled to get dressed, but Victoria was already to the door. To avoid embarrassment, Dustin scrambled into the adjoining bathroom.

Victoria cautiously opened the door and was greeted by her secretary. "Director, do you have the TV on?"

Victoria really didn't know what to reply and answered "No, we were just talking" as she unconsciously adjusted her dress.

"It's really bad! Put on the news channel!" her secretary demanded and then turned around and walked back to her desk.

"Dustin!" Victoria called out as she crossed her office and turned on the television.

As Dustin emerged from the bathroom, he walked over to Victoria and stood next to her with his arm around her waist. He listened intently, but like most people, he could not fully comprehend the scope of the disaster. As Dustin continued to listen, a feeling was growing within him. He knew what he had to do. Seeing a piece of discarded string hanging on the edge of the wastebasket, he scooped it up. Standing in front of Victoria, Dustin put the string around her forehead and held on tight to the spot on the longer piece that overlapped one of the ends.

At first, Victoria tried to swat his hands away, but then she kind of realized what he was doing and submitted. Dustin cut the excess off the string and held the piece he wanted in his hand. He then walked over to the office door, and as he opened it, Victoria asked, "Dustin, what in God's name are you doing, and just where are you going? You can't leave now!"

Dustin turned around and looked at his love and pointed at the television set. With determination in his voice, Dustin replied, "See all those people they are talking about that died. They had one thing in common. They all had hopes and dreams. My hope and dream are that we spend the rest of our days together. But we should also try and fulfill our dreams whatever they are. Not to do so, in light of what just happened, would be wrong." Dustin paused as he stared at Victoria and then added, "I'll be back." He then closed the door behind him and left the building.

Victoria stood there for a moment and stared at the door. She then went behind her desk, opened the bottom draw, and withdrew a folded pair of dungarees and a T-shirt. With a smile on her face, she then went behind the couch and retrieved her bra and underwear. Starting to giggle a little, she went into her private bathroom and took a shower. Victoria felt like she was a teenager again, about to go out on her first date.

ARE YOU REALLY, REALLY SURE?

SCOTTY RELEASED HIS HOLD ON Doreen and quietly asked her to go to the personnel department and determine if any of the crew had parents, siblings, or relatives that lived in the shore area of New Jersey or any of the other affected areas. Almost as an afterthought, Scotty also instructed her to gather the resident chaplains together and direct them to the crew members that may have been affected by the tragedy. Doreen suggested that it might also be a good idea to have a memorial service for the people that have died. She felt that it might give closure to the crew and allow them to refocus their energies.

Readily agreeing, Scotty asked her to set it up for tomorrow in the auditorium. After kissing Scotty on the cheek, Doreen left to begin her work, which would be no easy task.

"Admiral!" Mary let her presence be known, trying to get Scotty's attention.

Turning around Scotty answered her cry, "Ah, Mary. I'm sorry to keep you and Carolyn waiting. Now, what was it you were saying?"

Mary began searching through a stack of photographs. So to save the moment Carolyn spoke up, "Admiral, we have been monitoring the impact of the asteroids debris on the moon. As Mary predicted, the impacts have occurred and are occurring on the dark side of the moon. Since there is not a satellite within orbital range of the moon, we have kind of hijacked the deep-space telescope, Taurus II. We are receiving a live feed from Taurus II, and, sir, it's really weird."

"How do you mean weird?" Scotty asked his interest aroused.

"Well, sir. I have this photograph here that will show you what we are talking about," Mary replied and handed an eight-by-twelve photograph to Scotty.

Scotty turned the photograph to the left and then to the right, trying to determine what side was the right side up. Mary stepped alongside of him, reached out, and adjusted the photograph. What Scotty was looking at was a darkened picture of the moon with colored lights alongside of the right edge of the moon.

"Okay, I have no idea what I'm looking—" Scotty began to say but was interrupted by Jonesy.

"Admiral!" Jonesy called out as he turned around to face Scotty and then added, "We've gotten word on the Willow Grove group."

Scotty looked at Jonesy for a second, waiting for more. When Jonesy didn't add anything further, Scotty asked, "Well?"

"Oh, sorry, Admiral," Jonesy stumbled and then continued, "The hangar the aircraft are in collapsed. Two aircraft are damaged, but the other two are okay."

"Our people, Jonesy. I don't care about the aircraft. Are our people okay?" Scotty demanded.

"Everyone is fine, sir," Jonesy quickly replied.

"Okay. Commandeer another hangar for the good aircraft. Direct CAG to fly two more out there. Also beg, borrow, or steal a C-5A to pick up the damaged aircraft and get them to the manufacturing facility," Scotty ordered and then asked, "Did you have anything to do with these two hijacking the Taurus II?"

"Don't you think hijacking is too strong a term? Borrowed is more like it?" Jonesy answered with a grin on his face.

"Whatever!" Scotty replied with a grin also on his face.

"Sir, am I correct in stating that the admiral just ordered me to steal a C-5A, the biggest cargo plane in the Air Force?" Jonesy asked, laughing.

"Yes, you are correct," Scotty replied and in a stern voice added, "But give it back as soon as those aircraft arrive at the manufacturing facility."

"Yes, sir!" Jonesy acknowledged and then turned around and began doing what he does best, acquire someone else's property.

Shaking his head, Scotty smiled and apologized to Mary and Carolyn and then asked, "You were telling me about these colors on the edge of the moon. What do they mean?"

Carolyn and Mary looked at each other with grins on their faces as if they held a secret no one else knew. Carolyn then nodded to Mary. Mary looked at Scotty and declared, "You know how we've been trying to figure out where in the hell the aliens have been hiding? Well, we think that you are looking at the answer."

It was easy for Scotty to tell that they were deadly serious by the determined expressions on their faces, but he didn't understand. He was looking at a dark photograph of the moon with some bands of color on the side.

Anxiously, Scotty ordered, "Now that is going to take some explanation."

Carolyn explained that when they received the feed from Taurus II, they subjected the film to spectrum analysis. The process involved the assignment of different colors to a variety of gases. When they analyzed the photographs, some of the gasses they tested for were somehow present in the bands of color.

Mary pointed to the color bands in the photograph Scotty was holding. She explained, "See that orange band, that believe it or not, is oxygen. That blue band is carbon monoxide, a by-product of a fire. That pink band is from a gas that would indicate a polycarbonate material was on fire. See that red band there? That would mean that a biomaterial object is burning. And, lastly, that white band is from a mineral base material that is likewise burning, such as hardened steel."

"Okay. But am I correct in thinking that it was theorized that oxygen might be present in pockets under the moon's surface? And if debris from the asteroid struck those pockets, wouldn't there be a good chance that there would be a fire until the oxygen ran out? Also, mineral-based material has been found on the moon, and wouldn't that also burn?" Scotty asked, anxious to believe what they have said, but it was necessary to play the devil's advocate.

"All what you say is true, Admiral. But this has been burning for over three hours. And don't forget the biomaterial that is not found on the moon," Mary replied with conviction and then glanced at Carolyn.

"Admiral, the aliens are there. Their base is on the dark side of the moon. And right now, they are hurting. This is our chance, Admiral. Let's pay these bastards back for everything they have done!" Carolyn added.

Scotty stood there, staring at them and thinking about what they just said. He reasoned that if what Carolyn and Mary were proposing was true, then the aliens were indeed hiding on the dark side of the moon. And, if they were hiding on the dark side of the moon, and a fire had been burning for over three hours, then they were hurting. Could the tide have turned because of the asteroid? Now would be the time to attack. A thousand other thoughts crossed Scotty's mind as to what might happen if they attacked and the aliens weren't there. The United States would be virtually defenseless from alien attack if they went on a wild goose chase. But Scotty desperately wanted to believe what they were saying.

Reaching a compromise within himself, Scotty replied, "Okay, I'll tell you what. I want you to give a presentation to the group. Instruct my executive officer, Beverly Hocker, to gather herself, Doreen, CAG, Bone, JW, Jonesy, Vinson since he's back, and Arty in my office, in say two hours. If you can convince the group of your conclusions like you have me, then it's a go. Oh, and add JW's assistant, Captain Linda Clark, to the group."

Carolyn anxiously replied "Yes, Admiral! Don't worry, we'll convince them" as she looked at Mary, and then together, they walked away, talking among themselves like young schoolgirls discussing their first dates.

Scotty watched as they left the communications room. He then turned around and walked over to Jonesy. Picking up the telephone, Scotty dialed the number for CAG's office. When CAG answered the telephone, Scotty didn't give him a chance to say anything. "CAG, identify who is speaking to you!"

"Admiral, I know that it is you. What can I do for you?" CAG answered more than a little confused.

"Put the air wing on full alert! All aircraft. Weapons are to be a full load of hypersonic missiles for the X-aircraft as well as the F-18s," Scotty ordered.

"Will do, Admiral. But can you tell me what is going on?" CAG replied even a little bit more confused.

"Two hours in my office with full status reports," Scotty ordered and quickly hung up.

CAG was left confirming the order to a dead telephone line.

Scotty next contacted Bone and ordered him to prepare the plasma cannons for action and to fulfill the needs of CAG quickly. Scotty then dialed JW and issued the order to start sealing off the base and to go on full alert. Bone and JW were as equally confused as CAG was, but they quickly carried out their orders.

Jonesy looked up at Scotty and was wondering what was going on. He knew the look he was now seeing on his friend's face. It usually meant serious trouble. Thinking the better of it, Jonesy didn't bother to ask any questions. Instead, he watched as Scotty left the room and went off somewhere to think.

NOW I LAY ME
DOWN TO SLEEP

Tom and Lydia remained standing on the one piece of dry land in the parking lot. They watched as fire companies and rescue workers came and went. Some brave rescuers ventured into the flooded areas in small rowboats looking for survivors. But the story was always the same. The boats always came back without any survivors.

Toward the evening, a Red Cross paneled truck parked near where Tom and Lydia were standing. The volunteer workers quickly started handing out hot coffee and food. Tom and Lydia walked over to the truck and gratefully accepted the offering of hot vegetable soup and a cold ham sandwich. After finishing their precious meal, Tom approached one of the Red Cross workers and explained the predicament that he and Lydia were in. Within a few minutes, a Red Cross automobile appeared and transported the couple to a local high school well away from the carnage.

Arriving at the high school, Tom and Lydia were immediately surrounded by rescue workers and emergency medical technicians. It was as if everyone wanted to do something for them. New clothes were brought to them. Platters of hot food arrived, followed by platters of all kinds of sweet desserts. When they were showered, changed, and fed, Tom and Lydia were brought into a makeshift office. Here they were interviewed about where they live and their present economic condition. The answers came easy, without thinking. The Red Cross worker who interviewed them tried not to show emotion but failed. Lydia saw it immediately in his eyes and asked what was wrong. The man did not have the heart to tell them and instead asked them to follow him.

Tom and Lydia were led into another impromptu office. On the far wall were two maps. The first one was a map of the entire state with almost the entire coastal area highlighted in red. The other map was a large street map of Seaside and Toms River, New Jersey. Seaside was awash in red highlighter. The area east of the Parkway in Toms River was covered in red. The Red Cross worker walked over to the map of Toms River and pointed to a spot covered in red.

Clearing his throat, he nervously spoke, "Mr. and Mrs. Cathcart, your house is here. We have confirmed that this entire area is destroyed. Your house was crushed by the wave." Looking down at the floor, he continued, "I'm sorry. Your entire neighborhood is destroyed. Everything in the red zone has been destroyed. It's…it's…it's just gone. As you can see, the businesses where you both worked have also been destroyed." Looking up at Tom and Lydia, the Red Cross worker could only add, "I'm sorry. Let me show you where you can sleep."

Tom and Lydia were, needless to say, stunned at the news. Walking as if they were in shock, Tom and Lydia were led into the gymnasium of the high school. The gymnasium was filled with hundreds of cots arranged neatly in rows. On each cot were sheets, a blanket, and a pillow neatly placed in the center. In the comer of the gymnasium, case upon case of bottled water was stacked against the wall. In another corner of the gymnasium, coffee urns were placed upon a table accented by trays of doughnuts.

Lydia walked to the center of the gymnasium and began making her bed for the night. Tom followed her lead and helped in the effort to act somewhat normal. When they were finished, they each sat on a cot facing each other. Tom saw the look of sorrow in her eyes. He then stood up and went to her. Sitting down next to Lydia, Tom took her hand in his and placed his other arm around her shoulders and drew her near. Lydia looked up at her husband and then placed her head in the cradle of his shoulder. Together, they sat for hours, each to their own thoughts, but they were of one with each other. A few hours later, they began talking about the impending birth of their baby and their lives. Throughout the night, they were alone. There simply were not any other survivors.

SHOWTIME

Before the meeting, Scotty meandered around the base. He was trying to busy himself as he thought over the possibility of attacking the aliens. At the same time, Scotty was trying to sense the mood of the base. He needed those under his command to be alert with high morale. Scotty thought that the overall mood would be low since the asteroid crashed into the east coast. Sensing that just the opposite was true, the contagious character of the men and women of Space Command lifted Scotty's spirits. Instead of being depressed, a new sense of dedication and purpose was growing rapidly throughout the base. Most importantly, a battle plan began to take shape in Scotty's mind.

When Scotty arrived at his office, he was surprised to see everyone there thirtyfive minutes early. Everybody with the exception of Mary and Carolyn seemed to have questionable looks on their faces. Scotty realized that basically no one had any idea what the meeting was about. CAG, Bone, and JW had been going crazy securing the base, bringing the weapons online, and preparing the aircraft. But they had no idea just what this was about. Scotty went over to the snack table and bypassed the coffee and cookies. Instead, he munched down a brownie followed by a bottle of water. After wiping his face with a napkin, Scotty took his place at the table and stood behind his chair.

"I guess you are all wondering what you are doing here. I know that this has been a most trying day for all of us. I grieve as you grieve for the great loss of life of our countrymen. But as chance would have it, the asteroid may have presented us with an opportunity that we must discuss," Scotty began and then looked around the table to see their reaction to the bait he just dropped. Seeing that the looks on their faces changed from questionable to interested, he waited as a few of the individuals adjusted their sitting positions and then continued, "Ladies and gentlemen, we may just have located the base that the aliens have been operating out of."

Everyone around the table seemed to move around in their seats at this revelation. A few of the participants spoke up with questions, but Scotty remained still in order to let the news sink in for a few seconds and then continued, "Mary and Carolyn think that they have located their base. Their evidence is convincing, but before I commit this command to an attack, I am interested in what each of you think. I've asked Mary and Carolyn to present their evidence to you after which I want you to pick it apart and give me your evaluation. Mary and Carolyn, would you please..." Scotty then sat down and began to listen and reevaluate.

Carolyn crossed over to the DVD player and inserted a disc as Mary began, "As Admiral Scott was saying, we think that we have located the alien base. That is to say we may have the area in which their base is located. When the asteroid broke up, as you know, parts of it went into space, some came down on our earth, while others collided into the far side of the moon, or as you may call it, the dark side of the moon. Prior to this collision, Lieutenant Jones, shall we say, fulfilled my request to borrow for a period of time the deep-space telescope Taurus II. He was able to reposition it so that we could obtain a better view of the moon just prior to the impacts. My main interest was trying to determine what influence, if any, the pieces of the asteroid would have on the relative axis and gravitational pull of the moon on the earth.

"Before we discuss the possible location of the alien base, I want to give you a very brief introduction of the moon. It is a widely held belief that our moon was formed by material which was thrown into space when the earth, approximately a little over four billion years ago, collided with a massive object. This object could have been a planet, a monstrous meteor, or even a giant size asteroid much like DG122 that just passed by the earth. The material that was thrown into space became our moon. But the word moon may itself be misleading. The moon does not revolve around the earth, but rather, it revolves around the sun in accord with the earth's rotation. During the early *Apollo* missions to the moon, the astronauts brought back with them a wide variety of moon rocks for later study. After careful consideration, the scientists concluded that the moon rocks were very similar to the rocks of earth. By the way, the age of the moon rocks was dated at approximately a little over four billion years old. This is near to the age of the earth. So you can see the similarity.

"What I am getting at is the principle that the basic composition of the earth and the moon is relatively the same. The difference, of course, between the two bodies is that we have an atmosphere while there is no atmosphere on the moon. The moon is devoid of life, and the chemistry to establish life, as we know it, simply does not exist. There are two theories about the moon that I feel that I must discuss. The first is that when the earth collided with the heavenly body, four billion plus years ago, oxygen was also ejected as a result of the collision and became trapped in the material, which formed the moon. Is it possible? Yes, anything is possible. However, it is very unlikely. Over time, such trapped gas would more than likely have seeped up to the surface. Before someone points out that gas, such as oxygen, could remain trapped in the rock strata, I want to say that, that is also correct. In essence, there is absolutely no proof that oxygen exists on the moon, and correspondingly, there is no proof that it does exist.

"The second theory relative to the moon is that there are polar ice caps on both the northern and southern poles. This as well remains in the realm of speculation. What I am getting at is the fact that there is a possibility, and I repeat that word, possibility, that there is water to sustain and feed life. Also, there is an unlikely possibility that oxygen may also be present to aid in sustaining that life. I wanted to make this as clear as possible so that you may take those facts into consideration as you consider what Carolyn and I are about to tell you." Mary paused and nodded to Carolyn to start the playback of the DVD they had prepared.

Mary turned back around toward the group and continued, "What you are about to see are still pictures we took from Taurus II, put together in time sequence, and played back at sixteen frames per second. This film begins two minutes before the first pieces of the asteroid crashed into the far side of the moon and lasts through the event for a total of fifteen minutes. I would ask that you pay special attention to the right edge of the moon in about the upper-middle quadrant."

When the film first started, they saw the moon as it appears every day. Cold and desolate but a familiar friend. Suddenly, just where Mary had told them to watch, there was an explosion of some kind on the far side of the moon. The film portrayed a fireball reaching beyond the edge of the visible side of the moon and into space. As suddenly as it appeared, it disappeared. Then another fireball rose into space from the far side of the moon. This time though, one could readily see that a fire was raging since its flames reached beyond the edge of the moon. Eventually, the fire died out as it was no longer visible from the vantage point of the deep space telescope.

When the presentation was over, Mary continued, "As part of our investigation, Carolyn ran a spectrum analysis of the flames, and the results were quite surprising. I think it best to let Carolyn tell you the results of that examination." Mary exhaled deeply and thought to herself that her presentation was a bit harder than she anticipated. She was more than happy to let Carolyn finish.

Carolyn stood alongside of Mary and, after receiving a reassuring glance from her, began to talk, "As Mary was explaining, we decided to run an analysis of the flames because it was so unusual. One would expect an object that collides with another to produce some type of an explosion. Even a fireball, such as you saw in the film, is possible. But what piqued our curiosity was the duration of the flames. In a setting such as the moon, lacking an atmosphere, any flame should have died out within microseconds and not continue to burn. Therefore, as we all know, where there is air, or if you please oxygen, fire is a possibility, and if there is fire, then the objects that burn will produce trace gases. That caused us to examine the situation much more closely.

"Without going into very boring detail regarding how such an analysis is accomplished, I would like to skip forward to the results. But first, I would like to say the types of gases we found surprised the hell out of us. First and foremost, we found the presence of oxygen. The most important gas that was found, which would indicate the presence of a fire was carbon monoxide. Other gases we found which would indicate the presence of living beings were carbon dioxide, hydrogen sulfide, ammonia gas, hydrogen cyanide, nitrogen dioxide, sulfur dioxide, and hydrogen sulfide, to name but a few.

"What does this all mean? It means that there is a living presence on the far side of the moon. If the moon contained only oxygen, then that would be the primary gas we found, but many other gases were found which is inconstant with a purely oxygen combustion. For example, the presence of hydrogen sulfide in combination with hydrogen cyanide and some other gases indicate a fire coming from such items as a form of plastics, wool, and silk. Other gases found indicate the burning of organic material while some other gases indicate the burning or melting of some type of metal. Those facts taken together indicate the presence of living beings who may live in housing primarily constructed of some type of metal, dress in clothing not unlike our own, consume food, and utilize a type of plastic in either construction or service goods, such as a computer."

Carolyn paused and then looked around the table and concluded, "Ladies and gentlemen, the aliens are there. They obviously have been affected by the breakup of the asteroid and are more than likely weakened. This is the break we have been waiting for. It's time to pay them back."

"I take it that you are recommending we attack them before we even know their strength!" CAG declared, wanting to see just how convinced Carolyn was that the aliens were not only there but hurting.

"Yes, Captain Kendall. I would recommend such an attack. Let me explain. All of the science indicates that there was one hell of a fire on the far side of the moon. The emitted gases from that fire proves that the material that burned was put there by some sort of intelligent life. And it sure as hell wasn't us. At present, no country in the world has the ability or the finances to establish such a base," Carolyn replied in authoritative monotone voice.

Vinson spoke up next, "Carolyn, is there any possible way that the organic material that you spoke of can occur naturally on the far side of the moon?"

"No, Commander. The moon is devoid of life. It is a dry planet, with the possible exception of its pole. The surface is comprised of rocks and dust, a lot of dust," Carolyn replied with a kinder tone in her voice.

"How can we commit to an attack when there are so many unknowns?" Arty asked, with a smile on his face testing his girlfriend.

Carolyn, not to be out done, replied with an equally broad smile on her face, "Lieutenant, or is it captain now? I—"

Arty cut her off, the smile now gone from his face since she grabbed the upper hand. Somberly, he corrected Carolyn, "No, it's commander."

"Oh, I wasn't quite sure what rank you are since you seem to be out of uniform. As—" Carolyn replied but was interrupted this time by Scotty.

"Okay, children, let's get back on track!" Scotty ordered and then turned away, hiding his silent laugh.

"Yes, Admiral. I apologize," Carolyn replied, feeling her rebuke and then continued, "The question the commander asked was a fair one and deserves a fair answer. The question was to the effect how we could possibly commit to an attack of the aliens when there are so many unknowns. Anytime that adversaries take each other on, as we have done with the aliens, the only thing that one can be sure of is his own capability. Other than that, the entire spectrum of the forthcoming battles is unknown. Before battle, armies usually do extensive reconnaissance. But we do not have that luxury. If we were to send a recon patrol to the far side of the moon, the game would be up. Just keep one thing in mind. We have risen to the challenge and defeated the aliens in direct combat. Granted that they may have superior weaponry, but our weapons and our pilots and servicemen and women have demonstrated their ability. They have fought a superior enemy against superior odds and have defeated him. That then, Commander, is the reason why we should commit to a battle where, yes, there are unknowns. Have trust and faith in our ability, dedication, and human spirit. United with one purpose in mind, we will defeat the aliens," Carolyn concluded on an emotional level.

Arty very meekly answered, "Thank you."

"Carolyn!" Bone called out as he stirred in his chair and then announced, "Our hypersonic missiles are more than a match for the aliens. Added to that our aircraft equipped with lasers and plasma weapons, and we are one hell of a force." Bone looked around the table as he was talking and received agreeing nods from most of the people.

Looking back at Carolyn, he continued, "Given that our weapons are a match for the aliens, I do have a couple of concerns. First, if we were to attack, the battle would be on the far side of the moon. Therefore, Space Command would be out of contact for the duration of the battle. How would we know what was going on? Secondly, our pilots mostly depend upon an automatic weapons system. That system will acquire multiple targets, track those targets, and hold radar tracking until a missile destroys the object. Our pilots also have the ability to strafe any surface targets they may find. My question is this, is there any way to light up the surface so that our pilots can visually seek out targets of opportunity?"

"The answer to both of your questions is, yes. There are solutions to both problems. It's just a matter of applying current technology to the communications problem and new technology to the second problem. The second problem, by the way, was something I immediately started working on when I first arrived here and with the help of Doreen was able to bring it to completion. But first, let's talk about the communications problem. As you are all aware when a spacecraft or in our case the X-aircraft go to the far side of the moon, all communications are lost. This is due to the fact that in order to communicate, we must have some form of line of sight. We are not able to wrap communications around an object in space. In this case, the moon. What I would propose is two alternatives. The first alternative would be to have a fighter standoff within sight of the far side of the moon and earth. I know it is within the capability of the X-aircraft to remain stationary in space for thirty minutes. After that, the thruster fuels the aircraft carriers would be exhausted, and the aircraft would enter orbit around the moon. It would still have its forward engines, but it could not, if you will, hover.

"The second alternative is to have one of the fighters deploy a series of four satellites in orbit around the moon and adjust those orbits so two of the satellites are on the far side at all times. This would have to be done in conjunction with another satellite being placed in space within sight of the far side of the moon and earth. Its primary function would be one of a relay station. The second—" Carolyn began but was interrupted by Scotty.

"Excuse me, Carolyn. I agree with both of your alternatives. It would be great to utilize both at the same time. The X-aircraft or Pegasus, as Doreen christened them, should serve as a backup. But where can we get our hands on five satellites? We simply don't have the time to acquire them. If we attack, it has to be done immediately," Scotty inquired.

Carolyn looked over at Jonesy who just smiled back at her, thankful that she had to answer Scotty. Looking back toward Scotty, Carolyn answered in a nervous voice, "Admiral, we…ah…have…ah…" She took a breath and quickly finished, "The satellites, they have been tested and rigged to our communication frequencies." Exhaling a deep breath, Carolyn waited for the follow-up question.

"You mean we have five satellites just sitting around?" Scotty quickly shot back.

"Well, sir, we actually have ten," Carolyn replied, with a nervous tone in her voice.

"Ten! And just where did we get these from?" Scotty asked, afraid once again of the answer.

Jonesy stood up and motioned to Carolyn that he would answer. Turning toward Scotty, he began, "Admiral, do you believe in Santa Claus?"

"Lieutenant!" Scotty sternly answered.

Jonesy got the point and replied, "Admiral, an opportunity presented itself for us to intercept a shipment of low-orbit military communications satellites. They were built by an American company and were in the processed of being shipped overseas. We simply borrowed them for our future use should it become necessary."

"We seem to be, what you call, borrowing a lot things lately. What else have we borrowed of late?" Scotty asked, with a determined look on his face.

For the first time in his life, Jonesy was a little nervous in answering, "Well, Admiral, we have borrowed tanks, other military vehicles, a few airplanes, one train locomotive and some flat cars, and some new civilian automobiles. Oh, and we had to start an airfreight company to handle our acquisitions," Jonesy concluded and then as an afterthought added in a soft voice, "The airfreight company is turning a profit. In fact, we will be starting overnight delivery of business packages soon."

"Good, we can tell that to the judge at our trials. That will just make everything right!" Scotty replied in an angry voice. After exhaling deeply, Scotty continued, "Jonesy, when this is over, we are going to have a really long talk." Scotty dismissed the conversation and then returned to the business at hand. "Carolyn, would you please continue?"

Carolyn had momentarily forgotten what she had been talking about and then remembered. "Yes, sir. The second part of Captain Bone's question had to deal with the illumination of the target area. We have been able to develop an illumination system that will work in an airless environment. The system is based upon the use of magnesium as an illuminator. The light produced will illuminate a ground area of a five-hundred-foot diameter and a height of two hundred feet. We were able to tweak it so that the light remains constant and does not fade at the edge of the effective range. The system carries its own supply of oxygen and will burn for a period of fifteen minutes.

"The delivery package fits into a six-inch diameter rocket. It is capable of being delivered from a standard weapons pylon from the X-aircraft. The nose cone is shot directly into the surface. Upon impact, stabilizing legs are set onto the surface, and the light self-ignites. These can be delivered in clusters or aimed at a specific targeted area. I would recommend placing them in clusters at first, and then, if needed, we can go for specific areas. At present, we only have three hundred of these rockets, and they are on their way here right now as we speak," Carolyn concluded.

"When will they arrive?" CAG quickly asked.

"They are coming in on the afternoon supply run from our facility in Nevada. That's due to arrive within the hour," Carolyn answered.

"CAG!" Scotty called out. "Can it be done?" Scotty asked.

CAG thought for a long moment and then carefully answered, "There are a tremendous amount of things that can go wrong. If we go for an all-out attack, it will mean stripping our defenses as far as the X-aircraft go. But no matter what, it's a do-or-die situation. To answer your question, hell yea, we can do it!" CAG concluded.

Scotty then looked around the table and then asked, "Okay. The time for talking is over. If we are going to do this, we have go as soon as possible before they have time to stabilize their condition. We must begin planning the attack. I know how I feel, but I want to get your feelings on it. So let me see a show of hands. Those who agree that we should attack, please raise your hands," Scotty directed.

Scotty looked around the table and watched as hand after hand was raised in the affirmative. Doreen's hand was the last to be raised, and when she did so, Scotty winked at her. Doreen, though, sighed and lowered her eyes. Scotty then directed the group into planning for the forthcoming attack.

PLEASE SIGN ON THE DOTTED LINE

Tom and Lydia eventually began talking about their future. At the moment, it didn't appear to be much. Their home was gone. Their jobs were likewise awash in a sea of debris. But they had each other and counted themselves lucky. As the shadow of night passed into sunlight, no other survivors had arrived. In the morning, when Tom went to get two cups of coffee, he asked one of the workers if the survivors had been taken to another location. The man looked at Tom with a slight sad smile on his face and replied, "There are no other survivors in this area." The man then put his head down and busied himself with wiping down the coffee urns.

Before taking their morning shower, Tom and Lydia were taken into one of the classrooms of the high school. In this room was rack after rack of newly donated clothing. Tom picked out a pair of dungarees and a new open-necked blue golf shirt. Lydia picked out a full-length blue jean dress. Both then walked over to the underwear table and snatched up brand-new undergarments donated by a local department store. After showering and getting dressed, a representative of the Crisis Management Office of the federal government asked to speak with them.

To Tom and Lydia, this man was a savior. What he offered was a new life and the means to get started. Lydia, at first, wanted to go back to her new home. But after being reminded that the total area where their home had been located was destroyed, Lydia listened and mentally began planning their future. As the man from the federal government talked, Lydia envisioned a new home—a two-story farmhouse with a wraparound porch. Of course, there was a hanging glider for her and Tom to sit on and watch the sunsets with their baby cradled in Lydia's arms. There was also a wild flower garden and a small vegetable garden.

Lydia was still daydreaming when the subject of a no-interest emergency personal loan and mortgage came up. Tom asked Lydia what she thought. Lydia was lost to her dreams until Tom touched her and brought her back to reality. Lydia looked around and realized where she still was and thought to herself, *That dreams were indeed a better place.* By the time the interview was over, Tom and Lydia had a fifty-thousand-dollar check in their hands along with a promissory note of two hundred and twenty-five thousand to use for the purchase of a home.

Needless to say, Tom and Lydia were in shock. They went back to the gymnasium and sat back down on the cot. For the next hour, they talked about where they wanted to live.

That night, Tom and Lydia left the emergency shelter with only the clothes on their back. The Red Cross gave them a ride to Philadelphia airport where they boarded a plane to their new hometown. It was not totally unfamiliar to them as they had passed through the town a few years ago while on vacation. Lydia deep down didn't know why she wanted to settle there, but the hills and mountains of Vermont were beckoning.

Lydia came to live her daydream. They settled onto a twenty-five-acre farm. Lydia planted her wildflower and vegetable garden. The house was an old two-story farmhouse, but Tom had to build the wraparound porch. Five months later, Lydia gave birth to a beautiful baby girl. Together, the family swung on the porch glider. Over the next few years, their family grew with the addition of identical twin boys and another girl. The family was a loving one, where the interest of one was the interest of all. Together, they watched sunsets on the wraparound porch. Tom and Lydia never spoke of their experience to their children, and family vacations never included a trip to the seashore.

UH…DO WE HAVE TO HAVE A PLAN?

Looking directly at Mary, Scotty directed, "Okay, Mary. It's your show. Where are they hiding and how do we get there?"

Mary unfolded a large map of the far side of the moon and hung it on the wall. She then placed a small disc in the center of the table and pushed a button on a miniature remote control in her hand. Instantly, a 3D hologram of the moon rotated a foot above the table. Clearing her throat, Mary began, "From the photographic evidence we have, I believe that the aliens have probably established their base in either one of two locations. Both locations are in the equatorial region of the far side of the moon on the western side. This would correlate with the fire that we observed. In this area, there are only two locations that would offer a suitable landscape for the location of a base. The first one is Crater Hertzsprung and the second one is Crater Michelson." Mary pointed out the craters on the large map for all to see. She then pushed a button on her remote control, and two red dots appeared on the 3D image, showing the location of the craters.

Continuing, Mary spoke up, "The more likely of the two is Crater

Hertzprung. It's bigger, offers a smooth surface from which one could launch air operations, and at the same time, because of the height of the crater walls, be hard to detect. In other words, if you weren't looking for the base there, you simply wouldn't see it."

"Assuming that you are right, how do we get there?" CAG spoke up.

"I have taken the liberty of working out the navigational aspects of the flight and have them on individual discs for your use. The approach should be from east to west over the moon at an altitude of one thousand feet. I—" Mary replied but was interrupted by CAG.

"Excuse me. What is the travel time to the target?" CAG impatiently asked.

Mary looked through the notebook she had prepared and found the chart she was looking for. Referring to her work, she began, "Taking into consideration the fuel capacity of the aircraft and allowing for fifteen minutes of flight time over the target area at maximum speed, I determined the following time frame. The flight time from takeoff to rounding the moon is seven hours and twenty-one minutes. If the aircraft have, as I stated fifteen minutes of flight time at maximum speed over the target area, the return trip will be six hours and thirty-two minutes. I've prepared a notebook for you to use as you wish, with all of the data. Also, as I said before, I have all of the navigational information on discs ready for programming into the aircraft flight computers."

"Wow! That's a lot of flying for our pilots," CAG declared to no one in particular.

Carolyn spoke up at this point and offered a solution, "I have a proposal. It's a little radical, but it will work. During the flight to the target, it is possible to have half of the pilots asleep and the other half will be awake. If an emergency happens, it will be possible to awaken the sleeping pilots in as little as four seconds. On the return trip, the pilots who were awake during the first half of the trip will be put to sleep and awaken just prior to their entry into the earth's atmosphere. The pilots who were asleep for the outward-bound segment will be awake for the return trip." Carolyn paused for a second to catch her breath.

Scotty took advantage of the silence to make his opinion very clear.

"I don't want my pilots feeling the effect of sedation just before going into battle. That will be suicide," Scotty declared and awaited a response.

Carolyn lowered her head, took a deep breath, and gathered her thoughts. Inwardly, she knew that if the attack was to work, it was necessary that the majority of the pilots arrive at the moon refreshed. Carolyn admitted to herself that her plan might present a risk, but it was a minimal one. Reaching into her briefcase, Carolyn withdrew two things. The first looked like a square computer chip about half the size of a playing card and almost as thin. The second item looked like a large Band-Aid. Where the gauze would normally be, one of the computer chips took its place. Holding up the computer chip, for all to see, Carolyn began her explanation.

"What I have in my hand is a sample of a medical device that is implanted in patients. Generally, it is known as a biometric sensor and has a variety of applications. For example, in heart patients, the sensor is embedded under the skin in the upper-left chest area. Since the electrical field in the human body powers it, the device allows the patient to be free from repeated needles or the taking of oral medications. The sensor itself monitors the heart and, when needed, will dispense proper amounts of medication directly into the bloodstream. The sensor is capable of containing a one-month supply of medication before it needs refilling. In diabetes patients, the sensor is likewise implanted in the body. The sensor will measure blood sugar levels every four minutes and then, if needed, will dispense the proper dosage of insulin. As you can imagine, these devices have saved many lives."

"What I am proposing is this." Carolyn put down the sensor and picked up the Band-Aid with the device attached and continued, "The biometric sensors will be preloaded with two different drugs. The first drug to be used is a very light sedative, which is equal to one of the PM headache tablets that are sold over the counter. This will be administered as soon as the aircraft are headed toward the moon. The estimated time for the effectiveness of this drug is roughly five hours. Therefore, the effects of the drug will have worn off well before they round the moon. To be on the safe side, when the aircraft are near the moon, the second drug will then be administered. This second drug is undiluted caffeine. It is a very small dosage, about seven milligrams. It's not enough to cause any hyperactivity, but it will wake up the pilots and put them into an aware state. I think—" Carolyn continued but was interrupted by Scotty again.

"I don't know much about the application of drugs. And I especially don't particularly like the idea that we are depending on drugs to fight a war. I know that we are on unproven ground with this whole thing. But I agree that our pilots need to be refreshed before going into battle, and I agree with the sleep sedative. I've taken them myself, and I don't have a problem with them. But the effects of caffeine worry me," Scotty stated, seeking reassurance that the caffeine would not impair the pilots.

Carolyn turned toward Scotty and carefully framed her response before answering. "Admiral, it's like drinking about three cups of coffee. Not enough to impair the thinking process but enough to wake the dead," Carolyn answered and received light laughter with the comment about the dead. It was just enough to break the tension in the room.

"Okay, I'll agree to it," Scotty responded, still a little unsure of the plan but added one condition, "Provided the caffeine dosage be reduced to say two cups of coffee."

"Admiral, I really think—" Carolyn began to reply but was interrupted by Scotty again.

"It's two cups. No more discussion!" Scotty snapped back.

"Yes, sir." Carolyn responded in a faked submissive voice, trying to hide her smile. Silently she shouted yes to herself. All along, Carolyn had no intention of loading the sensor with the equivalent of three cups of coffee. She was going to load it with the equivalent of two cups of coffee from the beginning but knew that she would receive an argument. So Carolyn asked for the equivalent of three cups and hoped that Scotty would then order the equivalent of two cups of coffee.

VAROOOOM!

V ICTORIA WAS STANDING BEHIND HER desk looking out of the window across the parking lot to the twisted road leading up to the observatory. She was anxious for Dustin to return. She wasn't sure where he had gone, but in her mind, Victoria knew what he was busy doing. It had been two hours now since he had left. After staring out of the window for more than fifteen minutes, Victoria became frustrated and began to tum away when she heard the distinctive rumble of a motorcycle. Turning back around, Victoria scanned the road, and then she saw it. A motorcycle was definitely headed toward the observatory. She watched the bright light from the headlight of the motorcycle as it followed the twisted turning road and came ever closer. When it was less than a mile away, Victoria could not contain her excitement any longer and ran outside. Inwardly, she knew that Dustin was the driver of the motorcycle. It was, after all, part of their dream.

Victoria reached the end of the parking lot just as the motorcycle pulled in and stopped in front of her. Anxiously, Victoria waited as the driver carefully took off each of his leather gloves one at a time and placed them on the gasoline tank. He then reached up and loosened the chinstrap that secured his full-face helmet. Dustin then took the helmet off in one swift motion. Unable to contain herself any longer, Victoria put her arms around Dustin just as he was standing up.

"Dustin, I love it. Where did you get it? What kind is it?" Victoria hurriedly asked as she let go of Dustin and stepped back to admire the motorcycle.

Dustin stepped off the motorcycle and, as he unzipped his leather jacket, answered, "It's pure American iron. Definitely not a 'rice' bike. One hundred percent American made. It's called a Softail. And guess what? I bought you one too!"

"Get out! I don't know how to ride a motorcycle," Victoria replied as she stepped back with a broad smile and overwhelmed with excitement. Then it dawned on her, and Victoria demanded, "Since when do you know how to ride a motorcycle? I thought that we were going to take lessons together."

"I wanted to surprise you, so I took some lessons on my days off and went for the license. I bought you a bike just like this one and signed you up for the same lessons," Dustin answered, now believing that Victoria was a little mad at him. Knowing that he had to turn the situation around, Dustin added, "Think of it as an engagement present."

Victoria was stunned. All of a sudden, their dream of riding motorcycles had become a reality. She could only smile as she imagined herself riding a motorcycle alongside Dustin, down some open road in the middle of nowhere.

Walking to the back of the motorcycle, Dustin opened one of the saddlebags and withdrew a waist-length leather coat. Handing it to Victoria, Dustin explained that the coat was actually an important piece of safety equipment. Victoria eagerly put it on as Dustin went to the other saddlebag and took out a helmet and another pair of leather gloves.

Victoria took the gloves and put them on as she asked, "Do you think the helmet is going to fit?"

"Of course. That's what the string was for," Dustin replied as he reached up and put the helmet over her head. As Dustin adjusted the chinstrap, he gave her some quick instructions on how to ride as a passenger on a motorcycle. Satisfied that she understood, Dustin sat down on the motorcycle and pushed the start button. Reaching backward, Dustin put the passenger pegs down and motioned for Victoria to get on.

Once Victoria felt comfortable on the seat, she put her arms around Dustin and asked, "When do I get my bike?" But she didn't receive a reply. Dustin pulled the clutch in and applied pressure to the gearshift pedal, putting the motorcycle into first gear. He slowly let out the clutch as he applied the accelerator, and together, they rode away. All thoughts of the tragedy that took place that day disappeared in the small cloud of dust the motorcycle left behind as it raced through the countryside. Dustin and Victoria were together, and they felt true freedom for the first time in their lives. They had each other and from this day forward; that was all that mattered.

SO WE DO HAVE A PLAN

F OR THE NEXT TWO HOURS, Scotty drew upon the ideas of those in the room to put together a battle plan. The plan depended upon the number of X-aircraft that they could put into the air. CAG and Doreen explained that there were one hundred and twenty-six aircraft available. However, ten of those aircraft had not yet completed their flight testing for airworthiness. Scotty, however, accepted the risk and decided that those ten aircraft would remain behind and serve as a rear guard should some alien craft survive the attack and head toward Earth. Doreen and CAG again reminded Scotty that the aircraft couldn't really be counted on, but these were desperate times that required desperate measures. Scotty needed all the airworthy aircraft to fly the mission.

Scotty divided the remaining one hundred and sixteen aircraft into twenty-nine squadrons consisting of four planes each. The squadrons were assigned alphabet designations. For example, the first squadron was designated Alpha while the second squadron was called Bravo. These designations continued through the alphabet until the letter Z. Due to the fact there were three more squadrons than there were letters of the alphabet, the twenty-sixth squadron was called Zulu Alpha. The twenty-seventh squadron was designated Zulu Bravo while the twenty-eighth squadron was named Zulu Charlie. The last squadron was, by default, called Zulu Delta.

It was the Zulu squadrons which were to lead the attack. Two of the aircraft in Zulu Alpha were outfitted with small stationary satellites that they would release two hundred miles above the surface of the moon. Both of those aircraft would then station themselves within sight of the earth and relay radio traffic from the earth to the moon and vice versa. The other two aircraft of Zulu Alpha would act as fighter escort for the squadron. The men of Zulu Alpha were to be the first into battle and the last to leave.

Zulu Bravo squadron would arrive on the far side of the moon at the same time as Zulu Alpha. Their mission, however, was to sweep across the surface of the far side of the moon with their radar at an altitude of seventy-five feet and drop the flares that Carolyn had designed in order to light up the target areas. They would also provide the initial intelligence assessment of the alien base and defenses. The pilots of the squadron would be disappointed that they would be unable to carry any offensive or defensive weapons beyond their wing-mounted fifty-six caliber guns. Therefore, it was decided that Zulu Bravo squadron would leave the area and return to earth as soon as their mission was completed.

Zulu Charlie and Delta were designated as the fighter aircraft that would carry the airborne plasma-beam weapons. Their job was to maintain a presence above the far side of the moon and destroy any alien aircraft that may be present. The big fear was the possibility that there may be Z-2 aircraft present, much like the one that Admiral Laffey's flotilla tried to explore.

The battle plan required that exactly four seconds after Zulu Bravo squadron crossed to the far side of the moon, Alpha squadron would do the same and begin their bombing run. Each subsequent squadron would then likewise cross to the far side of the moon at four-second intervals. In case the aliens were able to launch their Z-1 aircraft, the plan allowed for every other squadron to enter the air battle.

Scotty ordered that CAG, who was to remain behind, be in overall charge of running the battle. The overall distance to the moon didn't matter as far as radio transmissions were concerned. Long ago, in the fledging days of Space Command, priority was given to instant communications over vast distances. With current capability, there would only be a one-second delay from the time a signal was transmitted to when it was received. Should communications be knocked out, the commander of Zulu Alpha Squadron, Captain Beth Foster, would be in charge and direct the battle as she determined. She was a personal friend of Scotty's from his days as an aviation cadet, and he could think of no one better qualified.

Relieved that the battle plan was finalized, Scotty directed the attention of the group toward other matters. He was concerned about the rescue craft that he knew were under construction. If a flyer should become stranded in space, Scotty wanted to be able to rescue the pilot. Turning toward Doreen, Scotty was momentarily stunned when he saw the look on her face. It was one of sadness and worry. He wanted to ask her what was wrong but knew that this was not the time.

Almost struggling for words, he asked, "Doreen, what is the status of the rescue craft development?"

Doreen cleared her throat before answering and in almost a strained voice replied, "Admiral, one of the rescue aircraft is nearing completion. But there is no way it can fly. The main engines have been installed and tested. However, the thruster nozzles have not arrived from the manufacturer yet. The reason for the delay is because the employees had shut the plant down for almost two months because of a labor dispute."

Barely displaying anger in his voice, Scotty commented, "So because of a labor contract and the reluctance of a company to increase the pay of its workers, there is no rescue vehicle. That's just great!" Scotty contained himself and then asked, "Is there any possible way to stage a rescue if one of our pilots should be stranded? I don't suppose we have one of those tractor beams handy that the space science-fiction shows always have."

Carolyn spoke up and answered, "Admiral, Doreen has been hounding the manufacturer for months to get the parts. We simply don't have them, and we can't get them." Carolyn glanced over at Doreen and smiled and then turned back toward Scotty and added, "And, no, we don't have a tractor beam, but we are exploring the possibility. We are probably years away from even understanding the elementary science of such a thing. And, no, there is no real way to rescue a stranded pilot."

"I know that you both have been working very hard, and I appreciate your efforts. I apologize for being short with the both of you." Scotty looked at Doreen and Carolyn and smiled. In return, he received a warm smile back from both of them.

Turning back toward the group and then looking at CAG and then at Mary, Scotty asked, "Mary, when is the earliest we can launch the attack?"

Mary looked at the clock on the wall, made a few calculations, and then responded, "The best time for the aircraft to take off will be in three hours and twentyseven minutes. I know it will still be daylight, but it will mean less flying time overall for the pilots."

"CAG!" Scotty called out.

"We'll be ready, Admiral!" CAG proudly answered and then added, "Pilot briefing will be in two hours. That gives us plenty of time to work out the details and program the navigational computers."

"Bone!" Scotty almost shouted in an excited voice.

"Aye, sir. We're ready now. All aircraft should be finished arming within the next thirty minutes. I will confirm with the other bases," Bone replied.

"Mary, you'll work out the rendezvous point and set the flying sequence," Scotty ordered rather than asked.

"All accounted for, sir," Mary replied and began to gather up her material and nodded to CAG as if to say "Let's get to work."

Scotty then turned toward JW and ordered, "JW, take care of our home!"

"All locked down, and my Marines are ready for anything, sir!" JW replied in a confident voice.

"Good! Ladies and gentlemen, thank you. You are dismissed," Scotty replied and watched as everyone left the room.

Doreen tried to linger, but Carolyn insisted that they leave and help Mary out with the navigation discs. Scotty watched as Doreen left and saw her turn back and look at him with a soft smile on her face. And then she was gone.

"Beverly!" Scotty called out.

Beverly turned around and walked over to Scotty. "Yes, Admiral."

"Beverly…I…just want to say—" Scotty struggled for words.

"Don't worry, Admiral. Everything will be fine. I don't suppose it would do any good to remind the admiral that his place is here and not up in space?" Beverly tried to reassure him and remind him of his main duty.

"No, it wouldn't. I just want to say thank you for everything. You are one hell of an executive officer," Scotty replied.

"Thank you, sir. Admiral, if I may from a woman's perspective. Make sure you bring that cute butt back here safe and sound. Give 'em hell, Admiral!" Beverly answered and then kissed Scotty on his cheek.

ALWAYS TAKE THE TIME TO SMELL THE FLOWERS

WITH LESS THAN FORTY-FIVE MINUTES until the briefing, Scotty sought out the solitude of the atrium. As he meandered the pathways thinking of the upcoming mission, his thoughts also turned toward Doreen. Scotty promised himself that if he survived the battle, he was going to take Doreen away for a weekend to some desolate beach where they could be alone. Once there, over a candlelit dinner, he would propose. Catherine, the ever-present romantic and mother, had given Scotty the engagement ring she had worn and three generations of Scott women before her. Reaching into a zipped pocket of his flight suit, Scotty withdrew the ring and held it up. He realized the tradition that went along with the ring, but he couldn't help wondering if Doreen would like it. *The ring was truly beautiful as light reflected off of the large diamond*, Scotty thought to himself. It was then that Scotty resolved to offer her the ring and at the same time he would buy her another engagement ring, which she could call her own.

While holding the ring, Scotty's attention was drawn to a budding rose bush off to his left. Walking the few steps over to the roses, Scotty admired their beauty, and another thought crossed his mind, *In a world of such simple beauty, why does there have to be war? Why doesn't right triumph over evil? And why do people have to die to prove that evil shouldn't exist in a world that is gentle enough to create a rose?* These were questions that Scotty couldn't begin to answer.

Leaning forward, Scotty put his nose up to the budding roses, closed his eyes, and deeply breathed in their fragrance. As he exhaled and took another deep breath, a vision of Doreen's smiling face appeared before his closed eyes. Holding the sweet smell of the roses within himself, Scotty dreamed of a life with Doreen. Slowly, Scotty exhaled and opened his eyes. Standing straight up, Scotty watched as two black butterflies with orange spots danced with each other as they flew among the flowers. Scotty wanted to remember the scene in front of him on the long flight to the moon. As he stood there trying to take mental pictures of the garden and the gentle butterflies, he heard Doreen call out, "Michael!"

Turning back around to look up the garden path, Scotty quickly returned the ring to the chest pocket of his flight suit. As Doreen turned the bend in the path and came into view, Scotty pulled the zipper closed on the pocket and reassuringly padded the pocket to make sure the ring was secure.

"Hi, Doreen!" Scotty answered as he walked toward her. The expression on Doreen's face was both warm, obviously irritated, and concerned at the same time. Scotty didn't allow her to say a word. He rushed into her arms, and they kissed a long, soft, passionate kiss as he held her strongly in his arms.

All the muscles in Doreen's body relaxed, and her worried emotions melted away as she felt warm and secure within his arms. When their lips parted, she could only utter, "I love you!"

Scotty looked deeply into her eyes and answered, "I love you, Doreen. And I always have from the first moment I saw you."

Not to be outdone, but coming from the heart, Doreen answered, "I fell in love with your photograph in the admiral's office and from the endless stories he would tell about you. And now, well, let's just say that I will love you until time itself doesn't exist."

Still in each other's arms, they kissed again. Their bodies melted into each other as they, for an instant, became of one spirit. Their thoughts and desires were the same. Their love was of each other, and their passion only grew. But the moment had to end.

Separating, they walked down the path with their arms around each other. Doreen buried her head in his chest and felt a circular object pressed against her forehead. She was about to ask what it was when Scotty spoke up, "You know I have to go."

"No, I don't, Michael," Doreen softly answered and then added "I don't want you to go!" in a much stronger voice.

Scotty guided Doreen to a park bench recessed into the garden. Here, flowers and large ferns on three sides of the bench surrounded them. Together, they sat on the bench facing each other, their legs touching, and their hands intertwined in each other's. Scotty again looked deeply into her eyes and felt a total and consuming love for this woman.

Doreen was his life, and he never wanted to leave her side. But he inwardly knew what had to be done. "Doreen, I love you more than my life. Since we met, you have awakened within me feelings I never knew existed. I want nothing more than to be with you, be part of you, and walk through life with you."

Scotty noticed a tear leave Doreen's eye and begin its tender journey down her cheek. Releasing his hand from Doreen's, Scotty reached up with his index finger and gently lifted the tear from her face. He then closed his eyes and placed his finger upon his lips and kissed the tear. As he reopened his eyes, his tongue softly took the moisture of the tear within himself. Scotty just wanted to forget the present and live within Doreen, but passion was a victim of reality.

Grasping Doreen's hands again, Scotty continued, "The world has suddenly became a warm and beautiful place. I hear the birds sing, and for the first time in my life, I can see a flower and wonder at its beauty. You have given me life, and I love you with a deep passion that only grows with each passing moment. But something threatens what is yet to be. I have to go. I will not let anything stand between us and threaten our life together. These aliens must be stopped and now is the time to do it. I want nothing more than—"

Doreen interrupted Scotty. "But, Michael, your job is here. Not flying off to the moon. You're in command of this base. All of the people here depend upon you. They know that your job is to stay behind and direct the battle. Not to go flying off and fight. They need you. Hell, I need you. Please, Michael, stay here and direct the battle. We need you alive and safe!" Doreen pleaded, knowing that it was useless.

Looking downward, searching for an answer and then looking up, Scotty answered her plea, "Doreen, I don't want to go, but I have to go. I'm a pilot in the United States Navy. A soldier's job is not to fight or kill. Hell, nobody likes to kill. Our job is to seek out and keep peace. That peace is now threatened by a force we don't know or understand. We know that they do not seek peace, but rather, they murder, no, slaughter innocent women and children. They don't care who or what you are. We have something they want, and they will stop at nothing to get it. They have to be stopped. We have an opportunity to hopefully stop them or put a really big dent in their plans. My job is up there. I will not ask anyone to do something that I wouldn't do myself. I'm not trying to prove something, it's simply my job," Scotty concluded and once again released his hand from Doreen's and touched her face as he added with a smile, "Now, wish me luck!"

Tears came to Doreen, and she softly cried. Withdrawing a tissue from his pocket, Scotty wiped away her tears. Doreen reached out and hugged him and told him once again of her love for him. Scotty likewise expressed his love. Together, they stood up and walked up the path. Doreen knew that it was time to let go of her love, if only for a moment of cosmic time.

When they reached the top of the path, near the exit, they kissed once again. Scotty said goodbye, and Doreen wished him luck. Doreen stood there and watched as Scotty went through the exit and disappeared but not before he turned around and smiled at her again. When Scotty was gone, Doreen remained standing there for a few seconds. But she couldn't hold the inevitable back. Doreen ran back down the path, sat on the bench they had just left, and cried. Not a cry of sadness but a cry of complete passion and hope.

IF IT'S CALLED A BRIEFING, WHY DOES IT TAKE SO LONG?

B EFORE THE BRIEFING BEGAN, CAG noticed that, while the main seating area was occupied by the pilots, other members of the base, who were off duty, stood alongside the walls of the room. Clearly, everyone wanted to attend the meeting. Some people were even standing outside the doorway, hoping to hear what would be said. CAG decided that it would be best to broadcast the briefing throughout the base. That way, everyone would feel that they, too, were in some way a part of the attack. The briefing was also simulcast to the other bases where additional X-aircraft would take off and rendezvous with the main fighter force from Colorado.

Scotty sat among the other aviators and listened for the next thirty minutes as CAG conducted the briefing. When CAG, joined by Carolyn, talked about the sleep cycle on the way to the target, they received a warm reception. Most of the pilots were relieved that they would get some sleep on the long flight. CAG further explained that each aircraft would be monitored, and, if need be, its course could be altered remotely from Space Command as the pilot slept.

When Mary joined CAG and, in detail, explained the actual mission that would be flown, the room became tomb-like. No one stirred in his or her seat nor was any comment made. If a pin were to drop, it would have been heard across the room. Every one listened intently, knowing full well that their lives might depend on a single fact or statement.

Scotty, however, was distracted for a moment as Doreen entered the room. His eyes followed her as she walked to the front and took her place at the briefing table. She still looked worried but somehow better and a bit more relaxed. Scotty hoped that the briefing would snap her out of it but knew that it wouldn't.

When the briefing was almost over, CAG did what Scotty had hoped he wouldn't. CAG called upon Scotty to say a few words. Scotty stood up from his comfortable seat and walked to the front of the room. At first, he paced back and forth, looking into the faces of as many pilots as he could. Returning to the center of the room and facing the pilots, he began, "As I look out among you, I see the look of raw courage. I also see a look of anger, and anger, as long as it is tempered and I can see that you have done so, is a powerful motivator. I also see a room of dogged determination. If you combine all three, well, that's a winning combination. There is one other thing that I see as I look out among you," Scotty raised his voice and added, "I see the best, most feared pilots in the entire universe. There is not a force in all of the galaxies and in all of the worlds in those galaxies that can defeat us. We own the skies, and we own space." Loud cheering at this point interrupted Scotty as the pilots were getting psyched for the mission.

Momentarily taken aback by the show of emotion, Scotty waited for the cheering to subside. Motioning with his hands for them to quiet down, Scotty continued, "As we go into battle, I want each of you to remember those people in Brazil. I want each of you to remember the men and woman of the HMS *Illustrious*. I want each of you to remember comrades-in-arms who paid the ultimate sacrifice so we could carry on the fight for another day."

Scotty paused for a moment and then cleared his throat. He began speaking softly but quickly raised his voice once again as he said, "These aliens, no, I mean these Bastards, have invaded our world and murdered. They have killed indiscriminately men, women, and, worst of all, defenseless children. And if that wasn't enough, they butchered the bodies of the victims in Brazil. Why? Because they want to be able to breathe our air, enjoy our sun, and live as we live. They don't come in peace. They come to kill. They want to reach down and kill all humanity so that they can take our earth. I say enough is enough. We have an opportunity right now and right here to give them a big kick in the ass. And that is just what we are going to do. We are going to blow their alien ass right off the moon and wherever else we may find them. We will carry the fight to them until the word alien becomes extinct in the languages of the earth. Let it be known, from this day forward, throughout the galaxies that Earth and the men and women of Space Command are not to be fucked with. The official designation of our squadrons is Raptor. You are named after the most vicious, the most cunning, and most feared animal that ever walked the earth. Today, the Raptors stalk space for the first time. Space, as we know it, will never be same again. From this moment until the end of time, space belongs to the Raptors. Good luck and good hunting, Raptors!" Scotty concluded his speech, which was met with loud cheering throughout the base.

In the briefing room, everyone stood up and cheered mixed in with whistling and catcalls. Then, suddenly, the chant of "Raptors! Raptors!" resonated throughout the room and into the hallway.

I DON'T WANT NO STINKING DIAPER!

CAG FOUND IT DIFFICULT TO regain order in the room. He let the chanting continue a little while longer, but CAG knew that the flights had to be airborne within thirty minutes otherwise the attack timetable would be off.

Regaining control over the crowd was not easy, but persistence paid off. Speaking in a very loud voice, CAG offered, "There's not much I can add to what Admiral Scott said. But I do want to first remind you all that it's a long flight. So hit the head. The Ds are available just outside the head for those who want them." CAG choked up a bit and then in a cracked voice hollered out, "I want to see each of your ugly faces back here. And you better take damn good care of my aircraft."

Swallowing hard, CAG hesitated and then hollered out, "Man your aircraft. Give them hell, Raptors!" CAG's last comment was met by more cheering as the pilots filed out of the room.

CAG stood there watching as the finest group of people he had ever known went off to war. Carolyn walked up to him and asked what the head was. CAG calmly replied that the word head was Navy slang for the bathroom.

"And what is a D?" she then followed up.

CAG looked at her for a second and then with a straight face replied, "Ds are diapers. It's a hell of a long flight. You wouldn't want them pissing in their flight suits, would you?" CAG turned around and walked away, laughing to himself as he heard Carolyn softly answer, "Oh, I never thought of that."

CAG kept walking and laughing.

OKAY, WHO TOOK MY AIRPLANE?

W HEN SCOTTY EMERGED ONTO THE hangar deck of Space Command, his first thought was that something was wrong. He was used to what could only be described as organized chaos on the hangar deck of an aircraft carrier as aircraft were readied for their ride to the flight deck. Once on the flight deck of an aircraft carrier, another ballet of organized chaos took place as the aircraft received their flight safety check and were moved into position for takeoff. But Scotty had never seen this many people milling around aircraft.

There were literally hundreds of people performing thousands of tasks. Everyone was busy doing their jobs. This was an effort unparalleled in military history. Nothing was being left to chance. Everything was checked and double-checked from the hypersonic missiles to something as simple as making sure the cockpit glass was clean.

As Scotty walked over to his aircraft, well-wishers must have slapped him on the back at least a hundred times. Scotty greeted each crew member individually by name or rank and wished them well. He accepted their cheers of "Good luck! Good hunting" or "Fly safe!" for what they were, a show of affection for the man in charge.

Approaching his aircraft, Scotty looked around for Doreen but couldn't find her. He was hoping she would come and say goodbye. But it was clear that she didn't want him to go and probably couldn't bring herself to say goodbye without crying. Scotty figured that Doreen didn't want him to see her upset, which in turn would have upset him.

Upon reaching his aircraft, Scotty paused as he was about to climb the small ladder up to the cockpit. It was then that he heard Doreen's voice softly call out, "Michael." Scotty turned back around, and Doreen was standing there staring at him. They didn't speak. After a moment, Doreen put her arms around Scotty, and he around her as they kissed. They didn't hear the whistling and cheering that erupted from those around them at first. For a whisper of time, they were in their own world, and no one else existed. Once they broke their embrace, Scotty noticed that Doreen's face was beet red. But who cared? Scotty reached over and kissed her again. Doreen inwardly knew that Scotty had made the right decision and breaking their kiss told him so. Scotty didn't speak but simply hugged her.

Doreen, once again, felt a round object pressed against her forehead as she rested her head on Scotty's chest. She was about to ask him what was in his pocket when Scotty kissed her on the top of her head and softly spoke, "It's time."

Lifting her head up, Doreen looked into Scotty's eyes and felt a deep feeling of love wash over her. "I know," Doreen almost whispered as she reached up and kissed Scotty on the cheek. Scotty passionately looked at his love and then turned around and climbed into the cockpit of his aircraft.

Once seated, Scotty looked down at Doreen with a smile on his face and mouthed the words "I love you." He then winked at Doreen as he put his flight helmet on. Within seconds, an aircraft-towing tractor pulled Scotty's plane to the flight elevator. In a few minutes, Scotty found himself parked on the runway.

After receiving permission to start the aircraft engine, Scotty looked up at the darkening sky and wondered what awaited him. His thoughts were broken by the flight controller who gave him permission to take off. A minute later, Scotty was airborne heading for the rendezvous point.

Doreen watched as Scotty's aircraft was taken to the surface. She stood there until it disappeared out of sight. She then ran into the control room to watch on closed circuit television as he took off. Beverly noticed the sad look on Doreen's face and walked over to her. Trying to offer words of encouragement and to snap her out of the state of mind she was in, Beverly offered, "He'll be just fine. There isn't a better pilot in the Navy than the admiral. But right now, I need you to help me run this base. We can't let him down. The admiral has a job to do, and so do we."

Doreen looked at Beverly and instantly knew that Scotty had chosen her well. There wasn't a finer executive officer anywhere. Doreen nodded to Beverly and turned around. In a firm voice no one had ever heard before, she ordered, "JW, lock this base down. Close all fire doors and station your men. Have damage control and firefighting teams on standby in case we are attacked. From this moment on, we are at war."

JW was taken aback a bit but quickly recovered and answered, "Yes, sir…err madame."

"CAG," Doreen continued, "Get an air cap (fighter planes patrolling the air space over the base) of F-18s up. I want them armed to the teeth."

"Yes, madame!" CAG quickly replied and relayed the order to his second-in-command.

"Bone! Bring the defenses up to full standby," Doreen ordered. Without waiting for a reply, she turned toward Beverly and winked. She then turned her attention to the fuel the Navy runs on, a large cup of coffee. Doreen and every member of Space Command who wasn't flying had the hardest job in the world; they had to wait.

IS IT NEW JERSEY OR NEW JOISEY?

A T THE VERY MOMENT THAT Scotty and his fellow pilots were taking off, Governor-Elect Patricia Greenfield was facing the hardest moment of her governorship. She found herself standing in front of a large group of reporters and television cameras. The group was assembled on the Garden State Parkway in the area of Toms River, New Jersey. It was at this spot that the force of the wave was broken due to the elevated height of the highway.

Patricia Greenfield approached the podium and grasped the two edges with her hands. Her normal coolness was gone. This was a news conference Patricia Greenfield wished she never had to give. How do you explain the unexplainable? How do you put into words the scope of the devastation?

"Good evening," she nervously began and then continued, "We are gathered here at the very spot that the tidal wave was stopped. It was here that the force of the wave was broken. Because of this highway, perhaps, millions of lives were saved. However, on the other side of this highway, millions upon millions of lives were lost. We cannot adequately comprehend the extent of the loss of life nor shall we ever be able to comprehend the extent of the devastation. We come here to honor those who have fallen. Collectively, their memory shall live through the pages of history. Individually, we will never forget what has happened here. Together, as a nation, as a state, and as Americans, we will dedicate this land, no, this resting place, in their memory."

Pausing for a moment, Patricia Greenfield took a sip of water. *Ironic,* she thought, *water is needed to sustain life and at the same time water took so many lives.* Looking out over the crowd that had assembled, she spoke of the future plans for the shore area.

The area north of Belmar, New Jersey, would be restored. An extensive search would be conducted for the recovery of victims. The same would be true for the area south of Brigantine to Cape May. For the area in between, there would be no recovery of victims. There would be no reconstruction. There would be no seashore. The task of recovery and reconstruction in this area was impossible.

The governor explained that a seawall would be constructed along this devastated area. The land from the seashore to the Parkway would be covered over with ten feet of soil. The area was to become a national park administered by the federal and state governments. Monuments would be erected to commemorate the loss of life. A museum would be built so that future generations would remember.

"The sun will once again shine over this area. Grass will grow tall and green. Trees will grow and spread their branches. Flowers will bloom and fill the air with their fragrance. Small animals will come to know it as home. Life will return," Gov. Greenfield pledged.

WHAT, NO CREAM AND SUGAR?

S COTTY AWOKE WITH THE TASTE of coffee in his mouth. *Somehow, Carolyn left that little fact out of her briefing,* he thought. Looking forward out of his cockpit, Scotty could just make out the silhouettes of the aircraft flying in front of him. Twisting and turning in his seat, Scotty tried to look behind him to check on the other aircraft. Since Scotty was the flight leader of Foxtrot squadron, the majority of the attack aircraft were flying to his rear. Barely able to see behind, Scotty was tempted to use the radio to check on the other aircraft. But radio silence was being maintained until the lead squadrons crossed to the dark side of the moon. As an alternative, Scotty thought about turning on his radar to check on the location of the other aircraft, but if he did that, the aliens might pick up the signal.

Not able to check on the other aircraft, Scotty, like the other waking pilots, reached into his flight bag for something to eat. Taking out a foil food packet, Scotty pulled the zip tab and lifted the attached straw. Sucking on the straw, Scotty swallowed a pasty mixture of vitamins and peanut butter with a slight trace of jelly. He then put the empty food packet back in his small flight bag and eagerly withdrew a foil container of water. After a quick drink, Scotty went to work. He ran a diagnostic check of the aircraft flight and weapons systems. Satisfied that all was well, Scotty, like all the other pilots, anxiously awaited the rest of the flight to the far side of the moon.

He constantly checked his mission clock. One part of the clock gave the total elapsed time of the mission so far. The other side of the clock counted down the time until his aircraft would cross over to the far side of the moon. When the clock read ten minutes, Scotty ran another diagnostic check of the aircraft, and, once again, all the results were normal. For the next few minutes, Scotty thought of Doreen and the life that awaited them. Unconsciously, Scotty felt the pocket on his flight suit that held the engagement ring. Touching the outside of the pocket, Scotty felt the reassuring shape of the ring through the material. For a moment, his finger lingered on its outline. His thoughts were interrupted when he heard a chime go off in his headphones. Reaching forward, Scotty turned off the two-minute warning alarm.

Attempting to shift his weight in the seat, Scotty could feel the adrenaline flowing through his body. His heart began to beat a little faster as every nerve in his body became alert. Scotty's body was preparing for battle. At the same time, Scotty's mind was on full alert. In seconds, he reviewed the battle plan and prepared his mind for battle. Scotty knew that modern air battles usually last for only seconds, and every one of his senses must be operating above capacity.

With twenty-four seconds to go, Scotty's aircraft became alive. His radar system turned on, his radio crackled, and his weapon system became active. CAG had decided to activate all the aircrafts systems remotely on the slim possibility that, in the excitement of a pending battle, a pilot would forget to tum on his radio, radar, and weapons. The results of such an oversight could spell disaster for a wayward pilot.

Immediately, Scotty's radio came to life as the lead attack groups called in to Space Command and each other. "Zulu Alpha, crossing to the dark side and beginning run," came the first call. Then a series of reports came in very quickly, "Zulu Bravo, beginning flare drop." "Zulu Delta, taking position."

"Shit!" an excited voice radioed in and then continued, "Zulu Delta, there's three, repeat, three Z-2s up here. Make that four about two hundred miles from the deck (surface of the moon)."

"Zulu Charlie, engaging! We have the two on the left. Over!"

"Copy Zulu Charlie. Zulu Delta attacking two on the right."

Often in times of heated battle, the best-laid plans go asunder. It was not because the plan wasn't well-thought-out but rather a battle plan has to be adjusted to fit the circumstances of the moment. CAG was faced with such a dilemma. The original plan called for squadrons to attack at four-second intervals over the alien base. It was anticipated that there might be Z-2 aircraft in the vicinity, but it was hoped that they would appear after the initial attacks were underway. The immediate presence of Z-2 aircraft was not a good sign. No one really knew their exact capabilities beyond the fact that they acted as a type of aircraft carrier for the Z-1 saucer aircraft. Now before initial reconnaissance reports could be obtained about the possible presence of an alien base on the moon, Zulu Charlie and Delta were engaging Z-2 aircraft. CAG knew that they needed help, and now.

Alpha squadron was charged with the mission of starting the initial bombing run on the surface of the moon and providing an overview of what the additional squadrons were going to face. CAG knew that this initial assessment would have to wait. Pushing the handheld transmit button on his communications headset, CAG ordered, "Alpha, Charlie, and Echo squadrons, disengage surface attack and join Zulu Charlie and Zulu Delta. Do not acknowledge. CAG out!" A few seconds later, CAG again pushed his transmit button, "Bravo, you're now lead. Provide recon report. CAG out!"

"Bravo leader. Beginning attack run. Will provide recon. Over," came a quick response.

"Zulu Bravo. Over flying area. They're right where they should be. Both craters active. Repeat both craters active. Target one, base is damaged. Wreckage everywhere. Crater two looks intact. Z-1's beginning to lift off. Repeat, Z-1's lifting off. I make it on the scope twenty-three unfriendlies lifting off. Bravo, out." A few seconds later Zulu Bravo transmitted again, "Bravo, did you copy?"

"Copy that. Crater one and two active. Z-1's lifting off," a calm but quick reply from the leader of Bravo squadron.

CAG heard the report from Zulu Bravo squadron and was thankful. Zulu Bravo should have been on their way out of the area after deploying the flares, but when they heard the radio traffic about the Z-1s, they performed the initial recon. *Thank God for quick thinkers*, CAG thought to himself and made a notation to put them in for a citation and the Navy Air Medal. It wasn't every day that fighter pilots in unarmed aircraft fly back over a target to provide a reconnaissance report while alien saucers are taking off.

The four naval aviators of Zulu Bravo squadron would never stand proudly before the men and women of Space Command to receive their medals and have them pinned on their dress uniforms. After Zulu Bravo squadron gave their report, three Z-1s chased them and fired upon the fleeing aircraft. In an instant, all four aircraft of Zulu Bravo squadron were vaporized into the void of space. No one except the members of Space Command would ever know of their bravery and sacrifice.

BUT, MOMMY, I KNOW MY ABCS

Zulu Charlie squadron immediately maneuvered into attack formation and targeted one of the Z-2 aircraft with concentrated firepower. All four aircraft fired at the same time perpendicular to the Z-2. The intense firepower from the attack aircraft penetrated whatever defenses the Z-2 had. Within a few seconds, the Z-2 exploded in a short but spectacular display of fireworks. It broke up in the vastness of space and tumbled toward the moon. Zulu Charlie squadron made it safely through the debris and once again went into attack formation on their other target. This time, the Z-2 put up a defense. As the aircraft of Zulu Charlie closed on their target, the Z-2 fired, and immediately, one of the attacking aircraft was vaporized. The remaining three pilots banked their aircraft to the right and then came up under the Z-2 aircraft. Together, they fired at the same time and danced their fire down the length of the craft. The plasma-beam weapons seemingly acted as a can opener. The Z-2 aircraft began to split apart down its underbelly from the fire of Zulu Charlie squadron. As the Z-2 came apart, it was engulfed in flames. One could readily see the bodies of aliens falling along with the tumbling parts of the massive aircraft.

Zulu Delta squadron began their attack on the third Z-2 at the same time Zulu Charlie attacked their first target. The commander of this Z-2 was a little more prepared than his counterparts. When Zulu Delta approached their target, Z-1s were being launched from the Z-2 aircraft. The squadron leader of Zulu Delta ordered his aircraft to realign on the target and concentrate their fire on the area where the Z-1 aircraft were emerging. When they were lined up for their attack run, the squadron leader then instructed his pilots to hold their fire until they were approximately one thousand yards away. As they were approaching the target, four Z-1 saucers came right at Zulu Delta squadron on a collision course. All of a sudden, the saucers banked their aircraft to the left and flew by Zulu Delta squadron as if they weren't there. Amazed that the Z-1s didn't challenge them, Zulu Delta pressed on with their attack.

When they were within range, the leader of Zulu Delta yelled over his radio, "Fire!"

Together, Zulu Delta fired their plasma-beam weapons at the same spot. Within three seconds, they broke off their attack. Two of the aircraft pulled to the right as the other two pulled to the left. As they pulled away, they could plainly see that the Z-2 was exploding internally as pieces of the alien craft broke off in a veil of flames. As if on cue, once Zulu Delta squadron was safely away from the Z-2, it exploded into millions of burning pieces.

Four Z-1 aircraft immediately set upon the two aircraft of Zulu Delta squadron that pulled to the left. The Z-1 aircraft began firing at them wildly, hoping for a lucky shot. The two pilots of Zulu Delta tried their best to come around and face their adversaries, but when three more Z-1 aircraft set upon them, the game was over. Both of the X-aircraft exploded when shot after laser shot hit their aircraft.

The element of surprise was lost when the remaining Z-2 aircraft continually launched her Z-1 saucers. The remains of Zulu Charlie and Zulu Delta formed up together to attack the last remaining Z-2. Together, they were five planes strong against what the radars were now showing as an enemy force of over one hundred and twenty saucers. But they pressed their attack. As they closed the range, ten saucers fell in behind them and lined up the X-aircraft in their weapon sights.

At the same instant, Alpha, Charlie, and Echo squadrons arrived on the scene and lined up to attack the saucers chasing Zulu Charlie and Zulu Delta.

HEEELLLOOO, DOWN THERE

As the air war was waging in space, Bravo squadron was beginning their attack run on the surface. "Bravo leader. Attacking crater one!" came the call to Space Command.

Everyone in Space Command seemed to look up at the computer monitor bank on the wall. They had followed the little yellow triangles, which symbolized the X aircraft, move against the little red triangles, which symbolized the Z-1 saucers. When three of the four blue triangles, which symbolized the Z-2 alien craft, disappeared from the screen, a loud cheer went up. Now the room was dead silent as suddenly the air war intensified, and Bravo squadron was beginning the assault on the alien bases.

Bravo squadron lined up abreast across the crater. Each aircraft targeted the structures within their zone. They expected to come under some defensive fire, but nothing happened. When they were within view and their targeting computers had confirmed missile lock, they attacked. Sixteen missiles slammed into the alien base. One missile hit the saucer hangar, causing it to explode into a fireball that rose six hundred feet above the surface of the moon. In seconds, they finished their initial attack and were on their way to crater two to unleash another barrage.

The leader of Bravo squadron called in, "Crater one aflame, multiple hits. Proceeding to second target."

Eight seconds later, Delta squadron attacked crater one. When they began their attack run, two Z-1 saucers crossed their flight path but were quickly destroyed. Arriving at crater one, they unloaded an additional twenty missiles into the already burning and exploding base. They could have easily made another pass at the base, but Bravo flight was coming under fire. Delta squadron pressed onward to crater two.

CAG decided to change tactics once again. He realized that crater two had to be neutralized as fast as possible while at the same time more aircraft were needed for the air battle. Before Scotty's group began their attack, CAG issued new orders, "Foxtrot, Hotel, Juliet, and Lima, attack crater two. Golf, India, Kilo, Mike, November, Oscar, and Papa, join the air war."

CAG would skip crater one for the time being since the reports indicated that, in all probability, it was incapable of posing a threat. CAG did what he had to do; he needed aircraft to fight the air battle, and, in seconds, twenty-eight X-aircraft would arrive and hopefully turn the tide.

Bravo squadron in the meantime lined up for their attack. When they were two miles away from their target, the sky lit up like a Christmas tree. The aliens were firing their defensive weapons wildly at the approaching planes. Their aim was accurate enough to destroy three aircraft of Bravo squadron. The squadron leader of Bravo received a crippling hit to his fuselage. All his electronics were out as well as his weapons systems. He knew that he was going to die but didn't want to do so in vain. He steered his aircraft toward a building on the alien base. The aliens saw him coming and tried to shoot him down, but their aim was off. At twelve hundred miles per hour, he crashed his aircraft into the top level of what appeared to be, not only the tallest structure on the base, but what looked like the main building.

The aircraft exploded on contact with the structure. Within seconds, the building began to explode and continued to do so downward. What the flight leader hit was an oxygen production facility. As the oxygen caught fire, it raced through the facility's piping, causing explosions wherever they led. The whole base erupted in fire with massive explosions.

Delta squadron made use of the chaos of the explosions and unleashed their own style of a living hell. They carefully lined up their targets and began their attack. Their missiles slammed into the base, causing even more destruction. Once they had completed their attack, Delta squadron flew off to join the air battle.

The alien base began to crumble, but a few Z-1s were struggling to become airborne. The defensive weapons of the base were all but gone. A few of the laser weapons fired after the fleeing fighters, but Delta squadron was out of effective range.

Scotty heard the reports from Delta squadron and decided to try a maneuver that he called the Compass Rose. It involved fighter aircraft attacking from the four points of the compass. One aircraft would first fly north to south over the base, firing its missiles. The next aircraft would fly east to west, firing off its weapons. Almost at the same time, another aircraft would fly west to east over the alien base attacking. The last aircraft of the squadron would then fly south to north over the base, firing at whatever targets were still available. All the fighters would then form up west of the alien base and sweep the target together firing at anything that remained.

Scotty began his north to south track and fired off his missiles at whatever structures looked somewhat intact. As he finished his ground attack, he edged his aircraft upward and almost immediately in front of him a saucer crossed his path. Taking advantage of the situation, Scotty locked his missile on the saucer and fired. He watched as the fire trail of the missile raced toward the saucer. In a few seconds, the hypersonic missile found its target and penetrated the saucer. Almost immediately, the saucer blew up in front of Scotty. He banked his aircraft to the right so as not to fly through the debris.

However, Scotty winced as he felt something strike his aircraft. At first, Scotty's aircraft seemed normal, but something was wrong. Quickly scanning his instruments, Scotty noticed that he was losing fuel at an alarming rate. The rest of Scotty's squadron finished their attack and left crater two in almost complete devastation. What wasn't burning was exploding. There was wreckage everywhere. What saucers were on the surface were destroyed, and their pieces scattered around the surface of the moon. Bodies of aliens were scattered everywhere. They apparently preferred to suffocate to death rather than die in the explosions and fires that consumed their base. The Compass Rose maneuver broke the back of the alien ground defenses.

Instead of sweeping crater two for a final blow, Foxtrot squadron formed a protective shield around Scotty. Safety procedures dictated that a disabled aircraft should try and make as much altitude as possible in order to establish a slowly degrading orbit around the moon. Scotty was just able to achieve orbit when his power ran out. The members of his squadron flew circles around Scotty as he entered high orbit around the moon. When they approached the air battle area, his squadron formed a V pattern in front of him and shot their way through the saucers that happened by. It was then that the call went out, "Scotty's down. Repeat, Scotty's down. Gather on him."

Scotty watched helplessly from his cockpit as saucers and X-aircraft chased each other around the sky. There didn't seem to be a pattern to the battle. Most of the squadrons stuck together and hunted down their prey. The saucers, however, seemed to be acting independent of one other. The aliens couldn't seem to coordinate an attack.

UH-OH

WHEN DOREEN HEARD THE TRANSMISSION "Scotty's down!" it was if a cold knife went through her heart. She dropped the papers she was holding and stared at the speaker on the wall. Beverly ran over to Doreen and placed her arm around her. Trying to comfort her, Beverly whispered, "I know he's okay. People like Scotty are different. If his hands were tied, he would try and kick you to death. He's a survivor."

Doreen had tears in her eyes and didn't really hear what Beverly said. Then a transmission came in, "He's alive. Scotty's plane is dead in the sky. He lost his fuel."

Doreen looked into Beverly's eyes and stuttered "There's no…no… rescue…craft!" and then fainted. Beverly caught Doreen before she hit the floor and called for a medic.

Beverly's attention quickly shifted when someone in the communications room called out, "Four saucers headed in. Their trajectory is directly at us. ETA four minutes."

Beverly sat Doreen down in a chair and pressed the transmission button on her communications headset, "CAG, talk to me."

"Four F-18s up. Two X-aircraft up. Will engage in three minutes. Over," CAG responded with a report and then turned his attention back to the ongoing battle.

"Bone!" Beverly next called out.

"Plasma cannons active and tracking enemy!" Bone quickly replied and then crossed his fingers.

Beverly watched the display as the saucers approached. They had half expected something like this for a long time, but it had never materialized. Now, what they had feared was happening. A direct attack by the aliens. Beverly glanced over at Doreen and watched as a medic held smelling salts under her nose. Almost instantly, Doreen made a face and coughed. She then opened her eyes and looked around. Beverly winked at Doreen and then turned her attention back to the impending attack.

"Fighters engaging!" a voice called out.

The vast communications room went dead silent again. According to the display, the aliens were approximately two hundred miles away and closing on the base fast. The display then showed the F-18s moving on an interception course directly at the aliens. In the comer of the screen, the X-aircraft were moving toward the alien ships from behind. Everyone stood or remained seated as if they were statues as the tension within the room heightened.

"Locked on targets!" came a radio transmission from the flight of F-18s.

"Tracking…locking on target!" a voice called out from the X-aircraft.

"Engaging the—" a voice began to speak but abruptly stopped as the people in the communication room saw what looked like straight lines come from the saucers aimed directly at the F-18s. The very next thing they saw were four large circles of light where the F-18s had been. People looked at each other, wondering what the circles of light represented before reality caught up with their thought process. Everyone in the room suddenly realized that the flight of F-18s had been destroyed without having fired a shot at the aliens.

The saucers were now less than one hundred miles from the base when they abruptly moved in the opposite direction to face the oncoming X-aircraft. That is, all except one. When the saucers reversed their direction, a fifth blip appeared. It was the same deception the aliens had used in the Pacific. Four alien saucers were now five.

This new saucer did not turn with the other four. Instead, it continued toward the base at over eight hundred miles per hour. The four saucers that were turning to face the X-aircraft began firing their weapons wildly. But this time, it was they who were surprised. As the saucers came out of their turn, they ran smack into a missile each. The pilots of the X-aircraft didn't hesitate or flinch when their fellow pilots were killed. All four saucers exploded within microseconds of each other in a spectacular display of pyrotechnics.

"Target acquired and fired upon!" Bone called out over the intercom.

The two plasma cannons fired at the oncoming saucer but missed. The saucer lowered its altitude and flew at the base at almost fifty feet above the ground. Onward, it came hugging the ground. The plasma cannons locked onto the target; however, the saucer was too low to the ground. As the saucer came over a small rise just west of the base runways, one of the cannons got lucky. One shot hit the saucer, but it didn't explode. Instead, the shot tore through its body, affecting the flight controls.

The saucer first rose slightly in the air and then plunged toward the earth. It crashed onto the number one aircraft elevator, which brings aircraft to the runway from the hangar deck of the base. Upon impact, the saucer exploded and burned. If it had hit the ground thirty feet in any other direction from where it crashed, the base would have just felt a small rumble or ground tremor.

But when it crashed onto the aircraft elevator, the impact caused a chair reaction. The elevator absorbed most of the impact, but the hydraulics, which powers the elevator, failed. Slowly, the elevator slid downward, allowing the burning remains of the saucer to fall onto the hangar deck. The burning debris first fell on the floor of the hangar deck, but some pieces fell onto an aircraft that was fully fueled and armed. The aircraft then exploded, spreading fire and death into Space Command.

THE BIGGER THEY ARE, THE HARDER THEY FALL

THE FIVE AIRCRAFT REMAINING FROM Zulu Charlie and Zulu Delta squadrons were about to begin their attack run on the last remaining Z-2 when they started to receive fire from the closing saucers. The shots were missing their aircraft, but sooner or later, the aliens would zero in on them. The flight leader was about to direct the other aircraft to break to the right when his radio crackled. Listening carefully, he heard Alpha, Charlie, and Echo squadrons calling him to let him know they were in pursuit of the saucers.

Alpha, Charlie, and Echo squadrons came in behind the pursuing saucers. Carefully, they closed the distance between themselves and the saucers. All at once, each squadron fired off four missiles and banked their aircraft off to the right. In one second of time, all the ten pursuing saucers blew up.

Zulu Charlie and Zulu Delta closed on the Z-2, and, together, all five aircraft fired their plasma cannons at the Z-2. The Z-2 tried to change its course and avoid the plasma fire, but it was simply too big and slow. As the Z-2 turned ever so slightly, the plasma fire ripped into its fuselage. Fire from one of the aircraft scored a lucky hit, penetrating the weapons storage area. The result was catastrophic for the aliens. When the weapons storage area ignited, the Z-2 disintegrated within moments.

Unfortunately, the attacking remains of Zulu Charlie and Delta were not far enough away from the area. As the Z-2 exploded, the shock wave it produced in the immediate space around it caught the fleeing fighter aircraft. When the shock wave hit the aircraft, they were thrown wildly around and collided with one another. Zulu Charlie and Zulu Delta squadrons no longer existed.

When the last Z-2 was destroyed, several more X-aircraft squadrons arrived to aid in the air battle. For a few more minutes, havoc seemed to reign in the space above the moon as X-aircraft targeted their prey. However, in rapid order, the alien saucers were destroyed through the determination and bravery of the men and women who came so far to fight for what was right.

I WOULDN'T LOOK UP
IF I WERE YOU

A S THE AIR BATTLE DREW to a close, Whiskey squadron arrived on the far side of the moon. They were closely followed by X-Ray and Yankee squadrons. Their assignment was to finish off the remains of the alien bases in craters one and two. After each squadron made their first pass, the alien bases were completely destroyed. Just for safety's sake, CAG ordered them to fire all their weapons into the bases. After Whiskey squadron made its second bombing run on the craters, it became apparent they were only destroying the destruction.

Radar scans confirmed that the alien bases were limited to the surface of the moon. There was no evidence that the aliens attempted to tunnel into the moon and hide part of their bases. CAG thought it logical, at least he would have done it, that they would hide some of their saucers under the surface. But the radar scans proved otherwise.

Concluding that it was alien arrogance to only construct bases on the surface, CAG decided that X-Ray and Yankee squadrons should go ahead and continue to entirely annihilate the remains of the bases.

While X-Ray and Yankee squadrons fulfilled their assignments,

CAG ordered some of the other squadrons to begin a grid-like search of the far side of the moon. He had a feeling that not all the aliens chose to die that day. And he was right. Every once in a while, as the aircraft searched the surface, a saucer would suddenly come out of hiding and attempt to flee. But the odds were against the aliens. Five times saucers tried to escape. But the members of Space Command thwarted their escape plans. Each time a saucer took off, it was quickly dispatched to alien hell, or so the pilots hoped.

Time and fuel, however, were beginning to run low. It was time for the aircraft to depart and head back to Earth. But there was a problem. Scotty's aircraft had lost all its fuel. He was adrift in space in a slowly decaying orbit around the moon. No one wanted to leave him. At the same time, however, no one could stay with him. Everyone tried desperately to come up with a plan to rescue Scotty, but there was no solution. CAG issued the order for the squadrons to begin the trip home. No one acknowledged it. He ordered them again to leave the moon, and again, his order was met with silence.

SMOKING LAMP IS LIT

THE HANGAR DECK WAS AWASH in flame and smoke from the aircraft that exploded. Like a snake trying to leap out and strike its victim, tongues of fire leaped into the air and across the cavernous area. Within seconds, a second aircraft exploded and spread its death and misery. And then a third aircraft caught fire.

An automatic fire suppression system self-activated when it detected the fire. The main fire suppression system was a clean agent system. This system utilizes a gas to extinguish the fire. When applied, the gas can seep into every nook and cranny where fire could possibly be. After the system puts the fire out, the gas, as well as any poisonous gases produced by the fire, can then be ventilated out and fresh air pumped in.

JW didn't panic. As soon as the fire from the crash of the saucer fell onto the hangar deck, alarms went off. He immediately scanned the fire control board and confirmed that the clean agent system was functioning. But the fire was continuing to spread. Knowing that the fire would be contained to approximately one quarter of the hangar deck, because Doreen had ordered the fire doors closed before the attack, JW felt a little relieved. What was in the back of his mind, which he didn't want to deal with at this point, was the fact that people had died during the explosion. According to the workboard, twenty-seven aircraft technicians had been in the area preparing the fighters for flight.

As an added precaution, JW decided to pump foam into the hangar area to help extinguish the flames. Once that started, he ordered his firefighting teams to attack the fire. As a last resort, he had the option of closing steel doors that cover the aircraft elevator opening when the elevator was down on the hangar deck. Once this was done, JW could then pump the oxygen out of the area and suppress the fire that way. That, however, was his last option and one he really didn't care to use. There was always a chance that someone may still be alive. If the oxygen were to be pumped out, then whoever was alive would quickly suffocate to death. Just for insurance, JW pressed the button controlling the steel cover. He was relieved when the status light turned green.

Counting to ten, JW pressed the button, which partially closed the cover.

TRAIN FOR HOME DEPARTING ON TRACK 3

S COTTY KNEW WHY NO ONE acknowledged CAG's orders. The last thing in the world a pilot wanted to do was to leave a fellow pilot in distress and unprotected. Pilots would rather give up their own lives than abandon another pilot. Realizing he had to do something to get everybody moving, Scotty keyed his microphone and began to speak over the pilot communication band, "This is Scotty. Repeat, this is Scotty... We did one hell of a job today. You all deserve a well done for your actions. And it is truly a day that will live in the memories of those who may have to fight this enemy in the future. Make no mistake about it. Today, you saved the lives of countless people and a way of life as we know it. But now it is time for you to return home. Our base and the people of Earth need your skills and your aircraft." Scotty felt a little uneasy laying it on so thick, but he had to get them moving. "I need you back home in case we have to fight this fight again, and I kind of expect it will happen.

"So, ladies and gentlemen, let's form up as per the orders and depart for Earth. It has been my honor to be associated with all of you. I have lived well, for I have been associated with the best of the best. I wish you well and a safe flight. You are truly America's elite, and right now, she needs you. So, Raptors, let's get moving immediately."

Scotty looked out the front of his cockpit and saw most of the aircraft gathered in front of him. Still, no one seemed to be moving. No one acknowledged his order. And then he saw it. One group of four aircraft began moving in formation. They flew in front of Scotty. As they passed, each pilot wagged (rocking their wings first to the left and then to the right) their wings as a gesture of respect. It was a pilot's way of saying goodbye.

Scotty sat still in his cockpit and accepted the salute each of his pilots displayed to him. When all the squadrons had departed for home, Scotty was still not alone. The other three pilots of Foxtrot squadron were right where they wanted to be, right beside their flight leader. Scotty talked to them over the intercom and thanked each of them for their loyalty, knowing full well that the bonds pilots forge with each other run much, much deeper than words could every express. Finally, Scotty ordered each of them individually to get going home.

One by one, each pilot departed reluctantly. When Scotty was alone, he took stock of his situation. No fuel for his hungry engines. His instruments were running on battery power, and that wouldn't last too much longer. When the power ran out, the heaters would stop functioning, and he would freeze to death. There was no rescue aircraft available. On the plus side, Scotty figured that he had eight hours of oxygen left, and, who knows, something might happen.

Scotty knew what he had to do. He desperately wished he was with Doreen but inwardly knew that was not to be. He wanted to say goodbye but didn't know how.

"Command," Scotty radioed.

"Pirate, this is CAG," Came the call back.

"How we doing?" Scotty asked.

"Scotty, we took a big hit. We have a fire in the hangar bay. The Marines are fighting it now and will have it under control shortly," CAG replied, feeling a bit foolish talking to Scotty as if he was in the room with him.

"Glad to hear that the fire will be under control. But were there any causalities?" Scotty asked, worried more about the men and women of Space Command than the base itself.

"We lost some people. Don't know how many yet though," CAG answered.

"Say, CAG, is Doreen busy?" Scotty anxiously asked.

"She's right here, Scotty," CAG replied and took his headset off and handed it to Doreen.

Doreen put the headset on and called out, "Michael!"

"Hi, Doreen," Scotty replied, his voice cracking a bit and then continued, "Are you okay?"

"No, you're not here!" Doreen replied with tears in her eyes.

"I know," Scotty quickly answered and imagined a mental picture of himself kissing Doreen. Trying to hold back his own tears, Scotty said, "Say, Doreen…I…I—" Emotion overcame Scotty, and he paused.

"I…know, Michael. I love you too," Doreen finished his thought as the tears rolled down her cheeks.

CAG then took the headset off Doreen as she sat down and buried her face in her arms and cried. "Admiral, listen up. We think we have a plan. There's an old Russian space station up there. Jonesy has hacked their system and is able to power it up and move it to your location. It has a supply of food and oxygen on board. Enough for at least three months. Jonesy and Carolyn are working on a plan now to get you into it. They mentioned something about the station having a flexible docking collar that will fit around your canopy. I'll let them explain that later. Right now, we have to do a couple of things. In order to stretch the power you have, we need you to turn off as much as possible. I want you to power everything down, even your radio. We also need you to save as much air as possible. No unnecessary talking and sit as still as you can. No moving around. It's the best we have, Scotty. Jonesy and Carolyn say that we can do this, and I believe them. So shut down your systems and let's go into a still mode. We will call you back in three hours. Turn your radios back on at zero one hundred (1:00 am). Do you copy?"

As CAG was talking, Scotty began to shut down his systems. As he reached for the switch to shut off his radar, CAG heard Scotty call out, "Ah, shit!"

Quickly, CAG asked, "What? What's wrong?"

"Search radar detected two saucers heading my way. I am shutting down. Maybe, they won't see me among all the debris up here. They might just think I'm a piece of space junk. Scotty, out," Scotty answered as he shut off all the electronics in the aircraft and waited.

SOMETIMES YOU HAVE TO SAY "WHAT THE HELL"

WHEN THE ATTACK ON THE alien base began, Arty and Vinson, like everyone else who was off duty, gathered together in the mess hall to follow the battle. CAG had made arrangements for the radio traffic between the fighters and the base to be broadcast in the mess hall so that everyone could feel like a part of the attack. He also had television monitors set up to depict what everyone was seeing in the communications room.

No one ate anything. A few people drank some coffee, but the buffet table that the cooks had set up went untouched. Like everyone else, Arty and Vinson sat on the edge of their seats, their attention riveted to every word they heard. While they sat there, suddenly, the entire base vibrated. It wasn't a very noticeable shudder but rather more like a ripple as the shock wave from the crashed alien saucer spread throughout the structure. Arty looked at Vinson, and they shrugged their shoulders at each other, not knowing what had just happened. They then turned back around, looked at the television monitors, and listened as the fighters directed each other toward the aliens.

Suddenly, the fire alarm went off, and everyone ran out of the mess hall to their fire duty stations. (On a military base, each person, whether on duty or off, has a fire station he or she must attend to.) Arty and Vinson found themselves alone in the mess hall. Since they usually operate away from the base, they were never assigned a fire station. Vinson walked over to the telephone hanging on the far wall and dialed the communications room. After learning what had happened, Vinson shouted to Arty, "A saucer hit the hangar deck. It's on fire. Let's go!"

Arty and Vinson ran up the stairs and reached the command area of the hangar deck. JW was busy directing the firefighting effort. He was openly discussing the option of closing the steel roof of the hangar deck and pumping out the oxygen. Arty spoke up and asked if anyone might be alive.

JW turned toward Arty and replied, "Yeah, there is that possibility. But if we don't stop this fire now, it could spread. And then a lot of other people might die."

Vinson grabbed Arty by the shirt and pulled on him. As they ran out of the room, Vinson turned back around and shouted, "Give us five minutes. And don't close that damn roof until then!"

Arty and Vinson ran into the equipment room and donned firefighting coats, helmets, communications gear, and oxygen tanks. Vinson grabbed a canvas bag and stuffed it full of pony tanks (a small cylinder with a mouthpiece that contains twenty minutes of oxygen). Together, they entered the burning hangar deck.

When they entered the area, Arty and Vinson were stunned by the scene. Fire was everywhere. Fire crews were dragging hoses and extinguishing the flames where they could. Firefighting foam was pouring onto the deck from nozzles mounted on the walls and the ceiling. In most cases, the foam smothered the fire only to have it reignite as heat and flames continued to spread. Vinson and Arty began their search for survivors. Walking along the wall, they immediately found one person. But he or she, they couldn't tell, was dead and burned beyond recognition.

After a few more minutes of searching, they came across another person or rather the person found them. As Vinson was walking by, he felt something grab at his leg. Bending over and pushing the foam away, Vinson uncovered a technician covered with debris. Arty and Vinson worked quickly to remove the aircraft parts covering the man's lower body. Both of the man's legs were broken, and he was slightly burned on the abdomen. Vinson quickly reached into the canvas bag and withdrew a pony cylinder. Placing the mouthpiece in the man's mouth, Vinson turned the knob on the top of the cylinder. Immediately, the man's lungs filled with fresh oxygen.

Vinson then motioned for Arty to grab his legs. Vinson took hold of the man's arms, and together, they carried the man to safety. As they were walking toward the safety hatch in the fire doors, a stream of fire suddenly blocked their way. Together, they ran through the fire and entered the hatch with their cargo. Laying the man gently down, they watched as medics tended to his wounds. It was a good feeling for them. They had saved a man's life.

Arty and Vinson then reentered the burning hangar. In the next few minutes, they pulled out an additional three people. Two other rescue teams had also pulled out four more survivors. Then JW sounded the Klaxon horn. Hearing the piercing sound, the rescue units and firefighters left the burning hangar and sought safety.

Vinson and Arty went to the triage center. Here, they grabbed a cold bottle of water and sat down on the floor against a wall. Arty unbuttoned the fire coat he was wearing and opened his water. Upon taking a sip of water and putting the bottle down on the floor next to him, a medic came running over.

"Let me look at your legs!" the medic declared.

It was then that Arty felt pain, real pain, for the first time. He looked down at his legs and almost went into shock because of what he saw. His pants were burned away from the kneecaps down. The calves of his legs were black. The skin had erupted and split open, exposing the tissue underneath. That tissue was blood red and, at the same time, yellow. Arty clenched his teeth in pain as Vinson grabbed his arm as a gesture of offering support.

"Give him some morphine. Damn it!" Vinson screamed.

The medic, however, continued to work on Arty's legs. When the medic finished washing the burned areas, he reached in his bag and withdrew a needle. The medic then withdrew a vial of morphine and filled the needle. Sticking Arty in the arm with the needle only caused him some more pain. In a few minutes, Arty became groggy and fell asleep. The medic had Arty put on a gurney and marked for evacuation to a burn hospital. Vinson couldn't understand how Arty could have been burned and not react to it. The medic explained that Arty was probably operating on pure adrenaline because of the work he and Vinson had been doing. He simply didn't feel the pain.

Vinson walked alongside Arty as his gurney was pushed to the far side of the hangar deck. There, a helicopter waited for him, its prop spinning. As soon as Arty was secured in the helicopter, the last remaining aircraft elevator began to ascend toward the surface. Vinson jumped onto the elevator and into the helicopter. Vinson would not let his friend go to a strange place without him. Through their ordeal, they had become brothers.

As the helicopter with Arty and Vinson on board took off, the large steel doors of the damaged elevator closed. Within a few minutes, the fire died as a result of the loss of oxygen. JW continued to pour foam into the damaged part of the hangar as an added precaution. After venting the area for thirty minutes, JW ordered the cleanup work to begin again.

OKAY, WHO'S THE WISE GUY? WHO DID THAT?

S COTTY SAT PERFECTLY STILL IN his cockpit. There really wasn't much he could do, but he wasn't going to wait for the aliens to find him. He had one thing going for him, however slight it may be. Scotty had some cannon rounds left. However, if he shot them off, the explosion of the shell, which propelled the shot, would then force a recoil and would move his aircraft backward.

Scanning the space in front of his aircraft, Scotty strained his eyes in an attempt to view the two saucers. He didn't have to wait long, for soon he observed them coming toward him, both at the same altitude. Instinctively, his hand grabbed the control column, and his index finger gently touched the trigger for the cannon. Scotty decided that if the saucers made a move to attack him, he would use his cannon anyway.

Ever so slowly, the saucers inched toward Scotty. They apparently didn't think he was alive. As the saucers came within a hundred yards of Scotty's aircraft, he stretched his index finger and brought it back down to rest on the trigger. Scotty was going to fire at the one saucer directly in front of him when it was within fifty yards of his aircraft.

Suddenly, a bright light appeared as one of the saucers shined a spotlight on his aircraft. Scotty pressed himself against the back of his seat and turned his head to one side. He kept one eye open to watch the aliens. Scotty again stretched his index finger and let it rest on the trigger. This time, though, his finger pressed halfway down on the trigger.

Scotty carefully watched the saucers edge ever closer. He was about to shoot when two arcs of blue light streaked over his aircraft and impacted on the alien saucers. The two saucers exploded in a spectacular shower of sparks and were instantly gone. Scotty at first couldn't believe what had just occurred. One second, he was preparing to die and the next second, his enemy was gone. Straining to look behind him, Scotty couldn't see anything. As he turned back around, off to his right no more than fifty feet away, was a very sleek-looking silver-colored aircraft with recurved wings.

Instantly, Scotty knew where he had seen this aircraft before. It was the same type of aircraft that had shot down his wingman, Ice, and the same type of aircraft he had unsuccessfully attacked. Scotty looked hard into the cockpit and saw the pilot of the craft tap the side of his helmet, motioning for Scotty to turn on his radio. Reaching forward, Scotty flipped the toggle switch, and his radio came alive. Immediately, Scotty heard what sounded like gibberish. It was as if someone was searching for a radio station and was moving the dial rapidly. There was silence for a moment and then he heard, "Earthman, you and your kind fight well."

Scotty pressed his transmit button in and asked, "Can you hear me?"

"Yes, I can hear you," Came a very quick reply.

"I suppose I should try to say something meaningful, this being my first verbal contact with an alien race. But the only thing I can think of is to thank you for saving my ass and all!" Scotty replied, feeling a little silly.

"The first word to pass between our civilizations is 'ass'? Wow! That will definitely go down in the galactic history books," the alien answered, followed by laughter.

Great, the first alien I meet is a comedian, Scotty thought to himself.

But those words also relaxed Scotty. Making sure that the alien heard him laughing, Scotty replied, "My friends call me Scotty. And again, thank you."

"You're welcome, Scotty. My name is Zalat," Scotty's rescuer replied.

"I have to ask you. Why did you save my life?" Scotty asked.

"Scotty, you and your kind are the enemy of my enemy. Therefore, you are my friend. I'm only sorry that I didn't get here sooner," Zalat replied.

Scotty wanted to ask a thousand questions, but he didn't want to push it. So he stuck to uncomplicated matters. "How did you learn English?"

"I don't know English. My translator, what you call a computer, has over forty thousand languages in it. I speak a word, and it translates it into whatever language I choose. In the same way, if you speak a word, it will translate it into my language," Zalat answered.

"How about 'friend'?" Scotty asked, testing the waters.

"That's a good word, my friend," Zalat answered.

For a few seconds, there was quiet between the earthman and the alien as they each thought of the possibility of their civilizations becoming friendly.

Scotty broke the silence, "Say, Zalat, you wouldn't have a force field or something that you could get me back to Earth with?"

Scotty heard Zalat laughing, and in between the laughs, he heard his response, "No, earthman, I do not have a force field. I know what you are talking about though. From time to time, we monitor your television. We find your shows, about what you call aliens, very funny. But I'll tell you what. I'm going to latch onto your aircraft and tow you back to your planet. We'll stay connected when we enter your atmosphere and all the way down until just before landing. I'm going to guide you to what you call the salt flats. But you have to promise me one thing. I want you to direct your people away. They are not to come to your aid until you call them. Agreed?"

"Sounds like a plan to me," Scotty anxiously replied and then added, "Of course. I agree."

Scotty watched as two clawlike clamps extended from Zalat's

aircraft. The two clamps locked onto Scotty's wing. Together, the two aircraft began moving forward very slowly at first. Their speed then increased as they emerged from the debris field. Scotty's heart was racing as together they began the journey toward Earth.

"We're going to arrive about two hours after the last of your aircraft have landed. Your base will have us on radar in a few of your minutes. Why don't you contact your base and let them know what is going on?" Zalat demanded more than asked.

Scotty did as was requested and contacted Space Command. The mood there was one of elation initially. But then the general mood changed. They didn't trust this alien, but Scotty was firm. Under no circumstances was anyone to come near him when he landed unless they received a direct order from him. The people in Space Command reluctantly agreed to follow his order. Before he signed off, Scotty request to speak with Doreen. When she came on the radio, Scotty told her what was going to happen. When he was finished, he told Doreen that he loved her and waited for her to reply.

Scotty heard her click on the microphone but couldn't hear her talking. Finally, he heard, "Michael, I…I…I love you." The next sound he heard was of Doreen crying.

Scotty wanted to wrap his arms around her and hug her, but that would have to wait. *Funny*, Scotty thought, *a couple of hours ago, I thought that I would never see her again, but now I'm on my way home.*

A TALE TO BE TOLD

As the two travelers journeyed toward Earth, Scotty started asking Zalat a million questions. He wanted to know where Zalat was from, what their diet consisted of, what it was like on his planet, if they played sports and, if so, what type of sports, how do they educate their children, and many, many more things, which allowed the time to pass quickly. What Scotty was most interested in was how this friendly alien became enemies with the not-so-friendly ones. Zalat explained that his people are known as the Yurlacks. Many Earth years ago, the same aliens, that are now making inroads into Earth, visited them. Zalat warned Scotty that these two alien civilizations would eventually kill everyone on Earth and then either populate it or take all its minerals and leave the planet devastated. In essence, Earth would become a dead planet. All vegetation will be gone, the seas will be emptied of their life-giving water, and Earth will die. Only a barren orb floating in space will be left.

Scotty asked Zalat what happened on his planet. For the next hour, Zalat talked without interruption. The Murlatots, which is the alien race that closely resembles earthmen, came to his planet. They said they came in peace. They were quick to share technological advances, but somehow, the advances they shared always seemed to lack something.

As months passed, the Murlatot's presence increased. Then one day, the Murlatots told Zalat's people that they were going to be joined by another race, the Gamatites, who were traders.

At this point, the military leaders of the Yurlacks became alarmed. They wanted to put the planet in a defensive posture. But the political leaders wouldn't hear of it. Rather, they welcomed the new race. The Yurlacks were encouraged to barter with the Gamatites who offered raw material in exchange for water and other necessities. All went well for a period of time until the long oval-shaped spaceships appeared (what Space Command refers to as a Z-2). In one night, over fifty of these craft arrived around the planet. The Gamatites told the leaders of the Yurlacks that these were freighters containing valuable minerals.

The following day at dawn, the Gamatites and Murlatots launched an attack that killed most of the Yurlack population. Those who weren't killed immediately were hunted down and tortured to death for the amusement of the Murlatots. Then the destruction of the Yurlack's home planet began. In the end, the planet was left desolate. All life had been wiped out. Most of the natural resources were gone. The oceans, rivers and streams were dry. The gentle balance of weather and life had disappeared. Life could not return to the planet. All was lost.

Zalat and a few hundred more, who had served in the air force, fought their way to freedom. They escaped into space and since that time have been observing the Murlatots and the Gamatites as they work their way across the galaxies. Whenever Zalat's people can fight these predators, they do, but Zalat pointed out that there just isn't enough of them. They can only conduct the equivalent of hit-and-run raids, hurting them whenever they can.

Zalat went on to say that they have been trying to raise an army against them but no one will believe their story until it is too late. Weaker civilizations have simply been attacked and destroyed. Stronger civilizations, such as Earth, are first infiltrated and then systematically destroyed from within until a final battle occurs.

Zalat warned Scotty that the battle he fought today was only the beginning. The force that Earth defeated was a scouting party. While the main force would not arrive for at least another two earth years, it was time to unite and be ready to stand against them. If possible, Earth should seek out the predators and destroy them before they come close to the planet.

Scotty listened to what Zalat had to say, but one thing puzzled him. He told Zalat that on Earth, there have been recorded sightings of alien spacecraft for thousands of years. Why, then, was it now that the Gamatites and the Murlatots were seeking to destroy Earth?

Zalat was silent for a moment and gathered his thoughts. It was hard to compress millions of years of history into a short lesson. "In order for me to answer your question, you must look beyond the confines of your galaxy. When one first looks up at the sky, one beholds a wondrous sight. Before him are millions and millions of stars and planets. Perhaps, in viewing this wonder, one's self-worth or importance is diminished somewhat due to the magnitude of what he sees. But then something magical happens. While standing on that planet and looking up at the stars, one begins to wonder if there isn't another planet with life on it. And if there is, could someone else be looking up at the very same moment wondering the exact same thing. Once this idea takes hold, an unquenchable thirst for exploration becomes the overriding desire. If life exists on other planets, we must seek it out. It is always an idealistic comfort to believe that we are not alone. In a universe of sixty-one million galaxies, it is hard to conceive that we are not alone," Zalat began, wondering if his new friend really understood what he was talking about.

Zalat paused and then continued, "When your galaxy was born, there were roughly forty-two thousand inhabited planets. Of those forty-two thousand planets, about nine hundred were sophisticated enough to have interplanetary transportation. The rest of the civilizations were in the developmental stages of growth and technology. It was decided millions of years ago that civilizations would be allowed to develop on their own. No one would interfere with that development unless those civilizations became a threat to the universe as a whole. That threat could take the form of technology, bioengineering, or social upheaval that could spread as a result of technological advances. If that were to occur, the loosely based federation of advanced civilizations would put a halt to such endeavors. I am no—"

Scotty interrupted Zalat. "But isn't that interfering?" Scotty asked.

"It is. But the overall goal was to preserve peace. You see, our civilization, like countless others, believes in what you call individuality. Each individual has a right to live and pursue his goals. Over time, peace reigned throughout the universe. You have a saying 'Beat your swords into plowshares.' Well, we actually did that. War became a word lost in history and forgotten. That is, until the Gamatites and Murlatots formed an alliance, bent on destruction, which we call Mugatot. It is because civilizations have known peace for thousands of years that my people are having such a hard time trying to convince the others of the threat. You are the first civilization to attack the Mugatot and succeed. This is something they have not faced before. But getting back to your question, if you take what I have discussed and keep it in mind, you will understand what I am about to tell you.

"At the time your galaxy was born, our civilization as well as many others were advanced enough to experience interplanetary travel. Your Earth offered a wonderful opportunity to the scientists and sociologists of the universe. Here was an opportunity to witness a planet as its terra formed from the beginning. It was agreed upon that your planet was off limits for colonization. No civilization would be allowed to establish a permanent base on your planet. The agreement was exploration for the sake of science. Scientific parties were allowed to observe as your civilization progressed but not allowed to interfere. One civilization made it known that they intended to settle on your planet and exploit its natural resources. They did try to do it, but other civilizations banded together and fought them off. Unfortunately, the battle took place over one of your cities long ago and was witnessed by thousands. But time turned truth into fable, and no one in the present truly believes what actually happened.

"Over time, you, meaning your civilization as a whole, became interesting but seemed bent on self-destruction. It was enlightening to see your civilization mature. You hold dear the life of a child but hold life itself cheaply. We have witnessed your endless wars. It was these wars that attracted the interest of the Mugatot. They thought that your civilization would destroy itself, which would leave your world open for easy conquest. For the past one thousand years, they have been closely watching your planet. It was only recently that we realized just what they were up to.

"During your Second World War, the universe, as a whole, became worried. Your world developed atomic power and used it for destructive purposes. Then there was a race to develop more destructive weapons. Finally, there were enough of these weapons to destroy your world many times over. It was then that many interplanetary civilizations came to your world to see for themselves what terrors you had wrought. It was also during this time that the Mugatot began their colonization of your planet in secret. Their aim, as I said before, is to exploit your planet. On Earth, they want to do this by fighting you from within. First, they will colonize by mixing in with your population, and when the time comes for an invasion, they will already have a substantial army on the planet. That army will confuse your world's response to the threat and will try and limit or destroy your ability to fight back.

"The best thing you ever did was to destroy their outpost on the moon. There is a slight chance that you may have saved your world. The Mugatot now know that they will have to fight for control of your planet. That fight will be costly for them, and they may not be willing to pay the price where the outcome is questionable. You and your kind have done well this day, earthman," Zalat concluded.

"Well, that certainly explains a lot!" Scotty declared and then lapsed into thought about what he had just heard.

During the rest of the journey, strangers became friends for life. They talked about their families and about their lives. They talked about their hopes and dreams. They talked about their planets and personal interests. They even talked about their childhoods.

Scotty realized that even though they came from different galaxies, they really weren't that much different from one another. It was almost as though their lives paralleled each other's. Their basic schooling was the same as well as the morals they learned. Their parents had the same wish: that their sons and daughters do better than they did. They both had talked about their first loves and about the one woman, or female of the species, if you prefer, out of millions that stole their hearts and desires. Most importantly, Scotty and Zalat desired the same thing— peace.

WHAT GOES UP MUST COME DOWN

A s THEY APPROACHED EARTH's ATMOSPHERE, Zalat reminded Scotty that they would stay attached during the reentry. Scotty was quick to point out the limitations of his aircraft during the reentry phase of the trip. Scotty had to keep the nose of his aircraft at a twenty-three degree up angle as he glided through the outer atmosphere. If not and the heat resistant fiber of his aircraft's underbelly failed to deflect the heat, his aircraft would quickly become a burning cinder.

Zalat listened patiently to Scotty's explanation without asking any questions. When Scotty was done, Zalat replied, "I know, my friend. I am well-aware of your aircraft capability during reentry. My people monitored the development and test flying of your aircraft. I must say, we were quite impressed with the engineering progress your designers made. Initially, we thought that you would fail because the design is way ahead of its time."

In a low voice, Scotty replied, "Oh." And then after a pause added, "I just thought that you needed to know that."

Zalat chuckled to himself and then declared, "Okay, ladies and gentlemen, buckle your seat belts and extinguish all smoking materials. Oh, and put those trays in their upright positions. We're going in."

Scotty didn't reply but looked toward Zalat sitting in his cockpit and shook his head in amazement. As they entered the outer atmosphere, Scotty felt the nose of his aircraft rise slightly. He then felt a few rough bumps as they penetrated the thin air. Scotty looked forward out his cockpit window and watched, awestruck, as a red halo of heat formed around his aircraft but away from its upper surface. Fifteen seconds later, they were through the outer atmospheric barrier and entering the super thin air of the upper atmosphere.

"We entered west of Hawaii and are on course for the salt flats," Zalat called out and then added, "I'm going to bleed off altitude at twenty thousand feet per minute and get us lined up on final."

"Copy that," Scotty replied as he scanned his gauges, which were all lifeless except for his altimeter, speed indicator, and compass. Scotty then flipped a toggle switch to deploy the wind generator. Wind generator is a small circular device embedded in the wing. When needed, it pops up, and the wind will turn a small turbo fan, which in turn will generate electricity for the instrumentation. Scotty, however, used it to charge up three of the aircrafts auxiliary power units (an electrical power storage device) so that the landing gear could be deployed.

Leaning a bit forward again, Scotty flipped another toggle switch, which turned on three gauges for the auxiliary power units. For the next few minutes, Scotty watched as the gauges went from red to full green, indicating that the units were fully charged. Scotty left the wind generator deployed and charged up his other batteries for the radio and navigation gear.

"Turning on final approach," Zalat radioed. After a few seconds he added, "Scotty, I'll release the clamps at five thousand feet. That will give us plenty of room for you to glide in safely."

"Release at five zero feet," Scotty radioed back and watched as the digital readout on his altimeter quickly went from thirty thousand feet down to six thousand feet. Scotty then looked over at Zalat as he radioed, "Releasing now!"

When the clamps were released, Scotty felt his aircraft rise slightly, but he quickly set it back on course. At two thousand feet, Scotty deployed his landing gear. The circuit board lit up green on all three wheels, indicating that the gear was down and locked in position. Scotty then slightly slowed his aircraft by deploying his air brakes. Looking forward out of his cockpit, Scotty lined up on the salt flats and began his descent. There wasn't time to think of anything else except landing his aircraft. He did allow himself a glance to the side and felt reassured that Zalat was flying alongside him, matching his speed and rate of descent.

At sixty feet above the ground, Scotty edged the nose of his aircraft down very gently and then flared it up a bit. He then he felt a hard bounce as all three wheels made contact with the ground. Scotty immediately lowered his flaps and held onto the flight control stick as his aircraft slowed. Two miles later, his aircraft came to a soft rolling stop. Sitting back in his seat and breathing deeply, Scotty let himself relax for the first time since the attack began. Gone were the pressures of command and the terror of battle. He was just glad to be alive.

FANCY MEETING YOU HERE.
DO YOU COME HERE OFTEN?

After a moment of relaxation, Scotty reached forward and pushed a button on the console, which activated the release mechanism for the cockpit canopy. Once his canopy broke the pressure seal and began to rise, a rush of steamy fresh hot air greeted his anxious lungs. After breathing pressurized air for the past fourteen to fifteen hours, the fresh air felt, no, tasted good. As Scotty was sampling this simple but precious delight, Zalat flew slowly by at no more than twenty feet off the ground. As if suspended by wires, Zalat then turned his craft around and faced Scotty. With an onrush of air and dust that obscured Scotty's view, Zalat lowered his landing gear and set his spacecraft down on the ground.

Scotty had hoped that Zalat would not immediately fly off and leave him as he wanted a chance to meet his mysterious savior. Bending over to the left, Scotty found and released the built-in stepladder, reaching from outside his cockpit to the ground. Before standing up, Scotty took off his helmet and placed it on the flight console. Once his helmet was off, Scotty stood up, swung his leg over the cockpit, and placed his foot on the first rung of the ladder. Very quickly, Scotty climbed down and walked over to Zalat's spacecraft.

At the same time, Zalat, too, was preparing to leave his aircraft. Scotty watched in wonder as, magically, steps appeared from the aircraft to the ground. In another second, the shiny metal material that Zalat's aircraft was made of seemed to separate. This allowed Zalat to leave his aircraft easily.

When Zalat stood up and looked at Scotty, Scotty's heart skipped a beat. Scotty had seen the little gray creatures and their almost-human counterparts, but Zalat, well, he was quite different. Zalat stood at least six feet tall with humanlike hands but with seven fingers, none of which resembled a human thumb. Scotty couldn't tell much about his overall physiology because his body was covered in a light rose-colored silklike flight suit. The only part of the body that was uncovered was Zalat's head. His skin was a smooth pale blue color, like the color of the sky on a bright day. He had a mouth, two eyes the color of deep green, a nose much like a human', and two ears that were embedded in his mostly bald skull. The only hairlike material grew down the center of his head much the same as a mohawk haircut. But it wasn't really hair. It was more like tiny quills similar to those on a porcupine.

As Zalat walked down the stairs of his spacecraft, Scotty remained still, following him with his eyes, with his mouth agape. Zalat approached Scotty with a slight smile on his face. He then reached into the pocket of his flight suit and withdrew two small silver-colored discs. While handing Scotty one, Zalat placed the other on his forehead and then withdrew his hand. The silver disc somehow stayed on his forehead. Scotty looked at the disc in his hand and then placed it on his forehead. When he withdrew his hand, Scotty expected it to fall off, but somehow, it stayed where it was. He then saw Zalat move his lips and hold up his arm in the old American Indian greeting of "How," but Scotty heard Zalat's voice in his brain say, "Greetings, earthman. How's your ass?"

Scotty and Zalat both laughed a laugh that took the tension away from the moment. While still laughing, Scotty replied, "You sure did save it." Scotty then stopped laughing and, in all seriousness, added, "I don't know how to thank you except to extend my hand in friendship."

Zalat stopped laughing also and shook Scotty's hand. He noticed that Scotty was, however, still staring at him. "Boy, you earth people sure are ugly," Zalat announced.

Scotty laughed and then replied, "I'm sorry. This is the first time I've ever seen someone like you."

"Well, now that your kind has shown that you can travel into space at your will, you will meet many fascinating civilizations," Zalat answered as he withdrew a round glass decanter from another pocket of his flight suit. Zalat took the cap off and offered the bottle to Scotty.

Scotty took the bottle of purplish-colored liquid and, without hesitation, took a sip. The liquid tasted like a sweet type of water, which Scotty liked. Zalat motioned for Scotty to drink again, and he did. This time, he took a much larger gulp, which pleased Zalat. Handing the bottle back to Zalat, Scotty thanked him. Zalat then took a large drink and put the bottle away.

It was then that Scotty realized something that he took for granted. Zalat was breathing the atmosphere of Earth. "You can breathe on Earth?" Scotty asked.

"Yes, the atmosphere on your planet is similar to my own. But your gravitational forces here are a bit more than I am used to. It feels as if a great weight is on me, and in a short while, it will be difficult for me to breathe. My flight suit helps relieve some of the pressure, but its effects are not long-lasting. I cannot stay long," Zalat replied.

Scotty was genuinely disappointed. He wanted to show Zalat his appreciation for saving his life and invite him to Space Command. "I'm sorry. I wanted you to meet someone special."

"Ah, that would be the beautiful Doreen you talked so much about. One day, you must visit with my people and meet my best friend, Minka. She would love to meet you," Zalat replied, offering Scotty a chance to travel to another world and forge a friendship between two galactic civilizations.

"I would be honored," Scotty answered with a smile on his face.

The two warriors stood there for a moment and then began talking about their common enemy. Zalat warned Scotty that the Mugatot were developing a new weapon in the form of robotic soldiers. So far,

Zalat and his people had been able to destroy the facilities that were producing these monsters. But Zalat feared that they might yet deploy a robotic army from some remote facility that Zalat does not know about.

Scotty found this curious and asked why his civilization does not depend on robots for pilots and soldiers and such. Zalat's answer was something out of a science-fiction nightmare. His people, like most of the galactic civilizations, developed robots a long time ago. Eventually, the robots became so ingrained in society that life itself became subservient. Zalat spoke of worlds where robots were entrusted with everything from military defenses to food production. Eventually, the robots simply took over and began exterminating life. For the next century, wars were fought to overcome and defeat the robots. When it was over, life was back in control but at a deadly cost. Some civilizations were completely gone while most saw their populations decline by as much as 80 percent. Zalat went on to say that no longer, throughout the galaxies, were robots given artificial intelligence to learn and develop on their own. While robots do exist, they are strictly limited in their programming. The Mugatot, however, were trying to revive the old ways and must be stopped.

Zalat then began coughing and wheezing slightly. Scotty asked Zalat if there was anything he could do for him. Zalat replied, "No, I must leave, but there is one more thing." Zalat reached into another pocket of his flight suit and handed Scotty another round disc, slightly larger than the one on his forehead. Zalat said, "If you need me, push the button, and I will answer. Together, our worlds will forge a friendship."

"Zalat, will your people help—" Scotty began to ask a question, but Zalat held his hand up, motioning for Scotty to stop speaking.

Zalat began wheezing a lot more now and struggled somewhat to talk. "My friend, I am going back to my council to petition them to share our weapon and flight technology with you. Your people have fought well, but without our help, you only have a slight chance to overcome the Mugatot. Together, we and others will overcome them."

Zalat began coughing again. Scotty put his arm around Zalat's shoulder and began walking him to his spacecraft. "It's time for you to go now my friend," Scotty pleaded.

As Zalat started up the stairs of his spacecraft, he reached inside and withdrew what looked like a small piece of paper. Zalat handed it to Scotty as he spoke, "This, what you would call a computer, contains information about the Mugatot and their plans. Just touch the symbols and the information will appear in your language. The star symbol will tell you the frequency code my ship will broadcast on when I come back. This way, you will know it is me. Look for me in three of your Earth months. I hope to have a favorable answer for you." Zalat folded the small device in half and then in half again and handed it to Scotty. "Do not give these devices to your engineers to study. They have a built-in mechanism that will cause them to self-destruct if touched by anyone but you. The moment you first touched them, they identified your DNA and became unique to only you," Zalat concluded and began coughing.

Scotty wanted him desperately to stay but knew that he could not. "You must go, my friend. Today, our people have taken the first step toward friendship. It will be a friendship that will span the galaxies," Scotty declared.

"Wow," Zalat began but was interrupted by his wheezing and then continued, "No mention of your ass this time? Now, that statement should go down in the galactic history books."

Both Scotty and Zalat laughed for a second, and then Scotty said, "Come on. Get out of here before you get really sick." Scotty then motioned for Zalat to get into his spacecraft and added, "Travel safely, my friend."

Zalat entered his spaceship and sat down. As the craft was closing, Zalat hollered out: "May your journey be a safe one."

Scotty stood there and watched as Zalat's aircraft self-sealed itself closed. In seconds, the spacecraft lifted off the ground and hovered a moment as Zalat waved, and then, in a flash, it sped off across the salt flats. As if transfixed, Scotty followed Zalat's craft as it arced upward and went into vertical flight with its nose pointed toward the heavens. In a few seconds, it was gone. Standing alone, Scotty continued to look upward and wondered at the marvels Zalat must see as he travels through space.

A few minutes later, Scotty tore his eyes from the heavens and looked around. He was truly alone and felt a little insignificant compared to the wonders of space. Shrugging his shoulders to dismiss his thought, Scotty climbed back into his cockpit and radioed for help. His thoughts then were not of the galaxy or even of the struggle ahead. He envisioned a beautiful woman with short brown hair and the cutest smile to be found in any of the galaxies. His thoughts were desires, and they were of Doreen.

EPILOGUE

WHEN SCOTTY RETURNED TO SPACE Command, he was given a hero's welcome. It seemed as though just about everyone was on the hangar deck as his helicopter descended on the remaining aircraft elevator. As he stepped out of the helicopter, Doreen ran to him. For a second, they only stared at each other. Leaping into each other's arms, they then locked into a long, passionate embrace. The large crowd surrounding them erupted in applause and whistles.

Scotty broke their embrace not only to save he and Doreen embarrassment but mainly because he wanted to be alone with her. Waving to the crowd, they walked arm in arm across the hangar deck to the elevator. As they walked, the men and women of Space Command welcomed Scotty back, cheering his rescue and return.

When the elevator doors opened near Doreen's quarters, they stepped out and quickened their pace. Doreen opened the door, but Scotty hesitated to enter. He reached into a pocket of his flight suit and withdrew a marking pen. Across the door he scrawled "Do Not Disturb Under Penalty of Torture and Death!"

For the next two days, Scotty and Doreen remained in her quarters. They had become the focus of affectionate attention throughout the base. Someone started a poll as to the exact time and day they would emerge. Seaman First Class Arthur Johnson won that bet. He was finally able to buy the car he had been saving for over the last two years. In fact, he would even have some of the twenty-three thousand dollars he won left over.

During the next few days, the men and women of Space Command honored their dead. In the atrium, a granite stone was placed among the flowers. No fancy words were chiseled upon its surface. In its simplicity, one could find solace. However, inscribed on it was the name, date of birth, and date of death of each member of Space Command who had paid the ultimate price for his fellow man. For those who never returned from battle, the words "Still on Patrol" were inscribed where the date of death should have been.

Arty remained in the hospital for the next four weeks recovering from his burns. Carolyn was given permission to leave the base to be by his side. She remained with him each minute of every hour of every day. Arty would never fully recover and would walk with the assistance of a cane for the rest of his life. Carolyn would share that life.

Vinson returned to Space Command when Carolyn came to the hospital. He became a jack-of-all-trades, trying to fit in anywhere there was a need for an extra pair of hands. Scotty, however, had other plans for him. Vinson would be given another mission with tremendous responsibility. He was to establish and direct an investigative office to uncover and eliminate, as best he could, any alien presence on Earth.

Bone worked feverishly restocking the weapons supply and even had ideas for modifications to the hypersonic missiles. He would have to wait for Carolyn to stop doting on Arty every minute of the day. However, a third plasma cannon was installed at the base. Like a child with a new toy, Bone was anxious to try it out. What pleased him most was the more sophisticated aiming computer. Bone knew that if he had that weapon when the aliens attacked, the base would have never been hit.

CAG, like Bone, worked extremely hard during the weeks following the battle. All the aircraft had to undergo complete diagnostic testing. It was the first time the aircraft had ventured into space for an extended period of time. Some of the examinations revealed stress damage to the wings that had to be repaired. This in turn led to the aircraft design being revised to eliminate the problem. All the electronics were tested and retested. Every system that made the aircraft function was likewise tested, and, in some cases, extensive repairs had to be undertaken. About 20 percent of the aircraft had received battle damage, mostly not from the aliens but from enthusiastic pilots who had flown their craft too close to the surface of the moon during the bombing runs.

Doreen and CAG worked closely together trying to rebuild the air wing. After a few weeks, a new fighter was arriving at the base almost on a daily basis. The X-aircraft combined with the hypersonic missile and newly mounted plasma cannons produced a very formidable weapon. The playing field was now pretty well-even.

Doreen paid particular attention to the final development of the rescue aircraft and ordered four more. It became her personal mission to see that these aircraft were available before another battle took place.

Beverly took as much of the workload off Scotty as she could. She was a working dynamo, running all over the base overseeing the rebuilding and preparations for the future. There was no job too big, too small, or too menial that she didn't involve herself in. Her crowning achievement was the design of a new circular station patch. In the center of the patch was a representation of a raptor dinosaur showing his teeth and about to bite. The raptor was colored a light brown against a field of blue. From the corner of his mouth, one could see a drop of blood. This symbolizes the blood of the members of Space Command that had died in the line of duty. In the field of blue was a circle of thirteen stars representing the original thirteen colonies of the United States. In the center of the stars was a representation of the star system of Pegasus, the official name of the X-aircraft. Around the outer edge of the patch was embroidered "Space Command Home of the Raptors and the Flame of Freedom." Each member of Space Command today proudly wears this patch.

JW was quite busy as well. He did everything he could to firm up the security around and in the base. Some members of Space Command would complain about the security precautions he instituted, but most realized that they were necessary. He vowed that as long as he was in charge of security, another spy would never infiltrate the base. Each

Marine under his command underwent relentless training in weapons and, especially, close-quarter combat. This was supplemented with endless hours on the firing range and physical training. The Marine contingent was the best there is, and they pride themselves on it.

In an effort to expand their capabilities for searching the heavens, Mary requested and received the funding to build an advanced astrophysics laboratory. With the help of Jonesy, she was able to tap into the world's best telescopes and radio telescopes. She also aided in the design of deep-space satellites that would become a network of early warning systems. When Dustin and Victoria returned from their trip of experiencing America from the seat of a motorcycle, Mary recruited them to become members of Space Command.

Jonesy? Well, Jonesy was in heaven. He was doing what he does best, "borrowing" what others don't have an immediate need for. Section chiefs would come to him with a shopping list of essential and dream equipment they wanted. The world was his warehouse, and he was the ever-present internet free shopper. Scotty let him play his trade but kept an eye on his "shopping." When Jonesy somehow acquired an armored limousine bound for the White House, Scotty felt he had gone too far. Although Scotty didn't return the automobile, he did place some controls on Jonesy, but not too tightly.

In the succeeding weeks, Doreen divided her attention between Scotty, work, and the little visitor from Brazil. Doreen and the little girl became inseparable. She would even accompany Doreen to work on occasion and delight in her company. Scotty even arranged for shopping trips to the local mall for the three of them. You see, Doreen wanted Scotty to become very fond of her. Doreen dreamed that she and Scotty would marry and begin their family by adopting the little girl whom they named Christina.

Admirals Morrison and Braddock would visit the base on unofficial visits rather than inspections. Scotty would always try and convince them that the president should be made aware of the base and their mission. Morrison, however, remained steadfast in his belief that it just wasn't time yet. His arguments gained strength when he learned of Zalat and the potential alliance with an alien race. Scotty remained true to his word and didn't reveal to anyone, including Doreen, the items Zalat had given him. Morrison didn't remain true to his diet and regained the weight he had lost.

In the quiet corridors of secrets in the Pentagon, the exploits of the battle in the Pacific were told and retold. Admiral Laffey became a living legend. Those in command recognized her dogged determination, dedication, and bravery. After some quiet pushing, she was made Chief of Naval Operations in the Pacific. She would always remain true to her friends and her fellow sailors. Most importantly, Maureen vowed to defeat the aliens. She embodied the new Navy.

When the USS *Rubin James* returned to Pearl Harbor, Captain Brian Webb retired from the Navy. He moved to a small island south of Bar Harbor, Maine, accessible only by a ferry service twice a day. It was not a life for most people, but for Brian, it was heaven. His days were mostly filled with sailing his new boat, and his nights were warm and comfortable in front of a fireplace. He longed to return to the sea, the first love of his life, but his footprints in the sand were not alone. Shelly Abrahms, the executive officer aboard the *Rubin James* joined him in his dream. Their love was complete and their lives fulfilled. Gone were thoughts of aliens as they rejoiced in their life as husband and wife.

To say that Catherine and Margaret led a quiet life would be a terrible understatement. Together, they became a force to be reckoned with. Their charity work overflowed into the social scene. Almost every Sunday, their picture was on the society pages of the newspaper. They had truly become the toast of New York social life and beyond. If they were not hosting a party for charity, then they were attending one; if they were not attending the opening of a Broadway play, then they were working in a soup kitchen for the homeless. One thing never left them, their smile and their hopes and dreams for Scotty.

Starlight, starbright

Things were progressing well at Space Command. The repairs were almost completed. The aircraft group was nearing full strength.

Replacement and additional personnel had been trained. Jonesy made it his mission to search the world and then procure whatever was needed.

At dinner this evening in the mess hall, Scotty sat back and listened to the sounds all around him. He realized that a new vibrancy had taken hold. There was excitement in the air and a renewed sense of purpose. People worked well beyond their duty hours to complete whatever needed to be done. For example, computer technicians were seen on the flight deck repainting the walls or helping to move aircraft. Doctors and nurses were seen scrubbing floors in their off hours. Pilots were all over the place helping out wherever they were needed. The battle had forged the men and women of Space Command together not only as a fighting force but also as a family looking after one another.

When Scotty finished eating, he went up to the hangar deck and asked JW for a Humvee. He just wanted to be alone. Scotty wanted to go up to the surface and look at the stars. JW had other ideas and assigned two Marines as a security detail to look after him. Scotty didn't protest but insisted on driving.

Once on the surface, Scotty drove across the runways and parked by a small hill. He instructed his Marine security team to remain behind. They protested at first but knew when to back off. Alone, Scotty walked up the hill and stood there looking at the stars. After identifying all the major star constellations, Scotty looked for the star cluster of Drago the Dragon. When he was a small boy, Scotty's father used to tell him that Drago was a magical dragon who would protect him. One only had to invoke his name three times, and Drago would come to his aid. Scotty always held his father's story close to his heart. As Scotty stood there looking up at Drago, he softly said, "Drago, Drago, Drago. Protect us this day." True, Scotty felt a little silly, but it always seemed to work.

Without looking, Scotty unzipped the top pocket of his flight suit and withdrew his mother's engagement ring. Holding it up to the light of the stars and a rising moon, Scotty admired the brilliance as the light pierced the diamond. "Drago, please let Doreen say yes. I love her so." As he thanked Drago, Scotty was interrupted.

"Admiral!" one of the Marines shouted.

Scotty lowered his hand and turned toward the Marine who was now running up the hill. "Yes!" Scotty answered as he put the ring back in his pocket and zipped it closed.

"Admiral!" the Marine shouted again as he neared Scotty's side. "Command called. Three Z-1s have been detected coming toward Earth. Fighters are being launched. We have to go, sir!"

"Okay, let's go!" Scotty answered as he ran down the hill.

What the Marine didn't see was the small, barely detectable smile on Scotty's face. Scotty didn't like the aliens and knew that they had to be defeated, but he loved the challenge. If the aliens wanted Earth, they would have to fight their way through him in order to get it. He'd be damned if he let that happen.

But that's a story for another day!